HARD
VENGEANCE

**Look for these exciting Western series
from bestselling authors
William W. Johnstone and J.A. Johnstone**

HARD ROAD To VENGEANCE

WILLIAM W. JOHNSTONE

PINNACLE BOOKS
Kensington Publishing Corp.
www.kensingtonbooks.com

PINNACLE BOOKS are published by

Kensington Publishing Corp.
119 West 40th Street
New York, NY 10018

First Printing: July 2022
ISBN-13: 978-0-7860-4872-4
ISBN-13: 978-0-7860-4873-1 (eBook)

10 9 8 7 6 5 4 3 2 1

Printed in the United States of America

Chapter 1

Two Months Ago

Denton I. Pulcross owned one square block of increasingly valuable real estate in the pulsing heart of downtown St. Paul, Minnesota. The proprietors of all manner of businesses paid sizable annual fees to Mr. Pulcross for the privilege of earning money in such a prime location—and in proximity to such a civic leader as Denton I. Pulcross. Yes, indeed, it was a much-sought stretch of storefronts.

But as popular as Millie's Millinery, Tumlin's Menswear, and the Circle Café were, none could ever hope to match the annual revenue generated by a business nested not along that lucrative face of the block, but behind a steel door on a side street twice removed from the bustle of commerce. This unlikely location was the beating black heart of Denton I. Pulcross's business dealings.

The establishment, The Dandy's Haven, Gentlemen's Club and Reading Room, was not advertised, was not spoken of by the privileged men who were its members, nor was its presence known by the general public.

Indeed, not even a sign nor number marked the entrance's location. The door itself was a batter-proof, plate-steel portal two-thirds of the way down the alley. A small, sliding panel at face height was manned from inside by a coarse brute in a tight necktie whose knuckles topped hands larger than the faces of most of the clientele. But it wasn't their head sizes Mr. Pulcross was concerned with. It was the girth of their wallets.

Once inside, members in good standing—powerful men all, with much money and a yearning to spend it on distractions unavailable to them elsewhere—entered a vast room with gaming tables, massage rooms, banquettes with curtains for intimate entertainments, and more. A vast assortment of the world's most sought-after libations were served by women, also from all over the world, a curated collection of beauties whose looks rated them among the most stunning specimens from their respective countries.

Flanked by two burly gents in tuxedoes and far to the rear stood a thick mahogany door with a brass knob that led to the outer office of Denton Pulcross, aforementioned owner and proprietor of The Dandy's Haven, Gentlemen's Club and Reading Room. Then came his office, a sumptuous, leather-and-wood-filled, high-ceilinged room with bookshelves and plush seating dominated by a massive desk.

Denton often sat behind it, puffing cigars and counting cash and bullying city officials and paying off policemen and ordering supplies and bartering for the same.

Through a door behind his desk was another room, with handsome wood panels and carpet. Unused much of the time, it was used for extra special events, and only his extra special clients were invited—only the wealthiest among the usual milling mass of tony members.

Tonight, one of those special events was taking place.

"Now, gentlemen," said Denton I. Pulcross, striding to

the middle of the room and thumbing his satin smoking jacket's black velvet lapels. "Who among you is interested in a taste of . . . the exotic?" He gazed upward as if in deep thought, and stroked a gray-flecked dagger beard that did less than he thought in concealing his double chin.

A rheumy, boozy smear of shouts of "Hear hear!" rippled through the room, along with much boot stamping and cane tapping.

He snapped his fingers and a narrow wood panel at the rear of the room swung inward. A flash of red appeared, seemed to hesitate before moving through the doorway, then was shoved forward. The flash stumbled, righted itself, and became a woman with bare limbs and wearing a rather short vermilion dress.

Behind her struggled a thin, not very tall, leering man in a black suit and hank of oily too-black hair that slipped down over his eyes above a long, bulbous, red-tipped nose. He struggled because she struggled, bound as she was behind her back at the wrist with wraps of a gold chain. This contrivance forced her chest forward and the result caused gasps of glee among the assembled jowly white men.

She was tall, slender, but not too slender, buxom, and her glowing skin was the color of powdered cocoa. Long, gleaming, midnight-black hair sat piled high atop her head. Her long neck, arms, shoulders, and legs were bare.

Hands holding drinks trembled, cigars drooped, lips were licked, and sweaty brows were dabbed with pocket kerchiefs. Denton I. Pulcross smiled. At least until a scuffling sound and a low, throaty growl from behind him spun him around, eyes glaring.

What he saw was what all the portly men in the room

saw, and they all shared surprised looks that grew horrified. The stately, chain-bound woman had spun on the greasy man bedeviling her. She growled and lunged and jerked and spun around, and in doing so, pulled the man toward her so they were face-to-face.

In eye-blink speed she bent down from her superior height and bit the tip of his bulbous red nose, then jerked backward, tugging the screaming man with her.

Blood sprayed, spritzing her face and running down her chin. She did not let go. She ground her teeth tight together and wiggled her head back and forth as if to sever the offending proboscis.

The flailing, shrieking man soon righted himself and pried her jaw apart enough he could jerk his face away from the snarling woman, though two of his fingertips suffered a similar treatment as his nose. He shoved her away and she stumbled once more, on shoes with heels that lent her already lofty height an impressive stature.

She quickly righted herself and stood with her bloodied teeth gritted, her breath heaving and her flinty eyes glaring at the fleshy faces ringing her. Strands of her hair worked loose from the impressive pile atop her head, lending her face an even wilder look as she stared through narrowed eyes at the men.

The man she'd attacked was doubled over and gripping his face. As blood leached between his fingers, his screeches were muffled by his hands, but the words were unmistakable—and they were nearly as shocking to the assemblage as the young woman's display. Nearly.

For several long moments, Denton I. Pulcross was uncertain what to do first. He could pull a gun on the woman, which would necessitate him having to lift his trouser leg and retrieve the single-shot derringer nested in a holster about his fleshy calf above his sock and shoe. It would be easier to whistle for his two mastiff men, but he wasn't sure he could even conjure up enough spit. While all that went through his mind, the two burly men appeared to either side of him.

"Oh, good. Control that beast." Pulcross nodded toward the glaring woman, who was in the midst of smiling and sneering and feinting a lunge at the tuxedoed gawkers.

The two big men bookended her, gripped her thin arms, and held her rigid. She whipped her head side to side, trying in vain to bite them. She kicked them each in the shins. Neither man moved. With a growl of surrender she once more stood still, breathing hard and glaring at everyone.

Meanwhile, Denton I. Pulcross had bent to the rocking, shrieking man. "Ellis, you damned fool, look what you've done! Get the hell out of here!" he growled through gritted teeth. Trying to shield the spectacle of the blood-faced idiot from the crowd had little effect.

"Me?" whined Ellis. "She bit my nose off!"

"If you don't get away from me, I'll bite your fool *head* off!" Pulcross shoved the blubbering man through the panel door, then slammed it shut. He turned and had to work to pull his gaze away from the bloody mess the fool had made of his carpet.

Emboldened by the presence of his burly men restraining the woman, he moved close to her right side. "Turn your face so they can't see that scar."

She acted as if she hadn't heard him.

He growled and once again walked to the center of the room, half occupied with thoughts of how to have Ellis killed. Looking over the crowd, Pulcross laughed. "Ah, ha-ha. What a show, eh? Imagine how fun she'd be."

Silence filled the room, save for the low growl from the woman's throat.

"All right now, who'll start things off? Who'll give me a . . . a thousand dollars for this dusky beauty?"

The group's taste for this particular dish had been lost in the frenzy. She smiled and stood tall, no longer looking any of them in the eye.

"Five hundred? A mere five hundred dollars would buy you more satisfaction than—"

"And a case of hydrophobia, I dare say!" shouted someone from the far side of the room.

It might have been the visiting Duke of Orrington, thought Pulcross. Or perhaps Chester Rockwood, the railroad tycoon. He couldn't be certain which. Didn't matter. The chance was lost. And his investment in the creature, too.

Denton pasted on an even wider smile. "For that money, I'm tempted to keep her for myself!"

"You'll need more chains, wot?"

Definitely that annoying Duke. Trust a royal to be that insufferable. Denton Pulcross stepped closer to the tall, beautiful woman in their midst and spoke loud enough for her alone to hear. "I'll have you chopped and ground up, then I'll feed you to my pigs. Then I'll feed you to this lot. That's what I'll do, you . . . exotic thing, you." He sneered as he turned away, but not before catching sight of the slightest tremor on the girl's lip. *Was that fear? Good.*

"I'll pay you five hundred for her."

Denton turned to see a trim man, not overly tall, with black hair and a sculpted black, waxed moustache standing beside the woman.

Who is he? Oh yes, I've seen him before. Previous infrequent visits. In town on business, he'd said.

Denton recalled the man was one of those who'd made their fortune out West. In the heathen lands. Some idiot who'd lucked into a gold mine and could likely buy and sell the lot of them.

Bet he doesn't know quality from quantity, Denton told himself. *Nonetheless, treat this one well. One never knows what the future might bring.*

He turned with a smile, hoping the man had not seen the scar running from her right eye and curving down her cheek to her chin. "Six hundred, sir." Heck, maybe it didn't matter to him. Some men liked that sort of thing. And the fact that she was bloodthirsty hadn't deterred the man from stepping forth.

When the man nodded his agreement, Denton said over his shoulder, "Come to my office for a drink and a bill of sale for the $600." He led the way.

The trim man followed with one backward glance at the woman. He winked at her.

Now that the fun was over, most of the other men had filed back toward the main room and other distractions. Pulcross and the buyer vacated the room as well, leaving the two burly brutes who held the arms of the tall woman in the pretty red dress with dark bloodstains smearing the front. They didn't move.

She did move, or at least tried to. Once more she kicked

at them, tried to surprise them with a lunge, twisting out of their grasp. Nothing changed, save for their tightening grips on her arms. Once more, she gave up.

What next? she thought.

Les than an hour later, she found herself seated in a sumptuous hansom cab, rolling through the rain-wet streets of St. Paul. She was still chained, although bound with her hands in her lap, and manacles of a thicker steel than the gold chain had been.

Couldn't break that one, she reasoned. *I'm not about to break this one.*

The man who had paid $600 for her had draped his wool cloak over her shoulders. She'd given thought to shaking it off, but it was warm. The last thing she wanted was to come down with a creeping, coughing sickness that would drain her strength. She'd need it, always had, always would. She sat rigid at the far end of the seat and did not look at him.

She figured she'd become his love slave or some such. It had happened before, three times, in fact, always to wealthy white men. They'd treat her okay, buy her things, expect a whole lot in return. One man's wife got wind of her and had tried to kill her with a knife. The old man had her sent away, sold her, she later found out, to one of his card-playing pals.

He'd not been nice at all, that card player. For a fellow who spent a whole lot of time gambling, he wasn't very good at it. He'd bet her one night and lost her. She wasn't sad to go, as he could be nasty when he was in his cups.

The night of the card game she'd ended up dragged

to the home of the winning player. He'd been the worst of all, so far. He was a man who liked to scuff his knuckles across a woman's body. He'd only hit her in the face once, though.

Guess he didn't like seeing her once-pretty face sporting buttoned-up eyes and a split lip. Instead, he took to punching and kicking at her body. She'd be stiff and sore, but she could still manage to do what she was supposed to do.

Eventually, he'd told her he'd grown tired of her. She'd overheard he was to be married. *God help that woman*, she'd thought. But to choose such as him? Maybe the fool didn't want God's help. She'd beg for it before long.

His impending marriage had led him to take her north to St. Paul and so, she'd found herself at Pulcross's Gentlemen's Club. Not without first being handled by the master of the place.

She'd tried to get the attention of the other women in the place, see if she could get help somehow. Not a one of them would even look at her. That had been two weeks ago. Then she learned she was being saved for a special event. That's what Pulcross had called it.

She got pushed once too often by that weasel-faced Ellis, always squeezing her and making nasty sounds behind her before jumping out of her way with a laugh. She got him, though, and that damn homely nose of his. She hoped he didn't have some sort of nose disease. But it had been worth it. Just to hear him scream had been lovely.

And there she was—bought and paid for once again.

The man spoke. "Aren't you going to ask me who I am or how I came to be there?"

She said nothing. Did not even look at him.

"Do you trust me?"

She shook her head.

"You're right not to, of course. You don't know me from Adam."

They rode in silence a moment more, then he said, "I trust you."

She looked at him with raised eyebrows.

He smiled and nodded. "Now, how about if I unlock those awful chains?"

She stared at him.

"It's true. Here." He reached into a vest pocket, tweezered out a skeleton key, and handed it to her.

Her sharp eyes regarded him with a somewhat softening look.

From her end of the seat, she regarded him with narrowed eyes. "Fine. How did you happen to be there?"

"Oh." He glanced at her and his eyes widened. "Oh, good heavens, no. I am not the sort to frequent such places. Rather, I was in town on other business and got wind of the frankly repugnant dealings taking place at that . . . that den of iniquity!" The man's face reddened and shook, and he spat the words as if they were hot coals in his mouth.

He glanced at her and saw that her brow had risen.

"My apologies, ma'am. That such things occur in this enlightened age is too much, really."

The young woman remained wary. And yet, something about him was different. She didn't quite know what made him so, but it was there.

Whatever he might turn out to be, he was different. And he had presented her with the opportunity to leave. It's not like she had anywhere else to go. No money, nearly no clothes, no friends, no kin, *no nothing*. Just like always. And so Zadie decided not to jump out of the carriage just yet. She'd stick with him, at least for a little while. At least until the train depot. And then she'd decide.

When they arrived at the depot, he made her button up the cloak. "So as not to catch a chill" he said. Then he held the door for her and bought tickets while she waited.

She hoped there would be food. It had been nearly two days since she'd eaten, and then it had been cold, boiled potatoes and the heel of a gone-by loaf of bread.

He bought two steaming cups of coffee from inside while she waited for him outside. "For obvious but unfortunate reasons," he said, then brought out the cups of coffee for them to sip. "While they ready my car."

And though she hated to admit it, that impressed her.

He handed her one cup. "I hope you don't mind, but I took the liberty of ordering yours with cream and a little sugar added. I guessed." He shrugged.

She decided that was a kindly gesture. They did not talk while they sipped their coffee. It was good, but too sweet. She would not say so, though.

He began to speak, looked down, said, "No, no—"

"What is it?" she said, maybe too quickly.

He touched the right side of his face with a fingertip and shrugged. She knew right away it was the scar. Always the scar they wanted to know about. Couldn't blame, them, really. It was not something everybody wore.

She sighed.

"I'm sorry," he said. "It's not any of my business. I shouldn't have asked."

"No, it's all right. It happened . . . when I was a child." But she did not want to say any more, could not bring herself to. She didn't know this man at all and the night was wearing on her. All she wanted to do was stretch out and sleep for a week.

Before he could say something else, a lean fellow in grubby work clothes came along and nodded to the man.

She guessed his rail car was ready, whatever that might mean. They followed the fellow, who didn't much look like a porter. He led them along a long line of cars down the tracks to where the darkness threw deep shadows.

She slowed her pace, and looked at the man.

He smiled, and nodded. "Here we are."

Round about then she began to feel ill, and not a jittery, jumpy sort of ill. But a bad, down in the gut ill. Before she knew it, whup! Up came whatever little she'd had in her gullet. She felt embarrassed and began to apologize, but the man laughed.

"That sometimes happens."

She fell right over onto her backside and he laughed some more. Before she knew it, the lanky fella who'd been leading them down along the train cars lifted her up and draped her over his shoulder like she was a sack of meal.

The worst of it was she knew it all was happening, could see it, smell it, hear it, feel it, but her sight blurred and buzzed like when you run too fast on a hot, sticky day. She tried to speak but the words came out sounding like mud looked, all thick and wet.

The kind man laughed some more, and the lanky man walked up what felt like a ramp. It was dark until somebody lit a lamp and the man carrying her lay her down.

Oh good, she thought. *At least I'll be in his train car and I can get some rest. It's been a long day, a long week, month. Heck, it's been a long ol' life.*

The lamp light came closer, making her sight all buzzy and blurry. Sound came and went like it was being pushed and pulled somehow to each side of her head. The light showed her the divan she was on was all raw wood and tall up the sides, like a box.

Like she was inside a wooden box.

She noticed she was laying on shredded straw or some such. *What's this?*

Voices, she heard voices. The two men were talking.

The man who'd bought her leaned down and looked at her. "You're feeling under the weather, eh? Well, you get yourself some sleep." He smiled and it was different from the way he'd smiled at her earlier. Yes sir, something was definitely different about this man.

Zadie tried to push herself up out of the mess of straw but her arms just would not do her bidding. Same with her legs.

A scraping sound stopped her feeble efforts. Like a door being closed above her, the light from the lamp in the man's hand began to narrow. Suddenly, she knew what it was—someone was sliding a lid on the box. The box she was in was going to be closed up. Like a coffin!

No, no. She thrashed her head side to side. *No, this can't be right, can't be . . .*

In a dusty corner somewhere inside her, Zadie found where her voice had been hiding. She grabbed it and used it, making it work once more. It wasn't a pretty sound, more like a squawk, but it worked. And she kept on with it until she was shouting pretty well. Not words, really, but sounds. Animal sounds, sure, but sounds.

It didn't seem to matter. That lid kept sliding, tightening the light, pinching it out.

Just before it slid into place, the man leaned close and looked through the gap, smiling. "See you in Deadwood, my dear."

The lid slid into place and the sound of a hammer nailing it down drowned out the young woman's muffled shouts from within.

Chapter 2

"Rise and shine, you dusky delight!"

Zadie had been awake for some time, perhaps hours. It was tricky to know. They hadn't been pleasant hours—her head thud, thud, thudded like a cannonade. Nor were they even comfortable hours, but at least they were enough to convince her she hadn't been buried alive in that crate.

Her last memories had been seeing that wooden cover slide over her, then the nailing, and screaming, screaming, screaming until she cold no longer scream. And then nothing until this morning.

She knew it was morning because it was cold and the light had barely begun to show itself when she first woke.

"I trust you've had a pleasant sleep. I rarely touch the stuff myself. Sleep, I mean. It has a nasty way of ruining a perfectly good late-night card game or drinking session or . . . well, anything at all." As the man spoke, he slowly walked in a crescent some feet before her hunched form.

For the first time, Zadie saw she wore not the tiny red dress that barely covered her, but some sort of sacking, like burlap. It itched when she'd shifted onto her backside.

Bound with thick manacles about her wrists and ankles, she was chained once more.

The chains might be attached to a ring in the wall. She'd leaned back from her hunched, sitting position once and felt something cold, perhaps steel, touch her back. The room had a plank floor, plank walls, and a window to her left, too far to reach, even if she could stand. She'd never felt so sore, so weak, so dried out, so . . . confused.

Since waking and coming into her mind once more, however raw and fuzzy it was, she had but one question. What did the man want with her?

And there he was—the same man who'd seemed so kind, who'd seemed, for a time anyway, there might be one good person in the world, one person who didn't want her dead or hated her because of her looks. Others had only wanted one thing—also because of her looks.

All that thinking made her head ache and pound like a war drum, right behind her eyeballs.

"Tipsy here will tend to you."

Zadie heard dragging footsteps draw closer. From beneath her hair, Zadie saw two feet, one in a shoe, the other, oddly shaped, wrapped in rags. Whoever it was set down a tin pail beside the feet. Water slopped out the side, slight steam rose from it in the cold morning air of the room. A work-reddened hand, a woman's hand, draped a grimy rag over the edge of the bucket and another hand set a hunk of lye soap onto the wooden floor beside the pail.

He walked forward, hunkered low before her, and spoke, his voice low and uncurling, like steel smoke, rust flaking from it. "A handy hint, my dear, before you get it in your pretty head to turn rogue once more and somehow fight your way out of this situation in which you find yourself—" He waited.

Long enough, she guessed, for her to look up at him. She did not.

He sighed and continued. "You will not, in fact, win. *Ever.* You will not escape. You will not do anything in your life from here on out but what I tell you to do. To illustrate what I mean, I'll tell you a little story, hmm? Let's see. Once, and only once, a long time ago now, a woman, let's call her . . . Tipsy . . . tried to run away. Actually, she succeeded. At least for a mile or so. But men, my men, in fact—yes, I have several men who specialize in such situations—tracked her. I'll wager you've come across them, or at least their kind, sometime in your . . . dark past."

He chuckled at his petty joke. "They used to be slave chasers. Tracked them down, hauled them back for their bounty. Sometimes, though, depending on the circumstance, they could only bring back a head in a sack. I forbid such behavior, though. Ruins a perfectly good investment."

He sighed. "At any rate, they tracked her and found her and brought her back here. By that time I had figured out two things. One, I needed a maid. And two, a maid really only needs one and a half feet."

Zadie heard a stifled gasp and sob.

The man chuckled. A low, grating sound like sand grinding between steel. "More or less. My aim may have been off that day. In my defense, axes aren't the most precise of instruments. But it got me my maid, didn't it, Tipsy?"

"Yes, Al." The voice was a whisper.

"It also stopped all that silly running away nonsense, didn't it, Tipsy?"

"Yes, Al."

Al, thought Zadie. *The man's name is Al.* Somehow, in her fuzzy mind she was desperate to make clear again, knowing his name seemed important.

He stood. "As I say, very simple rules, really."

Half turning, he said, "The sooner you understand them, the sooner you will begin to understand we are all one big family here. Maybe not the happiest you'll find"—he shrugged—"but then again, who really is happy, anyway? Maybe you'll be able to tell me, one day . . . Zadie."

That got her. Zadie looked up for the first time, wondering how he'd found out her name. She didn't recall telling anyone her real name . . . ever. Then again, nobody had ever drugged her before. What else had she said? What else had she done?

He laughed, a sound as low and menacing as his speaking voice, but without words. It reminded Zadie once again of the sound she'd heard as the lid on the crate slid over her.

"Oh, Tipsy?"

"Yes, Al?" The voice was scratchy, as if the woman had spend too much time shouting. Or screaming.

"Be careful of this one." He opened the door. "She bites."

Chapter 3

One month later

"And furthermore," said the chunky, red-faced mayor of the little mountain mining town of Boar Gulch, Chauncey Wheeler, "most especially on the Sabbath there is no call for showing such . . . such . . ." The little fat man scratched at his short, black-and-gray flecked beard and squinted up at the timbers of the ceiling in The Last Drop Saloon, as if the words he was searching for might have been carved there by some guiding hand.

"Blatant disregard? Heathenistic attitudes? Immoral behavior?" offered Nosey Parker. The slender scribe in a bowler hat sporting one bullet hole through the crown rocked back on his heels, pleased with his word choices.

"Yes!" Chauncey's pink, pudgy hands smacked together. "All of those . . . and more, no doubt!" The stout fellow stood facing the four men he'd been excoriating, his eyes wide, his chest heaving, and his pink fists balled at his sides. His silver watch chain swung slightly with the effort he'd just expended.

The men stared back, their eyes, too, slightly wide. The

man standing behind the bar was one Rollie "Stoneface" Finnegan, former Pinkerton operative and current co-owner of The Last Drop Saloon. His business partner, Jubal "Pops" Tennyson, a robust man, all bone and muscle, stood nearby with his corncob pipe clamped in his teeth, his thumbs hooked on the straps of his denim coveralls. His eyes glinted, and he was the likeliest among them to cut loose with a chuckle.

To his left stood the aforementioned Nosey Parker, and seated at the bar was Wolfbait, a wizened old fellow with long, gray beard and moustache, a hawk nose, and a piercing look in his eyes. All held cups of fresh, hot coffee.

Rollie broke the silence. "Chauncey?"

The mayor regarded him with a cold, imperious look. "What?"

"Would you like a cup of coffee?"

As if he'd been asked to throw a kitten off a cliff top, the mayor ground his teeth together tighter and sputtered a growl as he stalked out the door he'd stormed through not two minutes before.

He'd barely gotten down the half-dozen steps outside, back to the Gulch's dusty main street, when Pops let loose with a low whistle and a chuckle.

Rollie ran a callused hand through his peppered hair and smoothed his trim beard. "What brought all that on?"

The men, once more, exchanged wide-eyed looks of disbelief. All except Wolfbait, who sat wheezing out a silent laugh on his stool.

Rollie leaned on the bar with both hands. "Out with it."

"Oh, I would"—the old rascal offered up a couple of dainty coughs—"but I'm dry, son. Dry as a puckered plank in the middle of a droughty summer." He glanced up from beneath his furry brows, a look of hope in his rheumy old eyes.

Rollie sighed and poured the old-timer a beer.

Wolfbait sipped, smacked his lips, and said nothing.

The rest of the men closed in, verbally assaulting him.

"All right, all right," said Wolfbait, sipping once again. He dragged his cuff across his frothy moustache. "The reason Chauncey's got a knot in his knickers is on account of the fact before too long a new arrival's expected in Boar Gulch."

"Why's that got him all worked up?" said Pops, sipping his coffee. "We get new folks drifting through all the time."

"Not like this. It's a fellow wearing a collar and a black suit and toting a Bible."

"Since when did Chauncey Wheeler go in for religion?" asked Rollie.

"Doesn't," said Wolfbait, sipping his beer. "But he does give two figs for the ladies."

"Ladies? I don't follow your thinking," said Nosey.

"Who can?" Pops winked.

"If I wasn't so tough, I'd likely resent that remark, Pops."

"Good thing you're made of old boot leather, Wolfbait. I have a few such comments of my own if you don't get on with your story. I haven't gotten a beer's worth of satisfaction from you yet."

"Okay, okay. Boy, you three are about as impatient as a—"

"Wolfbait!" Rollie smacked his hands on the bar top.

"Yeah, well, seems that new sky pilot's got hisself a certain widowed sister."

That elicited a few raised eyebrows.

Nosey said, "What's that got to do with Chauncey? Most people in the world have close relatives, many of whom have lost loved ones in a tragic way. I imagine the poor woman's husband was taken from this earth in a most cruel fashion, perhaps a knifing or a skirmish in some brutal battle somewhere."

Pops shook his head, smiling "You best scratch that down in your journal, mister writer man."

"Ain't the woman's dead husband Chauncey is interested in, you ninny!" said Wolfbait. "It's the woman herself!"

Wheeler knew the preacher a long time ago as school chums, recalled his sister, too.

"That sly fox," said Pops.

Nosey's furrowed brow relaxed. "Ah, now I see."

Rollie knocked on the bar. "I wish the mayor luck."

"Why?"

"He's going to need it."

"Oh, I don't know about that," said Nosey. "He is the mayor, after all. A land owner and founder of the town."

"Yeah, but look around," said Rollie. "It's a hard sell for most women. There aren't that many about. Sure there's Mrs. Pulaski at the Lucky Strike."

"And there's Sal. She and Pieder seem happy up there on the hill at the blacksmith shop."

"And the women under Miss Madge Gladwell's care," said Wolfbait with a wink.

"Sure," agreed Rollie, "but how many genuinely enjoy living here?"

They all commiserated by nodding and saying, "That's true."

A commotion outside interrupted their brooding. Voices drew nearer, then they heard steps on the stairs leading up to the porch.

"Chauncey back to give us heathens a second dose?" said Pops.

All four men turned to face the open door and in silhouette, appeared a woman. She stood still, tugging off her gloves, then stepped inside slowly.

Despite the always dusty ride into the gulch, her dark blue traveling coat and skirts, rimmed with black piping, looked remarkably clean, free of dust, and . . . fresh somehow. She even wore one of those fancy hats pinned atop a pile of shiny auburn hair. With no use other than as a decoration, the hat appeared to have a spray of tiny white flowers pinned with a lavender ribbon. On her, such a frivolity worked like a charm.

Her figure was trim where it ought to be, fulsome in all the other right places, and her half grin, half smirk seemed to indicate she knew what men thought when they looked at her.

All four men stared at her a few moments too long.

She eyed them each, one at a time, her eyes landing on Rollie last, and they stayed there.

Finally, he regained his sense and in a husky voice said, "Ma'am?"

She smiled, strode the last few paces to the bar, and squeezed in between Wolfbait and Nosey.

Wolfbait slid off his customary stool. "Won't you have a seat, ma'am?"

She smiled at him as if he were a cute dog. She still didn't speak, but remained standing.

"You smell lovely," said Nosey.

Rollie rolled his eyes. Pops chuckled and drew on his pipe.

Finally, looking at Rollie, she said, "I assume you are Rollie Finnegan."

"Uh-huh." He nodded, then seemed to come to himself. "Yes, I mean. Why?" He was torn between gazing at this fetching young beauty and being wary of her.

She would not be the first pretty young woman to saunter on in there. He remembered just such a scene, not too many months before, with Miss Delia Holsapple, daughter of one of his former arrestees, an embezzler who'd hanged himself in jail. The young woman had, since her father's suicide, dedicated her life to vengeance, blaming Rollie for everything bad that had since happened to her and her family.

She'd come to a sad—and still somewhat mysterious— end herself in the Gulch. "Found" dead by Chauncey in a cabin he'd rented to her in exchange for . . . services everyone knew about but no one wanted to talk about.

The import of her presence in the Gulch had been her prepaid newspaper ads, which she'd taken out all over the country, telling every criminal everywhere just where to find Rollie.

He and Pops were still fighting them off.

Still, this young woman was . . . something else.

Pops stepped forward. "What my fumble-tongued business partner here is trying to say is yes, that's Rollie. I'm Pops Tennyson." He doffed his bowler. "And this here's

Nosey Parker, speaker of awkward statements. And that old, gnawed-on bone is Wolfbait."

"Are you a widow?" said Nosey.

She gave him a narrow-eyed stare. "What a silly question. Do I look like a widow?"

"You don't look like no widow I ever seen," said Wolfbait, smiling up at her.

She nodded and smiled at them all again, then she unpinned her hat and set it on the bar top. "I am pleased to make all of your acquaintances, I'm sure. As for me, I am Tish Gray. And I am here at the behest of my employer." She returned her gaze to Rollie. "You know him well, I am quite certain, Mr. Finnegan."

"I know lots of folks, ma'am."

"This one is your former employer—Mr. Allan Pinkerton."

Rollie's eyes narrowed and his slight polite smile disappeared as his face hardened before them.

"I can see it's true," she said, watching him.

"What's that?"

"You really did earn your nickname of Stoneface."

"Never liked that name."

"I don't blame you," she said. "It does a disservice to stone everywhere."

Pops let out a full-throated laugh. "She's got you there, Rollie. Oh, I like this young lady."

Everyone expected Rollie to ask her what it was the infamous Pinkerton wished of him, but he asked a different question.

"Would you like a cup of coffee, Miss Gray?"

Those words weakened her cool, amused demeanor.

She recovered quickly. "That would be most kind of you, Mr. Finnegan."

"Call me Rollie," he said, pouring a cupful.

"Rollie, then."

As she sipped, Pops went on about sliding chairs off the tables and righting them, busying for the day. Nosey and Wolfbait lingered, unabashed.

Rollie knew the old man no longer cared what people thought of him. Hell, he wasn't certain Wolfbait had ever cared about such things. He was a crusty old rock hound with an interesting past, the same with most folks squirreled away in the mountains rummaging for "color," the one nugget or pure seam that would change their fortunes forever.

Wolfbait had led himself one heck of a life so far, from a youth as a schoolteacher back East to a series of boom-and-bust strikes in the mountains of the West. His latter years had been filled with more bust, likely owing to the old man's penchant for beer and palaver. But he was a foxy old gent, handy with a gun, and fearless as a cornered badger when pushed.

As for Nosey, well, he was just plain peculiar. Odd behavior was not unexpected, nor uncommon where he was concerned. He wasn't even due for work until the late afternoon, which didn't deter him from lurking about in the mornings.

Rollie didn't much mind, as the man was astute and helpful, if odd. When he got up to his life's work, the writing of dime novels, Rollie wasn't certain. But considering that most mornings Nosey looked as though he'd been dragged backward through a knothole, Rollie surmised the young scribe spent his overnight hours writing.

"Well?" said Nosey, looking at Rollie.

"Well what?"

Nosey sighed. "Aren't you going to ask the lovely Miss Gray what it is that Mr. Pinkerton might want from you?" He turned a smarmy smile on the young lady. "Not that any of us mind the company of such a fetching emissary."

"You are a smooth one, Mr. Parker," she said, sipping her coffee. He smiled until she continued. "But then again so are river rocks."

"And baby's bottoms," said Pops from across the room. He followed it with a low chuckle and relit his pipe, then shook the match once and stuffed it down the oft-scorched front pocket of his bib-front trousers.

Tish Gray smiled at him, then nodded. "Mr. Tennyson, you appear to be on fire."

"Huh?" he looked down and saw that once again his overalls were smoking. He patted himself vigorously. "Thank you, ma'am."

"Don't worry," said Rollie. "He's too full of bull to burn."

"And you're too ornery not to," said Pops.

"Uh-oh," she said. "I appear to have touched off a fuse."

"Naw. They're forever going on in such ways. Like an old married couple they are." Wolfbait shook his head and downed the last of his beer, then rapped his hands on the bar top and stood. "Well, I have to get going." He touched his hat brim. "Nice to meet you ma'am. Got me a long day of sitting in the sun to get started on."

On his way out, he said to Nosey, "Tell me how all this

works out, boy. I can't stand the suspense." Waving over his shoulder, he left.

Miss Gray turned her attention to Rollie. "Well, Mr. Finnegan? How about it?"

"It?"

"Aren't you the least big curious as to why Mr. Pinkerton sent a messenger out here to track down the infamous Stoneface Finnegan?"

"I have a pretty good idea of what he wants."

"And that is?"

Rollie sighed and paused in wiping down the already-gleaming bar top. "He wants me to work for him again."

She smiled and nodded. "Yes, that's it in a nutshell, though he explained it in more detail."

"He would. Allan J. Pinkerton was always windy. Why say it in two words when he could pollute the air with fifty?"

She looked disappointed. "He said he had been wrong to let you go, regrets it, and hopes you will reconsider. I brought you a letter from him."

Rollie emerged from behind the bar and made for the back room where crates of liquor were kept. "Keep it. I'm not interested."

"Not at all?"

"Not in the least." Rollie left the barroom and once he'd closed the storeroom door behind them, he smiled a little. It was a flattering thought and something he'd long considered.

He'd loved his work, and he was very good at it. His thoughts flicked back to that early spring day a couple of years before when he'd been bushwhacked in Denver City after testifying in court against, ol' Chance Filbert, yet another arrestee. On his way to Hazel's Hash House to enjoy a celebratory slice of pie and a cup of bold, hot coffee he'd been knifed from behind several times and left for dead.

But he hadn't died.

He had, however been forced to retire from the agency, retire from the one and only thing in his life that pulled him from bed each morning. He didn't blame Pinkerton for his injuries, but he did blame him for not sticking by him. All Rollie had gotten from the man for too many years of unrivaled success as a manhunter was a pocket watch. Until now, that is.

"He let you come out here on your own?" said Rollie, emerging from the back room. "He's even more callous than I remember."

She narrowed her eyes. "Nobody *lets* me do anything in life, Mr. Finnegan, thank you very much."

"Then what is it you want?" Rollie smacked his rag to the bar and stared at her, hands on his hips.

For the first time, she looked flummoxed.

"What's the matter? I call your bluff, did I?"

She nodded. "Yes. But since you asked, I want to learn. From your experience."

"You hear that, Rollie?" said Pops. "That's what young folks say when they talk about old people."

"No, not like that." She rolled her eyes. "You see, Mr. Finnegan, for me and for a whole lot of others in the biz, Stoneface Finnegan defines the meaning of a true, no-nonsense operative. I want to be your apprentice. I want to learn every trick in your book, Mr. Finnegan. I want to learn everything about the manhunting trade."

Rollie groaned. Once again, he ran for the back door, knowing he had to get out of there before he said something in a woman's presence he'd regret.

"Apprentice. Foolishness." Rollie sputtered, moving a shovel and an axe from one spot in their old shed to another, then moved them back.

Nosey poked his head into the doorway. "You know, now that she's found you—her sage, her oracle—she strikes me as the sort of person who will not be denied. She will not give up until you teach her."

Rollie said nothing, but sunk the axe deep into the chopping block.

"If you ask me, that tenacity is perhaps the most important trait a person engaged in detective work could have."

"Nobody asked you, Nosey."

With a smile on his face, the writer had already turned toward the bar.

Later, in that quiet hour before the afternoon regulars began wandering in, Nosey was out back burning their trash pile, and Rollie and Pops found themselves alone in the bar.

"What do you think of our new visitor?" said Pops.

"I'm not convinced she came out here because Pinkerton asked her to. He's capable of a whole lot of weaselly behavior, but even he wouldn't send a young, inexperienced woman out here on her own. And on a fool's errand, to boot."

"She's out here on her own?"

Rollie shrugged.

"And what's she really want?"

Again, Rollie shrugged. "That's what I'm not certain of. Maybe it's as simple as wanting to learn how to be a detective. Hell, I don't know. I do know she bears watching. Or have you forgotten all those people who come here to hunt me down?"

"I haven't forgotten a thing. Still carry the scars from tangling with a few. I will say she certainly seems keen about learning your former trade."

"Yeah, well, she can go back where she came from and play with dolls or needlework."

"Oh, I think you're selling her short, Rollie."

"I know, I know. Look, it's not you she came out here for."

"Nor you, come down to it. She came out here to get information. To learn. What's the harm in that?"

Rollie grumbled something, but Pops just chuckled. The seed was planted in Rollie's mind, he could tell. The irascible sleuth was thinking about something and that was never a bad thing. It would come out eventually.

And it did, sooner than Pops expected.

Nursing a cup of tepid coffee, Rollie said, "You know, she sort of reminds me of myself at her age."

"Ha!" said Pops. "I can't believe you were as pretty as all that."

Rollie frowned at him. "Don't be foolish. I meant she's fiery and reckless and hungry. I don't mind that in a young person."

"This mean you're going to let her hang around, old-timer?"

"Who are you calling old?" Rollie growled. "But yeah, maybe. We should at least talk."

"Good!" said a voice from the doorway.

The two men turned to see Miss Gray once more.

"Don't get any ideas," said Rollie. "I meant me talking you out of being foolish. Nothing good can come of you pursuing this line of work, young lady."

"Oh, how sweet," she said. "You're already teaching me."

"Teaching you?"

"Yes, how to say one thing when you really mean another." She winked at Pops as she walked by him.

He smiled and shook his head as he chucked a few more sticks into the stove.

"I'm already regretting this," mumbled Rollie to Pops. "I'll blame you when it all blows up in our faces."

"Me?" said Pops, holding up his hands. "I'm just an innocent bystander here."

"Bystander, yep. But innocent? Ha." Rollie looked at the young woman. "I can tell you one thing right now."

"Anything," she said, pulling out a small notebook and a pencil.

Nosey walked back in and clutched his chest. "Ah, a woman who writes. You are a seductress, madam."

"And you are a cad," she said, but smiled before turning back to Rollie. "Now, you were about to tell me something about the sleuthing game."

"Yep. And it's this." He leaned forward.

So did she.

"I will never, ever, ever work for Allan Pinkerton again. Not even in death. Is that clear?"

"That's not a lesson, Rollie. And I'm not surprised, given the way he treated you."

"You're not?"

"No. And neither are any of the other detectives. Particularly we of the young breed of investigators."

"Why's that?" said Pops.

"Because among those who know about such things, Rollie "Stoneface" Finnegan is a veritable legend. You, sir, are an idol, and plenty among us fairly worship you."

"That's foolish," he said. "You don't even know me."

"If you did," said Papa, "you'd run from here as fast as your pretty legs could carry you!" That set him off on a chuckle lasting the length of the bar and farther. He swung the front door wide and in wandered a couple of early regulars, Bone and his son, Bone Junior. Barely scratching by and they were always about, eager to tackle the grimiest of chores for a dollar and a beer. Sometimes just a beer.

"Be that as it may," said Tish Gray, "I have my boot wedged firmly in the door and I'm not leaving until I learn everything I can from you, Mr. Finnegan, about the trade of manhunting."

Rollie faced the back wall and rubbed his temples hard.

Chapter 4

On their advice, Miss Gray rented a tiny cabin from Pieder and Sal, not far from the newer, larger cabin he'd built closer to his smithy. They'd mentioned to Rollie just the week before their intention to rent it out on a short-term basis to newcomers.

It had been Pieder's first abode when he'd come to town, then he'd met Sal, the woman who'd tended his wounds after the grievous, vicious battle Cleve Danziger and his band of men, one of the many headhunting hordes seeking the bounty on Rollie's pate, had brought to the town.

She'd tended Pieder's wounds, they'd hit it off, and her days of drifting from one man's camp to another had ended. What she'd sought and not found with any of them she finally found with Pieder, and he with her.

Though he never mentioned it to anyone, in an odd way Rollie felt responsible for them having found each other in such a manner. Their happiness brought him happiness. He'd not found it himself thus far with any woman, but then again he'd never sought it for longer than a quiet, humbling experience with a prostitute could bring.

Of late, he'd been keeping a regular weekly appointment with Madge Gladwell, the madame of the women who'd moved in and taken over Chauncey's aborted town hall. Madge had quietly paid off Chauncey's substantial outstanding debt on the unfinished structure.

She had also since come to terms—with Chauncey, who knew what that might mean—and purchased the land on which the building sat, ending his dreams of owning and operating a grand hotel or town meeting hall. No one knew quite what Chauncey's dream for the property had been.

It also meant she was committed to staying in Boar Gulch, at least for the time being. The thought of seeing the buxom, intelligent, handsome, and no-nonsense woman on a regular basis for the foreseeable future pleased Rollie.

Having Tish Gray up at Pieder's place, and under Sal's kindly but watchful eye would hopefully result in some sort of friendship with the slightly older woman that might keep the girl out of his way for more hours of the day than he cared to spend around her. She'd been in the Gulch less than forty-eight hours and already he was annoyed more by her questions than he had been by anyone in a good many years.

By late in the second day he'd managed to evade answering some of her more probing questions. "How do you obtain confessions from someone who, perhaps, has lost the ability to speak, whether it be an affliction from birth or, say, they had their tongue cut out by a band of rogues worse than they?"

He'd just stared at her after she'd asked that. He honestly had no idea how to respond. And he didn't want to ask what she meant, because she would repeat the question, word for nightmarish word.

It was Pops who'd saved the day. "Miss, you don't mind my saying, but you sound like Nosey Parker. He's a nice fellow and all, but he does have a way of making something out of nothing that can be annoying beyond belief."

She'd looked at each man, then said, "Hmm," and walked out. Rollie hadn't been certain how to take that, but he didn't think on it too deeply. It was a gift and he thanked Pops for it.

"Not sure what I said, but you're welcome."

The afternoon blended into dusk, which became evening and full dark. The two lamps in The Last Drop shed light enough for men to play poker by, but the lamps and tobacco smoke, as it did each night, watered the eyes and caught in the throat. Rollie and Pops spelled each other now and again and stepped outside for a breath of cool night air.

At one point, Rollie asked Pops if he'd talked with the stranger who'd drifted in a couple of hours before.

"Not much, no. He's been chatty about this and that, but nothing of consequence. Wanted to know about the town, any strikes lately, the same thing everybody new in town asks. He's a bit frayed around the edges, but he's been paying for his drinks right along."

"Good. We'll see that he does. Something about him feels odd."

Pops nodded, but said nothing. He'd learned to trust Rollie's judgment in such matters. He'd learned early on that being a Pinkerton man for decades tended to sharpen certain skills.

"Not to worry," said Pops, peeking back in the door. "I think Wolfbait just turned himself loose on the poor guy."

It was well known in Boar Gulch and in the various mine camps beyond that ol' Wolfbait was a talker. Few men, sober or near-legless, could keep up with him. When most men were so addled by drink they could barely join two words without losing their way, Wolfbait plowed on ahead with what he called "conversatin', " as if he were being paid handsomely for the task.

Pops and Rollie agreed that, through his chatter, the wily old fellow was single-handedly responsible for preventing even more serious brawls than The Last Drop saw. On this night, he'd shown up later than his usual dusk appearance, explaining to anyone within earshot he'd gotten so comfortable sprawled out on a sun-soaked boulder he'd been lulled into a particularly vivid dream. He'd discovered a gemstone the worth of which far exceeded all the gold in all the gold strikes ever made on earth. He'd been just about to discover exactly where on his claim, for of course it resides on his claim and his alone, that shiny gemstone was nested and waiting for him. But just at the crucial moment, he awoke, "needing to water a tree in the worst way."

He swallowed a long gulp of beer, set down his glass, and said to the stranger beside him. "What do you think of that, young fella?"

The man turned a bleary set of eyes on the hairy old gent. "Wish I had me some of that luck, I tell you."

"'Course you do," said Wolfbait, beckoning Pops for another round. "Ain't a man alive with any sense wouldn't envy me. Why, I'm sitting on a fortune!"

"How you gonna find it?"

Wolfbait recoiled as if he'd been slapped. "I thought that'd be as obvious as that oversize sniffer hanging off your face, son. I'm going to crawl back up on that rock soon as I get home and pick up where I left off. I expect by morning I'll have figured out everything I need to know." He sat back on his stool, a smug look pulling his voluminous gray whiskers wide.

"Huh. It's always somebody else has the luck, I tell you," said the stranger.

"What's your name, fella?"

"Name's Dinkum. Folks call me Dink. Dink Fricke."

Wolfbait held out a horned old hand. "I'm Wolfbait. Folks call me Wolfbait. Pleased to make your acquaintance, Dink. Though, you don't mind me saying, that ain't much of a name." He leaned closer. "I was you, when I got to a town such as this where nobody knows who you are, why, I'd change it to something like Melvin or Ezekiel or some such." He sipped his beer. "Just a thought."

"Thanks, I'll consider it. Maybe next town."

"You moving on already?"

The man shrugged and sipped his whiskey. "Don't know yet. I need me some luck, is what I need. Once I find it, I'll stick to a place. By God, I'll stick."

"No nuggets in your past then, eh?"

"Nothing to speak on, nope. I been all over, I tell you, keeping two steps ahead of those who'd see me swing and one step behind striking it big. I tell you, I'm a man caught in the middle."

"More like a muddle, I'd say."

"Huh?"

"Never mind," said Wolfbait. "Where you been lately? Maybe I've traveled through there myself. When the urge takes me, I set out, wear off some shoe leather seeing the sights, I do."

"Oh. Well, I just had me a time in Deadwood, Dakota Territory. Went there to see what all the fuss was about."

"And did you?"

"Did I what?" said Dink.

Wolfbait sighed. "Look, son. If you're going to converse with the likes of me, you best keep up your end. When you were in Deadwood, did you discover what that town's so dang famous for? I can't go to the outhouse without hearing somebody yammering Deadwood this and Deadwood that."

"Yeah, well," said Dink. "That town is something else. Full of hot times."

"Yeah, but how's the gold in those Black Hills? All I hear is how there are nuggets the size of baby heads rolling around on the ground soon as you walk into town. Thing is, I only hear that from sad sacks who never seem to have any cash themselves. Makes a fellow wonder, it does."

If Dink Fricke took offense to Wolfbait's comment, he never let on. He downed his shot, poured himself another, and pulled a wry grin on his face. "Tell you what, though. That town had some women in it. Not like this one."

"What are you talking about?" said Wolfbait. "I'm here to tell you Boar Gulch has some of the prettiest and kindest ladies you'll find this side of any spot on the land mass yonder east of us."

"Yeah?" The man wobbled on his stool and slammed back another shot. "Well maybe later I'll see if you're lying or not." He leaned over the bar, and as he talked, his voice grew louder. "Tell you what, though, they won't be nothin' like that woman I made happy back there in Deadwood, I tell you."

"Ha!" said Wolfbait. "I bet the only thing you made happy was the barkeep."

Rollie came back in from taking a short evening stroll up the main street of the Gulch. As unofficial town keepers of the peace, he and Pops took turns keeping an eye on the town proper.

"You just listen to what I'm saying, mister with the beard." Dinkum looked up at Pops, who was behind the bar, a few feet away, filling a glass for someone else, but listening.

"They called that woman the 'dusky maiden' on account she was like him," he nodded toward Pops.

"So?" said Wolfbait. "What's a person's color got to do with anything?"

"I'm telling you she was impressed with ol' Dinkum Fricke. I showed her a thing or three. Had her a body you can't even imagine, all of everything and then some, and not a stitch on her! And could she dance? Hoo-wee, I tell you what! Funny thing, though . . ."

The night hadn't been a particularly busy one and the half-dozen other men who'd come in, some playing cards, others talking at tables, all quieted. Intrigued by this stranger, they hoped to hear a lascivious story to wind up their evening.

The entire time the man spoke Pops and Rollie had been eyeing the man, wondering when to shut him up, shut him off, and toss him out. Neither man tolerated blue chatter in the saloon and the regulars knew it. They gave this fellow the benefit of ignorance . . . but not for long.

Rollie happened to look over at Pops, who'd been inching

down the bar, wiping with his rag the bar top Rollie had just wiped.

"Hey, Pops," whispered Rollie. "You okay?"

"Hush now," he said to Rollie, listening and eyeing the oblivious, nattering drunk before him.

Rollie's eyebrows rose. Pops had never talked that way to him before. He might be a lot of things, most of them admirable, but he was never rude. There's something in this, thought Rollie, trusting his instincts.

The drunk kept yammering. "She had her a welted scar running from up here"—he dragged a grimy finger up beside his right eye   "it curved down by her ear"—he traced his fingertip down a little more—"and ended there by her chin. Other than that, as I say, she was one of the prettiest women I ever did see. Even if she wasn't white."

Pops lunged over the bar, straight at the man. The empty whiskey bottle spun away and dropped to the floor and glasses upended. Pop's lace-up work boot kicked Wolfbait's half-filled glass and shattered it in the old man's hand.

Wolfbait was already sliding away from the unfolding scene before him. And what a scene it was. So taken by surprise, Rollie had barely enough reflex to snatch Pops' right pants' cuff, but Pops' momentum was too much for his grip. He watched as the wide-eyed drunk was overwhelmed by his business partner's tiger-flailing body.

By the time Rollie made his way around the bar, Nosey, Wolfbait, and two other men were tugging on Pops to peel him off the screaming drunk. He wasn't throwing punches but shouting something that was lost in the general ruckus.

Finally, with Rollie's help, they were able to pull the snarling, thrashing Pops off the mewling, drunk Dink.

"What's wrong, man?" said Rollie, wedging himself between Pops and Dink. "Hey! Look at me, what's wrong?"

Pops shook his head no and shrugged the men off. All tense, they waited to see what might happen next. Quick as a snake strike, he reached past Rollie and snatched up the drunk's shirt front and drew him close, face-to-face. Being taller, he ended up lifting the man up onto his toes.

Rollie held his arms up, keeping the others back. He suspected a far deeper reason than just being offended by this man's lewd descriptions of a black woman. It looked as though Pops had regained some of his senses. He was, after all, one of the most reasonable men Rollie had ever met.

"Drifter, I want details."

"Oh, oh, yeah. You're one of them kind, right?"

Pops yanked the man's face even closer and bellowed, "No! Don't you ever say that! Now more about this woman—tell me more. Now!"

"I . . ." The man's head sagged and he began to weep. "Look, I never knew her, not in that way. I lied. I only saw her once." He looked up again. "Man, I'm telling the truth! Anything I said was only stories from other men. Honest!"

"The scar, dammit! What about the scar?"

"Yeah, I only saw her the once. She was dancing. Tried to hide it, the scar, I mean. Look"—the man wriggled and pulled a sneer—"what's it to you, man? You like that sort of thing? Go to the Gem. She works there for Swearengen. Al Swearengen, he owns the place. Hell, he owns the town. You want a piece of her, go to Deadwood. Get her for yourself!"

Revealing his tight-set teeth, Pops drove a big-knuckled fist right into the middle of Dink Fricke's leering face. "I intend to." Then he dropped the man, who collapsed in a heap onto the floor.

Pops walked through a ragged gauntlet of stone-still men, and out the front door.

For long moments there was no sound in The Last Drop. Everybody knew Pops was the one most likely to chuckle and diffuse a situation with a wise crack. What they'd just witnessed was something else.

"Fighting over a prostitute?" said Bone. "Jeez."

Rollie fixed him with a hard stare and a finger. "Shut it."

Bone nodded once and looked at his boots.

"Nosey." Rollie nodded at the unconscious Dink, then to the bar.

Already in motion, Nosey was clearing up. Wolfbait pitched in to help.

Rollie walked behind the bar, lifted down a decent bottle of whiskey and fingered two glasses, then made for the door.

He found his pard sitting down the low porch a ways, feet planted in the dirt, arms crossed over his chest. Rollie sat next to him, popped the cork, and poured two glasses, then set the bottle at his feet. He held one glass out in front of Pops, who let out a low sigh, took the glass, and continued to stare straight ahead.

Each man sipped.

If Pops wanted to talk, he'd come around to it in his own good time. It took much of that drink and another. Rollie simply waited.

Finally Pops spoke, his voice low and cracking. "You remember when I told you about my family?"

"I do, yes." Rollie remembered much of the conversation of a year or so before, not long after Pops had come to the Gulch, chasing the huge and slovenly Dickey twins.

The two fat boys had been drawn to town by the bounty on Rollie's head, and Pops had helped dispatch them. Hitting it off, Rollie had offered Pops part ownership in the bar as thanks for helping save his life.

Parts of their long-ago conversation came back to Rollie as he sat by his friend, sipping whiskey in the dark.

"Some time ago, I had a wife and a daughter. That was back before the war. We were slaves, which I believe I have mentioned and which I am certain does not surprise you anyway. Near as I can tell my wife is dead. Things got tight for the Colonel who owned the farm where we lived. That's because he was an idiot, couldn't gamble to save his ass. He began selling off his moneymakers, the slaves. I reasoned my wife was safe, safe as any of us could be anyway.

"She had skills, knew three languages and could read them all, too. I figured that would put her in good in the big house. Turns out she was the first of us to get dragged off. She made me promise to look after our daughter. I needed to go after her, but our little girl needed me worse. Then I heard the caravan she was in was set upon, and whoever did it killed all the slaves, every single one of them."

Rollie remembered simply waiting for Pops to continue.

"I was out tending to the sorghum like I did every day with the rest. My little girl was too young to work, so she

was kept by an old woman too old to work the fields. Ma Grunt, we called her, I don't know why. She always had that name. This one night, we got back from the field, and all our babies, were gone. Ma Grunt was bruised up, stoved in like she'd taken a mighty kicking, which I am certain she had.

"We come to learn that the master shipped off all our babies to the slave market, and when Ma Grunt tried to stop his men, she took a beating, a hard beating. Died later that night, on a pallet on a dirt floor, all alone and blaming herself for those children being taken off like that.

"The rest of them, they talked big and cried and carried on. Me, I left. That night. Had to find my baby girl. I had nothing but my own two feet, pair of old trousers more hole than cloth, and a shirt with no sleeves. Then the war got in my way. I did my part, figured I should. But that left me as poor as ever, and with a couple of scars, and a cold trail. I been chasing clues and notions since. Never did find those babies. But then again, I ain't dead yet, neither."

Rousing himself from that memory, Rollie looked at Pops in the dark. "So you think this woman he mentioned is your daughter?"

"Damn right. There was always the chance she was still alive and now I know she is. That drunk's description of that scar. I know how she come by it . . ." His words faded as he stared into the dark before him. Behind them, voices bubbled up again from the bar.

"What are you going to do?" said Rollie, sipping his whiskey.

"What do you think? I'm going to Deadwood."

"And what are you going to do when you get there?"

Pops looked at Rollie as if he'd asked not just one, but two stupid questions in a row. "Free my daughter. What the hell do you think I'm going to do—hunt for gold? Gamble?"

Rollie grinned. "Not sure if you've noticed, but you're a black man. And you'll be angry. Everybody knows Swearengen's as nasty as they come. He didn't get his widespread reputation for being a nice guy."

Pops looked at him. "What are you saying?"

"I'm saying you won't get far."

Pops looked into the dark. "I don't care. I'm going."

Rollie sipped again. A moment passed, then he said, "That attitude will only get your daughter killed."

After a bit, Pops sighed. "So you believe me?"

"Of course I do. You're the only man I'd believe in such a situation. Nobody else would be as convincing. Well, maybe that drunk in there believes, too."

"Yeah," said Pops, rubbing his knuckles. "Sorry about that . . . I guess."

"I'm not. Now he'll move on somewhere else and we won't have to look at him or listen to him."

"I'll pay for his drinks."

"No way," says Rollie. "He earned them, sure, but he'll still pay."

Pops chuckled. "You are a hard man, Rollie. Some might say . . . stone-faced."

He shrugged. "It's not a name I like, but I never said it wasn't a useful trait."

The two men sat a moment longer, finishing their drinks.

"I'll be going with you, you know," said Rollie.

"My fight, not yours."

"That's not the way friendship works. You know that."

"Can't talk you out of it, then?"

"Nope."

"Appreciate it."

"Sure thing."

"First light?"

"Yep."

With a couple of light groans, they rose. Rollie carried the bottle and they walked back inside.

From the shadows at the side of the bar, Tish Gray smiled in the dark. She knew just where she was headed bright and early the next day. Whether they liked it or not.

Chapter 5

"It's been . . . what? Four days since we left Boar Gulch?" Pops stood for a moment in the stirrups to rest his backside from the saddle. He guided his roan around a washout in the well-traveled but poorly mended freight road. The horse he called Bud was successor to Bucky, his previous mount, who'd come down lame with swollen leg joints over the previous winter and never recovered.

Rollie nodded. "Yeah, four this morning. Why? If you know of a way to travel faster, you let me know."

"Naw, I will admit I'd like to have been there already, but I'll keep. Just hope Tish will."

They rode on in silence for a few minutes longer, then Pops said, "What I was going to ask is . . . how long are we going to pretend she ain't back there?"

Rollie glanced at Pops.

"Yeah, 'course I know. Don't look so surprised. You ain't the only one with eyes, you know."

"I was hoping she'd have given up by now."

Pops laughed. "That girl? Not hardly."

"I know. Stubborn."

"Like you said, reminds you of you."

They rode a minute more, then Rollie said, "We're coming into the mountains, the Absarokas and the Bighorns."

"And when we do?"

Rollie shrugged. "Been easy so far, but high country's a different story."

"She made it out here on her own, after all."

"Yep, but most of the way she took a stage, then got a ride to the Gulch with that odd drummer who sells tinctures and wigs."

"Yeah, that little fat man, calls himself Dr. Something-or-other. Sells two useless products. I don't know how he makes a go of it, but he does. Shows up every six months like he's married to that pocket watch."

Rollie grunted agreement.

"Something tells me she'd not put up with shenanigans from such a man."

Rollie looked at Pops. "You really think with that body that he's capable of . . . shenanigans?"

"Good point."

"I don't want anything to happen to her. She's not very seasoned. Luck will only carry a person so far in life."

"That's the truth," said Pops. "I guess every few hours when you've been saying you're going to 'scout our back-trail' you've been checking on her."

"Yep."

"You're a soft touch, Finnegan."

Rollie scowled and repacked his pipe.

"She outfitted okay?"

"Seems to be. Two blankets and provisions enough. She's been making a cold camp, though. Afraid we'll see her, I guess."

"That can't be fun," said Pops. "It gets nippy at night in the mountains, just like the Gulch."

"Mmm."

Pops said no more on the subject but suspected he'd gotten through to Rollie.

On through the long day, they rode higher into the foothills along the trade route, and saw no one, though they half expected to, it being a primary east-west trail.

The blue sky gave way to a mass of dark, low clouds moving at them from the east, urged along by a biting, bitter wind. Neither man needed to mention it. The horses began to shy as gusts pummeled in lower and lower.

"Other side of that ridge," said Rollie between breezes.

"Yep." Pops knew it would be a good place to camp.

It had been a long while since he had ridden through there, but even longer for Rollie. Nonetheless, the ex-Pinkerton man had a keen memory for landscape, trails, and such.

"Might be a soaker," said Pops.

"Yep. Good reason to find cover of some sort."

Pops looked at him. "And the girl?"

"Yeah, it's been long enough. We'll go a little further in, then I'll cut north and circle back on her."

Another twenty minutes brought them deeper into the treed hills.

"Used to be a lean-to of sorts up there about a quarter mile or so, on the right side of the trail. That was a few years back, though."

"Worth a look," said Pops as the men heeled their mounts into a trot. The clouds had darkened and left little doubt rain was on its way.

"Hey," said Pops. I think I see something up ahead, in the road.

"Yep," said Rollie.

Sure enough through the encroaching bluster and gloom, and around a mass of tan granite to their right, they saw a rider coming toward them. On a black horse with a white blaze on its forehead that shone in the murk like a patch of snow, the rider wore a brown slicker that snapped and whipped in the wind. The rider cut to right, to the other side of the road, indicating he or she had seen Pops and Rollie and was making way.

The move revealed a second rider who'd been in line with the first. Atop a smaller brown horse, this rider wore no slicker but had on a canvas chore coat with the collar tugged up high. And did not give way.

All four riders rode toward each other, closing the gap from hundreds of yards to ten, then half again. Rollie had already unthonged his revolver's hammer and made certain his short coat wasn't in the way. He was glad he'd not pulled on his own slicker yet.

"Howdy!" said the first rider. His hat, as with Rollie's, was tugged low, shadowing the face.

"Looks like rain ahead," said Pops, nodding up the lane.

Still, the second rider held his ground. He was a thin man, gaunt, and had a gray-flecked, stubbled face. He stared at them. Rollie did the same in return.

"Yeah," said the first rider. "Come through it not long ago. Headed this way for sure."

After a long pause in which horses pawed and snorted, Pops finally said, "We best get on. Don't want to hold you men up none."

"Oh, we ain't traveling together." The first rider glanced at the other man. "Just near enough, is all."

"Oh, my mistake." Pops touched the brim of his brown bowler and nodded. "Stay dry."

"You, too." With that, the first rider urged his mount forward and gave Rollie a long, slow appraisal and a nod as he rode by.

Rollie did the same, but neither he nor Pops rode forward.

Once the man was out of earshot, Rollie said, "Pops, that lean-to should be just past that rocky outcrop up there. I'll go just past that, then double back."

The second rider nudged his mount forward, finally crossing to the opposite side of the road less than ten feet from Pops' horse.

Pops nodded, but the man did not return the gesture. He kept an eye on both men as he rode slowly by. Rollie gave him the hard stare, unflinching, his left hand on the butt of his Schofield.

Pops rode forward and Rollie held his ground, angling his horse such that his left side faced the west road. For a moment it seemed as if the second rider was also going to stop. Rollie didn't care. He could wait. All night long, with full rain, if need be. The girl was a worry, but that would concern him after this fool rode on.

And the second rider did that, though he was not keen on having a stranger eye him as he rode away, for the man kept glancing back over his shoulder.

Rollie waited him out. He was good at it, had spent many hours of his past life waiting for such greasy fellows to ride in, ride out, to slip up in some way. He rarely had wasted his time. Finally the man disappeared down a low rise, and Rollie urged Cap, his longtime, trusty gray gelding, into a run to get around the boulder.

Pops had already dismounted and was toting his sawed-off, double-barreled Greener, what he called Little Miss Mess Maker, to inspect the lean-to.

The roadside shelter looked much as Rollie remembered, and as a pleasant surprise seemed to have been maintained by someone at some time. The roof was an odd mix of mismatched planks, thick wooden shingles, and halved lengths of pole. With all that effort others had put in, it should be good enough for them for the night.

Rollie rode up, but didn't dismount. "I have to go back."

Pops nodded. "You certain you don't want me and Lil' Miss here to accompany you?"

"If I don't make it back in a half hour or so, come to the party. Or if you hear too much gunplay. But they looked spineless, little more than starved wolves. That's why I need to go back for Tish. She's not that far behind us."

"Okay. Go on. I'll make a fire."

Rollie nodded and cut off-road, northwestward, paralleling the track, but far enough upslope and in the trees he hoped to beat the men to the girl's location.

As he rode off and disappeared into the treed slope, Pops said to the little clearing, "Well now, just how much is too much gunplay?" He shook his head and resumed investigating the lean-to.

Heading west as quickly as he could thread Cap through the sparse trees, Rollie made it to Tish's location sooner than he expected, but not before the two strangers. They were still on horseback and flanked her. She'd stepped down from her mount, a quiet gelding Rollie knew she'd rented from Pieder.

He needn't have bothered with the subterfuge of cutting through the trees. They saw him emerge and ride up to within a dozen feet of the nearest, the second man.

The first shifted in his saddle and nodded, offering the same hollow smile he had earlier. "Well, it's good to see you again."

"Is it?" Rollie had already glanced at the young woman to make certain she wasn't harmed.

She caught his look and offered a weak smile, but it was apparent she was in the path of danger. Or had been.

"This woman is traveling with us and I'd appreciate it if you men move along," he offered.

"Well now," said the first man, still smiling his toothy smile. "That don't seem too kindly of you. After all, we was just passing a greeting back and forth, wasn't that right, miss?"

She glared at Rollie and nodded. "That is correct, yes."

He sighed and kept his eyes on the nearest man, who had already lost one staring contest and didn't seem the type to go away bruised a second time. But it would be fun to try.

"Rollie, what are you doing?"

He didn't look at the girl, but her foolish slip of the tongue was not appreciated. It did have an effect on the face of the chatty stranger, however. For the flicker of a second, Rollie saw recognition flare in the man's eyes. *So he knows who I am.*

It was a stretch, but not much of one, all things considered.

"Yeah, well, with this weather coming in, we should make tracks," said the man, still staring at Rollie. "Lots of ground to cover."

"I thought you said you two weren't traveling together?" Rollie kept them both in sight. Any quick move and he'd have to be quicker.

"Oh, we ain't," said the man. "I'm talking about me and my horse."

"Okay, then." Still Rollie didn't move.

The chatty stranger in the slicker finally broke eye contact with Rollie and nodded at Tish. "Ma'am." He glanced once at his companion, then got his black horse moving westward once more.

The second man continued staring at Rollie.

Tish finally grew impatient. "Honestly," she said, swinging up into the saddle.

The man finally broke eye contact and rode off after the first man.

Tish wheeled her horse over to Rollie, who watched until the second man disappeared down the road. Wind shoved at them down the roadway from the east.

Finally glancing at her, Rollie insisted, "Don't you ever do that again."

"What?"

He shook his head. "If I have to tell you—Never mind. Let's go."

"Oh, now I'm worthy to travel with you?"

"Isn't that what you've been doing anyway?" Without waiting for an answer, he said, "Go—ride ahead of me. Now!"

His tone told her to obey and stop questioning him. At least for the present.

With Rollie lagging behind her and keeping watch on their back trail, they rode east toward the lean-to. He doubted the two strangers would make an appearance soon, but didn't think they'd seen the last of them.

"Hey," she said, calling back to him. "What was that all about back there?"

He glanced at her. "You seem to know so much about investigative work, you tell me."

"As it happens, I don't. Yet. Not until somebody teaches me."

"Nobody ever taught me, Miss Gray."

"Then you were lucky."

"No. I was—and still am—careful and observant."

She rode along a moment, pinching the collar of her coat tighter. "Okay, lesson one. Got it."

He shook his head and said nothing else on the short ride back to meet up with Pops.

Riding up they saw a small canvas tarpaulin had been strung between trees and Pops was busy rounding up dry wood before the storm arrived. Previous travelers had established a fire ring just under the outer edge of the short front roof of the lean-to.

"Storm's taking its time getting here!" shouted Pops with a smile.

"We got here as fast as we could!" Rollie shouted back.

Tish smiled, despite her annoyance with Rollie.

"What's so funny?" said Pops. "And welcome to camp, Miss Gray." He dumped an armload of snapped, dry wood and smaller duff he'd gathered to start the fire.

"You two sound like an old couple who've been married forever."

"Ha," said Pops. "Feels like it sometimes. I'm the pretty one, by the way."

If Rollie heard all this he didn't let on. He'd tethered

Cap beside Bud and had begun stripping off his gear. The lean-to had just enough room inside for their respective piles of tack and gear, and themselves to stretch out and sleep.

"You have a slicker?" said Rollie, looking at Tish.

She shook her head. "I'll be fine. Not to worry."

"You'll need one before tonight's up." He tossed her his rolled-up raincoat.

At the same time, Pops held out his own.

Again, she smiled. "You two are so kind, but really, we have a shelter. I'll be perfectly dry."

The partners looked at each other, then shrugged and went about their tasks, each man seeming to know what the other was doing without looking, and each getting up to a needed task without asking the other.

"What about the horses?" she finally said.

"What about them?" Rollie led hers over by Cap and Bud, then tied them, heads and necks angled somewhat beneath the tarp.

"You'd best deal with your gear, Miss Gray."

She set to work removing her saddle. "But they're going to get wet."

"Not their heads," said Pops. "The rest of them, why, yes they are. If you'd rather swap your spot in the shanty here with your horse, be my guest."

"Not on your life," said Rollie. "You're smelly enough."

"Ha!" Pops shook his head and lit his pipe with the same match he set light to his campfire. "Need more tinder. This wind's playing devil with my flame."

"Here." Rollie handed him another couple of handfuls of pine duff. "If the wind shifts, we'll get smoked out, you know."

Pops sighed. "And if it doesn't, we'll be fine. Time will tell. Don't you agree, Miss Gray?"

She shook her head. "I'm not getting in the middle of this."

Shortly after Pops began cooking, the wind dwindled. "Here it comes."

"How can you tell?" Tish was stirring the beans with a short wooden eating spoon.

"Sometimes—not every time, but sometimes—a big blow beforehand will calm itself. Not for long, mind you, but enough to let Miss Rain saunter on in. Almost as if the big, blustery wind is taking a bow and saying, 'After you, my dear.'"

"And then?" she said, eyeing the sky.

"Then he gets drunk and rowdy and ruins the whole thing." Pops chuckled.

"Or you could just wait to see what happens," said Rollie.

"I thought Pops' descriptions were poetic."

"Uh-huh," said Rollie.

"Aw, don't mind him." Pops dished up the beans into two tin bowls. "He's got his knickers in a bunch over them fellows from before."

"Well, I didn't think they were all that bad. Maybe a little curious, but not bad men. Just . . . down on their luck."

"They're the sort you keep away from, Miss Gray." Pops pointed a biscuit at her, then handed her a bowl of hot beans.

"Oh no, I can't take your bowl. I have a plate in my bags."

"No no, I'll use the pot. Besides, plates aren't a civilized way to eat beans with spoons. You spend too much effort chasing the things around the plate. Use the bowl. And get yourself one when you head out on your own adventures." He winked.

Rollie said nothing.

The rain began, a slow pelting at first. The horses seemed to grow smaller where they stood, curling into themselves as the raindrops came down faster, thicker.

A few minutes later, with the rain hammering like hundreds of knuckles knocking on the roof, they ate warmed biscuits and tinned beans.

After a while, Rollie spoke, still not looking at her. "You said my name."

"What?" she said, spoon paused in midair.

"To those two fools back there. You said my name."

"I—" Then she shut up as the potential weight of what she'd done came to her. "Oh."

Rollie sipped his coffee and looked out at the rain. "That's lesson two."

Nobody said anything for a long, long time.

As the wind picked up once more, they watched their hunched, droop-eared horses and felt a number of tiny droplets begin to drip from the ceiling.

Chapter 6

Hours later, in full dark, Pops woke from a seated doze to see Rollie sitting up, but not where he had been. *Man moves like a cat in the night.* "Spell you?" Pops whispered, noting the fire had gone out.

"No," Rollie replied, also in a whisper. "Wake the girl. Quiet."

Moments later, a close, harsh jag of lightning ripped apart the darkness and for the briefest of moments, raw daylight blared bright and awful.

Tish and Pops flanked Rollie and as the lightning flashed, followed by a slamming boulder of thunder, a jolting sound so close and so loud they all jerked as if shot.

Tish's scream was clipped off by Pops' big hand.

"Get your gun," he said low in her ear.

She did.

"Know how to use it?"

She nodded.

Rollie nudged Pops and then Tish to move, get away from the places they'd likely been seen squatting.

The horses still thrashed and whickered and Pops

low-walked over to them, gentling them as best he could without speaking.

Rollie bent low, reached back to his gear, then moved forward again. "Stay put," he said to Tish, then before she could reply, he was gone like a shadow.

Pops returned to her side.

"Pops, what's happening?"

"I'd say your friends are back. Now stay put." And he did the same thing Rollie had done, only out the other side of the lean-to.

"Pops?" Tish whispered. "Rollie?" She heard nothing but the rain pounding down and the stamping and throaty, worried sounds of the horses.

A flash lit the sky, farther away but still too close for her liking. She shoved backward to the rear of the shelter and steeled herself for the thunder. It came, but as with the lightning, it seemed to have traveled away.

The rain hadn't taken the hint. It pounded down harder, harsher, and louder than ever.

Tish gritted her teeth and gulped. "Okay," she said, licking her lips. "I should help. They might need my help." With no more thought than that, she tugged on her hat and crept low as she'd seen Rollie and Pops do, making her way to the front of the lean-to.

Squinting into the blowing, pelting gloom, she gulped once more and darted out of the lean-to. Keeping her free hand in front of her in the dark, her mind worked hard to recall where the big ponderosa pines stood.

Two things happened at once.

Her fingertips grazed the rough bark of a pine and she felt a slight wash of relief.

Then she realized it wasn't a tree—because it was moving.

She took a step backward just as a jag of lightning crackled downward, followed by the snap of thunder once again ricocheting back toward the curve in the road with the lean-to. The lightning turned the scene bright and for a flash of a moment, Tish once more felt relief.

A man was turning toward her.

"Rollie?" she said, loud enough to be heard over the whistling wind.

The light fizzled and a big hand snatched at her body, smacked her shoulder as if pawing for her, then grabbed her coat at the shoulder and jerked her forward.

She flailed her hands, forgetting one held a cocked revolver. The gun went off.

The sound of it buzzed and rang in her head, made everything about her feel muffled and padded, as if with cotton batting. Fumbling across her body with a hand, the man found the wrist of her other arm and squeezed hard, creating stabs of sharp pain as he jerked it up and down as if working a pump handle in a hurry.

As she howled in pain, Tish felt her revolver slip from her grasp.

The man pulled her close and growled into her face. "Shut it!"

She had a fleeting thought of biting him, but he whipped her around so she faced away from him and his arm pulled her tight to him, jamming into her ribs and pinning her arms to her sides.

She thrashed and flailed and shouted, "Stop it! Get away."

As she tried to pull in a big breath and shout for Rollie

and Pops, his lower arm squeezed even more and she could barely breathe. His left hand slapped hard on her face, mashing her nose and mouth and holding her head rigid.

Tish fought for breath, the panic of not being able to pull in breath jerked her body into a desperate frenzy of kicks and flailing. He clamped his arms and hands tighter about her, rendering her immobile. She twitched and wondered if she was going to die in this filthy man's hands, in a storm in the middle of—She didn't even know where she was.

She felt the man jerk, and heard a voice to her right.

"Let her go! Now!"

Sounded gruff, she thought. *Might be Rollie.*

The order only made the man tighten his grip on her. She bucked against him again, but it did no good. She felt what strength she had left was ebbing away.

Still holding her tight, her attacker shouted, "No, sir! I am going to snap her pretty neck if you don't back off!"

Tish heard a growling sound, then a harsh metal clicking.

"Let her go."

She had no idea if the man had been persuaded by that latest directive, for the man who'd made it didn't wait long enough to find out. The night exploded in sound and light and smell worse than anything nature had been dishing up. As her attacker's arms dropped away from her, Tish felt herself falling, and she collapsed beneath him.

What happened? she wondered. Thrashing to free herself, she quickly realized she could not hear but could smell a harsh, pinched stink. Something about it was familiar, but she didn't know what it was.

Rough hands grabbed her once more. She fought with feeble slapping efforts as the hands persisted.

"Hey! Hey! Tish!" said a voice, close to her ear, but sounding far off and under water. And muffled by bedding, lots of bedding.

Somebody or something lifted her up, and she felt her feet beneath her once more, but collapsed. Pulled up again, she was spun by the rough hand and was being shaken and shouted at. She wanted to tell whoever it was to stop it, leave her alone. She could take care of herself, thank you very much. Always had.

But could she? Could she now?

Her legs began to buckle once more and she was lowered to her knees where she swayed.

Lightning blew apart the night once again, brightening everything about her. She still couldn't hear so well, couldn't smell much but the rank stink that seemed to get right in her nose and mouth and throat and lungs. But what she saw was something she would remember for the rest of her life.

A couple of feet from her face, the blown-apart head of a man revealed its gory self to her. His eyeball hung by a glistening pink cord, his hair was missing from part of his wet and white head. Pooling thick redness was sopping something beneath it.

Suddenly she knew what it was—the man who'd grabbed her, one of the men from earlier on the road. The one who'd talked to her, not the second, quiet one. The nice one.

Oh no, she thought. *He's been shot because of me. Somehow . . .*

She felt herself pull in breath. Felt herself release it and push it out as a scream, a sound she'd never before made.

The full-body scream took all the effort she had in her entire body as it worked up and out of her mouth. She could not hear herself but could feel her hands clasping the sides of her head as if to help hold it together lest what happened to that man happen to her.

Her fear and anger and rage all smeared together in that one long scream, then she fell silent. Something touched her, a hand, maybe, and she jerked and shoved it away.

After a while, Tish felt a hand on her shoulder once more. It did not startle her as much, though she still jerked as if stung by a bee. She looked over, up the arm, and recognized the person who looked to be Rollie. His trim silver beard seemed to glow in the night. The rain, too, she noticed, had slowed a little.

"Come on now," he said, but not in an unkind way. "We have to go, Tish. Come on."

Once again hearing the rain spatter and thunder in the distance, she realized he was not angry with her. She also realized Rollie had saved her life. Saved her not from a kind man, but from a man bent on doing her harm. But why her?

Possible answers to that question flitted through her mind and she shook them off, refused to give them thought. As Rollie walked with his strong hand at her elbow, guiding her back toward the lean-to, she realized she hadn't gone far, not far at all.

He steered her inside and to the rear of the shelter once more, and got her seated.

"Now please stay here," he said, laying her sodden revolver on the packed earth of the floor beside her. "I'll be back."

Without glancing back, he went into the drumming rain

once again—the man those men were likely hunting. He went back out there, probably to look for Pops, his friend.

Feeling the weight of all that had gone wrong press down on her, she fought to keep from giving in to tears. She did not deserve them. She crawled to the front, sat, and watched the night beyond, the horses to her right standing sullen and drooped once again.

For the first time since she'd undertaken the journey from her home in Chicago, Tish Gray felt the creeping, gnawing feeling of doubt nibble at the edges of her thoughts. A tiny but constant voice chanted, *"You'll never be a Pinkerton agent like Stoneface Finnegan. Never. Not even half as good. Barely that."*

Crack sounded from far off in the night, then a second, more of a *boom*, somewhere to the right, beyond the horses. After a half minute, maybe longer, a third sounded. Another *crack*.

Tish Gray had no choice then, for her mind retreated to the darkest of possibilities in which she saw three faces of men, but only one of them was alive—the second rider from earlier. The one who did not talk, did not smile, only glared and looked as though everything he saw displeased him. In her mind, she saw him standing above two sprawled bodies, rain pooling with blood atop their stilled forms.

One was Pops and the other Stoneface.

Chapter 7

"Rollie!" gasped Pops. "That you? If it is, then shoot this good-for-nothing . . . !"

Rollie heard his friend's shouts, knew the voice, knew he'd recognized somebody else in the treeless patch. But it was too dark and too close to shoot.

Tucking low, Rollie ran fast to his left and came up on the man Pops was struggling with. Thoughts quickly flashed through his mind. Where was Pops' revolver? Hell, where was the shotgun? He'd had them both at the ready back in the lean-to. For that matter, why hadn't the other man shot Pops yet? Maybe Pops had disarmed him somehow.

As he ran around to get behind the attacker, Rollie figured the attacker was likely the second man from earlier, the one he'd had the staring contest with. The chatty one, he'd done for back with the girl. That had been luck to have stumbled on them. Another thought occurred to him. Maybe those two had only been interested in the girl and not in him.

As he closed the gap between Pops and the other man once again, Rollie had a fleeting thought of how Pops would have cracked a joke, something about how Rollie was always thinking it was him people were after. As if he wanted such attention.

The two struggling men danced in a circle, their grunting and fist blows loud enough Rollie heard them through the sluicing rain. It had let up a little when he'd taken the girl back to the lean-to, but it had gathered strength once again.

Nothing for it, he closed the last ten feet and did his best to come up behind the man through the dark and wet and hard rain that kept filling his eyes. He raised the revolver and brought the butt down on what he hoped was the man's head and not Pops.

The heavy gun's butt thunked and thudded hard against skin and bone, but no man went down. Rollie had delivered a number of such blows over the years and never had they failed to drop his man.

He raised the gun to give a second dose when he saw Pops had gained the upper hand. Then Pops disappeared.

Rollie dashed forward as the attacker staggered toward Pops, who had tripped over something—the edge of the roadway. Sprawled on his back, Pops hadn't righted himself before the man was on him. Pops flailed and kicked, shouting low sounds and growled threats. He snatched up a fist-size rock and swung it at the man, but it was mud slick and flew from his fingers, smacking Rollie square in the left shin.

He groaned and bit down hard to fight the pain about to lance up his leg.

Now that he could see the man in full, he stumbled to one side so as to not hit Pops, thumbed back the hammer and squeezed the trigger in one motion. The crack echoed and he watched the man stiffen as one arm clawed and crabbed for his back. But instead of falling down, the man pitched forward and set up on the now-upright Pops once more. As before, the two men grappled, though it was obvious Pops had again gained the edge. But they were too close, too tight for Rollie to attempt another shot.

He landed another blow to the man's head that jerked him up into a stiffened pose, giving Pops time to pull away and dash to his right. It also gave Rollie the chance for another clear shot. He cocked the Schofield and fired—and was rewarded with a dull click. He tried again. Nothing.

"Get back, Rollie!"

Rollie knew that meant Pops was back in the game. He dragged his throbbing leg away from where he thought Pops would be shooting. He'd made it about three feet off the roadway when Pops' Greener roared, belching flame and lead into his still-standing attacker.

The effect, as always, was magical to Rollie. The boom stilled the night as if the rain itself had been slapped across the face and stunned.

The waving man's thin form whipped backward into the air and slammed to a splash and thud about six feet to Rollie's left, smack in the middle of the flooding roadway.

Pops staggered toward him, the second barrel aimed and at the ready. Rollie ambled up onto the roadway and both men arrived at the body at the same time. With no warning, the blasted man whipped his right hand out and snatched at Rollie's leg—the same leg Pops had hit with the rock.

Rollie's instinct overrode the fresh stab of pain and he cocked and triggered—the sound decidedly louder and deadlier than a dull click. The bullet cored its way into the man's right temple and likely out through the rear left side of his head and into the muck-filled lane.

"I think you got him that time," said Pops.

"He sure didn't want to go."

"Don't blame him. Place he's likely headed, I'd be in no mood to get there myself."

The two men trudged over to where Pops thought he'd lost his hat. Rollie found it, then went back and dragged the dead man out of the road and into the rocks alongside.

"Thoughtful of you," said Pops.

"Nah, don't want him to shy the horses when we ride out in the morning."

"Tish okay?"

"Yep. Mostly."

"Huh." As they trudged back toward the lean-to. Pops asked, "Why you limping?"

Rollie smiled in the raining dark. "I'll tell you later."

Chapter 8

The rain hadn't stopped, but it had slowed again while they groped their way back to the lean-to by feeling trees, arguing, and barking their knees on what felt to Rollie like every rock in the region.

Arriving at the lean-to, Pops said, "Tish? It's Pops. You there?"

No reply.

"Tish!" barked Rollie in a low, gravelly voice. "It's Rollie. We're both fine. Trouble's over now."

"Okay," came the reply.

In the near-dark, the men looked at each other, then Pops set to work rekindling the blaze he'd built close enough under the front overhang that it hadn't gotten soaked.

Neither man bothered Tish for more information, but once the fire danced, throwing wavery, warm light on the log walls, they saw she had scooted tight against the back wall. Sitting scrunched up with her knees tucked under her chin, and her revolver close by her right hand, she barely looked at them. As if reassured by seeing them in the firelight, a moment later she stretched out in her blankets.

Pops asked once again if she was all right. She nodded, then put a hand over her face and didn't move.

The partners each raised eyebrows, but didn't ask another question. Neither was in any mood to go to sleep, however. The fights had sapped their strength, but left them nerved up. From numerous past experiences, they'd be that way for some hours yet.

Pops made coffee and each toasted biscuits on rocks close to the fire. Raising their mugs in a salute, they ate the last of the biscuits.

Eventually, Pops yawned and tapped Rollie on the shoulder. He whispered low that he'd take the first watch, and that Rollie should get some sleep, but the ex-Pinkerton man merely shook his head. Knowing it was a doomed effort to argue, Pops nodded and leaned back against a side wall and pulled his blanket up onto his lap. He kept Lil' Miss Mess Maker close at hand, as well as his revolver.

Rollie did the same with his weapons and gazed at the fire, fairly assured they would not be molested for the rest of the foul, drizzling night.

The day dawned bright and promising with no lingering hint in the sky of the night's vicious storm. The only water still falling were random drips off the roof edges into already-shrinking puddles.

Following their supper the evening before, Pops had set the dishes out in the rain to fill. By morning they were still where he'd set them, overflowing with random drops plinking the surfaces. And remarkably upright, given they sat inches from the comings and goings of their hurrying boots of the previous evening.

Not much was said as the three stretched, yawned, and rubbed their neck kinks and cramped legs. Rollie relieved himself some ways off in the woods, then dragged the first shot man off into the trees, well away from the camp. He kicked duff and wet soil over the remaining grisly bits.

He tended the horses, looking them over for any troubles they may have developed in the night of wild weather.

"Their mounts?" asked Pops as Rollie stepped into the lean-to.

"I looked, found where they'd tied them. But they're long gone, bolted westward in the night."

Pops grunted, then walked off to tend to his first requirements of the day, some distance from camp. Upon return, he washed his face and hands, and set about making coffee.

In the interim, Liz struck out behind the lean-to for a few quiet minutes, too. On her return, she helped Pops by cleaning the previous night's various rain-filled vessels. Soon, they were seated much as they had been at supper, sipping hot coffee and not yet saying much.

Finally, it was Tish who broke their silence. "I'm sorry to both of you . . . about last night. How I reacted." She looked away from them.

"Rollie told me what happened. And you have nothing to be sorry about," said Pops. "I'd be worried if you hadn't kicked up a fuss of some sort."

"It's just that I've never been in a situation that was so . . ."

"Intense?" said Rollie.

"Yes! That's the word!" She pointed a finger at him, then remembered who he was, at least to her, and blushed all over again.

Rollie smiled.

"You should do that more often," she said.

"What?"

"Smile. You look . . ."

"Less stony?" Pops let out a hearty chuckle, then whistled. "Oh, I wish I remembered to bring along a nice hank of bacon. Mm-mm, that would go down good about now."

Tish bolted from her seat and rummaged in her satchel, then handed Pops a forearm-thick, bundle about a foot long, wrapped in oilcloth and tied with twine.

"Aw, don't tease me, girl! No!" He closed his eyes, held it under his nose, and sniffed. "This is Pieder's pig. The one from last autumn, no?"

Tish's eyes widened. "How did you know?"

"I happen to be a connoisseur of hog flesh, mostly of the sort that's been smoked and rendered into tasty bacon."

"Yeah," said Rollie. "He also knows you were bunking with Sal and Pieder. I don't suppose you brought any eggs with you? A couple of clucking hens stuffed in that carpetbag of yours?"

She shook her head. "Sorry. Just this sack of coffee and another sack of something Wolfbait gave me." She tugged it free and held it out. "I didn't cook. Didn't want you to know I was tailing you."

Rollie snatched the sack from her and held it up under his nose. "Wolfbait's biscuits. I would commit more crimes than I have for one of that man's biscuits."

"Well get ready for jail, because that's what they are," said Tish.

He untied the rawhide strap and peered in, and smiled again. "Oh my. My, my . . ."

"They're good, I'll grant you," said Pops, feeding the fire and warming the fry pan. "But they can't hold a candle to my sainted mama's biscuits." He waved his fire-poking stick at them. "Now that woman could cook—"

"Oh, here we go," said Rollie, rolling his eyes.

They spent a decent time together over breakfast, though after a while, Pops grew fidgety and Rollie knew the man was eager to get back on the trail and make tracks for Deadwood. They packed up camp.

Before they mounted up, Tish said, "I assume we haven't yet buried the two miscreants from last night."

"Who's this *we*?" said Pops. "You got a mouse in your pocket?"

"What? Oh, no. I meant . . . shouldn't we bury the two men you—Those men who died?"

"You're correct about one thing," said Rollie. "We haven't done that. And we won't."

First time that day she looked at her arm where the man had grabbed her. Despite what he did, she felt she had to say more, do more. "But—"

"I went through their pockets, looking for anything telling who they were," offered Rollie.

"Did you find out?" she asked.

"Nah. Their type live lean. They're little more than starveling coyotes on the run. We get to a settlement, I'll mention them. Might be somebody who cares enough to come up here sniffing."

"But what will happen to them?"

"What do you mean?" said Pops.

"Bears, wolves, other critters." Rollie climbed into the saddle.

"So we're just going to leave them?" said Tish.

"Oh, we'd like to stick around, ma'am"—Pops smiled at her—"but I for one don't feel like being savaged by a grizz today."

"Same here," said Rollie.

"What?" Tish's eyes grew wide.

"Don't worry. He'll eat his fill and wander off."

"But . . . that's so savage an end."

"Well, nobody ever said living was civilized." Rollie looked at her. "Dying's even less. Now, if you care to quibble the point further, you can do it with the bears and the dead. In that direction." He pointed westward, toward where they'd come from. "You should be able to make it back to the Gulch before you're too hungry."

The two men clucked their horses into a walk downslope toward the muddied road. Tish Gray sat her horse before the lean-to, astonished at their lack of empathy. Then, as she looked around, the shadows of trees and rocks and the lean-to seemed to harbor wolves and bears and lions.

Before the men were out of sight through the trees, she followed.

After a time, Rollie said, "Sure you don't want to head back to Boar Gulch? Not but a few days hard ride from here."

"Not just now," she said, trying, but not succeeding, to sound flippant about the decision. As if she just might take the notion to turn back alone at any time.

Despite his light demeanor, Rollie was worried about having her along. He felt responsible for her, and resented the situation she'd put them in, even though he knew it was far too late to do anything but take her along.

As if reading his pard's mind, Pops said, "She might prove useful yet."

Rollie looked at him as if he'd been struck in the face with a dead fish.

Pops' eyebrows rose in equal shock. "I only meant *three* is bound to be stronger than two."

"Not if one of them slows the other two down."

"Ain't no arguing with you, is there?" said Pops. "But I will remind you I didn't ask you to come along."

"What's that mean?"

"Means I'm the boss of this traveling carnival show and I say she comes along."

Rollie sighed. "If that's how you're going to play it, I guess I have two choices. Go along or go home."

"Yep," said Pops.

"Hey," said Tish from a dozen feet behind. "I am right here, and I have two ears that work."

Both men turned and looked at her. And saw narrowed eyes and a hard look on that otherwise pretty face.

"Well," said Pops, patting his drum-tight belly. "I guess as long as you keep finding slabs of bacon and sacks of biscuits in that carpetbag of yours, we'll see how it goes." He tugged out his pipe and packed it.

He and Rollie turned around and looked ahead, aware that if looks could kill, they'd be writhing on the ground right about then.

With a night of grimness behind them, and a bright, blue day ahead, the trio rode on toward Deadwood.

Chapter 9

"How long they been gone?" Wolfbait looked over at Nosey, his bushy brows raised like birds in flight.

"Who? Pops and Rollie?" said Nosey, not looking up from the book he was reading.

"Who do you think I'm talking about, boy?"

Nosey looked at him.

"That got yer nosey sniffer up out of those pages!"

"Are you all right, Wolfbait?"

"'Course I'm all right. I just don't appreciate not being talked to when I'm talking to a person. You understand?"

"Sure." Nosey looked back at his book.

Another few moments passed. Wolfbait shook his head and stoked the stove, mumbling about fighting off chilblains and a worsening case of the rheumatics.

"A week," said Nosey, still reading. "And change."

"Huh?"

Nosey looked up from *David Copperfield* and sighed. "You know, you crotchety old goat, I wish you would listen when I speak. It's an annoying habit you've developed and I worry for you. I really do. They say as people age they go off the rails up here." He tapped his temple.

And raised the book just in time to deflect a stick of kindling the old man chucked his way.

Lowering the book, he was laughing so hard he began to tear up. "You should see your face, Wolfbait! Oh, and you thought I was serious. You see what we all have to put up with when you're talking to us?"

"You really think I smell like a goat?" Wolfbait sniffed at his armpits and shrugged. "I don't smell nothing. 'Course, that could be because I lost most of my ability to smell when I was working as a blaster on the Old Lonesome Mine, back a few years ago and a couple of valleys over. They were desperate for an expert and I felt like having a little adventure. I ever tell you about that?"

Before Nosey could do much more than look back at the pages of his book, Wolfbait was off on another story.

Not that it mattered. It was still late morning and they didn't expect any thirsty folks in much before midday. It would be the same each day for weeks to come, for they didn't expect Rollie and Pops to return from Deadwood any time soon.

Nosey tried to rummage back into the lines he'd been reading, but his thoughts kept turning to the pretty face of the lovely Miss Tish Gray. "You suppose she's okay?" he said, talking over Wolfbait's tale.

"Huh? Who?"

"Miss Gray. She had to have followed them. I don't see any other reason for her to have left town the same day they did.

"'Course she lit out after them. She's like a lovesick kitten tagging along after Rollie. She ain't about to let him ride off, especially not on an adventure, and not take her along."

"But that's just the thing," said Nosey. "He didn't take her along."

"See? That's why they left me in charge here. You was any dimmer, boy, your wick would snuff out. Smart one, that gal is. She kept her plans secret, elsewise she knew what ol' Stoneface would say."

Nosey set down the book and nodded toward the door. "That reminds me, we agreed not to use their names, especially You-know-who's while they were gone. Especially not around strangers. But we've done a poor job of it."

"Yeah, yeah, but I don't see any strangers hereabouts, do you?" Wolfbait craned his reedy old neck in all directions, like a turtle looking for a sunny spot.

"That doesn't matter. You know how folks are always turning up at odd times looking to collect the bounty . . . on his head. No sooner does one criminal bounty plot get foiled then another of the people he arrested years ago pops up and posts another bounty on his head. I don't know how he sleeps at night."

Wolfbait snorted. "Simple. It's 'cause he knows I'm always at the ready."

Nosey poured himself a coffee and held the pot out toward his companion.

Wolfbait scratched his chin. "I reckon I might do better with a glass of beer coating my insides. Settle me down a little before the rush."

Nosey looked toward the door, then jumped backward a step.

"What was that for?"

"I don't want to get trampled." Nosey sipped his coffee. "You know . . . in the rush."

Wolfbait mumbled something about getting no respect as he poured himself a glass of brew. And then the unexpected happened. They heard bootsteps on the stairs out front, in counterpoint with the light jingle of spurs.

Moments later, a wide-shouldered man centered himself in the open doorway, looking in. He was solid of frame resting on two tree-stout legs, and he stood skylined against the day's brightness.

"Come on in," said Wolfbait. "We're busy but we'll see if we can find you a chair." He thought this funny and slapped his leg.

Neither the stranger nor Nosey followed suit.

Spurs ringing, the man crossed to one of the poker tables along the side of the room opposite the bar and sat down with his back to the wall, angled to he could take in the full room and the door.

Nosey noticed the man wore a two-gun rig of dust-peppered black leather.

His spurs jingled as he stretched out his thick legs before him, boots crossed. "A bottle of whiskey and a clean glass." The stranger dug out a couple of coins from an inner vest pocket and tossed them on the baize-covered table.

"Clean glass'll cost you extra." Wolfbait chuckled and set a glass and the bottle on the counter.

The man stared at him.

"I ain't bringing it to you, fella." Wolfbait crossed his arms. "I may be a whole lot of things, but I ain't a servin' woman."

"Oh, for heaven's sake," said Nosey, snatching up the

bottle and glass. He set them on the man's table and picked up the coins. "You'll have change coming."

"Nah. Keep it." The stranger poured himself a glass of whiskey and smacked his lips. Then he held it up and smiled at the two men behind the bar. "Here's to you, gents."

He knocked it back and sighed, then poured another. "Name's Mace. Mace Matson." He looked at them. "That mean anything to either of you?"

"No more than it ought," said Wolfbait. "Which, since I don't know you from a tree, I'd say it don't mean a thing."

"Huh," said Matson. "I'll have to think on that."

"You do that." Wolfbait ran a rag along the top of the bar. He wanted to know more about this Matson fellow but didn't want to appear he was like Nosey. Particularly if the stranger was some sort of gunhand or outlaw.

The stranger sipped the whiskey, then sighed and leaned back farther in the chair. "Yep, mighty fine discovery I made for myself, stumbling on this little place. Why, a few miles back I about gave up hoping that awful trail led to anything at all but more of this forsaken wilderness."

"Well now, stranger"—Wolfbait drew himself up to his full height, which, given the bend in his back, wasn't what it used to be—"there are folks hereabout who might be offended to hear such talk about our little town."

"Oh." The man chuckled. "Settle down, old-timer. I ain't in the business of offending people."

"Well you sure are picking up the trade, mister."

The man didn't take the bait. "What'd you say this place is called?"

Nosey beat Wolfbait to the answer, shooting the old man a glare. "We didn't. But as you ask, it's . . . Ball Gulch."

"Oh? That's not what I'd been told. I was told I'd find a place called Boar Gulch if I kept on this trail into the Sawtooths."

"Then why did you indicate earlier you were surprised to find anything up here at all?"

The man settled the front legs of the chair back to the floor and poured himself another drink. "A clever fellow, huh?"

"The place you mentioned," said Wolfbait. "Boar Gulch? Why that's clear down the next valley and on the far side of the peak beyond."

"You don't say?"

"I do say." Wolfbait nodded.

"I guess I got my trails crossed somehow."

Wolfbait kept on drying already dry mugs. "Aw, don't fret. It happens. Mostly to old-timers, but it happens."

Nosey groaned, then looked up as a set of boots could be heard outside. They stopped halfway up the steps and a low voice could be heard murmuring in conversation with someone else.

"That'd likely be my . . . associate, Drake Keller." As with the mention of his own name, Matson let the words hang in the air like smoke and eyed the two men behind the bar. "Not heard of him?"

"No," said Nosey. "But that means little, as nobody gets out of the hills much these days."

"Oh? Pickings are good, are they?"

"Nope!" said Wolfbait. "They're so bad none of us can

stop for a breath! Got to keep mining and sluicing and digging just to stay alive."

"Yes." Nosey pulled a frown. "I can't imagine coming here just now and expecting to find any color in these hills. We're a dying town. What gold was here has long since been picked away and hauled out of here."

Another man darkened the doorway, paused, lifted free his hat, and ran his fingers through long, black hair. He eyed the room, the brightness of outside hampering his sight for a few moments. "Mace. There you are."

"Here I be." Matson kicked another chair at the table back a couple of feet. "Take a seat." He looked over at the bar. "Could one of you men bring us another glass at your convenience?"

Nosey nodded and took his time.

"Thanks," said Keller. "I know it was a long walk."

"You have no idea," Nosey said over his shoulder as he walked back to the bar.

The two men lingered a long time over that bottle, draining it, chatting low, and then calling for a couple of beers. With a yawn or a sidelong glance out the door, they asked questions posed more as a courtesy than for an answer.

Obvious to Wolfbait and Nosey, the men were *sniffers*. Since Rollie had bought The Last Drop, three types of folks showed up in Boar Gulch. The first were the people who looked as if they'd spent their lives behind a desk back East and had sold everything to bet on finding a hidden seam of gold. They were dew-eyed *seekers*, looking for something, anything that might change their lives.

The thing most of them were to learn the hard way, something men such as Wolfbait and Nosey knew, was that most of their lives would be changed, but not necessarily by finding a fortune in gold or silver. If they let themselves enjoy the freedom and the dream of waking each day in a pretty place, filled with the possibility of promise, that often was the fortune itself. Sadly, most folks didn't find much in the way of gold, and gave up—angry and bitter and poorer of mind and wallet than when they arrived.

The second type of folks were those such as Rollie, and Madge and her girls, there to *mine the miners*, offer goods and services to the men (and a few women) who dug all day and needed tools or food or libation or brief moments of companionship.

The third type of folks who showed up in the Gulch were *sniffers*—those eager to separate Rollie "Stoneface" Finnegan's head from his body, lug it back to whatever hole the bounty-posting revenge-seeker was waiting in, and collect a fat cash reward for their efforts.

The last time anybody'd seen such an advertisement, it had been in the pocket of a lone wolf, a bounty man by the name of Chigger who Rollie had had to fight off while he was otherwise engaged at the shaving bowl.

In addition to losing a nose and three fingertips, Chigger had also lost a whole lot of blood. The one thing he had gained in the encounter with Rollie's straight razor was a new mouth right in the middle of his throat.

The well-worn advertisement fished from the dead man's trouser pocket had said Rollie's head—nothing else required, though it specified it must be identifiable as Stoneface Finnegan's head—was worth $10,000. Rollie had spit, washed off his razor, and finished shaving.

Wolfbait and Nosey were pretty certain the two jokers—

Mace Matson and Drake Keller—had come to collect on said bounty.

Only trouble was, neither Rollie nor Pops, the town's officially unofficial lawmen, were in town, and weren't expected back for many weeks. As there hadn't been an attack of the Chigger sort in several months, all the town, save perhaps Rollie himself, had grown soft in their guardedness over such matters. It was largely considered, perhaps even hoped, such foolishness had finally become a thing of the past.

But here it was again, smack in their midst. And Wolfbait and Nosey, as seconds in charge, had to figure out just what they were to do.

Sipping his beer, Matson said, "Oh, by the way, my men should be here some time in the night. Any place in this *Ball Gulch* you recommend for a hot meal, a bath, and a little female affection?"

"Your men?" said Wolfbait, trying to keep his voice from sounding old and shaky. It didn't work.

"Yeah, another dozen or so." Matson drained his glass and turned it upside down on the table top. "Just like us."

Chapter 10

"Yep, they're my men. Well, I don't own them." Mace Matson laughed. "Not yet, anyway. Some of them get any worse at cards and I expect the only thing they'll have left to barter is their lives." He thought about that, then smiled. "You know, that's not a bad idea." He looked at his companion, Drake Keller.

Keller fiddled with building another smoke. "You can't own a man. Not unless he's a slave. That's a different story, though."

"Naw, now I can't agree," said Matson. "See, I'm thinking if a man wagers himself into a corner and he's lost everything and he ain't got nothing left to offer—"

"Your thinking's off, Mace." Keller interrupted as he lit his smoke. Man'll have his clothes, maybe even his boots. Don't tell me you'd take a man's boots and socks and leave him naked."

Mattson shrugged. "Yep. I said *everything*."

Keller blew smoke out his nostrils and shook his head. "This talk has turned foolish." He shouted over his shoulder. "Hey, old man!"

Wolfbait stiffened but didn't look.

"Don't let them get to you," said Nosey, loud enough for the men to hear him.

Boots on the steps out front broke the mood. Nosey and Wolfbait looked toward the door, expecting another dozen of these fools to descend on them. But in leaned Bone and his son, Bone Junior.

Nosey sighed. "Welcome, fellows!"

Bone and the boy looked at each other. As the self-appointed town scavengers and takers-on of tasks nobody else dared do—usually digging new privy holes and covering up old ones, burying dead folks and rendering carcasses and such—nobody ever seemed to have a kind word to say for them. But Nosey was looking pleased to see them. That was peculiar, no mistake.

"Come on, boy. Something's off. We'll come back later." Bone nudged his son.

"No, no, no." Nosey rushed over and nearly grabbed them by the arms to usher them to their preferred place, or rather the spot Rollie and Pops preferred to have them sit—a two-person table off in the corner, well away from the other customers.

Knowing they exuded a powerful, ripe odor on the coldest of days, it was a necessity Bone nor the boy ever balked at. On the scorchers, Rollie had decided it would be best if he brought their beers out to them. Bone thought that was downright respectable.

Nosey stopped just shy of tugging their sleeves, remembering at the last moment they were not the type a man wanted to get touchy with. He gently shooed them deeper into the bar and toward the accustomed table. Wolfbait took over a couple of beers, their usual first round. The number of jobs they'd had of late determined the number of drinks they got to have.

"You kidding me?" said Mace, eyeing the two newcomers. "Them two are little more than whiffy hogs. Can't a man drink in peace without having his nostrils savaged by such as them?"

Wolfbait had by then returned to his second-favorite spot, behind the bar. His first favorite, sitting at the bar and drinking, would have to wait. He was about fit to be tied. He reached beneath the bar to the topmost of the three shelves and his gnarled old hands closed around his weapon of choice—a single-barreled shotgun he'd come to rely on more and more in recent years. His eyes not being what they once were, the shotgun was good in a scuffle.

Wolfbait flopped the shotgun on the bar top. "Now look"—he eyed the two strangers—"it's one thing for you two to come on in here and yammer all manner of foolish talk to each other. It's what men do when they drink. I understand. Been there myself. And you can even insult me now and again. Okay, that's one thing. As you said, I'm old. I have suffered fools lo these many years. I can put up with a few more, I reckon. But when you light into my friends, folks who've been here doing work to build up a fine town such as Boar Gulch, why, I reckon I won't put up with it."

Silence draped over the room like a wet wool blanket. Bone and his boy looked at each other with wide eyes. It had been a long time since anybody had ever come to their defense, especially Wolfbait, who was always nagging Bone about this or that. Things like Bone's long-dead wife and mother to the boy. Pretty thing, but what a tongue! Keen as a honed knife.

Had she lived, Bone reckoned she would be one of those old women who likes the sound of their annoying voices. Just as well she left in a huff one night, claiming she needed to take some air as the stink off Bone's socks was enough to kill birds in midflight.

She was always wandering off in the wee hours to be alone for a spell, so it didn't cause him any bother. Trouble was, the day before, a storm had kicked up. A spring gully-washer, and that night, she lost her footing on a mucky bank of gravel just looking for an excuse to slough away. The excuse was right under her feet.

They found her at the valley floor, broke neck, her tongue stuck right out. He'd always imagined she'd died talking, likely cutting him down. He liked to think so, anyway. He expected that would have pleased her.

So when Wolfbait stuck up for him and the boy, it gave Bone an odd sensation, a feeling he didn't recognize at first. Then he did. Something lots of other folks had, *friendship*. He'd seen such folks together, all joshing and joking and helping one another in times good or ill. Bone had not felt that in many a long year. Perhaps not since his boyhood.

"Pop?" whispered the boy beside him. "You okay?"

"'Course I be!" Bone growled and turned away, trying to clear his eyes of their pesky new invaders.

Drake Keller raised his eyebrows, shifted in his chair, and regarded the old man behind the bar, the shotgun laid on the planking before him. With a smear of a grin held on Keller's mouth, he looked at Mace Matson, and the two laughed hard and long.

"You have to be kidding me, old man!" said Matson, smacking a hand on the green tabletop. "It ain't insulting to speak the truth. It's nothing more or less than the right thing to do. If I was to tell them smelly fellows just what I want to do to them for spoiling a fine afternoon for me, well, I reckon you'd think I was being harsh. And maybe you'd be right, for that would be an opinion. See?" The man warmed to his topic and several sets of eyes were on him as if he were about to speak some truth everyone else might ever only dream of attaining.

"One more word, jackass! Just one more word." Wolfbait hefted the shotgun and cocked it.

Bone and his son shoved farther into their corner, eyes wide and not feeling wholly comfortable this kerfuffle seemed to be about them.

Mace stood slowly, his hands held out to his sides, his fingertips twitching slightly as if they were snake tongues testing the air. Any trace of mirth on his face had slipped away. "Old man," he said, his voice low and even. "You think harder now."

His companion, Drake, hadn't so much as twitched.

"I've thought all I need to. Been thinking longer than you've been alive. I told you I didn't want to hear no more bad mouthing going on here. We were all fine and dandy until you and that one rode in and laid up in here as if you own the place."

"Now then," said Mace, standing full height. "That leads me to a question, old man."

Nosey laid a hand on Wolfbait's shoulder, but he shrugged it off with a growl and jerked the barrel toward the door. "Do all the asking you need to right on out that door and into the street, 'cause you ain't welcome in here no more."

"And who's saying that? You the owner of this place? Huh?" Mace asked this with a curious grin once more on his face. "I don't think you are. I think you and that other joker ain't nothing much at all. I think the owner of this place is none other than the celebrated, infamous Stoneface Finnegan."

"Comes down to that, does it?" said Wolfbait, returning the grin. "Yeah, I had you two pegged for bounty men from the start."

"Bounty?" said Drake. "Who said any such thing? Why, we're old friends of Finnegan, nothing more. Here to check up on him, for old times' sake, don't you know."

"Like we told you before, this here ain't the place you're looking for."

"No? Funny, I guess I won't believe you, seeing as how I know you've been lying to me all along. Yessir, this place isn't called Ball Gulch or whatever you claim it to be. It's Boar Gulch good and proper, because you said as much not but a few minutes ago. And as for not knowing about Stoneface? Bull. Now, I'll gladly leave, but you tell me where I can find him, since he's not here, in his very own bar. The Last Drop, the very bar he owns. Now why is that, I wonder?"

Wolfbait's beard fluffed in the light breeze that sneaked in through the open door. He motioned toward the outdoors.

Again, a long moment of silence filled the room.

Finally, Matson said, "Come on, Drake. Let's go see what's keepin' the boys."

The other man grunted and shoved up from the table,

pitching the chair backward and clunking it to the floor. "Yeah. Might as well."

As they walked out, Mace stopped in the doorway. "We'll be back . . . old man." He touched his hat brim and followed Drake out onto the porch, then down the steps.

Nosey, Wolfbait, Bone, and the boy all heard the cold laughter of the two men as they descended the steps and walked down the street.

Chapter 11

Nosey had been asked by Rollie and Pops to stay on premises while they were gone, and as their employee, he was in no position to refuse. However, given the visit of the two rogues, he gratefully took Wolfbait up on his offer of staying overnight with him at the bar.

Besides, working for Rollie and Pops was a whole lot easier than digging for gold. He'd bought a claim a half mile or so from town and managed to cobble together a tiny cabin with the help of a couple of fellows he paid with the last of his cash. The cabin had served him well since his arrival in the Gulch years before.

Digging at the site was an altogether different challenge, and one he loathed. The odds his claim contained a useful amount of gold were not in his favor. So he wrote instead, which had been his goal since roving westward after an ouster from his home back East where he'd been a stink-stirring journalist.

Dallying with the daughter of a crooked businessman, he had discovered her father had been up to little good. He was also being chased by hired thugs of another big-city fellow to whom he owed a substantial amount in gambling debt. Deciding it wasn't worth sticking around Nosey had headed west.

"Been a dream of mine for years now," Wolfbait said suddenly.

"What's that?" said Nosey, hoping the old man didn't snore.

"Why, to spend a night locked up in a bar!"

"Just to clarify, you won't actually be doing any drinking."

"Aw, now don't go and spoil my fun before I even start!" Wolfbait winked and lugged blankets out of the roomy accommodation Rollie and Pops shared out back behind the saloon.

"Where are you going with those blankets?" said Nosey.

"Out to the bar, where do you think?" Wolfbait ambled past him and dropped two wool blankets on the newly swept floor behind the bar. "It's the only place those savages ain't soiled with all their chaw juice. Honestly, you'd think they were all raised in barns."

Nosey double-checked the front door was locked, then peered over the bar. Wolfbait hadn't bedded down yet, but was lifting free one of the better bottles of whiskey, something tucked in the back called "Mama's Downfall." He winked again and poured two shots to the rim. "Always have me a slug before I retire of an evening."

"Just as long as it's one slug. I'm not convinced those two bounty hunters won't circle back tonight." Nosey sipped the whiskey Wolfbait put in front of him. "I think they believe we have Rollie tucked in here somewhere, hiding from them."

"Rollie hide? Ha. That proves they don't know the man a single little bit. Why, Rollie Finnegan would no sooner hide than I'd no sooner bed down in here without my trusty old gut shredder here. Now, you going to gnaw on that glass all night or can a hardworking fellow such as myself get some sleep around here? I got me a feeling we'll have a day full of those two rascals. And more, if that Mace fool ain't lying."

Nosey smiled and set down the empty glass. "And don't forget the supply wagon's due tomorrow . . . or any time in the next few days."

"Knowing Chauncey, it'll take a week longer than he promised and we'll have to listen to how hard he worked."

"Yes, with Rollie and Pops gone, he hated to hear we'd be too busy with the bar to make the run."

"Since he doesn't trust anyone, he was stuck doing it himself!" Wolfbait slapped the bar top. "Oh, we take our jollies where we can get 'em, eh, boy? Well, good night."

"Good night to you, Wolfbait. Shout if you hear something."

"Same to you."

The night passed without incident, though Wolfbait swore he heard a scuffling outdoors in the narrow hours, so he poured himself a drink and eased back into slumber.

The morning began as so many days did in the high peaks of the Sawtooth Range, clear and blue and fine. After ample cups of coffee and a quick trip to Geoff the Scot's for a slab of mock-apple pie for each of them, Nosey and Wolfbait settled down on a bench out front to watch the rest of the little main street awaken. There was Wheeler's Mercantile and Emporium, and the Lucky Strike, and Horkins' Hardware and Horkins' Assay Office.

Bone and his boy sauntered down the street, nodding and actually smiled at them.

Seemed the first smile Wolfbait could recall. "He acted odd the whole time he was here yesterday."

"He thinks you and he are now bosom pals."

The old goat jerked back as if Nosey had slapped him. "Why would he get that idea?"

"The way you spoke of him as a friend. I don't think he hears that too often."

"Bah! I meant that about the entire town."

"Too late, I'm afraid," said Nosey, nodding past him.

Wolfbait looked to see Bone and the boy making for them. "Oh no."

But movement far beyond the southern end of the main street caught the old miner's eye. Up in the treed slope behind Geoff the Scot's eatery, Horkins' Hardware, and his brother's assay office. *Mule deer?* he wondered. *No, that shadow is too tall for a muley.*

Bone's boy had seen the old-timer visoring his eyes and staring off into the trees, did the same. As if he were reading Wolfbait's mind, he said, "Riders up there."

Bone spun and squinted toward the trees. "You're right, boy. There ain't nobody got better eyesight than my boy. Got that from his ma, rest her."

For a moment, Bone's son straightened his usually slouched shoulders. "More than one rider."

"And that's not the road in," said Nosey.

"Fellas," said Wolfbait, looking eastward. "I expect there's trouble a-brewing. I see more men on that slope."

Bone nodded, looking westward and up the bare hill behind the bar. "Uh-huh. I expect yonder'll be more."

"Good morning," said a voice coming to them from the north end of town.

The group of four tense men spun as one to see Mace Matson trotting toward them. He rode a fine, high-stepping gray adorned with simple but shining black leather tack. He also held a rifle balanced across his lap. Looking fresh as a new daisy, he reined the horse to a halt before them and smiled as though he'd slept the sleep of angels.

Wolfbait didn't like him any better than he had the day before. "What do you want?" he said, wishing he'd brought his shotgun out to the porch with him.

"I thought I made my intentions somewhat clear yesterday." The man controlled the dancing horse and didn't let his smile slip. "I want Stoneface Finnegan, here and now, and then me and my boys will be on our way. And no, I didn't buy for a moment your story about this being Ball Gulch or whatever foolish name you fed me yesterday. I also don't believe he's not in town. From what I've heard, he never leaves this dismal hellhole.

Nosey shook his head. "As we said yesterday, Mr. Matson, the man you seek is not here."

Matson shook his head and looked briefly past them, up the slope toward the western edge of town. "I lied a little myself yesterday, too, so I'm not going to cast too much blame. Remember when I said I had a dozen or so men due to come in any time?" He looked at them all in turn, then his eyes settled on Wolfbait.

The old man returned the look but with no sign of a smirk. "What? You plan to hoorah the entire town?" He snorted. "Take more than however many men you claim to have. Been tried before and not a one of the attackers lived long enough to brag on their stupidity."

"Well, the big difference is that my sixteen men well technically with me there are sixteen—haven't yet lost a fight." Mattson nodded as if agreeing with himself. "It's a fact. Mm-hmm. And we don't plan on breaking our streak hereabouts. Now, where oh where is Stoneface?" He stood in his stirrups and shouted, "Oh, Stoneface! Stoneface, you hiding from ol' Mace?"

"You idiot!" shouted Wolfbait. "He's not here!"

The insult slid off Matson like water off a frog. "Okay, okay, I'll play the game, but not for long. If he's not here, where is he?"

Nosey smiled. "If I were to tell you, I wouldn't be much of a friend, now, would I?"

"I admire your dedication, but Finnegan ain't worth it. He's a wanted man with a substantial bounty on his head. I will be doing the work of the law, of justice, and of right."

"Oh, so you're a lawman, huh?" said Wolfbait. "Well, why didn't you say so?"

Mace canted his head to the side. "Would that make the difference?"

"With you? Nah. You ain't anything but a fool. And a liar, to boot!"

For the first time, Matson's patient façade slipped. He ground his teeth together. "I will not leave town without his head swinging in a bag off my pommel."

Wolfbait crossed his arms. "Tell me this. Since you're such a burr under my saddle blanket, why can't I just shoot you right now and be done with it?"

"You can. Go ahead." Matson shifted in his saddle and nodded southward with his head. "But you should know my associate—you remember Drake Keller from yesterday, I expect—is convincing a strange, haggy, little pinch-faced woman to accompany him back to our camp yonder in the hills.

"Now, Drake prides himself on being a popular gent with the ladies, but if this woman, I believe she's the wife of Pulaski, proprietor of the Lucky Strike gambling hall and rooms for rent, should not find him as handsome as do other women, he will drag her by the hair. He'll make some effort at keeping her alive, of course, until such time as Stoneface Finnegan shows himself to me."

Nosey held up his hands as if he were being arrested and looked the man in the face. "I tell you here and now, with God as my witness, Rollie Finnegan is not in this town. He's gone and we don't know how long he'll be gone."

"Nor when we can expect him back!" added Wolfbait. "So stop harassing people. Leave that woman alone!"

Matson shifted in his saddle. "If he is as you say, not here, then you must know where he is. You'll just have to tell me . . . or that woman will die a hard, cold death. But not without screeching like a trap-caught weasel first."

"We can't tell you where he is," said Nosey, still holding up his hands in a vain effort to show honesty. Uncertain why it seemed like a good idea, he made an attempt to somehow prove his truthfulness. "We don't know where he's gone. If you know him so well, you know he's a detective, and as such he'll often go off for stretches of time hunting fugitives."

"Liar. He ain't a detective no more and he hasn't been since he was gutted and left for dead back in Denver City."

Nosey shrugged. "That's where you're wrong, but suit yourself. You're such a genius."

Matson shook his head, the annoying smile once more

on his face. It seemed to say to them all *I know so much and you know so little*. Before riding back toward the north end of town, he turned and said, "Oh, by the way, until you tell me where I can find Stoneface, me and my men will be here, picking off one townsfolk a day, maybe more. I haven't decided yet. If we get bored with that, we'll set to taking this town by force.

"My men have a powerful thirst and we could use some food, too. I count two establishments that sell liquor and at least one mercantile. Oh, and two other places where we can buy a meal. No, what am I saying? We'll be taking what we want. That's the beauty of traveling like this—I don't need to carry any money on me!"

A staccato of barking laughs followed him up the street.

Nosey had to hold Wolfbait back from rushing inside for his scattergun. "All you'd do is anger him. He's already enough off the beam, as you might say."

Chapter 12

It was an awful time for a band of mercenaries to descend on little Boar Gulch. The most recent gold strike hadn't amounted to much, just enough to whet the hunger for the roving hordes of seekers looking for the next sure spot. If not fizzled, it had at least whimpered along, offering the ardent among them enough color to keep the tantalizing dream alive, dangling before them each day.

And so the Gulch, as the locals called it, managed to cling to its existence season after season, the shops developed in the first big flush stayed. Others came, a few others went.

The brothel, run by Madge Gladwell, stayed in business and kept the single, drunk, lonely, and frustrated miners from shooting at each other every night of the week. Sullen gunplay was down to every few nights of the week.

The arrival of Mace Matson and his band of renegades couldn't have come at a more inopportune time. Not only were the town's de facto law keepers—Pops and Rollie—gone from town, but the mayor, Chauncey Wheeler, as well. Stalwart, reliable Pieder and Sal, had also decided to leave on a camping trek deeper into the mountains.

Pieder had been an avid angler much of his life, beginning in his youth in his native land of Sweden. Since emigrating to the United States, he'd had precious little time to pursue his interest. Most of his time had been spent in search of whatever future the promising new place might offer the bold young man with all before him and nothing left alive behind.

Nosey, Wolfbait, Bone, and the boy all moved inside The Last Drop. The thought of all those gunmen roving the hills felt downright spooky.

"You want a marksman, you can't do better than my boy," Bone said, nodding his long, stubbled, horsey face. His big red ears got redder, unaccustomed as he was to being a braggart.

Nosey nodded. "Well, you did say he had good sight."

"What about gunplay?" said Wolfbait. "Seeing's one thing, but lining her up and squeezing on that trigger's a whole other deal. Especially focusing on a man."

While looking at his scuffed boot toes, Bone's boy Junior said, "That don't bother me none. Back home, we mixed it up with the Doolittle clan all the time. I laid a passel of them low." His own set of ears, the equal of his pater's, bloomed crimson.

"And a gun?" said Wolfbait, suspecting where the conversation was headed. He squinted through the knot hole in the back wall of the living quarters behind the bar.

"All we got is the squirrel gun," said Bone. "She's a muzzle loader, but she'll shoot true enough."

"No, no, that ain't going to be near good enough for a situation such as this," said Wolfbait. "Got to have a modern weapon or none at all. Might as well throw rocks at them as rely on something that needs that much attention with every shot."

"Can't help you then," said Bone, miffed at the rebuff of his family's most cherished possession.

"Here," said Nosey, tugging free a spare rifle Pops had left behind on two pegs above the foot of his cot. "I'll look for bullets."

The kid held the polished rifle and shook his head. "I can't take this."

"Good," said Wolfbait. "Ain't nobody offering it as a gift. Just a loan, see?"

The kid smiled and his father responded for them both. "That sounds good to us."

Nosey and Wolfbait departed the bar, making for different directions to spread the warning word and round up volunteers.

Less than ten minutes later, gunfire south of town brought Bone and his boy back outside.

They had little time for examining the situation. A shot came in from the ridge to the south, fast and hot, and quicker than they'd expected. It chewed a dusty furrow about a dozen feet too short of its intended mark—namely the kid.

Instinct forced the father and son to jerk low, even though a wall kept them hidden well enough from all but the luckiest shots at that distance. From its poor placement, they figured it had been fired in haste. That didn't mean the next one, expected any second, wouldn't find its home in somebody's skull.

The kid had quickly gotten the feel of the strange new rifle and with a nod to his father, who nodded approval, the kid whipped off a solid shot in the direction of the shooter. It brought no tell-tale shrieks, but it did beckon another shot down at them. Another poorly placed effort.

The kid eyed the hillside and shot again. His victim shrieked, then toppled. A slow-rising cloud of blue smoke wafted and rose, teasing apart among the black-shaded trunks of the Ponderosa-riddled slope.

"All okay?" shouted a voice from behind them. It was Wolfbait, still picking his way up the street toward the north end.

"Yep!" shouted Bone, quick and clipped, knowing the value of keeping palaver to a minimum in such a situation. "I reckon that was good shooting, son, but we need to recall how it was back home in the green hills of ol' Tenny. You know what I'm driving at?"

The kid nodded, his Adam's apple bobbing as the words came up thick, pride of memory misting their eyes. "Shoot and move, shoot and move," he whispered.

"That's it, son. Now, you see that stack of barrels yonder?"

The kid nodded, easing the hammer back once more.

"Good, 'cause that's where we're bound once that fool lets another shot fly. I'll go first. You lay into them with a fine round, then join me. We'll leapfrog it from one spot to the next. Get ourselves to that log stable Chauncey owns."

"I know every log of it," said Junior. "We all-but built it our own selves anyhow."

"This ain't no time for prideful thinking, son. But yes, we put a powerful bit of sweat into that stable. It's solid. We'll hole up there. Got us plenty of bullets and we can poke free the chinking enough to deliver a few choice shots, I reckon." That was all Bone had to say. He nodded once, his squirrel gun gripped tight in his right hand, his big knuckles white, his stubbled face pocked with sweat. "Give the word, son."

"Git her!" said the boy, his rifle leveled on a suspicious dark hump poking up from behind a gray granite knob. He was certain the hump was the hat of one of the raiders.

Bone bolted and the kid made the funny little piggy noise with his left nostril, same noise he always made a hair of a second before he tightened his finger on the trigger.

The bullet bored a hole in that black hump and the black hump jerked up, then dropped back out of sight behind the boulder. No shouts this time. But then again, the kid didn't wait to cock an ear. *Time for crowing later,* he thought.

He tucked low and followed his father's path, catching up to the man as a bullet whizzed in like a fire-plagued bee, pocking the dirt where his trailing leg had been.

"Good to see you, boy," said Bone. No smile, just relief.

"And you."

"See that wagon?"

"Yep."

"Let's go again."

The boy nodded, licked the ball of his thumb, and grazed it over the foresight. "Yes, sir." It took him a moment to line up a target. But he found one—a knee, and just below it, the toe of a boot. He was tempted to shoot for the boot, then remembered it was no time to toy with his quarry. This situation was worse than any with the Doolittle clan. Far worse. Back then they'd slap-and-tickle each other before tiring of such antics and call forth blood. Shooting at outlaws, it was kill or die, right off quick.

Having decided on the knee, he set the shot, said, "Git her!" and on the exhale, the piggy sound preceded his shot. He saw the man's kneecap explode at the same time his father's screech pierced the air to his right. The boy drew back behind the dense heap of barrels and was already down and running toward Bone.

His father, a collapsed heap twenty feet from him, halfway between the barrels and the wagon, shouted without rising, without moving. It was a leg wound. The boy saw blood squirting, then spraying in a mist, then squirting from somewhere hidden, somewhere on his father's sturdy body. Maybe the Maker was telling him enough was enough. Eye for an eye, leg for a leg.

"Stay put, boy! You stay there! He thinks I'm dead. He'll not shoot me twice, but he's a-waiting for you to poke your head out of that hole like an adder, and then you're done, boy."

"But Pap—"

"No, I say!"

The boy had come to a place in the path of his life he could no longer avoid. He recognized, if not for the first time, his father might not always be right in his thinking. Coming to a decision of his own he was confident in, Junior shouldered the rifle, bent lower than someone looking down on him from a hilly refuge might expect, and eyed the terrain.

The only clue to where the shooter might be—no doubt savvy and on the move, too—was the drifting, disappearing cloud of smoke lifting up and off westward.

The breeze was slight. He looked higher up that high rock face, then lower than the last shot had been. He saw the remnants of a manmade cloud . . . there. And behind it, less than a shadow, more than a shadow. A man's shoulder, or the shade of one. Good enough if it chipped stone, good enough to buy time to haul Pap back here.

"Better behind barrels than a gappy wagon," he muttered, lined up the shot, worked his nostril, and touched her off. Not waiting to see if the shadow become powdered rock, he leaned the rifle between two barrels, crouched low, and dashed for Pap.

Junior's worn boots crunched gravel and his father's head moved slightly. "Boy, no! Get back!"

"No, Pap! Hush now!" As fast as he was able, Junior snatched the ragged cuffs of his father's trousers, dragged him backward, and jerked him to the right, guessing a bullet might be winging its way toward them.

He was right. A bullet smacked hard right where his father's chest had been, but the boy kept pulling. His father screamed, and though all of this took but seconds, he imagined his father's grievous wound filling with grit and somehow killing Pap. That thought made him pull all the harder, and before he knew it, Junior had Bone safely behind the barrels again.

His father had always seemed so much larger than he. Of course, he had lifted the man up from the ground any number of times when he'd had too much corn liquor, but somehow his father felt as light and as stiff and awkward in his own big bony hands as a sun-puckered plank.

"Pap!" He straddled his father and tugged him to lean back against the barrels.

His father's head lolled a moment. Just when the boy

was about to smackcd him hard across this grizzled face, Bone opened his eyes. "You best think twice before you strike your Pap, son." Then he smiled.

Junior knew it was going to be okay. Had to be. Just had to be, elsewise, what would he do with himself?

Chapter 13

"This can't last for long," said Wolfbait, before remembering he was alone.

Nosey had said he was going to take the east edge once he peeled off from Bone and his boy.

Wolfbait sorely wished Rollie and Pops were about. He understood deep down how every single one of the folks in town felt. It had been a couple of years since Rollie had come to town and had dragged behind him a whole wagon filled with troubles. Not that he meant to, of course, but that hardly mattered any more.

Trying to concentrate on the task at hand, Wolfbait gave thought to the situation. The fact remained that all their lives were in danger once again because of Stoneface Finnegan. All the other times—that first was a humdinger, with killing Cleve Danziger and his gang—Rollie had been around, and had never asked anybody to do anything more than defend themselves.

Wolfbait knew the man felt powerfully guilty about it all, but once more they were in the same boat. The difference was Rollie was nowhere about. Wolfbait hated thinking this way because the man—a good man, to boot—was his friend. "Dang it, Rollie," he muttered, doing his best to low-walk around the far side of the hall, where Madge and her ladies had taken up residence.

Chauncey, the goober who had hired it built, had meant the building to be a town hall of sorts, a meeting place, a church, a little bit of everything. Even a "cultural center." That had raised a few eyebrows and chuckles. Not that Wolfbait could fault the little fat mayor for wanting to "bring the outside world in," as the man had put it. Boar Gulch could be a mite trying at times, filled with people who were there for one reason only—to make a fortune. The ones who left were those whose desire to keep seeking that fortune had grown stronger than their desire to sink roots and keep trying.

Wolfbait had been one of those, too, at first. That had been many years before, as a younger man. His past included, among other occupations and experiences and adventures, a run as an instructor of the classics at a boarding school back east in Connecticut. "Ha," he muttered, letting the humor of that notion pull a smile on his old, whiskered face. "If they could see me now."

Shaking his head and glancing about, he reached up to the back door atop a small landing He rapped hard and quick, hoping at least one of Madge's girls was in the kitchen where they took turns cooking for themselves, family style.

While Wolfbait didn't have much use any longer for the finer points of female companionship, at least not those a man willingly paid for, he did enjoy the company and conversation of these tender ladies and would often bring a heaping mound of hot biscuits in exchange for a couple of hours of chat and cups of coffee. He knew he was sometimes looked on as a nuisance by some, but several of the girls, Julep and Tansy, in particular, seemed to genuinely enjoy sitting around the table with him and chewing the fat. He didn't think they got much kind talk from the half-drunk miners who came a-calling at the front door.

When no response to his knocking came, his first thought was they'd maybe peeked out a window and had seen he wasn't carrying a plate of biscuits, so they were ignoring him. Shaking that away, his wry smile slipped. *Could the invaders have already gotten here?* He'd been watching for a while and had seen no sign of comings or goings, which any time before midday was not in the least unusual.

His neck hairs prickled. He bent low and crept to the hinge side of the door and rapped again. Nothing. Then he heard steps inside the kitchen. Heavy and heeled. Not the usual soft sounds of the women wearing their woolen socks or house slippers.

The thumb latch on the outside door handle depressed and the door creaked open a few inches. Then a few more. He still couldn't see up into the gap.

"Hello?" said a woman's voice, low and husky.

That would be Madge, thought Wolfbait.

But if things were all right with her, she'd not be so wary. She was a boisterous, intelligent, opinionated woman who had more brains than most all the men in town put together. With some to spare. She'd drawn him out on several occasions and they'd gotten right down into the dirt, talking about all manner of philosophy and such.

"You don't fool me, Wolfbait," she'd said. "Somewhere

beneath that hunched old back and long beard and 'shucks' this and 'by golly' that, there's a scholar and a gentleman.''

He'd pulled back as if slapped about the chops, but couldn't help being honored and even a little embarrassed by the fine woman's assessment. She was right of course, in a manner of speaking. But that had been some time ago.

Currently he was a gun-toting, mountain-dwelling rascal who was trying to protect his friends from an invading gang. "Madge?" he said, licking his lips. He said it again. The door opened another couple of inches.

"Wolfbait?" Her voice was low, his name a forced whisper.

"Yeah! You all okay? Bad men on the loose. Need you to hole up and—"

"Can't!" was the only response, then the door clunked shut.

He froze. Trouble inside, no doubt. Madge never acted so rude, so odd.

Maybe by knocking he'd put her in danger! Wolfbait backed up a step, then another, glanced behind himself and toward the corner of the building. Should an unsavory bolt out that door he could open up on him.

Nobody came out.

But he heard a muffled shout, a woman's voice, then another, a man's voice, as if responding. The second voice rose into a shout, barking out obscenities.

Wolfbait got his back up. That was just not acceptable.

Those women inside were his friends, and in a world where such things as friends were few and far between, especially in the mountains, it was a fellow's responsibility to take care of said friends. But what to do? How many vile dogs were inside? Had they caused harm? Were they waiting for him? And where?

Good thing few windows were along the south side, where he was angled. His first question was how to get in? Then he remembered the firewood cubby hole Bone and his boy had built at Madge's request.

It led from the woodshed lean-to off the north side, just the other side of the kitchen. From hugging their cookstove in the winter hours, Wolfbait knew for a verifiable fact come decent weather the ladies often left that wood box door unlatched during daylight hours so as to let cooling breezes drift into the kitchen from the shaded north side.

Only a light, gauzy cloth was left to hang over the opening to keep bugs from pesking on in. That meant he would be able to nose his way in, and with any luck he'd not be seen or heard. Trouble was, between where he was and where he needed to be—in the woodshed—were the back kitchen stairs and to the left, a window.

He bent lower, readjusted his grip on his trusty old gutshredder, and made it around the base of the steps, his eyes on the window the entire time.

The blue-flowered curtains were closed, but gappy, so he couldn't be certain if anyone was watching. No movement of the curtains gave him the confidence he needed to peel his eyes from looking at the window long enough to once more hug the back wall. Scooching to his right, he slid beneath the window, decided nobody inside could very easily see him, and hustled faster toward the corner.

Another shout sounded from deeper in the building. Hard to tell if it was a man or a woman. Maybe from one flight up of the three floors above.

He quickened his ambling, lopsided pace and made it to the woodshed, where he lifted the bent nail stuck in the hasp holding the door pinned closed. He eased the door open just wide enough to slip in, but the sun-dried wood and oil-deprived hinges squawked. He froze, half-in, half-out.

Hearing no sounds other than his own thudding heart, he licked his lips and pulled himself fully into the darkened interior of the woodshed. He paused once again, heard nothing, and, inch by inch, closed the door. Stepping with care, he made his way through the thick layer of wood duff, old bark, chips, and chunks of wood.

The musty, off-season smell reminded him of the woodshed of his childhood home in New England, but Madge's shed was still about one-third filled with stove-length splits. The woodstove was in use year round, it being how the ladies cooked their food, boiled their coffee and tea water, and gave them something to crowd around in the early mornings of the off-seasons.

In the near dark, Wolfbait squinted and groped his way along the wall with his fingertips until he felt the edge of the little wood-framed opening of the wood box that led to the kitchen. He felt in the space and his fingers touched wood. Fire wood. *Of course*, he thought. *What else would be in a wood box?*

Then he cursed himself for following through with such a fool notion. He should have just kicked in the back door and leveled on whoever wasn't a woman. About to go back out through the squawking door and try his luck at a proper entrance, he heard voices in the kitchen. A man's voice and a woman's. It was Madge, that much was certain. The man's voice wasn't one he was familiar with, and he knew everybody in town.

Whoever it was hadn't left, or had come back into the room. Wolfbait listened carefully.

"Now look, you. Me and the rest of the boys got a right to do as we see fit, seeing as how you and them others are our prisoners, so to speak. We get through with this town, you'll be begging us to take you with us anyways. Won't be nothing left of this fly speck!"

Evidently the man thought he was mighty funny, for he set to braying at his own joke like a donkey.

Wolfbait sneered and gripped the shotgun tighter. He bent lower, remembering the wood box was about knee height, and then he saw slivers of light show between the logs, and realized there wasn't as much stacked wood as he had thought. An idea came to mind. Nodding to himself, he thought it might just work. If not, well, it beat doing nothing.

He held the shotgun aimed toward the kitchen and balanced the barrel's end on a chunk of firewood. With his right hand he reached in and jostled the stack.

The man kept yammering, so Wolfbait jostled the wood again. A top piece dislodged and tumbled a few inches, enough to make a scraping, clunking sound as another piece thunked against the side of the box.

That shut the fool's mouth. Then he mumbled, "What the—" Louder, to the woman, he said, "What was that?"

"Oh . . . it was probably our tomcat. He keeps the mice scarce. But I wouldn't go near there if I were you. He's tougher than any man I've ever come across, by far. He'll tear you a whole new face."

Wolfbait's bushy eyebrows rose like a couple of startled

birds taking flight. *Madge knew he was in the wood box.* They didn't have any ol' tomcat! She was banking on Wolfbait to dose this devil. He peered in again and figured she was to the left of the box, likely over by the dry sink.

He heard bootsteps draw closer. Then the light he'd seen between the logs winked out, shifted as the man angled his face side to side. Then the fool reached in and moved a piece of wood. He peered in and Wolfbait saw the man's face half lit. It was a homely face, a big nose that had been broken more than a few times. Two piggy eyes, dark and beady, sought in the darkness.

Time for this fool to feel the tomcat's claws, thought Wolfbait, and just when the man began to straighten up and say, "Bah!" Wolfbait jostled a log once more and did his best tomcat voice. It was not impressive, he had to admit. Been a long time since he'd been called on to imitate a critter, least of all a cat. But it worked.

The man bent down once more and leaned in.

Wolfbait said, "Meow, dirtbag," and triggered his trusty old shotgun.

The man whipped backward, not even able to get off a scream. Wolfbait felt bad about the mess in the kitchen, but he had not time for such niceties, as Madge was there in an instant.

Chucking firewood out of the way, she said, "Get your skinny old backside in here, Wolfbait! Other men are upstairs with the girls, but I hear them thumping around. They'll be down here any second. Hope you have more shells!"

"You bet I do. Help me now!"

The woman was as strong as she looked, and yarned him through that wood box, skinning up near every part of him as she dragged. He managed to gain his feet beneath him and dash to the side by the dry sink while she rummaged at the shot man, boots still twitching, fingertips jerking, but his head was nearly gone. She rose up with his gunbelt and revolver, strapped them on, and took the other side of the door.

Just in time, too.

A large man shoved his way through the kitchen door, cutting quite a figure in new red longhandles and wearing his guns. A tall sugarloaf hat squashed down a drape of long, black hair, and on his feet were dog-eared boots. He sent the door spasming to a stop against the toe of Madge's boot where she stood behind the door.

He didn't notice. "What's happenin' in here?"

Just before he responded, Wolfbait noticed that the man's back was thick with rolls of fat that jounced as he stomped into the room.

Any second and he would see Wolfbait to his right. Partly in shadow.

Wolfbait beat him to it. "Here's what's happening, jackass!"

Freed by his gnarled old trigger finger, the shell Wolfbait had thumbed into his beloved old single-barreled blaster slammed into the man's breadbasket and tore it wide open.

The force of the shot at such close distance shoved the fat man into a wall of shelves laden with canned goods, sacks of meal, flour, beans, coffee, and pots and pans.

As the big, flailing lummox slammed into them, his hat popped off and the wall of shelves collapsed, sending the contents flying in all directions before clattering to the wood floor.

The red-clad man with the gaping wound in his chest big enough to fit two fists into stared with glazing eyes through the smoke and flour dust. A thin but steady stream of cornmeal drizzled down onto his head from where a sack had snagged on the edge of a high shelf. The last of the pot lids spun and settled with a clatter.

"Good Lord, Wolfbait. That was loud," whispered Madge.

"Yeah," he said, rubbing his chin. "And a right mess, too. Don't worry. I'll clean up after myself."

"That's the least of our woes," she said, offering him a grim grin.

He rummaged for another shell. "How many more up there?"

"Ah, let's see . . . four that I know of. Others might have come in once I was cornered in here by that fool." She nodded toward the first dead man.

Their quick, whispered conversation was cut short by a shout from atop the staircase in the hallway beyond. "Jed? What you doin'?"

Wolfbait and Madge didn't move.

"Jed? Aw, hell." Another set of feet made their way down the stairs, this time in socks.

Madge had closed the kitchen door and Wolfbait shook his head, but she'd already taken her place behind the door. He resumed his spot near the door, still in half shadow as another man came down the hallway.

He nudged the door open with a knuckle. "Jed?" Peering in, he saw Wolfbait through the crack in the door. "Oh, hell!" The man jerked backward and the door slipped closed.

Knowing the outlaw was snatching for a gun, Wolfbait

whipped open the door with his right hand and ducked down, leveling the shotgun on the man in the hallway. Fully clothed save for a hat and boots, the man had drawn a long-barreled revolver and had just about brought it up to bear on whoever might be opening the kitchen door when Wolfbait jerked the trigger.

He heard a small dead thud from his gun, then nothing happened. Wolfbait looked down at his old shotgun as if he'd just been handed a sack full of spiders, then up again at the man in the hallway. The hatless, bootless man smiled and laid his thumb on the hammer, but a gunshot to Wolfbait's right caught the stranger in the throat and shoved him into the hallway closet door. He slammed hard as if he were trying to break down the door with the side of his head.

Instinct jerked Wolfbait to a crouch, but he looked up to see Madge behind the door. She'd jammed the tip of the revolver's barrel through the crack on the hinge side as it had opened.

She looked at Wolfbait and nodded. "There."

"Well, I'm obliged," he whispered, cracking open the shotgun and picking out the shell. He leaned the gun against the wall. "She never let me down before, but I can't risk that happening again." He looked up at the staircase. "This keeps on, won't be no need for us to climb the stairs and go after those rascals!"

"What's the matter? You afraid of a little exertion . . . old-timer?" She winked at him.

"I'm just saving my strength for more important matters, that's all. I'll show you later."

"I look forward to that."

The sound of more stomping upstairs reached them, then a door slammed and a woman screamed.

"I best get up there." Wolfbait ducked into the hallway, looking up. His spot was not visible from above, nor could he see to the top of the stairs. Didn't mean he wanted to dawdle, though. He stripped the gunbelt off the man who'd fallen and slid the long-barreled revolver from beneath the man's knee, where it had wedged when the man met his end in a crumpled heap.

"Too damn long and fancy," he growled, looking at the weapon.

"Here," she said, handing him the two gun rig she'd strapped on. "Long, I like. I'll swap with you."

"I can't take that. You'll need it. There's that other one, off the fat one, but it's all covered in flour."

She'd already unbuckled the gun belt and thrust it at him. "Stop arguing. We have to save my girls!"

He grabbed the belt and strapped it on, checking both guns and loading five empty chambers. "Lazy fool," he muttered, then drew one, cocked it, and hugged the right wall, aiming upward.

He saw nothing and advanced toward the bottom of the stairs. He sensed more than saw Madge's presence just behind him and figured no point in telling her to stay downstairs. She wasn't the sort of person who took orders too well. Keeping his mind on the task at hand, he slid one hand along the railing and the other on the gun aimed upward, ready to go. He took one step up and felt softness beneath his boots then recalled the stairs had a fancy carpet runner down the center. He continued up. One of the steps squeaked and he winced and gritted his teeth. *Can't have everything.* He climbed.

Another scream came from above.

Madge, close behind him, whispered, "That was Julep!"

"Hush." Even in that tense moment Wolfbait felt the woman's flinty stare burning twin holes into his back.

Recalling one of Rollie's favored phrases, *In for a penny . . .* he hustled upward. Reaching the top he swiveled his head left then right, his long, wispy gray beard following like a scarf. All of the doors were closed. Just his luck, each one could be hiding a killer.

Madge nudged him and nodded toward the nearest door.

He nodded in return and licked dry lips. He hadn't thought just what he'd do if he had to burst into a room. Didn't work too well for the fellows who'd tried to barge into the kitchen. A high-pitch sobbing came from that room, quickly cut off as if the woman had been jerked hard.

That did it. Any wavering Wolfbait had felt a moment before evaporated like a puddle in the desert.

He kept the revolver pointed, jerked his head down the hall, and Madge nodded. She turned to face the other doors, her revolver cocked and ready. Wolfbait raised his left boot and was about to kick in the door when Madge leaned close and said in a kitten of a whisper, "No locks."

He nodded and stood to the right of the door, reached over, turned the knob and thrust the door in, then jerked his arm back.

A bullet whistled out past them and punched a tight, little hole in the front wall.

He thought he heard Madge growl beside him. Her place was receiving a beating. He guessed it would see a whole lot worse before they were done.

"Come on in, damn you!" said a low Southern voice.

"I heard your ruckus, but we was just commencing our party. And I ain't stoppin' for nothin'.''

Wolfbait peered low around the doorframe and got a finger snap glimpse of a naked man, save for his boots, seated on the bed, his back to the headboard. He had his left arm about the neck of a wide-eyed, tearful and red-faced young Julep, and he looked to be choking her tighter with each second that passed. She struggled, and the man delivered another shot.

Wolfbait didn't dare fire willy-nilly with the girl half atop the man. He gnawed his lip a moment while the man spoke again.

"Seems to me you ought at least respond to a gentle-man's kind invitation." Another shot buzzed past them and the man howled with laughter.

Wolfbait snatched off his hat and winged it into the room. At the same time the man shot at it, Wolfbait dropped to his right knee and brought the revolver to line up nicely with the part of the man farthest from the girl—which happened to be the man's right boot.

Wolfbait's bullet did what he hoped. It punched right through the wide part of the boot sole and passed out through the top, then out the window. Glass shattered, but the sound was nothing compared with the man's screaming.

In his frantic flailing, he dropped his gun and let go of the girl, who dove to her left and off the bed. Wolfbait charged in, confident Madge would keep an eye on the other doors.

"Julep, you okay?" Wolfbait glanced at the near-naked woman who'd retreated to the far wall, massaging her neck which, he saw, was deep crimson with thick handprints.

The man had stopped just short of choking the life from her.

Instant rage welled in the crusty old miner. Stepping close to the yowling man, he snapped him hard on the side of his face with the butt of his pistol. Wolfbait hadn't thought the blow would do anything more than annoy and shut him up for a moment, but it did. The fellow's eyes popped wide and he stiffened as if he'd just remembered something very important. Then he jerked to his side and nearly toppled from the bed, unconscious or dead.

Wolfbait didn't care which.

The whole time the man's shot foot squirted blood, then dwindled to a slow pumping. But he was past caring, and Wolfbait took grim glee in seeing the wound. "Help me truss him, Julep." He snatched up the man's blue-checked shirt, then tossed a dirty green kerchief also from atop the pile of the man's shed clothes. "Here, gag him. I'll tie his arms and feet."

Julep had tugged on a flimsy robe, for which Wolfbait was grateful. He didn't need distractions just now, even if they were interesting ones.

"Is he dead?" she asked.

"We can only hope. But if he ain't, when he comes around he's going to be ornery and thrashing." He finished binding the man, then handed the woman her tormentor's pistol. "Here. If he comes around, shoot him."

"What if he doesn't?"

Wolfbait grinned. "Do anything you want to him. He sure as heck did to you."

"Hurry up in there!" whispered Madge from the hallway.

"Don't nag me!" Wolfbait growled in a low whisper, half kidding, as he crept up beside her once more.

"I heard that. I also heard noise from Annette's room." She nodded toward the door directly across from them.

"Same thing," he said, trying the knob. Again, the door swung inward. And he was attacked by some sort of snarling creature. As he ducked and tried to shield his face, it occurred to him said creature smelled a whole lot like rose water.

Madge came to his rescue with one free arm. Still holding the revolver trained on the hallway with the other, she growled, "Settle down, Annette!"

The attacker eased off just as she was about to sink teeth into Wolfbait's upper arm.

"My word, girl," he said. "I thought we were on friendly terms!"

Recognition of the old codger widened her eyes and she eased off. "Oh, Wolfbait—I'm sorry. I thought—"

He shoved past her, but saw only an empty room, the rumpled bed, a tidy dresser top with various items he figured ladies seemed to value—a hair brush, bottles of scent, other odd items he didn't dare want to ever know about. On the far wall was an open window he looked out.

Annette walked up behind him. "He was in here, but when he heard the shooting downstairs, he left through the window."

"Mighty big drop," said Wolfbait.

"I think he hurt his leg when he landed."

"Good." Wolfbait risked a farther look to both sides, but saw no sign of anyone. "He'll probably warn the others, which given how we've been operating, might be a good thing!" He smiled at her, hoping to show a confidence he didn't particularly feel.

She didn't look convinced. Also looked as if she'd taken a nasty backhand to the face. "How?"

"Well, it'll let them know we folks of Boar Gulch ain't pushovers!"

A ruckus behind them at the door made them both look up. The rest of the girls were peeking in.

"No others up here," said Madge.

"We were afraid to open our doors," said Tansy.

"Don't blame you." Wolfbait grinned. "After this, I might be afraid to get out of bed every morning."

"I'm going to check the rest of the place," said Madge.

"Not without me, you ain't." He took the lead, checking his revolver and scouting the rest of the rooms, just in case. "That one on the end." He nodded toward a last closed door.

"My room," said Madge. "Should be empty."

"That's a shame," said Wolfbait, waggling his eyebrows.

"Down, fella."

They checked her room, which though slightly larger, was outfitted much the same as the others. Unlike the room where clothing appeared to have been tossed in a rush, Madge's possessions were all tidy.

Wolfbait offered some instruction. "We'll head back downstairs. Check every corner as we go."

"You girls help Julep, Madge put in. "She's still got one of them. But he's tied."

"Don't go easy on him," said Wolfbait as he descended the stairs, the biting end of his gun held ready before him. He didn't think any more gunmen were about, but it was no time to be sloppy.

He wondered how Nosey and Bone and the boy were

getting on. And where in the hell were the rest of the townsfolk?

The rest of the building was empty of any more living outlaws.

"I hate to leave you," he said, looking at Madge again. "But I have to see how the boys are faring."

"Go," she said. "We're fine. We'll drag the dead out back."

"Maybe wait until we know we've got rid of the rest of the devils first."

She nodded. "You sound confident."

He checked his bullet supply, retrieved another revolver from a dead man, and smiled. "No sense thinking the opposite. We'll get the bums." But he was far from certain. Nosey was not much of a shot and Bone and the boy, well, he just didn't know. They were likely decent bush fighters, but he'd not yet had to rely on them in a fight.

He tipped his hat to Madge.

She leaned close and kissed him. "Take care, Wolfbait."

"You, too."

He thought maybe she looked a little sad to see him go. He hoped so. He was right fond of spending time with her. Figuring the doors might be watched, he left through the woodshed, going slow the entire time. And leaving through the woodshed might give him a few extra yards of head start should lead come raining in on his back trail.

Chapter 14

Once he left Bone and his boy behind, Nosey kept Wolfbait's suggestion in mind and, keeping low, made for the north end of the street. Wolfbait had been going in the same direction but had made a narrower route of it.

Nosey scampered straight up the hill behind The Last Drop as if he were going on the trail up to Pieder and Sal's. But before reaching the top he angled right and paralleled the main street below.

It didn't take him long to come up on one of his fellow Gulchers, a man known to all for his baked goods and tasty dinner fare. Geoff the Scot, proprietor of Geoff the Scot's eatery, a diner he'd built up from a tent-and-stump affair in the early days to a hard-sided shack with tables and benches.

Geoff urged Nosey to draw in closer. "How you made it up here without getting shot is a miracle."

"I'm just lucky, I guess. Where is everybody else?"

"Those outlaws caught everybody by surprise," said the burly cook. "Pulaski and his wife slammed the doors, bolted them tight, and locked themselves in, but the invaders broke down the back door and dragged her out of there. We sent a few shots after them, but then the fellow who had her used her as a shield and we didn't dare risk firing any more."

Nose could tell by the look on Geoff's face the incident had rattled him.

"Pulaski, he's not so good with a gun, as you know, and while she's a sharp-tongued thing, she's not too scrappy. I only hope they don't hurt her. Pulaski, he lit out after them, but I got pinned down, couldn't go on." He rapped on his left leg and winced.

"What happened? Did you get shot?" said Nosey.

"No, I fell, bunged my knee up in good shape. Can't hold much weight on it just yet."

Nosey eyed the man's leg, swollen as big as a head in the middle. "I'm sorry to hear that, Geoff."

"Nah, could be worse. At least I'm not shot."

"True."

Geoff sighed and looked into the hills. "Oh, what a mess."

"Where's everybody else?" said Nosey, looking about for the dozen other townsfolk he should have seen.

"That's the thing." Geoff shrugged. "They're everywhere. They were either rousted by the invaders or just up and rabbited on their own at the first sign of them. I wouldn't be surprised if they were up there in the trees, watching us right now."

"A shame," said Nosey. "But I can hardly blame them. This sort of thing has become too commonplace in Boar Gulch." He felt bad saying so, but he, too, was tired of being harried because of the bounty on Rollie's head. It was a tough situation for the ex-Pinkerton man, to be sure, but it was even worse for the innocent folks of the Gulch, particularly because it wasn't attention they earned or deserved.

"We shouldn't have to defend their homes and businesses, too, dammit." The big Scot growled his annoyance as he eyed the hillside for sign of movement.

Nosey understood, but he knew, too, that Geoff was solid. And he baked a mean mock-apple pie. That alone endeared him to most everyone who knew him.

Prairie-dogging up to look for sign of Wolfbait or Bone and his son, Nosey wondered how they were making out after all that shooting they'd endured earlier. A shot whistled in, and before he knew it, he was facedown in the gravel with Geoff dragging him backward behind a boulder.

"Nosey! You okay?"

"I will be once I get this dirt out of my mouth."

"Sorry about that. Had to get you to safety."

"I appreciate it, Geoff. What happened?" As soon as he asked it, his right leg began to throb.

"You caught lead."

"I did?"

Geoff nodded, looking around the low near edge of the rock. "Your right one."

"Huh," said Nosey. "Other than the pain, I'd never know."

The big cook looked at Nosey. "Wolfbait was right about you."

"What did he say?"

"That you're an odd duck."

Nosey ripped off the right sleeve of his shirt and wrapped it tight above the little wound on his lower leg. "I'll take that as a compliment.

"Fine by me." Geoff leaned close and inspected the wound. "I can't be sure, but it looks like it barely caught you. Likely passed right through. If you were fat, it'd be a whole lot worse."

"Oh, well," said Nosey, beginning to feel a little green. "That's good. Perhaps we could talk about something else?"

"Sure thing," said Geoff, noticing the writer's paling pallor.

Not long after, the cook looked down the street, past the north end. "Aw, hell."

"What?" Nosey grunted and shifted on his elbows, looking in the same direction. Then he said the same thing as he spied none other than Boar Gulch Mayor Chauncey Wheeler wheeling his supply wagon along the last stretch of trail that led to the north end of main street. It would bring him up beside his own mercantile. "There's no way we can warn him off.'

"They'll eat him for lunch."

"Nosey shrugged and closed his eyes. His head was pounding like a locomotive fighting an uphill grade. "Maybe. But that man has an odd kind of luck. The thing I'm worried about is he'll tell them where Rollie and Pops have gone."

"You think he knows?"

Nosey looked at him. "Only four of us—well, five if you count the girl—were supposed to know. But you know."

"Well, yeah. Most everybody in the Gulch knows. And Chauncey didn't leave on the supply run nearly a week after Rollie and Pops and the girl left town. That leaves a lot of time for somebody to tell somebody."

"Or lots of somebodies," said Nosey. "Well, one of those somebodies blabbed and it wasn't me," said Nosey.

They looked at each other and at the same time said, "Wolfbait."

"It's not his fault," said the burly café owner. "He's . . ."

"Just Wolfbait," said Nosey, smiling, despite the pain in his head.

They watched as Chauncey rolled down the last decline in the north road behind his mercantile to his back door and loading dock. He'd unload his goods, then drive the team up to The Last Drop to unload crates of booze, then on up the street to Geoff's diner and Horkins' Hardware.

And at each stop he'd sit in the wagon with his arms crossed until someone would come out and begin to unload the wagon. He'd say, "No, no, no, no." Then he'd hold out a fat pink hand and waggle his fingers. His hauling fee, he'd say.

Funny thing was, Pops and Wolfbait, sometimes Nosey, would usually do a freight run, with Rollie and Pops' wagon and team, and nobody ever got charged, not even Chauncey. Such kindness on the part of his neighbors didn't matter a whit to the chubby mayor. He viewed everything in life as a business opportunity.

Once he was unloaded, he'd drive back to his barn and make whoever he'd coerced into riding shotgun with him unhitch the team. He'd also make them rub down, feed, and water the team, and then grease the hubs on his work wagon. Then and only then would he pay them the pittance he'd promised them for making the trip.

Nosey felt that whoever was stuck sharing a wagon seat with Chauncey for days on end should also be paid an endurance fee. Rollie always paid Nosey and Wolfbait amply, though neither man ever asked for such.

But now here was Chauncey riding right into hell, with no clue.

Somehow, Nosey wasn't particularly bothered. Sure, if either he or Geoff were able to get word to him without risking their own necks or the necks of others, they would. But unless he could think of something fast, there was little chance of getting Chauncey to turn around.

Then it was all decided for him as Mace Matson tore down the street on his black horse, dust cloud following, and headed straight for the pudgy mayor. As if a festering wound had been pricked open with a rusty knife point, three more riders, Nosey thought he recognized that devil, Drake, among them, emerged from all directions and closed in on Chauncey.

By then the fat mayor saw them coming at him and reined to a halt. His shotgun rider, a stoop-backed miner named Jimbo Teets, crippled and old far before his time by rheumatism, also saw them, and knew them for what they were—strangers with fast horses and guns drawn. No fool, he bailed off the wagon and made for the pucker-brush northward toward his cabin and claim faster than anyone would have thought possible given his bent, gnarled body.

Chauncey's curses and shouts chased him for a few steps, then Jimbo outran them and left the chubby mayor sitting alone in his wagon, turning red and wondering just what it was he was supposed to do.

About the same time he saw the guns the strange men held, he cursed himself for not wearing more than his customary two-shot derringer, which was inside his inner coat pocket.

The newcomers thundered up and Mace stared him down.

"How . . . how do?" said the mayor.

"You a drummer?" said Mace.

"What? Me, a common salesman?" Chauncey puffed up and fired a look of superiority, or what he hoped was one, at the coarse buffoon before him. "I should think not. I am Chauncey Wheeler, mayor of Boar Gulch. And who, sir, are you and your . . . minions?"

"Oh," said Mace, ignoring the question and whipping a sloppy stream of chaw juice across the wagon's front wheel. "So you actually choose to live in this rank hole, huh?"

"I beg your pardon—"

"Won't get no pardon from me, fatty."

"Uh! Be that as it may, I must ask you to back away so I may finish my supply run. It has been a long day and I am played out."

"Supplies, huh? What-all you got under that tarp? Boys!" He nodded to the men about him and they rode close, whipping out daggers and slicing through the taut ropes binding down the load. With Chauncey cursing and grunting and flailing his arms toward them as if he might somehow land a punch through thin air, they whipped back the tarpaulins and let out whoops and howls at their discoveries.

"We got booze, boss!"

"And all manner of food, too. We are set, we are!"

"You most certainly are not set, you . . . brutes!" Chauncey stood and worked to hoist a leg up onto the wagon seat, looking as if he might launch himself toward them somehow. "Unhand my goods, you thieves, before I . . ."

A rifle hammer cocked all the way back and the snout of the barrel poked the fat mayor in the side of his face, dimpling a pink, whiskered cheek. "Before you what, Fatty?" Mace Matson shoved the rifle harder, knocking Chauncey to his seat once more. "And take off that stupid bowler. Can't abide a man in a bowler hat."

Chauncey obeyed.

"Now, whilst my men rummage your goods, I have a couple of questions for you, Fatty. How you answer will determine whether I kill you or let you limp home and thank your lucky stars Mace Matson was in a forgiving mood. You got me?"

"I . . ."

Mace shoved the barrel harder. "Got me?"

"Yah, yah!"

"Good boy, Fatty. Now, the most important question. Where have you all hidden Stoneface?"

"Who . . . who?"

"You an owl, Fatty? I said where's Stoneface Finnegan?"

"Oh, oh . . . but . . . but . . . he's not hidden! Rollie Finnegan's gone off with his business partner, Pops, and that silly Pinkerton girl! They've gone to rescue some hopeless fool over in Deadwood!"

Mace scowled. "Deadwood, eh?" He sat his horse a moment as he thought over this situation. A slow grin spread over his face. "Well, why didn't anybody say so? That's all I wanted, after all. But no, everybody else in this rat hole of a mine camp had to make up stories and lie to me and treat me as if I was some sort of criminal. You ever hear of such a thing, Fatty?"

Emboldened by the slight change in Mace's demeanor toward him, Chauncey drew back, away from the gun's barrel. "Is Rollie Finnegan why you're here? My word, man, we're sick of Rollie Finnegan here in Boar Gulch! Good riddance, I say! Go get him—and with my blessing!" Chauncey nodded, a benevolent look on his fleshy face.

Mace leveled a cold stare on him. "I don't need your permission to do a damn thing, Mr. Fatty Mayor Man. And just to prove it, I will enjoy watching your face as we ransack your new haul. Already been through that store yonder and took what we needed from it anyways. If I'm guessing right, and I am never wrong, you're low on coffee beans. Out of 'em, in fact. I hope for your sake you brought more."

Chauncey's wide eyes and trembling bottom lip brought a hearty laugh from Matson.

"But . . . you can't . . . that is to say . . ."

Behind him something smashed on the ground, something made of glass, and Chauncey jerked, wincing as he took in the damage. For the moment, he forgot himself. "You idiots! Do you have any idea how much it costs me to haul in those oil lamps? They were specially ordered for—" He clipped off his speech.

Matson leaned close. "What was that, Fatty?"

Chauncey looked down and shook his head. Matson snatched him by the coat front and spurred his horse. The beast lurched and Matson held on to Wheeler. The fat man sputtered and bucked, but Mace's grip was as tight as sun-shrunk leather and he dragged the yowling, flailing merchant off the seat and let him slam to the ground.

Before Chauncey could get his feet under him, Matson had slid from the saddle and was on him, delivering a series of hard, tight punches to the mayor's sputtering, jowly face.

"Why . . . ?" Chauncey repeated the word a number of times in between punches.

The question only broadened Mace's grin. Finally, he paused. "Because."

Mace snatched a bottle of whiskey from a pried-open crate in the wagon and jerked the cork out with his teeth, then spat it on the ground. He swigged long and hard. When he finished, he let out a long belch. "Somebody get that gut pile out from in front of the wagon. Then drive it yonder to the back of the mercantile. Be safer to go through it back there." He eyed the surrounding hills as he took another long pull on the bottle. "Never know if one of these townies will grow a backbone and take it into his mind to lay more of us low. Then get back to hoorah-ing this town. We ain't through yet."

Chauncey winced and tried to scoot backward along the ground, but one of the men leaned low in his saddle and dropped a loop around Chauncey's upper arms. He dragged the still-dazed man, screaming and flailing away toward the back entrance of his store. Reaching the loading dock, the man slid out of his saddle and jerked Chauncey to his feet, then shoved him hard. Chauncey fell over once more. "Seems to me we ought to give you a little reward for being the one person in this rat hole of a town who had the stones to tell answer that simple question with a truthful answer."

Chauncey weaved and got to his feet. He was most definitely not used to such rough treatment and he thought perhaps a mistake, some oversight had occurred. All this had happened so quickly, he was confused. Then he was reminded that yes, indeed, it truly was happening. For the men not far away were smashing and slashing his goods— sacks of flour and corn meal lay gutted and thrown to the earth, tins of fruit and canned milk tossed and rolling, a few stomped beneath the hooves of the mounts of the prancing, drinking devils.

"What say we have a little fun, boys?" shouted the man who'd dragged him over to the store.

A couple of the other men shouted and joined him. Soon, they were passing a bottle and trading hard-knuckle shots at the the face of cowering, blubbering Chauncey Wheeler. The harder he sobbed and shrieked, the more vigor they put into pounding on him.

Soon, his eyes were puffed and buttoned up. He weaved, wobbled, and flopped to his side on the dusty earth. He had a sense he was leaning against something solid, perhaps it was his own building, but he couldn't be certain.

Doesn't matter, anyway, thought Chauncey as he slowly lost consciousness.

Chapter 15

"Either of you men seen Bone or his boy?" It was the first thing Wolfbait said to Nosey and Geoff once he heeded their hisses and whispers to get over to them, under cover and out of the line of fire.

Nosey shook his head. "No, but not long after they set themselves up with the rifle, I heard shots and then I heard cries far up in the hills. I'd say the boy's as good a shot as Bone let on."

"Good. We'll need him. We aren't done with these rascals. I guess they aren't convinced Rollie's not here." Wolfbait sat down with a sigh. "Oh, my bones ain't made for such foolishness. Keeping up with all the folks who want Rollie's head is wearing me out."

"You and me and the whole rest of the town," said the big restaurant owner.

"That's a problem for another time," said Nosey. "Right now we need to figure out how to help Chauncey and the women at the town hall."

"Seeing as how I'm the only one of us who still has both his pins under him," said Wolfbait, smacking his knees and raising dust. "I reckon that's up to me, huh?"

"I can help." Nosey shifted his sore leg to show he was still able. His face turned gray and he squeezed his eyes shut tight. "Oh, Lord . . ."

"See?" Wolfbait shook his head. "You're of no use to me! You can't even hop, boy. You aren't fit to do a damn thing other than stay here and take pot shots at anybody who's a stranger."

"Well, I can go, dammit," said Geoff. "I've been worse off. Just you watch me." He nodded and tried on a smile, but Wolfbait saw the sweat running down his face, stippling his top lip.

"Yeah, well, we'll see, mister. I need a couple of minutes before I'm ready to hop on out of here anyway. Just keep an eye on the ladies' building. Madge is a tough thing, and they have an assortment of guns now, but I don't like leaving them like that. I only come up here to check on you goobers. Now I'm pinned here."

Random blasts of gunfire increased throughout the next couple of hours, with Nosey and Geoff and Wolfbait holed up mid-slope behind a big tumbledown of sun-bleached boulders. Every once in a while one or another of them would poke his sniffer out from behind a jag of rock and eye the scene in town.

Not much to see, they reasoned, and yet whenever Wolfbait tried to amble away from the spot, a shot would whistle in from one of two directions. The couldn't get a fix on the shooter, and realized they might be in the foolish situation for a good while yet.

"How many do you reckon there are?"

Geoff pooched his lips and counted, grimacing at the pain in his swollen knee whenever he moved. "I only ever saw four or five, not all at once, but at different times."

"Me, too," said Nosey.

"Well, that Matson said he had what? A dozen or more men? I guess he wasn't lying. Might be he was holding back some on that estimation, too."

"I sure wish Bone's boy would have worked his magic on that Matson when he was romping along the street, bold as all get out." Geoff shook his head.

Nosey wiped his nose with a grungy old hanky. "Does it strike you odd that as poorly organized and as slipshod in their approach to this town takeover as Matson and his men have been, and I do believe they have shown themselves to be fairly inept, the town was in even more of a pathetic condition?"

"More like sad than odd," said Geoff, his dry voice deep and tired.

"Yeah, *sad* is the word for it, gents," said Nosey. "The rest of them have all gone off and don't appear to be coming back to help any time soon."

"Getting on toward that time when some of the boys will wander into town from their diggings for a night of fun at The Last Drop, too." Wolfbait's bushy eyebrows rose in concern. "Hmm. I ain't seen anybody yet. Wonder how they know to stay away?"

"I know how," said Nosey.

The other two looked at him and he nodded and forced a thin smile. "Jimbo Teets."

"What's ol' Jimbo got to do with it?" said Wolfbait.

"Oh, he just got back from riding shotgun for Chauncey and he skedaddled as soon as he sniffed trouble."

"That's why he's still alive," said Geoff. "You don't get to become a gimpy old miner with rheumatism by being careless."

"He ain't that old, you know. He just looks it. That blasted rheumatism." Wolfbait frowned. "He must have warned the other miners. At least from the north end of town."

Nosey agreed and said, "Must be somebody else warned them off up at the pass for the south trail."

"Or they heard the shots and decided they could live without a slice of pie or a trip to the assay office," said Geoff.

Wolfbait snorted. "A day passing without a wedge of your pie? No sir, not a rock rat in all these hills would stand for such a thing."

"I appreciate your words, Wolfbait, but I'd rather my pie wasn't the cause of somebody dying."

"Yeah, there is that."

The three men fell silent once more, keeping low and waiting out the afternoon.

After an hour of inactivity, Wolfbait told his two companions that, as he was the only one among them still able to walk, it was high time he made it back to Madge and the girls. He'd hated leaving them high and dry as he had, and couldn't do a thing sitting up there in the rocks with Nosey and Geoff the Scot, who seemed safe for the moment, if not happy about it.

The men tried to talk him out of it, but it only emboldened the old goat. He gave them a quick salute, then picked his way back down through the rock-strewn hillside toward the bordello.

And he nearly made it.

The back door was cracked and he made for it, deciding against another entrance through the wood box hole.

"Hello?" he shouted cautiously at the door from the top of the steps.

A shot cracked the stilled, hot afternoon air.

He felt something shove his right shoulder forward, as if he'd been punched from behind. The blow whipped him nearly around and he slammed forward, colliding with the door and falling face-first into the coolness of the kitchen.

He heard a woman's voice shout, "Wolfbait!" The last thing he saw was the angelic face of Madge Gladwell, surrounded by several younger angels, all gawking down at him with worried looks.

With such heavenly visions before him, Wolfbait drifted into blissful— if increasingly painful—unconsciousness.

Chapter 16

"Pap, you think you can make it out of here?"

Bone looked at his son. "Boy, they done shot my leg. So, no, I do not think I'll be leaving this here spot for a while yet. Lucky for us these barrels were here."

The boy nodded. "If they hadn't, we likely would not have come this way, though. Too far to the wagon from the barrels."

"That's true, boy. You know, you're starting to sound like your ol' Mama. She was a contrarian, too. Always liked to pick apart what I was saying, then tell me why I was wrong."

"Oh, I didn't mean it like that, Pap."

"Well, you should have. I never said she wasn't right. That's the thing, son, she was right pretty much all the time, you see?" Bone chuckled and leaned forward to readjust the strip of his son's shirt they'd used as a tourniquet to keep the blood from oozing out. A flash of pain whipped up his leg like a snake strike. Bone's face grayed out once more and he sucked wind through his teeth.

"Here," said the boy. "Let me do that." He set to it and

in short order the pain in his father's throbbing limb had
eased.

Bone sighed. "Appreciate it, boy. You know, we get out
of this, we ought to give thought to pulling up stakes. We
ain't amounting to a hill of farts stuck up here in the hills.
Living like dump rats half the time."

"Don't talk like that, Pap. I like it here just fine. Better
than anywhere else we ever lit, and that's a fact."

"It's good to hear you say that, son, but the fact remains
you ain't had near enough schoolin'. Now that you're
nearly a man, why, it's time we live somewhere you can
set to sportin' the young ladies." He watched as his son's
face bloom deep red.

"Aw, Pap . . ."

"I know what I know son, and that there's one topic that
even your mama couldn't best me on."

"How's that?"

"'Cause she was a girl and I was a boy. Ain't no way
she could know what a boy thinks, now is there?"

"No, sir."

"That's right. Now, we can talk more about his later.
Right now, you best take up that rifle, 'cause I just saw
one of those rascals cat footing behind the saloon. See that
far corner?"

Quick, and making no sound, the boy raised the rifle
to his shoulder, cocked it, and held it at the ready. The man
Bone had seen didn't emerge from behind The Last Drop,
but they both knew that could mean any number of things.
He might have entered the building through the back door,
might be in the outhouse, could be sniffing around the
little outbuilding back there.

After a minute or so, during which neither Bone nor

his boy so much as flinched, despite the sweat drops trailing down their faces and tickling like walking flies, their patience was rewarded. Just not where they'd expected.

The man's head emerged slowly, step by step, up the trail that switchbacked up the hill behind the buildings lining the west edge of the main street. Bone nodded his head once, but he needn't have. Junior saw the man.

Soon the fellow emerged from the waist up. Taking precautions, he skulked low and jerked his gaze left then right, and back again. He held a rifle high at his chest and wore no hat. His shoulder-length, sandy hair hung lank and unmoving, even in the breeze that riffled his shirt sleeves.

They waited and waited some more and the man became visible from his knees up, still slowly zig-zagging his way upslope away from them.

"Boy, you can take him down any time," said Bone in the barest whisper, not glancing at his son. "Less'n you're working on your skills." He smiled, pride in the boy's abilities evident on his wide eyes and smile.

"Can't."

The word came to Bone as barely a whisper, and he thought maybe he'd not heard it right. "What's that, son?"

The boy began to move his cheek from the stock.

"You best explain yourself, boy."

"Ain't never shot a man in the back before, Pap."

"Oh. I see." That hung in the air a moment, then Bone said, "But he's one of them who're terrorizing our town, son."

"I know." Then the kid snugged his cheek to the stock once again.

Bone barely had time to look back toward the man halfway up the slope and fully visible, before his son had squeezed off a shot. A cloud of dust spurted up beside the man's right boot. The man spun, crouching low and firing a shot of his own . . . at nothing and everything. His eyes were wild and he cranked another round, but the boy's bullet cored a hole in the center of his forehead, driving a hank of greasy hair deep into his now-even-more-useless brain.

He stood upright a moment, his mouth a circle of surprise. Then he slowly pitched forward, a tree giving way to a final bite of the axe. He hunched as he toppled, dropping the rifle and rolling in a sloppy tangle of flailing arms and legs for the better part of twenty feet before sprawling to a stop. His left leg was the last thing about him to come to a rest, clunking down as if he had decided he was too tired to take another step.

He lay faceup on the slope, his right arm wedged beneath his torso and his neck bent at an odd angle. He did not move.

"You pulled that first shot," said Bone, glancing at his son.

"Yep."

"Proud of you, boy. Some proud."

The boy's face bloomed crimson once more. "Thanks, Pap. Say, you think you can make it to the saloon if we hustle around back?"

"When have I ever not made it to the saloon?"

"Good, 'cause I got me an idea." Junior nodded toward a sloppy pile of planks, several of them at least a foot and a half wide and four or five feet long.

"Son, you just keep getting smarter all day long. You're a credit to your mama, you know that?"

"Well, all I know is we got to get under cover where we can defend ourselves and get that leg doctored."

"True, boy, true. But how you gonna tote a shield board and a gun?"

"Little at a time. That jaggedy trail he took upslope yonder give me the notion we might make the trip from here to the saloon in fits and starts."

"True enough," nodded Bone, wincing at his throbbing leg. "Ain't any straighter than a dog's hind leg."

"You'll have to go first. That way I can cover you."

Instead of arguing, Bone surprised the boy by nodding. "Yeah, that's wise. I'd only slow the works. I'm going to make it to that other wagon, but I ain't gonna stay put. Then I'll make it to the old trough. From there I should be able to make the north side of the bar."

"You'll be easy pickin's then, Pap, so—"

"I know, I know, boy. I won't dawdle. No more than this gimpy pin will allow, anyhow." He selected a dry plank about a foot shorter than he was tall, and keeping low, he shoved upright once more. He tested his leg, found he could put a little weight on it, but didn't trust it. "Okay, boy?"

"Yep," said the kid and they repeated their effort of earlier, though with a different destination in mind. "Git on it." And he watched as his Pap made the first run without any ruckus.

Bone rested a moment, then bolted for the trough. Again, his post-legged amble, with the board clunking, attracted no attention from bullets.

They could just see each other if they each leaned out a bit, which they did, nodding. Bone waited. The boy waited.

"Boy!" Bone beckoned him with a quick hand wave toward himself.

The kid hesitated, then lowered the rifle and ran toward the wagon, holding the rifle at the ready to deliver a quick shot. The entire short run toward his goal, pictures flashed through his mind of the man he'd just laid low jerking a wild shot then tumbling dead down that slope.

He slammed to a halt behind the wagon, letting out a breath he hadn't known he'd held.

"Boy!"

He looked toward Bone, who was beckoning him. "Don't stay there—too open!"

The boy nodded and ducking low once more he bolted for the trough where his Pap crouched, hunched and awkward with his plank shield and his bum leg hidden beneath it.

The boy nearly fell on top of Bone, who held out his arms and tugged the kid down. "Watch that gun, boy, you're liable to take off yer Pap's topknot."

When they'd pulled in a couple of deep breaths each, Bone made ready. "Same thing—I'll go, you follow. I'll make right for the back door. Only thing to do now is get to it!" With that, he shoved himself forward, into a crouching shuffling run, the plank held before him, facing southward, the direction most of the shooting had come from earlier.

The boy covered him until he disappeared around the back corner of the saloon. Then the kid pulled the rifle down and waited a few seconds. He held his breath, half-convinced he was going to hear a shot or two telling him someone had laid his Pap low.

But the boy heard no shots. Heartened with that knowledge and with the increasing suspicion they were no longer being watched, he repeated his earlier run. Rifle poised, finger dancing near the trigger, he bolted like the hounds of Hell were gnawing his heel bones.

And he nearly made it.

About the same time he heard a thin, pinched gunshot, Junior's left leg whipped wide as if determined to take off at a run on its own. Digging in harder, he managed to make it to the far back corner of The Last Drop and knew he'd been shot. It came to him, through a haze of hot, slicing pain, that he'd taken it in the opposite leg his father had.

"Boy," said Bone, appearing beside him as if he'd been in hiding. "Got to get us both in the saloon before we bleed out. We bind these wounds tight, then we sip and splash whiskey inside and outside of us. Why, I reckon we can take turns doctorin' on each other's legs, get the bullets out. Then we'll be in tall cotton."

By leaning against each other and ambling with their good legs, they managed to hobble through the saloon's back door as he spoke.

"Reckon together we make one good man, Pap."

"Naw," said Bone. "You're a hell of a man all on your own, son. Never could a father be prouder. Now let's find us that whiskey while we still have strength left."

"You think Pops'll want this here rifle back? I've grown right fond of it, I have."

"And never has a weapon claimed its rightful owner like that one has, son. I reckon we can come to some arrangement with the man. I reckon so." He winked and popped a cork.

Chapter 17

Seven men thundered along the north road out of Boar Gulch, then took the east cut not far from town, Mace Matson at the lead and Drake Keller riding drag. Mace didn't care for a single one of the idiots he rode with, Drake included. And since he cared about such things, he was disinclined to trust any of them, too.

Long ago he had realized he was going to die at some point. Unaware of anyone who'd ever been able to avoid that ultimate conclusion, he refused to get fretted up over such things as trusting people or not trusting them, regretting past deeds . . . or misdeeds, as often seemed to be the case with him. Nah, he was through with all that.

Mace Matson rode where he wanted to and took what pleased him, be it money, land, horses, gear, or women. And since he'd begun that way of conducting himself in the world, he had slept easier, never been richer, and had more women fawning over him than he'd ever known before.

How this had come about remained a little bit of a mystery to him, but not enough of one to stop him from shrugging and smiling and enjoying the hell out of it.

He'd once tried to explain this simple way of thinking

to Drake, but the hard-bitten fellow never even smiled, let alone trusted anyone, Mace included. And they were as close, friend-wise, as either of them would ever be to anyone else. Even so, Drake's reaction didn't much surprise him. Mace had snorted back a laugh and shook his head. That was all.

Didn't matter. He was content with chasing down soon-to-be dead men for the bounties on their heads, not so much for the money as for something to do. He enjoyed the challenge of outwitting his quarry.

He also knew, deep down, he wasn't all that intelligent. Keller was a smarter, wilier man than he was. But with everything in life, Matson did his best to make like a duck and let it roll right off his back. For he knew he had something nobody else had—he had the fire inside. The fire of not caring. And that made him the smartest man in any room, any ol' time.

Even losing what he guessed was about eight men back there in Boar Gulch didn't much matter. He had begun with fourteen men, not counting himself and Drake, and now they were seven. That meant nine had died or were howling and bleeding out in the woods somewhere around the nasty little mine camp. Die and be done with it, he had said as they rode on out.

What had stuck with him were thoughts of some of the locals, who had surprised him with their gumption and willingness to fight back. He expected they'd been stirred up by that mouthy old bearded fellow from the saloon, the one who couldn't lie worth a fig, and that bookish one in the bowler. *Nosey* was his name. Suited him. But Matson gave them credit—they were dung stirrers, and likely fighters, to be sure.

Mostly, though, he was pleased to be shed of that dismal hole in the hills. And as a bonus, they were loaded up with solid food and enough booze to keep the men stupid and dozy for a spell.

One of the men, a sloppy, fat-gutted fellow name of Shub, with dark, short hair and darker circles beneath his eyes—maybe a Mexican had sneaked into the bed of Shub's mama's bed—had ridden up close off Mace's right side. Knowin Shub was a chatty one, Mace felt like spilling a word or three, so he said, "Finally making for Deadwood. Yep, I do believe we're on the trail to a sure thing, Shub."

"Yeah? Why's that, Mace?" said the sloppy man beside him.

"Because, you fool, even if Stoneface concludes his business in Deadwood, he'll be headed back this way. We're bound to meet up with him sooner or later." Mace smiled as if he'd finally solved the question as to why the sun stayed up in the sky without falling down on their heads—another of the many such things he'd always wondered about.

After a few moments of cogitation, Shub shook his head in disagreement. "Well, what if he don't head back to Boar Gulch right off? Maybe he might decide to make for the East to do some visiting or some such? No, sir, it's tricky to know what folks will get up to nowadays."

Mace sighed, reached over with his right hand, and punched Shub on the side of his head hard enough that he slid rightward in his saddle, nearly spilling out.

He reined his horse to a stop while he worked his way back upright. "Ow! Why'd you do that, Mace?"

"I should think that was obvious, Shub. That was for spoiling my good humor." Matson swigged a little whiskey and set to whistling a jaunty tune he made up as he rode east-southeastward for Deadwood.

As the last of the Matson gang rode out of town along the north road, which actually angled east toward Deadwood, Nosey and Geoff stood awkwardly and stretched, the bitter tang of anger and shame polluting their mouths. A town-wide meeting would be held soon. A meeting in which each townsfolk would rant about how they once again had had to put up with Rollie's problems.

Nosey could almost hear it coming. "It's always his fault we get hoo-raahed!" Or "he wasn't even here this time to defend us nor protect us!"

And neither he nor Wolfbait would be able to argue. How could they when Rollie and Pops had been voted on by the townsfolks to be their lawmen? Why, Rollie himself had nearly *speechified*, as Wolfbait put it. Rollie reckoned it was only right he take on the duties of lawdog as he was responsible for so much of the town's newfound woes since he'd arrived.

And it had worked, for a time, mused Nosey. But it was the third time a gang had ridden in and ransacked the place in a big way. All because they were looking for Rollie. Or more to the point, because they were looking for Rollie's head.

Nosey knew the people could not defend their friend, nor could they disagree. It was, as someone wise once said, a hell of a spot to be in.

Chapter 18

Pops had been silent since they broke camp after breakfast. As he had for the past couple of days, Rollie had tried to draw him out as to a plan of action once they reached Deadwood, which they might do in a day or so.

He had certain ideas what he thought they ought to do, but kept reminding himself it was Pops' venture. Since he was along only to help, Rollie ended each subtle suggestion with a question to Pops, something along the lines of, "But what do you think, Pops? It's your game after all."

The man would shrug and mumble something, then bury himself in some little camp task. Rollie knew he'd have to figure out Pops' mood before they got to Deadwood, but kept hoping Pops would come around on his own.

As for Tish, she had turned out to be a rather pleasant, if a chatty, companion. She was also a conundrum to Rollie. One minute she'd seem rather flighty, twittering on about some notion she'd heard in a city—the latest odd fashions in ladies' hats—as if he'd care one whit. Then a few minutes later she'd angle back to an earlier odd comment. Somehow she'd tie in hat fashions with how she'd made a careful study of them and deduced certain styles would be more conducive to undercover work.

She'd filled their journey with such notions, peppering the miles with random facts and figures. He had finally decided she was likely one of the more intelligent people he'd ever met, and also one of the most tiring. Not unlike Nosey Parker.

He and Pops had left her to tend a campfire a few nights into their journey with her along. As they gathered wood for the fire, Rollie looked over his shoulder to make certain she wasn't within earshot, and said to Pops, "I think we finally met Nosey's match."

He'd chuckled. "Yeah, but a whole lot prettier. And slightly less annoying."

"We aren't to Deadwood yet," said Rollie.

That brought another chuckle from Pops. "True. I'll check back with you when we get there."

Now that their destination was near, it was the normally good-natured Pops who had grown somber, serious and maybe even a little dour. Definitely not a common mood for jovial Pops.

Later that day, Rollie slowed Cap to wait up for Pops, who had slowed his pace, lagging behind Rollie and Tish, who also had grown silent. Not that Rollie minded the silence.

He'd noticed his pard looked haggard. "Hey, Pops."

The man looked up at him. He'd been riding with his pipe stem clenched in his teeth, and though the bowl had been packed with tobacco, Pops had not yet lit it.

"You out of matches?"

"Huh?"

Rollie nodded toward the pipe.

"Oh." Pops took the pipe out of his mouth and stuffed it in the pocket of his bib front trousers.

"Pops, are you going to tell me what's going on with you or not?"

"What are you talking about?"

"You've barely spoken the last day or two, and when you do it's grunts. I get a head shake or a shrug to a simple question like, 'Do you want more coffee?', and if I ask about Deadwood, you get, well, stone-faced. Like you're doing now."

Pops didn't look at him.

"The stone-faced look? That's my job."

They rode side by side in silence for a few moments. Tish rode ahead of them by a half-dozen yards.

Finally, Pops said, "My wife. Been thinking about . . . how it was. How it used to be. I been pretty good so far, not thinking about who or what I might find in Deadwood. Truth is, I don't really know if that girl up ahead is her—my daughter." He finally looked at Rollie.

Rollie merely nodded. He knew from long experience when it was best to keep his mouth shut. People usually need a little priming to get their talking pump working, then they need to be left alone. More often than not, they'd fill in the gap of silence and come around to what it is they really want to tell you. And so, he figured, it was proving to be with Pops.

"What if it isn't her, Rollie?"

It was Rollie's turn to shrug. "Then it's not her. Doesn't mean your daughter's not out there somewhere. It's a big world, but we'll find her. Besides, that girl in Deadwood is somebody's daughter. That's all that matters."

They rode in silence a few more minutes, then Pops said, "You're something else, you know that?"

"I hope so," said Rollie. "Otherwise, I'd be like everybody else. And I damn sure don't want to be like Nosey or Wolfbait."

For the first time in days, Pops smiled—genuinely smiled—and chuckled.

She must have heard the sound, because Tish looked back at them, then held her horse while they caught up to her. "What's all this? Are you two conniving ways to get rid of me again?"

"Nah," said Pops, tugging his pipe out once more. "You seem to be doing that all right on your own."

"We were just discussing what our plan might be once we reach Deadwood."

"Oh, is that what we were doing?" said Pops, eyebrows raised.

"Yep. And if nobody else has any ideas, I have a few."

"I bet you do," said Pops, shaking his head. "Okay, let's hear them. Me, I'm more of a ride-in-and-see-what-happens sort."

"That kind of thinking will only get you killed," said Tish, giving Pops a harsh look.

"Whoa! Now I know you've been spending far too much time in the presence of ol' Stoneface here."

"You two about through?" said Rollie. "Since it's getting late in the afternoon, we might make camp early. By my reckoning we have another day of travel. That should see us arriving in Deadwood just about nightfall tomorrow."

"Why night time?" said Tish.

Rollie smiled. "You tell me."

"Oh oh," said Pops. "I sense another lesson coming on." He urged his horse off the trail and over to inspect a likely camping spot. "I'll be over here, doing anything but listening to another Pinkerton session."

"So you're afraid of what you might run into in Dead-wood?" asked Tish.

Rollie squinted over the rim of his cup of steaming coffee. The firelight reflected in the center of his eyes as he sipped, still regarding Tish. "I never said I was afraid."

"Of anything?" she said.

That's when he knew she was toying with him. He found it annoying. As Pops watched the two and said nothing, he seemed to be half enjoying the repartee. The other half of him was mired in thought and ignoring his coffee.

Rollie stretched his legs and rubbed his side, feeling the knobs of scar tissue beneath. His old wounds still pained him now and again. "Any man who isn't afraid of something in life is a liar or an idiot."

"What about women?"

"Doubly so."

"I'm not sure I like that," Tish said.

Rollie shrugged. "You don't have to. But like it or not, we're mired in a man's world. Men ride roughshod over everything nowadays and women seem to be stuck putting up with more than they ought. It's not fair, but there it is."

"Not forever." She frowned. "Not if I have anything to say about it."

"Good for you, girl," said Pops, lifting his cooling coffee again. "I happen to know a thing or two about living in an unfair world. And I'd add to what Rollie said by saying it's a white man's world right now. At least hereabouts. Doesn't mean it has to always be that way, though."

"I'll drink to that," said Rollie.

"Speaking of," said Pops, drawing out a small cork-stoppered bottle of whiskey from his saddlebags. "I reckon it's time for a little medicine. These nights get cold."

"Oh," said Tish, smiling. "That's your excuse?"

"Don't need one, but it's nice to go through the motions. Otherwise, we'd be reduced to savagery."

They all took a splash, then Pops raised his cup. "To friends. I appreciate . . . well, whatever it is we're about to do."

"Hear, hear!" Tish raised her cup high.

Rollie and Pops looked at her.

"Sorry, I get a little carried away sometimes."

"You don't say," said Rollie, hiding a grin behind is cup. "Good whiskey. That the stuff we keep away from the riffraff"

"Yep," said Pops. "Wonder how they're getting along back there?"

"Oh, I expect they're fine. As dozy as Boar Gulch has been lately, the worst that might happen is Wolfbait gets too cozy with his stool and his beer glass. Other than that . . ." Rollie shrugged.

"You mean you don't care?" said Tish. "What if it burned down?"

"Already happened once," said Pops. "And we're still here."

"But it's your business!" she said. "Your investment, your future security. It's all tied up in that place. Don't you care?"

Rollie sipped the whiskey. "Be nice if it didn't burn down or explode or went away somehow, but . . . I don't know. If it did, as long as nobody got hurt, I guess, to answer your question, I don't really care, no." He looked at Pops. "You?"

"Nah. There are things in life t more important than money, girl."

"Like *family*," she said, but her tone was somber, as if the very word was distasteful to her.

Rollie was curious about her past—who she really was, where she came from—but unless she offered to tell them, he wasn't about to tug it out of her. He knew Pops felt the same way. A man's—or a woman's business was their own until they chose to share it with you. And if he never fond out, so be it. She had reasons for keeping her life a locked trunk.

The quiet and lost mood she'd slipped into, likely nudged by the whiskey's calming, warming effects, was bookended by Pops' own reverie. Rollie looked at one, then the other, and sighed. He liked the quiet, but he also wanted to get some thoughts on what they would do by the time they got to Deadwood.

"Maybe tomorrow," he said and finished his whiskey.

"Huh?" said Pops.

"Nothing. We'll talk in the morning."

They had talked, but nothing much was decided on. By the time they took to the trail once more, Rollie had given up and figured he'd leave Pops alone to go with his usual way of dealing with situations see what happens. But that didn't mean Rollie had to.

The mountains, hills, and shadows they'd seen on the horizon, not an unusual vista for their journey so far, drew them in, and the day slowly aged.

"It's what I was trying to get at last night," said Rollie later, as they discussed what to do once they reached town. "I'm known in all manner of places, mostly in sink pits like Deadwood, and mostly by the sort of folks you don't want to be acquainted with. We have to keep a quiet presence." He turned to Tish. "And no names, you hear me?"

"Why pick on me?" But as soon as she said it she recalled their run in with the two men on the trail, which might have been avoided or at least softened if she had not said Rollie's name.

"As I said, it's likely I'm known here in this foul haven of fools."

"Don't hold back," said Pops. "Tell us everything you think of this town."

Rollie continued. "Every owlhoot, former convict, and wanted man in the West would love to see me dead and swinging, or bleeding out in the street." He nodded at his pard. "And Pops, as a former slave, will only get so far himself."

"Where does that leave me?" said Tish.

"Sticking close by us. Doing what we say. And keeping your gun strapped on."

"That serious, huh?" she said.

"Yep."

Just as he had expected they would, they drew close to Deadwood. At dusk, with shadows beginning to nibble the edges of everything, they noticed more roads and tracks and dirt trails spidering off in all directions into the Black Hills. Also noticed was a marked rise not only in the number of ore wagons and men a-horseback passing them on the road, to and from the direction of town, but foot traffic had increased as well.

They passed hovels tucked into the hillsides. Some roadside rock debris, broken tools, and the savaged carcasses of trees, cows, deer laid about the premises. A couple of times the inhabitants were out, sitting on rocks or stumps, chewing, spitting, puffing, drinking, and doing little else, campfires smoking before them.

A number of them took no pains to disguise their bald interest in these newcomers—a curious trio of a white man, a black man, and a young woman—but the men—they'd all been men so far   returned their nods of greeting with a nod in reply or a hello and a one-fingered salute off the flop brim of their worn toppers.

"Won't be long now," said Rollie.

"Tish, might be best if you wore that big wool cloak you've got stowed behind your saddle," said Pops.

Rollie nodded. "And take care to cover up your head and face."

"Why?"

That sparking glint came into her eyes and Rollie suppressed a sigh. "Because you're a pretty young woman and towns like this, well—" He didn't want to elaborate on the cruder points of where his thoughts had headed, not in the least because he didn't want Pops to get moody again. But in that, he was surprised.

"Towns like Deadwood are full of men who make towns like Deadwood so notorious for very few things, none of them savory. I don't think I need to tell you why we came here, do I?"

Tish sighed and pulled out her cloak. As she tugged it on, she said, "So you think I'm pretty, Rollie?"

"I guess." He looked off toward the growing gloom of the black hills seeming to close in all about them.

"Does he say that to all the girls?" she said to Pops.

"Oh, sure." He set fire to a pipe. "Heck, he's even said it to me a time or two."

That brought a laugh from Rollie.

By the time near dark came, they had reached the western end of downtown.

"It's busier than I expected it to be," said Tish. "Bigger."

Rollie nodded and tugged his hat brim lower. "A whole lot more to it than the last time I was here."

"First stop." Rollie nodded toward a sign that read SHERIFF and they rode up to the hitch rail out front. He stretched his back before climbing down, and said, "Sit tight. I want to see an old friend. I'll be right back."

As he climbed up onto the boardwalk, Rollie let the fingertips of his left hand brush the walnut grips of his Schofield. He'd already checked it and made certain it was ready to pull before they rode down Main Street.

He knocked on the door, then turned the knob and walked in. He had expected to see his old friend, Seth Bullock, sheriff of the Deadwood region, at the desk before him. Not the stripling with the oiled, black hair and moustache who sat there with his boots up on the desktop.

A thin sliver of wood for picking his teeth protruded from his mouth, and his clothes were creased and spotless. The man thumbed through a thick stack of wanted dodgers. It took him a moment or three to look up.

"What can I help you with, old-timer?"

Rollie rested his hands on his waist and bit back a sigh. Another young fool who thinks he's more impressive than he ever will be. At least not until he gets a knock or two, a scar, and a broken nose along the way. If he had to lay odds, he bet with himself the kid wouldn't last long in the job. He'd be taken out of it for good with a bullet or run for the hills with his tail tucked.

"Looking for Seth."

"Oh?" said the young man, swiveling his chair slightly so that this grizzled stranger was sure to see the badge pinned to his chest.

"Yeah, I can see it, son. Nice, shiny badge. Now where's Seth Bullock?"

That got the kid's back hair up. He shoved away from the desk and jerked to his feet, a practiced sneer forming beneath his oiled moustaches.

He was tall, but not much taller than Rollie. And he was bird-chested, despite his efforts to puff himself. He rested his slender hands on his double-gun rigs, also well oiled, noted Rollie.

"He isn't here right now. Been called out of town on important business. We expect him back before too long. But none of that matters, 'cause I'm in charge."

"I see. And who are you?"

The kid puffed a little more. "I'm Deputy—acting lawdog—Hawkins."

They stared at each other a moment.

Finally, Rollie said, "Look, son—"

"That's the second time you've called me that. I have a father, thank you very much. And judging from what I see, you wouldn't make a patch on the seat of my old man's trousers."

Rollie straightened. "Well, good. As long as we know where we stand . . . boy. When the sheriff comes back, you be certain to let him know one of his oldest friends, *oldest professional friends*, stopped by." He held the stare long enough to watch the hubris drain from the kid's face. As he turned for the door, he let a grin creep onto his mouth.

Behind him, the kid said, "But . . . you didn't tell me your name."

Without turning, Rollie said, "You're right. But that's okay. I have yours." He turned the knob and walked out.

As he mounted up, Pops said, "How'd you make out?"

"No help there. Bullock's out of town."

"Too bad. Where to now?"

"I think we ought to ride through, camp out past the far end. There's a stream, used to be a good spot in the trees, unless somebody set up shop there since."

"Well, let's find out." Pops clucked his horse back onto the street.

"We're not staying in town?" Tish looked at Rollie with what he swore was alarm.

"Nope."

"I thought we might clean up a little. Have a meal somewhere."

Rollie smiled. "There's a little shop at the far end, should still be there. Maybe we can find something that's more tolerable than what we've been eating."

"You have a problem with the way I cook deer?" said Pops.

"Nope. Just been a lot of it."

* * *

Back inside the sheriff's office, a man walked into the front room from out of a shadowed hallway in the back. "Hawkins, you're a fool."

"What?" The young man spun on the other deputy Bullock had left in charge.

"You heard me. You don't even know who that was, do you?"

Hawkins looked toward the door once more. "No, why? Should I?"

"Nah, not unless you been living under a stone most of your life."

"Who is he?"

"That fella, the one you called 'old-timer'? The one you said didn't make a patch on yer pappy's backside? Why that's none other than Stoneface Finnegan himself."

For the second time in the last few minutes, the color drained from the young man's face. His puffed chest deflated and he seemed to sag in on himself as he stared out the glass in the door. "Stoneface Finnegan," he muttered. "I am a fool."

"Ah, it ain't nothing, kid." The other man, not much older, but all muscle and bone, black shirt, and squinty eyes, clapped a hard hand on the kid's shoulder. "I happen to know of a fellow who'll pay handsomely to know who just rode into town. Yep," he said, plopping his hat on his head as he strode for the back door once more. "Yes, sir. Handsomely."

As the door closed behind him, Deputy Hawkins heard Deputy Beaucaire whistling a jaunty tune.

Chapter 19

"Won't help us if you get yourself caught . . . or worse."
Rollie was arguing with Pops.

"But I want to see my—I need to see that young woman.
What if she's my daughter?"

"If she is or if she isn't won't matter if you're dead, Pops.
Think about it."

"Then what do you suggest? 'Cause sitting here drinking coffee isn't getting me any closer to why I came." Pops
had set down his cup on a warm rock about the fire and
scowled, half at Rollie, half at the creeping darkness settling
about them like a wool blanket. "So how we gonna get in
there and out again?"

"I don't know," said Rollie.

From across the campfire, Tish leveled her gaze at them.
"I do."

She knew what they were going to say, but before they
could speak, the fiery young woman held up a halting
hand. "I have all the required assets a pig like Swearengen
could want. You said so yourself, Rollie."

"I never did!"

"Sure you did. Both of you did. When you said I should cover up before riding into town."

"That's not what we meant."

She shook her head. "Close enough. Look. I know how to handle myself in certain . . . situations."

"I don't think you do. Those men back there on the trail? You were naïve and that was going to land you in a world of hurt."

That shut her up, but only for a moment. She stood, hands on hips, and paced back and forth on her side of the campfire. "I know what you're thinking, but it's really not up to you, now is it?" She stood facing them, her hands balled into fists at her sides.

Oddly enough more than anything at that moment Rollie wanted to laugh. She looked so determined, yet she was acting like a four-year-old child. He hid his grin behind his coffee cup.

Tish glared at them a moment longer, then stomped off.

"Hey!" he said, but Pops put a hand on his arm. "Leave her be. She's frustrated, stuck with two old-timers like us. She wants a little adventure in her life."

"Deadwood is not the place to find it."

"I know. But you know how she can be. She'll walk back here in a little while all sullen and by morning everything will be forgotten. Meanwhile, what sort of plan are you thinking about? 'Cause I'm about ready to ride on in there and make things happen."

"Take it easy. I know Bullock isn't around, but he wasn't the only ace we have up our sleeve."

Pops sipped his coffee. "Well?"

"I'm thinking," Rollie growled. "And besides, what

makes you so interested in plans all of a sudden? I've tried for days to get your thoughts on the matter."

"Now that we're here, as I say, I don't want to waste a single minute. I'll take this town apart board by board if need be."

"Well, let me think some more. In the meantime, I think we ought to make sure she hasn't wandered off."

"She's not a child, Rollie."

"She's not my child, but she's somebody's kid, and I feel responsible for her. She's out here because of me, after all." He turned and shouted in the direction she'd walked. "Tish! Tish?"

No reply came for long moments. The two men exchanged glances. Then they heard, "What?" from a distance away.

"Down by the brook, I'd say," said Pops.

Rollie cupped his hands about his mouth. "Just don't go far, okay?"

"Can't a woman have some privacy?"

Both men shut up then, eyes wide.

Rollie sat down. "Maybe I am being too protective."

They laid out their bedrolls and settled in.

"I know you'd rather bust on in there right now, Pops, but I need a few hours of shut-eye."

"I hear you. Fresher in the morning. See if we can do it your way first."

"What's my way?"

"Nice and polite."

"And if that doesn't work?" said Rollie, knowing the answer he was about to receive.

Pops chuckled in the dark. "Then me and Lil' Miss

Mess Maker will tend to things in our own way. We got a lot of practice doing such together, you know."

"I know. Let's hope it doesn't come to that. But if it does, I'm with you. I want Tish to stay out of the line of fire."

As if on cue, the young woman walked back into the dwindling glow of firelight. "You're talking about me again. Don't you know that's rude?"

But they could tell by her tone she had gotten over her momentary anger. She climbed into her own bedding and said, "Good night, gentlemen." Just as she had every night on the trail.

"Good night, Tish."

"Night, Tish."

The three of them had proved to be light sleepers. Rollie was confident any one of them would hear any unwelcome sounds in the night. He was also certain that by morning they'd have a plan of action figured out and would be back in town, negotiating somehow. *Heck,* he thought. *Maybe it'll go smother than we figure.* After all, in his experience, with enough threatening, most folks folded like a poor hand of cards.

His thoughts circled like that until they fizzled, pinched off by deep slumber, punctuated by Pops low soft snores, an old bull grizz deep in hibernation.

One of the three wasn't asleep. The youngest lay awake for a long, long time. Waiting for just the right moment to make her move.

Chapter 20

It took Tish a full half hour to climb from her bedding and walk in a low crouch away from the campfire and the two snoring men. At one point she froze because both snorted nearly in unison, as if they'd been startled. She held her breath but had a hard time of it because she wanted to laugh.

For all their bluster, in some ways they were not what she expected of two burly fighting men, certainly not Ol' Stoneface Finnegan, the legend. She had to remind herself during the years he'd built that legend through deed and daring, she'd been but a child, and indeed many of those years had taken place before she was even born.

Steeling herself, she kept on, not daring to breathe deeply until well away from the camp. The horses whickered low as she approached. She'd considered riding back to town on her horse, but she reasoned saddling and leading the horse away would make too much suspicious sound, especially if a horseshoe struck stone.

Rollie might well be sleeping the sleep of the dead, but

that didn't mean he wouldn't be up and running, gun drawn and cocked, by the time she swung into the saddle.

The thought of his flinty, fiery eyes staring her down in the dark shivered her spine. She pulled in a deep breath of the cool night air and shrugged her cloak up higher over her shoulders and headed toward Deadwood.

As she walked, Tish became aware of all the night sounds she'd been hearing for weeks, and it occurred to her it was the first time she'd ever been intentionally moving away from the unspoken safety and protection of Rollie and Pops.

Even after she'd followed them away from Boar Gulch thinking she hadn't been seen by them, they'd been just up ahead on the trail. She'd been certain they'd catch sight of her if she kindled a fire, and so she'd slept in a cold camp.

Come to find out, they'd known she was there from the start.

And she was not only venturing willfully away from them, but without their knowledge, and toward something she was petrified of and excited about. Petrified because she'd heard, as most people had, of the cutthroat, boom-bust thrill that was Deadwood, and certainly she'd heard of the Gem Theater owned by the notorious Al Swearengen.

But thrilling, too. It was a chance . . . no, it was *the* chance for her to do exactly what she'd sought out Rollie Finnegan for in the first place—to show him what she was made of, to show him she was capable of going under-cover, using a fake name as a disguise, and snooping for information about Pops' daughter.

She had no doubt the woman they were seeking was

his daughter. The way Pops had acted, the glazed, far-off look he got in his eyes when he was left alone for more than a couple of minutes. Something told Tish the woman had to be his daughter, yet she ignored the tiny, niggling voice in her mind that kept saying she was being wishful, that she had no proof.

She would go there, march right into the Gem, demand to see this Swearengen fellow, and convince him somehow that she was . . . what?

Tish slowed her pace. Intentionally, she had not given much thought to the notion of passing herself off as much more than what she was—a pretty face. But to work in a theater one had to do something . . . theatrical. Could she act?

Well, Tish, she told herself, *that was the entire point wasn't it? To pretend. To assume a false identity and play a charade, all in the name of lawful conduct.*

She picked up her pace. Of course, she would act, and even sing and dance if she had to. She'd done a little of that in finishing school, at the pageants and mummery shows each season. Theater class had been her favorite undertaking at school. It suited her, she liked to think. Though she readily admitted she was not much of a hand at carrying a tune.

A snuffling sounded twenty or so feet off the road to her right followed by a harsh growl and a rustling, then a drawn-out squeaking that ended in a tiny, near-inaudible gurgle. Something died. She had mere seconds to consider it all before the yips and howls of coyotes began up on a hillside somewhere in the dark to her left, inciting what sounded like dozens more all about her.

A man's voice from somewhere ahead bellowed, "Shut up!" and the coyote song yipped and skittered to a close.

Carefully, Tish moved on.

Far too soon, she saw lights—random yellow glows—ahead and to either side, then to her left the low glow of a campfire. *Town,* she thought. *I am coming to the town.* And for the first time since she'd left the safety of the camp with Rollie and Pops, Tish Gray felt a stab of regret about her decision.

More than that, a sense of foreboding curled over her. The same creepy feeling she'd gotten the day before she'd found out her Grandmama, the woman who'd raised her, had died in her sleep, yet different. The feeling was not so much one of sadness and gloom, but of raw, stark fear, all blood-red and violent. Tish swallowed back a hard knot in her throat, pulled in a deep breath of cold night air, and hurried forward into the increasingly bright night, ever closer to the unknown that dawn in Deadwood would bring.

Chapter 21

Though she wore her cloak's hood up over her head, she had to keep her gaze upright in order to see where she was walking. It had been easier to hide riding on a horse. Even at the early hour a number of men were about and nearly every one paused in their tasks to stare at her as she walked by.

She half stared at the first few and nodded in greeting. One man looked as if he might have taken that for a welcome, a chance to sidle up to her, but she hustled onward, tense and worried. Should it come to it, she might not be able to pull her revolver as Rollie had shown her on the trail.

That had been an interesting lesson. One he'd insisted on. Pops stood by, chuckling and rocking back on his heels, now and again offering pointers. Helpful as he was, they all knew Rollie was the most experienced when it came to handling guns. He'd been coy about pointing to the gun when she had it hung on her hip in the simple but robust brown leather holster.

Her thoughts drifted back to the lesson.

"You're goin to want to, um." He nodded toward her waist and turned red. "Take your time when you draw that. One of the biggest mistakes folks make is they rush it. It's all well and good to be the first to draw, but if you do it in haste, as I've seen far too many folks do, you are guaranteed to end up at best with a hole in your boot. At worst, you'll have a snagged gun that will leave you dead."

"That was a chipper thing to say." Tish stood with her legs apart and her hands poised as she'd seen two angry, drunken men do once in a saloon.

"What is it you're doing there?" said Rollie.

Chuckling, Pops said, "You look about ready to start a foot race!"

Tish reddened and dropped the stance. "I thought that's what you were supposed to do."

"Only if you're a regular gunhand with a reputation as such. And a high-falutin opinion of yourself that won't quit." Rollie's hard look softened. "What you want to do is go slow and easy. Don't pull the gun, but repeat over and over letting your right hand find that revolver's grip, over and over."

He watched her and nodded. "Yep, just like that, slow and easy. You're forcing your mind to do what you want it to know. It makes more sense in the doing than in the explaining."

"I hope so," said Pops, returning back to the campfire. "Because I never heard such twaddle in all my days."

"Well," said Rollie. "By all means, why don't you show us how you pull a gun with accuracy every time."

"Not a problem," said Pops. And walking over he hefted Lil' Miss Mess Maker, cradling it across his chest *as if it were a baby. He paused before them. "And that's how it's done."*

Rollie sighed and rolled his eyes.

"Oh," said Tish, wishing there was more shooting and less folderol.

It had taken them hours of slow, boring practice, but they finally got to the shooting part. Pops had set up pinecones along the top of a log and they'd paced backward from it twenty paces.

"Okay, we'll try it from here." Rollie turned and faced the row of pinecones, with nothing but a few spindly trees and a gradual slope that allowed them to see the mountains beyond for miles. The farthest peaks were purple, those closer in and still a day's ride eastward were darker.

"How many more days until we reach Deadwood?" she asked Pops.

"Oh, about two, maybe three, tops. That is, if I'm remembering right. Rollie, what do you say?"

"That's about right, yeah. That's why we need to get you proficient at drawing this gun, leveling, pointing and squeezing that trigger."

She pulled it out as Rollie had shown her, slow and measured, hefting it with the sore muscles in her forearm and hand, tensed and accustomed to the weight of the gun. It was surprisingly heavy, but after all that practice, it was not so noticeable. She actually had grown to like the heft of it, the reassuring weight of the gun in her hand.

"You're trembling," said Rollie, in a tone telling her he was not impressed. She did her best to not reply, but instead to take the remark as useful criticism. It didn't work. His comment rankled her, but she did her best to keep her hand from trembling. That didn't work, either.

"What say we take a break for a bite? I'm feeling peckish and I bet Tish could use some of my fine cooking to steady those nerves," said Pops.

"I'm steady," she said, trying to concentrate instead on the pinecone she wanted to kill.

"No, you ain't neither," said Pops. "And I don't blame you. I'd be the same way if I had a grizzled old goober like Stoneface Finnegan glaring at me and mocking my every move."

"I didn't mock anybody. I have been trying to help her develop a skill needed to protect herself when the time comes."

"If the time comes, you mean."

"Where we're headed?" said Rollie, shaking his head. "No, it's when. My guess is you'll want to keep your hand on the gun under that cloak of yours. It's a good way to disguise the fact that you're heeled like a man."

She lowered the revolver and slid it back into the holster. "What's wrong with my feet?" she said, looking down at her boots. "I admit my boots are a little dusty, but I do not have feet like a man."

"What?" said Rollie. "No, no, no."

Pops laughed so hard he stood with his shoulders working up and down.

Rollie shook his head and stalked off toward the campfire. "Time to eat," he said over his shoulder.

Pops rubbed his tear-filled eyes and sighed. "Heeled is one of those words folks use in a silly way, near as I can figure. In this case, it means you're wearing a gun."

"Oh." Tish looked down at the holster and the gun belt, shining the brass buckle with the cuff of her sleeve. 'Why didn't he just say so?"

They walked toward the fire.

"With Rollie Finnegan, you never know what's going on in that mind. Best to do as he says. I find it all works out, even if it doesn't seem to make sense at the time of the doing. You follow me?"

"I guess so." Tish rubbed her arm and looked back toward the pinecones.

"Don't worry, plenty of daylight left for you to lay low a few of those deadly cone critters yet. Just now, though, I'd be more worried about getting a biscuit before Rollie polishes them all off."

Rollie looked at them and stuffed a second biscuit into his mouth. "Too late," he mumbled. Then he winked.

Shaking her head of the memory, Tish continued her walk through Deadwood.

Chapter 22

Even in the early morning light when most of the businesses on the main street of Deadwood seemed to be closed and awaiting the abhorred morning to begin again, there was no mistaking the Gem Theater for anything other than what it was—a saloon and dance hall.

Folks in Deadwood, as in all mine camps, kept an ear cocked for the rare shouts of color, yelps bedraggled miners made as they ambled into town and plunked down a sack of dust or nuggets of promising ore at the assayer's office. Everyone in town, the merchants, the floozies, the barkeeps, the liverymen, all of them, would mark that man in their minds as one who could pay outstanding debts or one who might be amenable to a card game. *And* if one were to get him drunk enough, he might be willing to forfeit his proven claim on the promise of a winning hand. And of course, a winning hand never made its way to any man.

But winning hands did seem to pop up with regularity into the fists of certain men in the Gem. Certain men who then reported back to the man who many considered ran the town.

In the early morning, Tish Gray was unaware of much of that as she stood before the Gem. What she saw was a solid edifice with a long, low covered porch, wide front steps, and a sign shouting the wonders of the exotic women within who performed all manner of dance and song. And all for a small fee.

She knew it was still far too early for any such business to be open. And yet, walking up the broad staircase, taking slow, hesitant steps, she heard voices from up top, the low mumble and murmur of men talking quietly. Reaching the top, she saw two men sitting on a long, low bench. They stopped talking and stared at her, each holding a steaming cup of coffee.

Bold or not at all, she told herself. What she'd promised herself years ago once taking to life's open roads alone as a wide-eyed youth.

"Good morning, gentlemen," she said, hating her voice sounding higher than she liked. Beneath her cloak, her right hand gripped the comforting, hard walnut grip of her revolver.

They stared. One of them, a fleshy fellow, wide of face, with black beard stubble poking out like a bristle brush, let his mouth sag open as if he'd been asleep and lost all control of his facial muscles.

She cleared her throat and continued. "I . . . am looking for a Mr. Albert Swearengen."

"Who?" said the other, thinner man. He leaned forward and squinted. "You mean Al?"

She nodded. "That appears so, yes."

He leaned back and spoke to his cup. "Huh. Didn't know his name was Albert. Huh."

Tish waited for him to continue. He did not.

"Perhaps you could tell me if he is currently here?" She nodded toward the double doors before her. Black shades were drawn inside the top glassed portions of the doors.

"I guess he'd be in there. He lives there! Don't he, Moe?" This struck the thin man as one of the wittier things he'd ever uttered and he laughed, a ragged, wet and raw smoker's laugh. He followed this up by spitting over the railing and into the dusty earth out front. His gobbet did not make it over the rail, clinging to the edge and oozing down to the porch's plank floor.

That struck the heretofore silent, fat fellow as humorous and he chuckled in silence, his wide, round shoulders jerking up and down as if he were being tickled.

Tish tried to work up a smile but found it impossible. With her left hand she reached for the large, brass door handle, but she hesitated before her thumb depressed the latch. From her right, the thin man said, "Ain't open yet, but the door's unlocked. Al's in there somewheres. Always is."

"Unless he's gone," said the fat man in a soft, wheezy voice, speaking for the first time since Tish found them.

"That's true, that's true." The thin man nodded and gazed into his oracle of a coffee cup once more.

Tish half smiled at them and was about to say thank you, but both were looking into their cups. She clicked the brass latch and nudged the big door. It swung inward with a slight squeak.

Chapter 23

As Tish's eyes adjusted to the dim interior, her nose wrinkled at the stink of the place. She detected the pungent, sourness of stale beer, of too many unwashed men in too small a place, and smoke from too many cigars, cigarettes, and pipes. Over all hovered the sickly stink from last night's oil lamps, blazing away until likely just a few hours ago.

She stepped into the room and gently closed the big door behind her. The floor was sticky and crunchy—sticky, she guessed, from spilled beer and poorly aimed spurts of tobacco spittle and blood and the Good Lord only knew what else. The crunchiness, from what she could gather without kneeling and inspecting—something she had no intention of ever doing—looked like wood chips, though she could not be certain.

Why was it that men enjoyed spending so much time in such disgusting places? She suspected during the business's open hours, the smells leveled off and mingled with the raucous din emanating from all the yammering drunken mouths.

Contributing, too, would be the piano she was certain the place possessed, the clatter and cacophony at the games tables, the shouts and shrieks of the women getting pinched and fondled while serving the men. And there were sure to be shouts at the bar, yelling to be heard over the din.

She finally felt as if she understood what Rollie had meant when he said he was in business to mine the miners. To him it hadn't seemed rapacious or unkind, merely business. But she understood it was precisely because there are people with money and business people want that money. Simple commerce.

"Hey."

Tish looked up.

"Who are you?"

The voice drifted toward her from far to her right, somewhere behind the long, dark-wood bar. A brass rail shone in the dull light, scuffed and worn dull.

Footsteps, slow and measured sounded. "I said"—the voice was slowly moving closer to her, though in no hurry—"who are you?"

Tish cleared her throat. "I am . . . looking for Mr. Albert Swearengen."

"Oh you are, are you?"

The walking stopped. She could just see the faint glow of a white-ish shirt twenty or so feet to her right, behind the bar. A sleeve moved and she heard a cup being set down in a saucer.

"And what, may I ask, do you want of him?"

"That is my business and his, sir. Now, would you be so kind as to fetch him for me?"

"Fetch him? Hmm, I suppose I could, but—"

"But?" she said, tiring of the endless parade of fools. She needed to get the subterfuge underway, else she might lose heart and the entire affair would somehow become obvious somehow. Desperate to turn and run, she concentrated on the fact that Pops' daughter was likely hidden away in the place somewhere, for what purposes, she knew not, though she could guess. First she had to find her. That was the job, the reason, in short, the key to both their futures.

"But?" The man behind the bar sighed. "It is rather early, don't you think for a woman to come calling?"

"Sir, I can assure you there is nothing untoward in my arrival here. I am . . . I have a business proposition for Mr. Swearengen. Nothing more."

"Ah, I see."

"Good. Then please tell him I am here."

"Fine." Another sigh. "Who may I tell him is calling at such an early hour?"

"Please inform Mr. Swearengen that Miss Letitia Rose is here to see him."

"Letitia Rose. Hmm. Pretty name. It's difficult for me to see if it suits you, seeing as how it's rather dark in here and the cloak you are wearing is hiding your face. It's a nice cloak, by the way. Very . . . distinctive."

She thought that an odd thing to say, but she treated it as a compliment. "Thank you. It was a gift from a dear friend a long time ago."

The hired buffoon didn't sound like a buffoon. Unlike the men she'd met on the porch, he seemed capable of putting enough words together to form coherent sentences.

"Hmm," he said. "Yes, well, friends can be like that. Kind and generous one moment, and then . . . ah, but I'm certain my experiences in such matters are of little consequence to you. What is it Mr. Swearengen can do for you, ma'am?"

It was a repeat of the same question she had rebuffed a few minutes before. Somehow, something had changed. Although uncertain what it was, she felt she could no longer hold him at bay. As if not answering that very minute, would result in him seeing she was an undercover operative. Somehow it could happen and, though she did not know how, it unsettled her.

Something occurred to her, something obvious, so much so she felt the hot flush of shame heat her face. "You . . . you're Mr. Swearengen, aren't you?"

There was a pause, then the man walked down the length of the bar, sliding his cup along beside him. He reached the end, fiddled with a latch, raised part of the bar top, and walked through, stopping a dozen feet away.

He walked closer, his boots sticking and crunching on the floor. "Oh, this floor. I don't know why I put up with those fools. I suppose Moe and Skip are out front, drinking my coffee and warming my chairs and not doing my bidding for which they are paid." He sighed. "Yes, Miss . . . Rose. If you haven't yet figured it out, I am indeed Mr. Swearengen. But please, don't call me that. Call me Al. All my friends and even my business acquaintances do so."

He stepped closer and she could see him. He wasn't at all what she had pictured in her mind, what this demon should look like.

He was trim, swarthy, but with a hint of handsome about his mustachioed face. And though he looked as if he'd had a late night, apparent by an air of weariness on his face and general demeanor, something else was there, too. Dare she say it, a kindness about the eyes and mouth? How could that be?

Steady Tish, she told herself. *That's merely what you are supposed to think. To be drawn in now is to abandon everything you've ever worked for.*

Realizing she was still gripping the revolver tight beneath her cloak, she relaxed the grip and with her free left hand she reached out and offered him a handshake. "It is my pleasure to make your acquaintance, Mr.—Al."

He smiled and, holding his cup aloft, he clicked his brogans' heels together and offered a sharp, if slight, bow from the waist. "It is all my pleasure, ma'am. Now"—he turned back to the bar—"may I offer you refreshment? A cup of freshly brewed coffee, perhaps?"

In that moment, her thoughts flashed quickly to Rollie and Pops, likely awake and making their own coffee. Or, more likely, already frantic and looking for her.

She should have left a note. Of course she should have. What had she been thinking? Oh, foolish, foolish girl. Then she looked at Mr. Swearengen, his back to the bar, one boot against the brass rail, and a half smile on his face, his head canted slightly to one side.

"It's just coffee, Miss Rose. While we discuss your business proposition."

"Of course," she said. "I should like that very much."

He smiled a wide, wide smile. "Good. Me, too."

Chapter 24

It was a low-flying crow hacksawing its way through the barely purpling sky that woke Rollie. "Hey . . . Pops."

Nothing.

"Hey!"

He heard the familiar groan and intake of breath as Pops, before he even opened his eyes each morning, rubbed his face briskly with his hands.

"Mornin', Rollie. Mornin' Tish."

"That's the problem," said Rollie sitting up in his blankets and looking over at her blankets across the cold fire.

'Huh?"

"Tish . . . she's not here."

Before Rollie could gain his feet, he was wincing. Stiffness from a dozen wounds over the years kept him from hopping up and into his boots as he still expected of himself.

Pops did the same, rubbing his back and stifling a yawn. "Maybe she's down by the creek dealing with her morning ablutions."

"Her what?"

Pops looked at Rollie. "Did you not pay attention in school, mister?"

Rollie muttered some dark words and Pops tugged on his lace-up boots and clumped into the cover of nearby pines.

Rollie felt her blankets, at first with timidity, then more aggressively. He growled and cupped his hands about his mouth and aimed a shout toward the creek. He was about to shout her name when Pops shuffled back into the clearing.

"Easy now, don't get all worked up . . . yet. Finish getting your boots on and I'll go down to the creek and see if she's about."

"Her horse is still here," said Rollie, bending to pick up a boot.

"See? If her horse is still here, it can't be she's gone anywhere." Pops walked down toward the creek, chuckling and shaking his head.

Rollie grumbled a little more until he got his boots mostly tugged on, then he stomped about the campsite breathing deep of the piney air and working out the kinks. He was sure Pops was correct. He hoped so. Yet there was a worm of doubt twitching in his brain somewhere.

That girl had been more damn annoyance than she was worth. Trouble was, he liked her. She was a good kid. He didn't want anything to happen to her. And he damn sure didn't want her set loose in a town such as Deadwood.

"Rat hole," muttered Rollie as he followed Pops' lead and found a spot in the trees to relieve his bladder. He figured a few minutes either way weren't going to matter, so first and foremost, he wanted a scalding hot cup of coffee, black and thick.

He crouched by the fire pit and held a hand over the black coals. No hint of warmth. They hadn't had much of a fire the evening before—too tired by half. All of them. He scrunched up pine duff and dry grasses, then teepeed twigs and larger snapped branches about the soft, dry heart of the fire.

By the time he heard Pops' boots stomping back up the path from the creek, the young fire was beginning to crackle and snap and Rollie could almost taste the coffee.

"Lay off that now, Rollie!" Pops nearly hissed the words, crouching low and speaking close to his face. Rollie noticed his pard's face was wet. "Men down there by the creek, up to no good, and I think they're looking for us. Won't be long before they're headed this way. Especially if they smell the fire."

"Damn it all to hell. There goes the coffee."

Rollie didn't need to hear any more. He went for his gun belt, which he'd uncharacteristically left looped about his saddle horn, as the saddle had served as his head rest for the night.

"They say anything?"

"Yeah, they did," said Pops, thumbing shells into his ammunition bandolier and slipping it over his head. "Said something about how Al—I'm guessing that means Swearengen, so they might be his boys—has all the luck. Something about seeing *a tasty new piece*—their words not mine—with red hair walk right into the lion's den earlier this morning."

"Oh no, Tish. Oh my word, what has that girl gone and done?" Rollie bit back anger.

With a nod to Pops, each took a side of the campsite, Rollie toward the horses, Pops to the pines at his left. They flanked the site and eyed the path from the creek, waiting for the newcomers.

They exchanged glances a couple of times. Pops eyed the fire and felt, as Rollie did, despite their situation he sure would have liked a cup of coffee before the kerfuffle kicked off the day. He indulged in a sigh and waited.

They'd been silent for several minutes, eyeing the entire southern edge of the trees and the path from the creek in the midst of it. Each tensed when a man wearing what looked to be an oddly tall black hat emerged from behind the trees. As he stepped into the edge of the clearing, they saw he wore a dusty, battered top hat.

Close behind him walked a short fellow unburdened by a hat or hair, but sporting scruffy ginger whiskers. Each man walked with care, the short man in boots, his taller, behatted companion wearing knee-height buckskin moccasins, long fringe rimming the tops. Swaying with each slow step, they looked left, then right, and back again. Each was armed, the tall man in the lead position with a rifle held across his chest, ready to level out and shoot. The short man behind kept licking his lips. His revolver, held in his right hand, trembled.

Pops guessed the little one might be the easiest to deal with. He'd seen men a whole lot more frightened in less dangerous situations. He and Rollie hadn't had the chance to chat about what to do about Tish, not how they were going to deal with these fools. But if he knew Rollie, ol' Stoneface wasn't going to waste too much time with them.

From the edge of his vision, Pops saw Rollie shift. From being in many such situations with the man over the past couple of years, Pops knew Rollie was about to make his play. That usually meant a full-on, immediate confrontation. It also meant doing something the invaders, whoever they might be, would not expect . . . something like stand up.

Suddenly Rollie jerked back down again. And there were more voices.

Pops had heard two, maybe three, down by the creek but had seen only one man through the trees. But he knew the men were after them. After he'd splashed his face down by the creek, they'd said something about a *him* traveling with a black man, except they'd used a word that he despised.

Like it or not, thought Pops, *they were talking about me.*

Still, he couldn't swear to any more than two, maybe three men, one of which he'd seen through the trees. But they were hearing more voices. At least three more, and using no caution about how loud they spoke.

Strength in numbers, Pops thought, readjusting his grip on the shotgun then touching the inside of his left wrist to the butt of the revolver he wore. His back-up plan.

"Why you two moving so slow?" asked a voice.

"'Cause they're about here somewheres," said Top Hat in a hoarse whisper.

"I see the horses and the smoking fire, but I don't see them." The speaker finally made himself seen, stepping into the clearing. "Besides, we got men fanned out all around. What good will two do against five?"

Top Hat looked at his short companion.

The short man eyeballed the entire scene before him, slowly raking his gaze over everything, then back again, settling his gaze on Pops. He squinted and lowered his head as if deciding what was there was not what he saw.

Then convincing himself, he shouted, "I see one!" and pointed.

The men scattered.

A couple of seconds later, the first shot ploughed a furrow into the sandy soil close by Pops' right foot. He sidestepped and used a close-by ponderosa pine as a shelf for a heartbeat of time. Then he stepped to his left once, squatted down lower than he hoped they would expect, and jerked his shotgun straight outward from his gut.

Pops touched off the trigger and a swarm of deadly lead bees drove straight and true at the shooter close enough the shot would mess up his day. He'd been in the midst of shifting to his own left, and the blast caught him on his right hip and jerked his leg out from beneath him as if he were trying out some exotic dancing technique. His scream of sudden agony did not match the pirouette. He ended up slamming into a slab of sandstone as if set there by a giant's hand in some long-ago time. He caromed off the stone and slopped face-first to the earth, flailing and howling and writhing.

Pops saw no one else about, but heard scuffling and shots not far northward in the trees. He wasn't too concerned for Rollie, as the man had skill and experience enough to fend for himself. But as there were five of them, and he had only taken care of one, he doubted the other four would all go for Rollie.

And then he had his answer. A lone figure darted between trees over by the horses. And it wasn't Rollie.

Pops cut down toward the creek, angled westward and up once more toward the horses. If any of the attackers were behind him, he'd be laid low with a shot to the back.

But he did what he always did in such situations—he took in the risks to know where the bad men were. Thus, he knew where they were likely to be next, and then he moved like hell, staying low and keeping a finger poised before the trigger.

Cap whickered and Pops knew the man was hiding near their three horses.

A shot cracked the near-silence and a low, gagging sound bubbled up from the trees close by the horses. The beasts danced and thrashed and stretched the picket line. The recipient of the shot staggered out from between two trees and dropped to a knee, kept trying to walk, and reached at the air before him, clawing at something invisible. With more of the gagging sound, he dropped forward.

Pops guessed he was done for. He also recognized him as the short, bald man who'd walked just behind Top Hat.

"That leaves three," said Pops. He made it to the horses, patting them and making soothing, clucking sounds.

"Hey, Pops!"

Pops peered over Bud's back and saw Rollie hunkered behind a tumbledown boulder.

"Get on your horse and get gone while you can!"

"No way, man! I'm not leaving you to deal with three of them!"

"There aren't three any more," snarled Rollie, glancing about. "And they'll be back here soon enough."

"How many left?" said Pops, not heeding Rollie's command one bit.

"I counted four more. Don't know where they all came from, but I have a plan."

"That's what I'm afraid of. Too many for you to handle alone."

"That's offensive, even from you, Pops. Now get on that horse and get to town!"

"I'm not leaving you to deal with—"

"Dammit, Pops, if you don't go, we could both be lost, and then where would Tish and your daughter be?"

"But—"

"But nothing. Tish is a good kid but she doesn't have the seasoning, nor the spine for this type of work. I never should have let her come. Look, if you won't do it just for her, then do it for your daughter. Otherwise, this whole trip will have been for nothing. Your entire life searching will have come to naught. Now go!"

"Okay, okay, but don't do anything foolish!"

"Ha! I'm going to lead them on a chase into these Black Hills. I've spent a fair amount of time in these parts. I fancy I know it better than they do. Now get gone so I can gather my gear before they circle back. They still think I'm in that draw down back there."

"What draw?"

"That's what I'm talking about. I know these parts, Pops. Now we both should go for our gear. Cover each other. Grab only what we need to do the job. Shouldn't take long. You go first. I'll cover you."

Pops nodded and darted back into the clearing, eyes peeled wide for sign of movement as he snatched up his essentials—his brown bowler hat and denim coat, his saddlebag, saddle, blanket, and the rest of the tack.

He lugged it back to the horses as fast as he was able and set to saddling the horse right away. "Okay, your turn, Rollie. Do it up. I'll cover your sorry backside."

Already on the move, Rollie had begun the same hasty gathering of goods vital to his upcoming merry chase. Within a half minute, he was back at the horses, having lugged his and Tish's saddles.

The men saddled in silence, each watching for the intruders.

"I'll take Tish's horse," said Rollie. "Might have need of him. He'd only slow you. Where I'm going—and where I'm taking those fools—they might catch sight of two horses and think we're together. They won't expect you to head into town and into the lion's mouth."

"Right. So glad you put it that way, Rollie." Pops rolled his eyes. "Listen, you just take care."

"Yeah," said Rollie. "You, too. You're not the sort who will be treated easy in town, if you know what I mean."

"Don't worry about me. I know better than you think. Been this way my whole life."

"So have they. Save Tish and your daughter." Rollie turned away, then looked back. "See ya soon."

Pops nodded and swung up into the saddle. He looked back once to see Rollie doing the same, with Tish's mount on a lead line in tow.

Pops gave an off-the-brim two-finger salute and a smile and nod.

Rollie nodded—no smile, not a surprise—and then the men rode in their respective directions.

Pops didn't look back and realized after a hundred yards he was tensed, riding as if he was trying to balance glass balls on his shoulders. He was waiting, he knew, to hear gunshots. Rollie's tough words and blunt talk didn't fool him. He knew the man he called a friend was going up against it, with at least four rouges still out there hunting him. And he was riding right into their midst, hoping to lure them on a chase to keep them from heading back to town, hopefully forever.

Pops didn't doubt Rollie knew the hills from adventures in the past, but he hadn't pointed out the thing Rollie was not mentioning—those adventures had been years before, back when Rollie was younger. And most importantly, when he hadn't been knifed without mercy and left for dead in an alleyway in Denver City.

No sir, Rollie "Stoneface" Finnegan was one tough guy, but he was not the same man he was back then.

"Am I the same man I was in years past?" Pops whispered aloud, doing his best to keep his mind off Rollie's welfare and giving his own worries hard thought.

Years past, so many years before, he'd been a father and a husband. He hoped he was still at least one of those things. He was pretty certain his wife was dead and gone from this world, but his daughter? Could it be her in Deadwood?

Just because he wanted her to be, felt something deep inside telling him it was her, didn't mean it was. Not until he met her. And what would he find? He refused to believe she was a foul slattern, crushed by the merciless power of oppressors. But what if she had become something too far gone to bring back?

"No," he growled. "Don't think that way, Pops. Don't do it!"

Concentrate instead on Deadwood, on getting there, and on what he was going to do once he got there. Maybe first he ought to see if Sheriff Bullock was back yet. What if he wasn't?

Pops couldn't rely on others. Especially not a white

lawman, no matter how much Rollie might think of the man. He didn't know Pops from Adam, might not feel kindly toward a free black man.

People were different, from one to the other. If he'd learned anything in his years on the road, he'd learned that lesson, and sometimes it came hard and quick.

So, what was he going to do in town? His usual way of dealing with this sort of thing, of riding in and seeing what happened, might not be the smartest way. Not if he wanted to get in there fast.

Not if he wanted to get in there, then out of there, with himself, Tish, and his daughter, all alive.

Chapter 25

Rollie didn't let up on his dash to get from that camp and spider-leg it onto a trail he vaguely recalled. It was his best hope to lead his pursuers far into the Black Hills. He intended to get them far enough away from the camp they'd almost give up on him. That's when he'd tease them into showing themselves. Unless he was able to get shots at them before then.

Despite his situation, he had to admit the day had dawned fine—clear, blue, and bright as only days in the mountains can be. The air was sharp with the homey tang of pine. Something chattered, then skittered—a squirrel—upslope to his left.

"I'm no threat to you, little one," he whispered as he cut a raw trail, switchbacking up a steep, sparsely treed slope. He was exposed from below and didn't much like the feeling. If he could make it across and into that stand of thicker pines ahead, he'd feel a whole lot better.

As if on cue, he heard a shout from below and looked over his right shoulder to see a gray hat moving among the trees some few hundred feet below. Rollie had hoped to keep from their sight, at least enough so they'd see at best two horses working through the trees, as if he and Pops were both on the run from the menace of the pursuers.

The farther away he lured them from town, the more time he could buy Pops. And if he got them far enough away, he intended to circle back around them and kill them, one by one.

What charity he might have felt toward them had drizzled away with the conviction the coarse brutes would have gladly shot him and Pops in their blankets, then looted their goods, divvied the spoils, led their horses to town, and sold them to the first livery they came to.

He had other reasons for laying them low, all four of them. Given what Pops had overheard, they were likely in the employ of Swearengen. And something was not quite right with that deputy, too. Could he have known who Rollie was? He'd seemed clueless, but maybe Rollie's old ability to read faces was faltering with age.

Might be the kid was innocent enough, and little more than a youth trying to act like a big deal while the competent boss man, in this case Seth Bullock, was out of town. Yet when he was in that office, Rollie had felt a familiar old drag of annoyance and caution creep up his backbone.

But then again, all of Deadwood was something to feel cautious about. He'd never liked such places, dens of grubbing fools and thieves and lazy men with ill intent. It was ironic that he had come to live in a place that in many ways was a young Deadwood in the making.

Boar Gulch was a raw mine camp blooming into a less-raw mine town. The only reason it hadn't gone to seed was because he and Pops had ridden roughshod over folks who wished to prey on others. He himself had been responsible for bringing the worst of the worst down on the heads of his fellow Gulchers, causing Rollie to feel a guilt he'd never shake.

That was something Bullock didn't have to worry about. He didn't show up in Deadwood with a price on his head and a string of folks looking to kill him for money or revenge. Or both.

It was also possible Rollie was thinking a little uncharitably toward Deadwood. There was a whole lot more to the town than the seedy spots, swill saloons and gambling dens, pits that attracted the lowlifes. Deadwood had grown quite a bit in the short years since he'd last been there. Even on their short tour through the main street last night he'd seen prosperity and promise in the form of paint and people who weren't necessarily there just to gamble and drink and fight.

He swore he even heard children shouting. Maybe Deadwood stood a chance of becoming a genuine town with long-term prospects.

"A little early to make such guesses, Rollie," he told himself, nudging Cap into a scrambling climb up a last stretch of scree.

They made it to a copse of pines when a shout from below sounded something like, "There! He's there!" and was followed by two snapped shots. The first sizzled far ahead of him, the second buzzing much closer, a lead pill parting air and looking for a heart to stop.

He muttered under his breath, called them profane names, and bent lower, making for a mass of pink and tan boulders large enough he might be able to make it around them. Play a game of cat and mouse up in the high rocks.

The sun baked the backs of his bare hands and felt good on the right side of his face. A breeze up riffled his shirt.

Under any other circumstance, it would be a place he'd enjoy spending the day doing little more than making a tight fire, brewing up coffee, and smoking a pipe or two while letting the sun warm his sore, scarred carcass and heat his bones. But it was not to be that day.

He glanced back once to see three riders stringing along, giving their poor mounts hell with snapping reins. One with a quirt lashed his beast's flank without mercy, even as the horse lunged and slid and struggled upslope.

Not for the first time did Rollie feel horses got the rawest deal out on the frontier . . . or anywhere for that matter. Plenty of milk beasts lugging delivery drays in cities, little more than canker-covered bone racks too tired to die.

He, Cap, and Tish's mount leveled off at the top—highest land for a good quarter mile around as the crow flew, though to the east and north, it wasn't by much. He guided the horses around a wagon-size knob of rounded-off rock and noticed sign of previous visitors, not so trammeled it was a popular picnic spot—he wasn't even certain many folks in Deadwood got up to such indulgences as picnics—but perhaps the Sioux used it as a lookout post.

Hearing the desperate neighing of two horses working in lathered counterpoint to each other meant he had no more time to speculate. Ignoring a man's growled urgings, the crack of a whip on a flank, and the hard, flat smack of a palm on skin, Rollie bit back a sneer and tugged his two mounts around a far corner of the rocks. Seeing nothing to tie them to and no time for hobbles, he contrived a picket line of the lead line he'd been guiding Tish's horse with. Just long enough, he tied it off around a narrower, jutting snag of rock.

"Have to do," he said, tugging free his ammunition and long gun. "Now stay put. No shenanigans, or I'll leave you here." That thought was a grim one—for it meant he, too, was likely to be dead, a true resident of that place with a squirrel or a snake for company in the hereafter.

He took stock of the vista, gave a quick glance toward his hunters, but could not see or hear them. That worried him momentarily, then he knew what they were up to, for if he were in their boots and part of a group, he'd split up, try to come at the top from several directions.

He recalled a bit ago seeing only three of them, but he'd sworn there had been four back in the draw. He should have worked harder to lay them low then, but he'd wanted to get back to Pops, not certain if the gunfire he'd heard was from him or for him.

Besides, the draw had been filled with trees. The men seeking him had either been good at hiding or were so poor at tracking him they'd remained hidden out of bald stupidity. He hoped it was the latter. He hadn't had any coffee yet and his tolerance for matching wits was low at the best of times.

Within moments he heard the quick click of a horse-shoe striking stone, but it was down the far slope, across from where he'd come up. He glanced to his right and his horses, though not pleased to be wedged into a rocky declivity, were nonetheless not too fidgety. Yet.

He finished stuffing shells into his short work coat's pockets, then catfooted low and wide behind them. He'd hole up at the highest spot, a little above the horses, which looked to have a crack wide enough to hunker in. From there he hoped to see all about him. But first, he had to get up there.

As he scrambled across the last rocky face to gain the spot, he heard a rifle levering behind him, not far from the horses. There he was, halfway across the rock and exposed to half the directions he was likely to see from up there when a bullet pelted a foot to his right, sending hard chips at him. He growled and dove the remaining eight feet to what he hoped was a gap in the rocky crown wide enough to conceal him.

If he'd been wrong about it, he might as well get used to the idea of bleeding out right where he was.

A second bullet nicked his left boot heel and sent his leg whipping outward. He cursed, made the gap, and rolled into it. Just right if he kept his head down. Problem was, he needed to prairie dog up to see what he was shooting at.

Still, it was protection, and he wasn't going to complain (much) about it.

Thoughts of Pops and Tish and even of Pops' as-yet-unknown-about daughter kept Rollie tight-faced and grim as he wormed around in the gap to face the hunter who'd shot at him. He cranked a round into his rifle and didn't have long to wait.

Something light-colored moved downslope, right about where the shooter should be. A blond head had poked up then jerked back down again.

With his right eye squinted in deference to the sun, Rollie held his rifle trained on the spot and waited a little longer. Then he saw the same thing rise up once again.

First it was the top hair, then forehead, then two eyes roving left, right, and finally up toward him.

As soon as Rollie saw recognition on the face of the man, he squeezed the trigger. Too late, the man tried to pull his head back down. The bullet punched into the center of his forehead.

The man jerked backward, arms whipping high as if he were at a church revival, then he flopped away, out of Rollie's sight, but not before giving voice to a strange, quick barking sound.

Rollie knew folks made odd noises at the end, as a bullet caught them unawares and forced air in, out, or through. A thrashing, scratching sounded, then something slid along gravel. That, too, ended quickly. He imagined the man's life had finally left him.

"Merle?" shouted a voice down below along the trail Rollie had come up.

That would be target number two. He waited, not liking the itchy feeling he felt between his shoulder blades, the one a man feels when he knows he's being watched. Hopefully not by the deadly, single eye of a gun barrel.

Rollie tucked lower in the rocky gap and saw movement to his right at the same time the huffing voice someone, he assumed it was the man who'd asked about Merle, was making.

He glanced to his right and saw a rattler as thick as his wrist slowly gliding over the hot rock face toward him. He wanted to say, "Oh, no," but with killers about he didn't think giving voice to any words was wise. The grunting fool was farther from him than the snake, but bullets the fool could send his way would reach him quicker than the snake.

A drop of sweat slid down along his moustache and tickled his top lip. Rollie shifted and with his right hand felt for his sheath knife. It was a tight fit, as was everything, given that he was wedged in between two mammoth boulders.

For all he knew his genius plan might have landed him smack on a rattler's den. Maybe this gap was somehow the main travel route of a couple hundred of the freakish fanged things.

Steady, Rollie, steady. He knew letting his mind unravel in the presence of a thick, big-headed rattler that hadn't yet discovered him was not wise. The only thing he really wanted to do was get out of there.

It was yet another reminder of how weary he'd grown of killers, intentional or otherwise, and over the past few years he worried he'd become little more than a killer of men himself. Mostly out of defense, but it was a worry. A Chinese laundryman had once told him he had a black soul and would spend forever alone, wandering in a very cold, windy place.

Right about then Rollie wished he was anywhere but where he was. But wishing wouldn't change his situation. Pops and Tish and Pops' daughter were counting on him. By the time he drew out the knife, the big snake, easily a six-footer, was less than four feet from him.

It slowed its side-to-side, curving, silent progress. It paused, flicked its tongue, and wound its way to its left. Figuring out Rollie wasn't something it wanted to tangle with, it veered to Rollie's left. With a last slip of its not-yet-rattling tail, adorned with more buttons than any Rollie had seen in all his years as a Pinkerton agent, it slid out of sight in a gap in the rock.

Meanwhile, off to his left, a sudden blast of heavy breathing was followed by a gasp from someone unused to climbing anything higher than a saddle or a bar stool.

A shaggy, black-haired head popped up not ten feet away, followed by two wide, wet eyes, and a leering face. Rollie saw right away it was because the man faced eastward, toward the sun. And so Rollie, if he was visible to the man, must be somewhat hidden and difficult to see. The head pulled back down.

Rollie eased the rifle back to where the man had emerged and glanced back at the snake. It still sat there, but had definitely begun to sense him and his actions had made it wary. The snake was beginning to coil. Its head was raising up.

If Rollie snatched with the knife at the snake and thrust himself up at the same time, he risked getting shot. No way could he look left and right at the same time. But that didn't stop him from trying.

The man poked his head up once more, and Rollie triggered his gun. He wasn't certain he hit anything other than air or rock, and he didn't wait to find out. He ducked lower and as he pivoted, he saw sudden, dark movement even before he fully faced right. He pulled his right elbow inward and slashed sideways with the big blade.

The snake had seen the sudden movement and hadn't been interested in doing much other than striking at him. It tried again, its big spadelike head rising up off its coiled body, the rattling din louder than any Rollie had ever heard. The brute's mouth was wide, pink inside, and the fangs gleaming white and pearling at the needle tips with venom.

Everything on Rollie's body contracted and tightened

as he began slashing again with his arm. A good three feet of the serpent's body, which Rollie saw was far longer than six feet, launched at him and he jerked himself as low as possible while arching his knife stroke upward in a whipping crescent. All he saw was the knife's gleaming blade nearly blinding him with reflected sunlight and felt something thud on his right shoulder, right beside his head, then glance off. He jerked forward, northward, out of the gap.

He whipped his head to his left, needing to see what path the striking snake would take next. He'd been hit by the rattler, that much he knew, but didn't have time to worry about it, for the thing was riled and would give it another go.

He saw the thing on the rock, but across from where it had been. Then he didn't see the rest of it. But he saw blood gushing from the severed half. He looked back to his right. Same thing there, only it was the lower half. That huge rattling tail was still going at it, but less, and whipping on the rock like a tree-root-thick rope being whipped and jerked by a crazed child.

He looked to the other side and there was the forward half of the snake, the head was as vicious as ever, the thing directionless, but its rage had, if anything, only increased. The massive jaws and wet-looking head whipped and thrashed, leaving a trail of blood behind, spraying into the air, all over the rock, all over Rollie, speckling his face and beard with gore.

At that moment, the gasping man chose to poke up once more to see what the commotion was all about. Rollie saw him at the same time the man saw Rollie. The man's big red face broke into a sneer and he raised a revolver, both hands extended, gripping it tight.

Rollie ignored the gruesome thrashing lower half of the snake behind him and was about to hurl the knife at the man when the snake's head, still bucking and twisting in its reflexive death spasms, and looking very much alive and bent on revenge, flopped over the barrel of his rifle.

As much out of revulsion as instinct, Rollie jerked the rifle up and away to get rid of the vicious, still-deadly half serpent. The snapping, swinging head and thick length of blood-spraying, ropey snake arced end over end. Rollie jerked himself low, watching as if time had slowed, as the foul thing smacked across the gunman's arms and chest.

The man's pistol went off, driving a bullet zinging by Rollie's right temple, then the revolver whipped upward out of the man's left hand and spun away against the blue sky. But it was the man Rollie was interested in seeing. He couldn't look away, for the dead snake, driven by freakish reflex, as if possessed by Ol' Scratch himself, sunk fang hard and fast over and over again into the man's arm, chest, and finally lodging in the fat, sweating red face.

The thick snake body wriggled and roiled with its slowing but still frenzied movements. Then the girth of it wedged in the man's screaming mouth.

Rollie scrambled to get upright and deal with the fool, but something touched his right arm. He swung around, raising his arm at the same time, ready to slash with the knife. And he did, because it was the still-roiling body of the snake. If anything, it appeared to have swelled since he'd lopped it.

"How long"—he used the blade to shove the thing away—"are you gonna keep on"—he tried to flick it away with the blade but the rock was sloped toward him and the squirming carcass rolled right back at him—"moving?"

He shoved at it again, finally sending it northward, where it rolled off the lower slope of rock.

At the same time he glanced toward the left, where the man had slipped from view. He still hadn't risen, but Rollie heard him, gagging and weeping and screaming and thrashing, all at once. *What a racket over a dead snake,* he thought.

As he shoved against the rock to remove himself from the crevice in which he had somehow become wedged, he wondered if the bite of the dead snake's reflex-driven jaws could deliver venom. Was there already enough poison in the vile mouth of the snake that it infected the man? Would it kill him?

All that and more darted in and out of Rollie's skittering mind as he grunted and cursed and wondered why he couldn't get out of the crevice. Never far from his thoughts was the fact that one, maybe two other men were out there hunting him. And the snake wrangler to his left, given the godawful woeful sounds he was making, was far from dead, though likely no longer a threat to Rollie.

As if in answer to those latest thoughts, he heard a voice, again from the left, westward, shouting. "I hope all that racket means you got what we came for! If not, I'm going to be one pissed off boss, I tell you true." The voice paused for a moment, then resumed, closer.

Rollie growled low and tugged. His left boot was caught. Perhaps the boot heel that had been shot had fouled him up somehow. He didn't need the boot half as much as he needed his life, and that yammering fellow was getting closer. He could hear his mumbling voice.

"Tell you what, if I have to deal with Finnegan on my own, I aim to keep the whole pile and you fools can grub for the leavings. I ain't even inclined to share with that fool deputy. Maybe I'll even tell Al where he can find his money. But he's going to need a candle and a big ol' pair of tweezers where I'll jam it!" The speaker thought his words as most humorous. He guffawed and howled as if he hadn't a care in the world. He certainly didn't sound like a man stalking another man, a deadly foe.

Rollie grunted and laid himself prone, letting go of his rifle for a moment to grip the rock face and drag himself forward. The angle was just right and his left foot slid neat as you please out of the wedged boot. He snatched the rifle up once more and headed downhill, off the north edge of the boulders.

It was at that moment he heard the talker say, "Milty, what in the hell have you gotten up to?" Then he whistled.

Rollie could just see the top of a hat, a black top hat that belonged to one of the first men they'd seen back at the camp. Immediately he regretted he had not sniped him when he'd first laid eyes on that foolish hat bobbing up from the creek.

"Lord a-mighty, but it looks to me as if you are trying to eat a snake, boy. Anybody ever tell you that ain't a wise food!"

Suddenly Rollie's hat popped off his head and pin-wheeled down the rock. It didn't make much noise, a sort, scuffing sound as he edged forward. He'd been hoping to make it to the drop-off edge of the boulder, about three feet above ground level, then he could swing himself around and ease to his feet, all the while keeping his rifle trained in the direction of the chatty man. But it didn't happen that way.

The chatty man said, "Hey!" and bolted around the boulder, rounding the scant trail not but a dozen feet from Rollie.

On hearing the man's shout, Rollie knew he'd been seen, thanks to the scuffling, clunking sound his hat made as it fell.

The man appeared in time to see Rollie crabbing forward, his chest and face to the ground, his legs up on the rock, one foot bootless, a big knife clutched in one hand, a rifle in the other. As Rollie jerked and shoved and grunted to get the lower half of his body down off the rock face, he locked eyes with the chatty man.

"Hey!" the man said again, and stood hands poised as if he were about to draw down on Rollie, but the man didn't snatch at either weapon on his double-gun rig.

Maybe he was shocked at seeing Rollie, and in such disarray. Maybe he didn't think Rollie could inflict much harm from such an awkward position. More than likely, the man had not seen much close-up gunplay before. Whatever the cause, he remained confounded long enough for Rollie to pinch off a shot.

It whipped wider than he intended, catching the man low in the throat, about where the neck stalk meets the chest. Surprisingly for such a distance, while he spasmed in place, the man remained standing. His long hands jerked and his fingers trembled, but the confused look on his face stayed in place. So did his tall hat.

His lips began working as if he were a beached fish,

and finally the word *Hey* leaked out as a long, wheezed sigh.

Rollie held still, one leg laid against the rock face, the other pinned uncomfortably beneath his body. He had witnessed many men and a few women die. Too many to count by his own hand. Though he had seen a number of odd, drawn-out moments of death, it was rare for anyone to remain upright after being shot in the throat.

Quivers in the man's arms traveled up to his elbows and shoulders. They sagged and slumped and hung there, useless. The man's eyelids twitched and he swayed back and forth. Finally, he said, "Hey" in an even quieter whisper and pitched forward, smacking his unprotected face against the sun-hot rock.

Rollie finally got his feet under him, eyes on the dropped man the entire time, and ambled over. He looked down at him. "Hey," he said, and with the rifle pointed at the back of the man's head, he bent. He lifted free the revolvers, first the right, then the left and tucked them into his own belt, then walked around the rock to look at the man who'd been playing with the snake.

What he saw forced a grimace onto his face. "Wow," he said, eyeing the still-spasming man.

The thick body of the snake, which now looked to have blackened, had stilled—finally died—as far as Rollie could discern, though the man beneath it twitched. He was still gasping, a thin, wheezing trickle of air was being pulled in and forced out through a thin slice of flesh that had been a mouth in the once-red, fat face.

The man's nose was a dimpled pock nested in a mass of doughy dark flesh the color of the sky in a ripping late-day summer thunderstorm. The face was no longer recognizable as one.

Overall, the face had gone purple and was tending toward black all over, like a bad bruise, a bruise that would never heal.

Rollie marveled at the fact the man had been bitten by a dead snake. Killed by it, for that matter. He looked down at him, wondering whether to end his suffering.

One of the man's eyeballs rolled in its puffed socket enough that Rollie saw white. The eye opened wide and stared at him. In that moment he saw whatever was left of the man, a man mired in some personal hell, unable to do for himself, a man with a family somewhere, some time in his past, maybe his present, perhaps a future that would never be.

Sure, the fool had chosen a poor road at one point, but nobody deserved to die like this. He saw in that eye a begging, beseeching look. He was certain of it. And as he pulled his Schofield and thumbed back the hammer, the eye seemed to soften, to say thank you, then it closed, even as the foaming from the mouth spurted harder and the man's chest and body spasmed.

Rollie's bullet drove into the man's forehead and the rigid, jerking body softened, sagged, seemed to sigh and relax against the hard, rocky ground.

"Be at peace, you poor excuse for a man," he said, knowing he'd given the murderous fool more quarter than he would have been given had the tables been reversed.

Rollie looked at the dead man beneath the head of the snake, then over around the corner of rock at the facedown dead man. "Pops'll never believe this. Hell, I don't believe it, and I lived through it."

"Don't count your hens just yet!"

Chapter 26

Rollie stiffened. Somebody had the drop on him, somebody who sounded haggard and angry and raspy of breath.

"What can I do for you?" said Rollie.

The man laughed. "That's rich. You offering to do something for me! Well, you already did that, man. You got rid of these morons for me."

Rollie eased his right hand toward his belt and the revolver he'd just tucked in there.

"No, no, no," said the man, then cranked off a shot that had Rollie's right arm been one inch farther out would have ripped off his elbow.

He winced and held his hand still.

"Good boy. Now, first thing you're going to do is toss that rifle you got in your left hand. Yeah, that left hand."

Rollie gritted his teeth. He felt like more than a fool and twice an amateur. Caught unawares from behind with one boot missing, his hat gone, and covered in snake blood.

"Who are you and what do you want?"

The man laughed. He sounded to Rollie like he wasn't

too old, early twenties? Might be that arrogant whelp
filling in for Bullock he'd met in the office. Nah, the voice
was off. And besides, that kid was all talk. Had not yet
seen action. This one sounded more confident, seasoned
somehow.

Again, the man laughed. "I'll give you this, Finnegan.
Never mind that face, you got yourself a set of stone
sweetmeats, that's for certain. As for me," the man sighed
theatrically. "Oh, I'm the awfulest thing that has ever
happened to you."

It was Rollie's turn to laugh. "I doubt that, kid."

The man continued as if Rollie had not spoken. "As for
what I want, why, not much. Not much at all. Your head
will do. But I got a feeling there's somebody wouldn't
mind laying out cold cash to have you alive, whole and
kicking."

That was interesting, thought Rollie. Might mean the
fool would keep him alive long enough to let him get a
few licks in. All he needed was one sliver of a slip to shoot
or gut or club the idiot.

Hadn't Top Hat said something when he was running
his mouth about who he wasn't going to share the reward
money with? The deputy? If that's so, there was more
than one. That made sense, since Bullock wouldn't likely
leave town with one deputy in charge of such a powder
keg as Deadwood. And certainly not such a green whelp
as the kid he'd met.

"My guess is you're a lawdog," said Rollie.

No quick laugh that time. That told him as much as if
the man had admitted it with a hangdog look.

"Time for you to shut up, old man, before I have me
another think. Might be you'll need to die sooner than

later so I can hack off that homely head of yours and stuff it in a sack."

Rollie sighed. "I wish you'd make up your mind about what you plan on doing with me. I'm wore out and I haven't even had my morning coffee yet."

"Oh? That's a crying shame, old man. If you could look deep into my eyes you'd see there ain't a living soul in there who gives a care. Now shut it while I figure out a few things."

Okay, for all the puffy chest bravado, this one wasn't necessarily a deep thinker. What was he, then? In all his years dealing with such men, Rollie had come up with a handful of ways to classify them. Most of the time they were little more than weasels, annoyances who preyed on others merely for money. Then were the next order, also out for money, but with a taste for blood. That usually meant some sort of creeping sickness in their families, maybe they had a pap who'd behaved viciously toward them. They would, in turn, do the same to critters—rip the legs off frogs, snap the wings of chickens, set living things alight.

He'd met them all, seen their handiwork, and when he caught up with them, he'd heard their whimpering and sobbing as if they weren't responsible for their actions.

He'd used other levels of classification in the little crude system over the years to get a picture in his mind of what sort of men—and sometimes women—he was dealing with. That in turn helped him in figuring how to deal with them. In the end, it was little more than a sometimes-useful game. But still a game, and it nearly always came down to being fast and close enough that accuracy with a revolver, always a dicey affair at best, wasn't vital.

"You still ain't tossed away that rifle, old man. I'll give you until I count to three."

"Don't test those limits, son. I expect you'd end up on a detour." Rollie dropped the rifle, though not far from him, thinking there might be a chance he could drop low, snatch up that rifle, turn, and set to blazing.

"Shut it, old man, and raise up that other hand," said the man, foiling Rollie's feeble plan to grab the revolver from Top Hat and turn and fire.

"Hold it up where I can see it. Higher, both of them. Now, slow as you please, turn around. But keep them hands high. I am a crack shot and no mistake."

"I've heard"—Rollie slowly complied and turned around even slower— "that bragging about a thing usually means you aren't worth a bean at it. What do you think about that?"

"I think you need to shut it, or die where you stand, you bootless old sack of crap."

Rollie heard a quick few steps of boot soles crushing gravel. He ducked low and spun, clawing for the revolver still tucked in the front of his gunbelt, but the man was quicker. Rollie dropped to his right knee and held his left arm up, the revolver in his still-capable but less-used right hand.

He got a glimpse of a wry, medium-height man with dark hair, squinty eyes, and wearing a black shirt and trail dusted duck cloth trousers. That was all, for the man had closed the gap between them and was on him, swinging something long and steel.

As he dropped farther, Rollie thumbed back the hammer, touched it off, and felt a brutal explosion of raw, hot pain flower up the left side of his head. At the same time, whatever it was had burst as if packed with dynamite. He weaved and staggered on his knees, his head buzzing and ringing as if he were hearing church bells clanging. Catching sight of the man who'd attacked him, he realized the man had swung his rifle barrel at him and it must have gone off at the same time.

Standing awkwardly several feet away, the man held his upper left arm with his right, the rifle sagging from a cradled position in his arms. He was shouting, no, he was screaming. Hearing nothing but bells, Rollie could tell not what. But the man's mouth was opening and shutting, his head was shaking back and forth, and he was jerking his torso up and down like a pump handle.

It was definitely not the lippy whelp of a deputy from Bullock's office. Not that it mattered much. Whoever he was, he was trying to kill Rollie, and so Rollie had to do the same in kind, and first.

Rollie was dimly aware his hasty shot had clipped his attacker. *Good.* He tried to ready a second shot, but somehow his mind was no longer in control of what his hands were up to. He looked down at his hands, saw the gun in the right, and tried to force it to cock the thing, aim, and fire. Nothing happened.

The man was coming at him, wounded wing or no.

Rollie vaguely wondered how, if he couldn't get his hands to work, could he ever get his legs to muster up the courage to stand again. But he did. At least one of them, his left. It jerked out stiff and straight and he noticed it still didn't have a boot on. That's right, he'd lost it somewhere.

A shadow fell over him and he looked up again. His

right eye wasn't working so well. It felt funny, sort of hot and wet.

Something poked him on the face and he saw, too late, it was the man with whom he'd been tussling. He shook his head again. *Of course it was. Who else would it be? Rollie, you have got to get your mind right.*

He squeezed his eyes shut and forced them open again. It did little to help. It felt almost like how a fellow feels when he's had far too much to drink, and regrets it, but knows he can't do a thing about it until he sobers up. *Time,* he thought, *That's it. I need time.*

The gun barrel had poked him. He looked up the length of the gun and the man was still shouting, Rollie could hear some noise other than those blasted bells tolling in his head—sounds that matched the man's yowling mouth— shouts and screams. The man was red-faced and crying pitifully as if he'd eaten a wad of hot chiles.

Was he trying to shoot Rollie? If that was the case, he wasn't very good at it. He looked to be fumbling with it. Yes, his left arm hung limply and in his screaming, crying rage he couldn't figure out how to operate the lever. *Good.*

The man lunged again and Rollie knew he was out of time. He dove to the right and rolled, the world a whirl about him. His head knocked against something and the clanging bells leveled and became a flat low hum. He could hear grunts and shouts and voices. One of them was his own. He shoved up away from whatever it was he'd rolled against—rock. It was the rock face, and he remembered the gun in his hand.

If he was hearing better and maybe seeing better, maybe his brain would figure out how to work the revolver again.

That's when the man slammed into him. Rollie got a glimpse of the young, wiry fiend as they collided. He'd lost the rifle or had given up on it. He was bare fisted and in his anger, lunged and thrashed and shouted at Rollie.

Rollie felt no gun in his own hand any longer. He must have dropped it, but he did feel his fingers closing in on themselves, forming into a fist. He swung it around hard, landing a solid punch, a lucky one as it turned out, for it hit the crazy man's bloodied, limp arm, and he bent at the waist, clutching himself anew and howling in agony.

Rollie heard those screams and added his own voice to the ruckus. "Shut up! You'll scare my horses!"

It didn't seem to matter, for the man hopped in a circle and howled louder than ever.

As quickly as he began his hubbub, the man seemed to come back to himself, and though he remained bent over, holding his useless arm, he glared at Rollie in anger, but also with a near-grin on his red face. Strings of snot swinging from his nose, he growled low and beastlike, and staggered toward Rollie, who was pinned against rock.

But Rollie had a notion he could end the foolishness.

One, two steps closer, then the man snatched at his own revolver, which he'd just realized he possessed, and yanked it free.

They were about six feet apart.

Rollie knew he had to get this right the first time or he was sunk. As a fresh wave of dizziness washed over him, he forced his eyes to stay open and tugged free his sheath knife. He kept low. Gripping the knife tight, he made to lunge right then jerked back to his left. The man with the gun lurched a foot too short to cut him off.

As Rollie ran by, the mouthy kid spun, cursing and

shouting garbled words more at home in a cave than a town.

Well, thought Rollie, *we are in a rocky place. Might be he's feeling at home.*

As he lurched past, he held out the knife gripped tightly in his fist and slashed outward, feeling it connect with something that nearly stopped it. But he shoved it forward hard, and the blade worked its way on through.

Just past the kid, Rollie swung around. If he was going to get shot, he wanted to see it coming. But the kid had barely made it halfway around in his own turn to face Rollie.

His revolver had fallen away much as had his rifle. With his right hand once more clasped over his blood-drenched upper left arm, he stood, spraddle-legged and heaving as if he'd been forced to run alongside a stagecoach. He wasn't looking at Rollie as he lifted his right arm away from his chest and squinted down at his right side.

His blue shirt, already covered with dark red staining, was quickly soaking up more blood as it gushed from a gash in the kid's side, midway between his gun belt and his arm pit.

And the blood kept pumping out of him. He whimpered, a childlike sound, and it was the first time Rollie felt a little pity for the fool. It didn't last long.

The kid growled again, and, perhaps sensing he had nothing to lose, he lunged at Rollie. Holding his slashed-open side with his right hand, his left arm swinging red and wet and useless, he sought to throw himself at Rollie, weaponless and fueled by seething anger.

The crazy young man shouted even crazier sounds as

he reached Rollie. At the last moment, Rollie jerked to the left and gave him another slash with the knife, intending to cut up high but his blow carved a bleeding groove in the fool's thigh. A fresh scream rose up and the kid tried to turn. But he'd reached the edge of the vast rocky outcrop.

Rollie had tried to maneuver the fight closer toward that spot, for it looked as if the drop off, while not so steep it wouldn't be climbable using a series of light-footed switchbacks, it nonetheless made staying upright a wholly impressive feat of endurance.

However, knowing he'd reached some sort of boundary, the young man tried to force himself backward with his one good arm, whipping it in a circle. His eyes arched wide, as did his mouth, but he'd fallen silent. And then he fell backward.

Rollie didn't know how far that rocky slope went before leveling off, but he knew stunty pines pocked it twenty or thirty feet below.

Rollie heard him scream once more, heard a wet thud and a slopping, slapping sound, then nothing. He let out a long breath and, still holding his big knife, he lurched forward, bloodied and ragged and half deaf. With a pounding, throbbing head as if in the midst of a cannonade, he neared the edge of the slope, a gradual enough curve that could get him into trouble before he realized it. But he saw below all he needed to see. No need to creep any closer.

He whistled and shook his head. Thirty feet down, the mouthy kid who'd come closer to killing Rollie than most had in recent years, lay facing upright, snagged in the pines. *Impaled* was more the truth. Three spiky, bloodied spires jutted from his body—one, through the belly, glistened with entrails. One poked through his upper right chest, just below the armpit, and the third missed his mouth by a couple of inches and protruded through the man's cheek, forcing his mouth into a wide leer. His open eyes stared up, straight at Rollie.

For the first time in many, many years, Rollie had to look away from a fresh death. It was one of the most brutal, sickening things he'd seen in a long time. He felt his gorge rise and felt his body cool down, and he knew he might throw up, pass out, or both.

"No sir," he said, gently shaking his head. And that was that.

Once he decided a thing, he was done with it. He pulled in a deep breath and limped back up across the rock to where his boot sat wedged in the crack. He looked around, reasonably confident nobody else was going to pop up and attack him, and knelt at the crevice.

Before he reached down, he looked in. Ignoring the stilled, half carcass of the big snake he'd sliced in two, he tugged his boot free.

Chapter 27

A half hour later found Rollie booted up once more, albeit with a wobble due to that shot-up heel. He gave thought for about two seconds to dragging the bodies together and lining them up, make it easier for whoever from town would end up fetching them.

Then he felt the crusting blood on his head and the pounding inside it, and figured had any of them been any more talented in the brute art of killing and savagery, they would have treated him a whole lot worse. And would have started by hacking his head free of his neck.

"To hell with them," he muttered and limped down to the horses.

Tish's horse had somehow worked itself loose from the tie-up and had wandered downslope a few hundred yards to a grassy glade. Rollie figured Cap would gladly have joined in the fun, but he'd been tied too securely. He couldn't blame them, what with all that shooting and shouting and blood not but a few dozen yards up the rocky slope.

Oh, but he was sore. It took him three tries to mount

up on Cap. "Damn horse—you keep getting taller," he muttered.

He caught Tish's horse without much fuss and left the four men who'd attacked him where they lay. Counting the one Pops had laid low at the campsite, Rollie was feeling better that no others would be coming for him. At least not for a little while.

Still, in case these fools were expected sooner than later back in town, he decided to cut northwest. He'd find a spot along a stream he remembered up that way. It wouldn't take him too far from town and he could clean up, get some coffee in him, a few hard biscuits and dried apple slices, then he'd be ready to ride into the hellish maw that was Deadwood.

Not sure how much more of the madness he could take—traipsing all over the hills, getting shot at and lunged at by snakes and men, sworn at. All of it.

My word, he thought.

All those years ago all he wanted to do was make a living legally. Joined the Pinks and did just that, arrested miscreants and lowlifes for years, and they all seemed to be coming out of the wormy woodwork for his hide. The ones who were still alive, anyway. Plenty of them, as it turned out.

Some of them had somehow ended up with deep pockets and deeper needs for vengeance. As if he had been the one to break the laws in the first place. To a man—and some women—they all seemed to conveniently forget the fact *they* had been the ones engaged in criminal behavior.

His head hurt worse than ever and he wished he had some sort of headache powders. Water, though, would do the trick. He sipped from his canteen while they rode and hoped they'd find that stream soon.

It took him several long minutes to thread his way through the sparse ponderosas before he heard a faint gurgling sound. Cap perked his ears and his nostrils quivered.

"Yep," said Rollie. "I hear it and you smell it. Let's go find us some water, you two."

A couple more minutes of easy riding led them to a low, grassy glade with shade close by the water's edge. It wasn't a big flow, but it didn't need to be. It was flowing and it was clear and it looked really good.

Rollie climbed down and led the horses to the stream. They drank with pleasure and greed and when they'd finished, he led them back up to the somewhat lush, grassy growth and unsaddled and hobbled them. Then he walked down to the water's edge, glanced around with slow, cautious care, and stripped to the waist. His head was pounding and throbbing and thudding, but when he fingered his temple, his fingertips no longer came away wet with blood. The cut had crusted over.

His vision was mostly back to normal and his hearing, never great these past years—too much gunplay too close to his head—was nonetheless better than it had been a half hour before. He even thought he might have heard a raven hacking its way through the afternoon air.

He had made certain his Schofield was loaded and ready to lift free and fast should the need arise. His knife, likewise, hung crusted with snake and man gore, but ready to swing or fly.

He hoped such shenanigans were past him, at least for the next couple of hours. He'd see what Deadwood brought when he arrived to find Pops and join in a fresh round of fun. But at the moment, he was in no mood for further foolishness.

He knelt and though his knees got soaked, he didn't care. He slopped water over his head and face, scoop after scoop, until he was a sodden mess. But the feeling of relief was immeasurable. Eyes closed, he didn't care if someone walked up behind him and snapped a bullet in his head. He reckoned he'd die closer to satisfied than he'd come many times in his life. Quickly, he cracked open his eyes and knew that was foolish thinking.

A sudden weariness drifted down on him like a quilt settling and he didn't have the strength to fight it. He needed rest. Just an hour or so, and he'd gain back what strength he woke with. Or a solid measure of it, anyway.

He walked over to his stack of gear, the two side by side saddles and saddlebags, and lifted out a squat bottle of whiskey, which Pops referred to as a "medicinal dose." He swore it was the only thing a man really needed. Well, that and a woman's comforts now and again, and a good pipe of rich tobacco.

"I'm inclined to agree, Pops," Rollie said with a grunt and a sigh. He settled back, resting his head and shoulders against a blanket roll and saddle seat. He sighed again, popped the cork, and sipped. Just enough to smooth the rough bits off that blasted ache in his head. Couldn't get any worse, he reckoned, so he took another swig.

Within a few minutes, he was out, the bottle upright in his hand at his side. His other hand, out of long habit, rested atop his revolver.

Chapter 28

"You're a damned little fool. Prettiest one I've ever come across, I'll give you that, but you're a damned fool." Swearengen slid out of his chair and kept his eyes pinned on Tish's face as he stalked around the desk, moving slow and even, a slight smile nearly making its way onto his mouth.

Tish felt herself breathing harder and she couldn't stop it. The man was the same man she'd met in the bar out front, but now that they were in his office, she saw a harsh change in how he spoke to her, how he carried himself. Starting with the obvious . . . calling her a damned fool.

"I . . . I beg your pardon, Mr. Swearengen."

"Al, please. I thought I told you that?" He was halfway around the desk and slowly making his way in her direction, but not quite straight toward her. She tightened the grip on her revolver.

Maybe she should just shoot him now, right through her cloak. No, that would only get her embroiled in a terrible trial situation at best. He hadn't actually done anything wrong yet. She, on the other hand, had blundered in here and all-but demanded he see her.

How could she claim self-defense when he all-but owned the town? No one would believe her.

He was nearly behind her. She turned her head to the left to see him edging closer.

"No, no, no. A pretty girl like you shouldn't have to beg anybody for anything." He was behind her then, and she felt his presence, knew he was leaning close to her left ear. "I'll need you to take off the cloak, Miss Rose, and . . ."

She spun her head toward him, eyes wide. "I beg . . ."

"Uh uh uh, we already discussed that. Besides, you have me all wrong, pretty lady." He touched her hair, smoothing it beneath the back of his hand. "I'll need to see both hands make certain you aren't . . . deformed, or anything such as that. So I can be certain you'll be able to function . . . on the stage. This is a theatrical palace, after all, Miss Rose."

Her breathing was rapid, but shallow. "Yes, of course. I see."

"Good. Now, please stand, lose the cloak, and we'll see what we have here. Okay?"

She hesitated, and her breath caught. *It's now or never,* Tish, she told herself. But she fumbled trying to get her feet under her without taking her hand from the revolver nested beneath her cloak.

She felt his hand on her back as if to help her, and then it snatched at the cloak and managed to jerk it down about her shoulders, pinning her arms. The revolver dropped from her hand and clunked to the floor.

He did not speak.

She said, "I'm a woman traveling alone. I . . ."

Leaning close to her face, he spoke in a whisper into her left ear. "Do you take me for a fool?"

She heard a thick, metal *click-click*, then felt something pressing into her cheek in front of her ear. She knew it for what it was, a gun. Small, maybe a derringer. A hide-out gun, she thought. Perfect for Al Swearengen.

He gripped her tight, half spun her toward him, and, with his face still close to hers, said, "You honestly thought I wouldn't know you came to town last night? In the company of a Pinkerton man and some other fool? Hmm?"

"I . . . I don't know what you're talking about."

"Oh come on now, woman." He chuckled and eased her back to a sitting position in the chair. Then he walked in front of her, holding the gun.

She saw she'd been correct in her guess, a derringer, two snub barrels one atop the other.

He looked down quick enough to toe away her gun then backed to his desk once more. "You should also know, Miss Rose, if that is your name"—he sat down—"that the men you rode in with, one of them being Stoneface Finnegan . . . interesting company a pretty young lady such as yourself keeps, by the way. You should know they are, even as we enjoy each other's company right now, are dying. Or, hopefully, dead."

Tish shoved upright out of the chair, eyes wide.

"Ah ah ah." He jerked the little gun's snout at her. "Calm down now, Miss Rose. There's little you can do about it, save mourn them. My men have by now taken care of them. And"—he leaned forward—"by *taken care of*, I mean they will have shot them and left them for dead. That you were able to escape this is most impressive. In retrospect, I am pleased you did, my dear Miss Rose. For if you had remained in that squalid camp you no doubt had with Finnegan, you would be dead now, too. So, in a way, I assume you have saved your own life by your boldness, Miss Rose. Misguided though your efforts are."

She shook her head, unable to think clearly, unable to do much more than force herself to not tear up in the presence of this monster.

Swearengen pulled a theatrical frown, then grinned. "I am somewhat toying with you, Miss Rose. Of course, the world is a much better place without Stoneface Finnegan in it, trust me. He was among the lowest of the low, and inflicted untold damage to many of my acquaintances. Likewise goes for anyone who dares to share a campfire with him. Well, all except for you, my dear."

"You shut your mouth! You—"

"Yes?" his eyebrows rose. He leaned back, never moving the gun from aiming at her, never taking his eyes from her. His chair squeaked. "Oh, I thought for a moment there I was going to hear sweet whisperings of passion and longing."

"Never."

"Oh." He leaned forward and, without looking away from her, selected a cigarillo from a wooden box on his desk. He leaned back and the chair squeaked again. He moistened an end of the cigarillo, placed it in his mouth, then struck a sulfur match and lit it. He blew a plume of blue smoke in her direction, then said, "I think you will change your mind about me, Miss Rose."

"Ha." She crossed her arms and looked about the room, noticing her revolver still on the floor a dozen feet from her and to the left. She looked away from it, back to him.

"No, no, no, Miss Rose. That will not do. I'd have to shoot you before I'd let you lunge for that gun. Now, where was I? Oh yes, I am quite confident in saying you will come around in your way of thinking about me. Indeed, every woman I've ever met has done just that. You'll soon see."

"How is that going to happen?"

"Oh, you'll meet a building full of them, Miss Rose. A building full."

She wanted to shout, to leap the desk, punch him hard in the face, and flip him over in his squeaky chair. Her anger must have shown because his eyebrows rose once more and he paused in puffing on his smelly little cigar.

"You know, Miss Rose, for a moment there you looked as if you actually wanted to harm me somehow." He shook his head. "That would be ironic, since very soon you will look upon me as your provider. As someone you cannot live without. And in many ways, that, my dear, will be the bedrock truth of the matter."

"No. That will never happen."

He laughed, "Good, a fiery spirit. I like that." He poured himself a short tumbler of whiskey, sipped. "I would offer you a glass, my dear, but I'm afraid I need to see those two hands unmoving in your lap. In fact, very soon, I'm going to ask you to turn around, then I'm going to tie those pretty hands behind you. And then we're going to march you over to what I like to call the newcomers' suite. Really, it's not that fancy, but we do our best here in little ol' Deadwood. We really do."

He regarded her a moment with his head to the side as if coming to some decision. He winked at her and sipped his whiskey.

Chapter 29

"Foolish girl," muttered Pops as he rode slowly into Deadwood. He wasn't really irked with Tish so much as he was with the feeling that had crept up on him the closer he drew to town. It was the early pricklings, the buddings of something he'd not felt in a long time. It was fear, and that made him angry and disgusted with himself.

He was a man as good as any of the others running around town playing their silly card games and bedding sad-eyed women and getting ripping drunk and shooting each other and maybe, just maybe, leaving a little time in their busy lives for dragging back to their claims and putting in a pinch of work. He swore all men were little more than large children much of the time.

The worst of it was he was one of them. And yet he was apart from them, too. Because of his skin color. "Fools all," he muttered, hating even more the lousy attitude he'd pulled on over the past couple of miles. It felt like a too-tight sweater.

A little, fat, brown yipper of a dog trotted close up to him and began its expected tirade, as if it were the mayor and was telling him the dos and don'ts of the town.

"You remind me of Mayor Chauncey Wheeler, you little belly with hair. Get along now. Git before Bud stomps you flat."

To Pops' surprise, the dog tucked his ears down and trotted back toward the shanty he came from, glancing back at Pops over his plump little shoulder.

The encounter and satisfying result, slight as it was, buoyed Pops' mood a pinch. He noticed the shacks lining the road out of town didn't look any better in day's light. If anything they were worse, leaners with rags stuffed in holes, chimneys smoking from more than their intended top holes. But it was the men and a few women lingering out front that made him bite back a grimace and force a slight smile and a touch of the hat brim.

Not a one returned the subtle nicety. Then one did, a woman with long black hair and a dirt-smudged face and a baby dragging on one teat and another wrapped about her rag-wrapped leg. She didn't look any older than thirteen or so, but she'd smiled and nodded back.

"Good luck, little girl," whispered Pops to himself and looked ahead to the buildings of Deadwood proper.

It didn't take long before he received a whole lot more than stares. Other black folks were around, and some Chinese, too. But as a stranger and a black man, he guessed he was a curiosity. He heard the usual words hooted his way, fool names and descriptions that had long ago ceased to cut him. Well, not too deep anyway.

Not about to lie to himself and pretend he was past all such caring, the words were always uttered once he'd ridden past and barely out of eyesight. He sat plank straight in the saddle, ground his molars tight, and could not help bunching his jaw muscles.

It was either risk powdering his teeth from clenching them so tight or shuck free Lil' Miss Mess Maker and set to work on the swill-faced fools. *Let it settle, Pops,* he told himself.

Up ahead, to the left, he spied the lawman's office and angled toward it through the nearly empty, dusty street.

Just before he drew abreast of the office and the sign out front that read S. BULLOCK, SHERIFF, a young man wearing a badge and looking too dapper by half, stepped out, closed the door behind himself, and cranked a skeleton key in the lock before dropping it into a vest pocket. Walking up the boardwalk with a slow gait, he leveled an assessing gaze on everyone he met. Turning his head to his left, he saw Pops watching him and he stopped. The young man faced him, hands hovering in the air like two tiny dogs, waiting for a chance to dance, to yip, to perform.

Nearly fluttering, thought Pops, *to draw down on me?*

Not hardly. He touched his hat brim and rode on. Looked like Bullock hadn't magically arrived in town overnight. That had to be the rude kid Rollie had said he'd met.

Just as well. Last thing Pops wanted to do was play legal games when a man like Swearengen was, at that very moment, maybe hurting not just one, but two young women Pops knew. The thought snapped him back to why he was in town in the first place. Had to find a livery, then track down Tish.

She was a bullheaded young thing, and dead set on going undercover smack into the mouth of the lion himself. Right at the Gem. Pretty enough, no doubt she'd be invited in. Maybe even given work. And then what?

Did you think that through Tish, girl? Hmm? Pops bet the lawdog was still staring at him, hands twitching, eager to shoot him down, but decided to not give the young fool any more reasons than he thought he already had. No, sir. Pops had work to do. He had to take Swearengen down.

How he was going to do it was something he hadn't yet figured out. It would come to him. Solutions like that always did. No choice. But first, he needed to find a place to lodge Bud.

By the time Pops found a livery, the morning had warmed as it nibbled its way toward midday. He'd left Bud in the care of a skinny old man, half Mexican, half black, with a curious way of speaking, and even more curious accent. He'd told Pops he was "from the islands." Given they'd been standing in the midst of a raw landscape that looked to have no end, Pops wasn't certain which islands those might be. It didn't trouble him for long.

He made tracks for the Gem Theater, and when he was once more within throwing distance of the place, he cut down a side lane. The rear of the place was busier than the front as most such businesses were. He saw the comings and goings of deliveries, of the slops house, a reeking couple of outhouses, a shack for chickens, and beyond, what looked like a hog wallow and shade shelter. Intermittent thick gruntings confirmed his guess.

A squawking wagon pulled up. A couple of men climbed down and set to work lugging in sacks of meal and kegs through a propped-open back door. From the clatter inside, Pops guessed it was a kitchen. He waited until they entered for the second time, then followed on their heels with a sack from the wagon of what smelled like corn meal balanced on his shoulder.

Inside the dim interior, the tang of stale beer, grease, and wood smoke filled his nostrils. It reminded him of meat gone off and greening in the sun. He breathed through his mouth and made it about a dozen feet inside before one of the men from the wagon showed up.

He was a burly fellow wearing brass-frame spectacles that looked too small on his sweating, bristled red face. He lumbered back down the passage toward the door. "Hey, what're you doin'?"

"Me?" said Pops, not quite turning his head to look straight on at the man. "I'm new here. Just hired."

"Yeah? Well, yonder's the kitchen." He shook his head and muttered as he shoved by Pops and made for the door. "What is Al thinking? Last thing we need's somebody like that running around back here."

Pops gritted his teeth and kept his face hidden and made for the kitchen, knowing his ruse would only carry him another minute, at best. He had to get shed of the kitchen. But where to go? Maybe the upstairs? Surely that's where Swearengen would keep the women. Place this size had to have plenty of rooms upstairs, plenty of places to hide women away, keep them pumped with laudanum or whatever else men like Swearengen used to keep women from knowing what was being done to them. Keep them beholden to him, make them look on him as their savior.

Two voices were arguing in the kitchen, one a woman's, the other a young man's, arguing as they slid pans and clapped lids on pots. He heard a rooster crow out back as he hustled past the kitchen door. Nobody said anything that sounded as if they were surprised. They kept on yammering at each other, so they must not have seen him.

Pops made it past the kitchen and into a dark space with doors along one wall, then a narrow stairwell stood before him. He wished he had Lil' Miss Mess Maker with him. but he'd figured a black man toting a sawed-off in town might attract more attention than he was looking for. Inside the lion's den, he was less certain than he had been a few minutes before out in the dusty street.

He sorely wished Rollie was there to help him then wondered if he was faring all right with those vicious killers in the hills. Was he so well known he had enemies in Deadwood, too? Wouldn't be a surprise. Rollie was one well-known—and one well-loathed fellow.

Pops heard bootsteps thudding somewhere behind him, and nearly at the same time, light footfalls sounded upstairs somewhere. Though it had been full daylight outside for hours, the hallway was narrow and dark. Stuck with it, no use fighting it, he pulled his revolver, trusting nothing about it had changed sine he'd checked it in the alley a few minutes before.

"In for a penny," he nearly whispered, keeping in mind he was about to open a ball he would not ever be invited to.

One step at a time, he ascended the stairwell, placing his boots with care and wincing each time a tread squeaked, which was every one. He had made it halfway up, hugging the shadows of the right side of the stairwell, and doing his best to not dawdle, when a door opened somewhere up above and a woman's voice said, "I'll get us coffee, then I'll help you fix your dress."

Pops dithered a moment, knowing she was likely about to walk down his staircase. Her voice had sounded as if it came from far along a hallway. He walked up the rest of the steps, about ten in all, taking two at a time. He reached the top and held, slightly crouched, getting his bearings. To his left stood one door at the top of the stairs.

A woman rounded the corner to his right, and they faced each other. She was thin, with too-black hair and the vestiges of heavy rouge and eye makeup on her face. The morning light slanting through a poorly curtained window to his left showed tiny wrinkles where smooth skin had once been.

Beyond her he saw doors lining a long, shadowed hallway.

Instead of shouting, she put a hand to her chest and said, "Oh, you startled me, man. Are you lost?"

For a moment, Pops didn't know what to say.

She looked at his drawn revolver. "What are you doing up here with that thing?"

He advanced on her and for the first time saw the spark of fright in her wet, red eyes. By then it was too late. He was on her and backed her to a wall, holding the revolver up under her chin while clapping his big left hand over her mouth. Her eyes rose wide.

"Ma'am," he whispered. His face close to hers, he smelled camphor and whiskey. "I'm not here to harm anyone, I'm here to find someone. Well, two people, actually. A black girl, pretty, looks like . . ."

Like who, Pops, he asked himself. *You wouldn't know your own daughter if you passed her on the street, would you?*

He shook his head. "Look, she's been here a while. Pretty thing. I been searching for her for a long, long time. Another one, she come here this morning, red hair, long, pretty, too, won't take no for an answer. She'll be saying she's looking for work, I think. You seen either of them?"

The woman kept looking at him, air puffing her nostrils with each short breath.

Pops felt terrible, but he'd been forced into it.

She struggled, and he squeezed his hand tighter for just a moment. "Come on now, please," he whispered. "I need your help."

She stopped struggling.

"If I let go of your mouth, will you tell me where I can find them? I'm sorry I had to do this, but they're in danger."

She looked at him and nodded.

"Now don't yell, you hear?" He wagged the gun before her face.

She nodded one more.

"Okay." He slid his hand away and she didn't move. The lower half of her face was crimson where his hand had been. He wanted to apologize again, but she was opening her mouth.

"Easy now," he said.

She jerked to her left, out of his grasp, and ran back down the hall toward where she'd come from. He growled and hurried after her as she commenced to shout. "Help! Help! Help me! Help me!"

Within seconds, the doors lining the hallway swung inward, letting in light to the dark hall, as well as women of all shapes and sizes. Most were white, one Chinese, one Indian, and two black—neither of them looked close to young enough to be his daughter. They all emerged, one and two per room. One of them was naked, the others wore flimsy nightgowns, a couple wore loose robes.

Most recoiled and retreated back a step or two, but three of the women advanced on him, unafraid of the gun in his hand. They bent to help his escapee to her feet.

One, a short, round thing with brown hair tending toward gray, stood sideways to him and held a pudgy finger at him as if accusing him of something. "Don't you move, mister!" she growled, then called over her left shoulder, "Linny, fetch Al. Now!"

A black woman at the far end of the hall opened a door and disappeared, stomping down another stairwell.

He hadn't expected another set of steps. Place was bigger than it looked from outside. He spun and bolted for the stairs, ignoring the closed door behind him. Likely it led to a room where he'd be trapped. At least bounding down the stairs he stood a chance of getting back outdoors. Might lose them somehow.

Halfway down, he heard shouts from that burly angry woman from above and boots from below. *Uh-oh. This is what you get for not having a plan, Pops.*

He was so much better at fighting outdoors. Give him a rangy hillside, some rocks and trees, a few decrepit mining buildings, and he could play this game all day long.

"Hold, mister!"

He'd almost made it past the kitchen entrance when the flesh-faced, spectacle-wearing man from the wagon advanced on him from the bright-lit kitchen doorway ahead, his destination, the exit from the crazy place back to the outside.

Pops still held his revolver, but the man carried a shotgun, cocked, and aimed right at his chest or head. He'd seen plenty of men get a dose of shredder blast from close range, and hoped it took his head clean off if he was going to get shot. He'd delivered it to many, and it was never pretty, all smoke and blood and meat and bone and cloth puckered into it.

He stood breathing hard, revolver drawn, aimed right at the man's spectacles, glinting in the light. Behind him, Pops heard footsteps thundering quick and hard, the steps of men. He backed to the left wall so he could see front and back. The man with the shotgun looked steady. He even chewed a quid slow, like a cow chews cud. Like he was hired to do just this thing.

Damn, thought Pops.

The footsteps from behind him drew closer and the door at the bottom of the stairs squeaked open. He glanced back over his right shoulder as three men emerged.

The one in the middle drew to within six, eight feet of Pops. He was of medium build and wore dark hair and clipped, trim moustaches. He stood with his fists on his hips, seemingly unafraid of the revolver in Pops' hand.

In a way, it told Pops they weren't going to shoot him. At least not yet. Not inside, anyway. The shotgun blast would also catch the man who had the look of a boss about him.

"Well, looks like we've caught ourselves an intruder, boys."

"What you gonna do with him, boss?" said one of the men who'd come in with him.

The man who'd spoken first said, "I'm getting to that, Skip. Shut your stupid face."

The man who received this ire was a thin, wiry-looking fellow with squinty eyes. The third was big, wide of shoulder and of head, but with a dimwitted, slow look about the eyes. He reminded Pops of a dozy bull. Both bore watching.

But the man out front, the speaker, had something different about him.

Must be Swearengen, Pops thought.

As if he'd read his mind, the man smiled. "I'm shocked to see you."

Pops' surprise must have been evident on his face for the flicker of a moment, for the man continued. "Yes, you. You are the man who traveled with Stoneface Finnegan, aren't you?"

Pops didn't reply. Just shared at him.

"Silent one, eh? Well, don't worry about that. We'll work it out of you. Right, boys?"

The two goobers behind him chuckled, the skinny one wheezing out a thin laugh, the thick, dim one a low, breathy guffaw.

Pops shook his head. "You sent those men, then?"

Swearengen shrugged.

"Well, they're dead." Pops wasn't certain that was true, but if he was a betting man—he was sometimes—he'd put all his chips on Rollie Finnegan.

It had an effect on the smug boss man—his eyes widened and his smile slipped—but it was momentary. His eyes narrowed once more and the smile that crept onto his lips was thinner and crueler. "Put down your gun . . . boy."

It was Pops' turn to smile. "If you think calling me that ruffles my feathers, you don't much know me, pal."

"Put down the gun or I'll stand aside and let Martin there"—Swearengen nodded past Pops toward the bespectacled man with the shotgun—have at you."

Pops sighed, thinking, *What the heck. I have nothing to lose.* "Look, Mr. Swearengen. I'm not here to cause a fuss. I am here to find two women."

That brought a sudden bark of laughter from the boss man. "In that regard, you are not unlike most men who come to the Gem. But they visit through the front door." His smile slid away once more. "One of those women just arrived." He nodded. "Yes, yes, I know who you seek. Red hair, easy to look at, full of pepper."

"What did you do to her?"

"Do? Me?" said Swearengen. "Why, sir, you cut me to the quick. It's not me who's done a thing to her. Well"— he shrugged once more—"I suppose, in a manner of speaking, I am responsible for what has happened to her."

Pops bolted toward him. "What have you done to her?"

Swearengen sidestepped and the big man behind him, followed closely by the skinny one, closed the gap. Pops pulled up the revolver but before he could fire, he was clubbed from behind. He watched the wall slide by, then the ceiling seemed to waver, pulse. A dark-haired man bent close and looked at him, smiling.

Swearengen.

He looked up, then spoke to someone Pops couldn't see. "Time to feed the pigs."

A muffled sound, a voice Pops couldn't hear, then Swearengen looked at him again. "Two down, one to go." He stood and walked away.

The buzzing in Pops' head gained in strength and was joined with a shaft of hot pain right down the middle of

his head, as if he'd been cleaved apart. Faces moved in and
out of his eyesight. He tried to move his arms but somehow they wouldn't do his bidding. Soon he was traveling
down the hallway toward brighter light. He wasn't walking, though. He was sliding along on his back.

I'm being dragged, he thought.

Whoever was doing the dragging wasn't cautious, for
his throbbing head bounced and clunked, and then he was
crossing the threshold and being dragged down the few
steps to the backyard.

Lifted up by rough hands and shoved along on something hard and narrow, Pops fetched up once, and was
shoved harder, then felt himself dropping. He hit hard into
something stiff, yet soft and thick and smelly. A stink, a
harsh, harsh stink.

The last thing he saw before he lost consciousness was
a big face staring down at him. Not a human face, but a big
one. The long snout and thick, yellow tusks of a boar pig.

Chapter 30

Rollie awoke slowly, and with a groan that leaked unbidden from his mouth. By the time he came to his senses, he first felt a coldness all about him, even before he opened his eyes.

He cracked them and thought perhaps he'd gone blind—that hard knock to the head by the devil's own rifle barrel. He couldn't see a thing. Then he knew if for what it was—night had fallen.

He opened his eyes wide and saw that, no, it wasn't full night, but it was on its way. The purpling sky provided enough visibility he could get to where he need to—town—if he got moving. And that meant getting up.

Though his instant urge was to jerk himself into full wakefulness, training over many years had taught him to stay calm, move only his eyelids, and keep his breathing level. He didn't hear any sounds other than a high-up breeze soughing though the tall pines. Closer, Rollie caught the momentary gurgle, splash, and slap of the shallow river.

Every moment of his day's travails came back to him, doubly reminded by an all-over body ache and a dull thud in his head that rivaled any hangover he'd ever felt from too much whiskey and not enough sense.

He heard no other sounds, save for one, the soft whicker of a horse, and he knew it to be Cap. He and the horse had been through a fair bit together and he knew the beast's sounds as surely as he knew Pops' voice. With thought of Pops, Rollie had to get up. He'd frittered hours, precious hours, sleeping on the riverbank when he should have been making for town to help his pard. As he shoved up onto his elbows, slowly because his head thudded so, he heard a clunk and looked over to his side. He'd knuckled the whiskey bottle.

Luck was with him, though for it had tipped over against a small hummock of grass, no bigger than a fist, and hadn't spilled much of what was left of its precious cargo. He rummaged, found the cork, and stoppered it. He'd take a swig or two once he'd had a long, deep drink in the stream.

It was another ten minutes before he was ready to mount up on his saddled horse, with Tish's mount in tow. Once he oriented himself and was making his way toward town, he hastened while he had some ability to see, however dim and fast-fading the day's light was. He managed to reach the trail they'd taken to the camping spot of the night before by the time full dark came down. From there, he was confident of his direction. The moon complied, better than half, though not quite full, and offered glow enough to guide him and the horses.

They reached the road and he was glad for the darkness, for he passed several people. One fellow, a broke-down old miner, looked like he could have been a cousin to Wolfbait. Riding a sag-backed old donkey, it moved slower than if both of them had stepped along under their own steam. They were headed to town, presumably to drink away the man's meager mined profits.

Seeing the old miner reminded Rollie of why he'd gone to the Gulch in the first place. Initially it had been to try his own hand at digging, though he'd still been recuperating from a near-fatal knifing back in Denver City. He'd showed up in Boar Gulch at the right time. The proprietor of the saloon had been shot right in front of him and he'd bought the place almost without thinking about it. The number of people drinking in the place at that time of day—afternoon, full light—convinced him of the prudence of this venture. A perfectly good day for digging at their claims and yet they were in town, such as it was, spending their money at the saloon. Rollie had quickly realized mining the miners was far more a sure-thing money maker than engaging himself in working at mining.

He caught up to and passed three more men afoot, all headed to town, none of them talking to one another, all looking forward to a first beer and a place at the baize table.

Good luck boys, he thought. *You'll need it in a place like Deadwood.*

Not a one gave him more than a nod and a passing glance. One man lugged a lantern, wick turned low enough for them to all share the road and not wander off. The old-timer on the donkey had seemed to let his big red whiskey nose guide him.

The closer Rollie drew toward downtown proper, the more worried he became, for even though it was night, strollers and early drunks and clusters of folks, mostly men, became more numerous. He drew a few long stares, though he wanted no attention at all. Most of them were armed and had the look of living a life at the edge of desperation. Not a one looked any different from the pile of carcasses he'd left back in the hills.

Rollie guessed some of them knew what he was about, tipped off by the wrong-headed, now-dead lawdog and his ilk. They might even have been urged by Swearengen to be on the lookout for him, in case his men failed to lay him low. That would account for the few hard stares he'd gotten in the preceding minutes.

Time for a different approach. Night's cover was not enough.

Rollie tugged his hat even lower and cut northward once more along one of the many numerous trails veining the rocky landscape surrounding town. When he'd traveled a sufficient few minutes, he angled westward once more with the intention of coming up behind the Gem. He knew where it lay along the street and made for it.

About where he figured the backend of the Gem to lie, he heard sounds of commotion, quiet but louder the closer he rode. He came upon a welter of planks and stumps and rocks and logs that looked to be materials left over from a building job. Plenty of that going on in Deadwood. He reckoned a fellow skilled in carpentry and with a small selection of tools might do well for himself in any of the mine camps bristling throughout the puckered hills and valleys, mountains and low, dry areas of the West.

The noises of a couple of men sounding like they were having a grand old time attracted him. In fact, he was headed that way anyway. He'd satisfy his curiosity without giving himself away, if possible. He tied Cap and Tish's horse tight, hoping no one was fool enough to steal them.

He double-checked his bullet loops, filled his revolver, and slid his rifle from its sheath, then checked and loaded it as well. He didn't like lugging it, but it was effective and didn't slow him much.

Walking tight around the side of the building backing up to the lumber stack, the louder the men became. And more intense the stink of pig became. It had long been one of his least-liked smells. He supposed a pig might well like it, but he couldn't imagine any other creature in the world would.

Then he heard another sound, a man's voice, low and weak at the edges. Tinged with fear, if Rollie was right. The worst of it was . . . the voice was familiar. He stepped closer, placing each boot step gently with deliberate care.

The two voices he'd first heard were fuzzy at the edges, probably due to his still-buzzing, ringing head. But he wasn't deaf and those men were close. Their words were becoming clear. He figured he wasn't but a dozen feet from them, hidden as he was around the side of the little shed he had been edging along.

"You think we should have shortened his chain?"

"Naw, now don't get stupid on me, Moe. You know well as I do we got every right to have ourselves a sporting time out here. All them hoo-has inside are having their drinks and card games and we got to stay out here and tend this fool prisoner. Well, sure. I figure we earned the right to give him a bit of play, make it last longer. More fun for us to watch. Besides, we got ourselves this here bottle. We're good."

"Yeah, but it sure is taking a long time, Skip."

"Yeah, might be you're right about that. Been hours and that pig ain't hardly tucked into his meal yet."

"Could be he don't like his color," said the thicker, slower voice.

The chattier one thought that was prime humor and giggled before drowning the giggle in a gurgle of booze.

Then Rollie heard chain slide and clink on itself, and another voice, close by the others, sounded right through the little barn's wall from him.

"You boys want to speed . . . the plow, you come on in." The voice coughed and spat, sounding as if the man behind it had run too far, too fast, and couldn't catch up with his breath.

"Come on." The chain shook and rattled again with more force, though still weak.

Rollie knew who the voice was—Pops. He sounded haggard, slurred, and slow, but it was him. Rarely had Rollie been so certain of something. He moved the rifle up, held it out before him, and stepped around the corner. The two men who'd been talking had their backs to him and were leaning on a chest-high railing and looking down into a dimly lit byre. Had to be the pig pen, given the stink of the place.

They passed a bottle between them.

From beyond them, Rollie heard the chain, heard a deep grunting sound, then muck squelching and chain links dully clunking one another.

"Get the hell away," said Pops' voice.

"You, two," said Rollie in a low voice, thumbing the hammer on his rifle. "Do as the man says and get away."

The effect of his voice on the two of them was immediate and impressive. They spun, facing Rollie, their eyes wide. One of them, a thin man, held the bottle in one hand. The other hand he held beside his waist as if he had a gun on him. And he did.

The other man was a wide-faced, slab of a man with more girth and muscle than brain. He stood facing Rollie with a dropped-open mouth and watery, bloodshot eyes. From the look of the pair, Rollie guessed they'd been drinking much of the day.

"What you want?" said the thin one.

"Tell you what I don't want," said Rollie, jamming the gun barrel at the big one's ample slop gut. "I don't want to waste my time. Turn around and drop to your knees. Face the pig sty. Now!"

They looked at each other as if the other might somehow explain whether they should comply.

"Now!" repeated Rollie.

"Rollie . . . that you?" came a voice from beyond the railed enclosure. This was followed by a squeal and a rattle of chain. "Back. *Back!* Hurry—can't do this much longer."

"What you gonna do, mister?" said the big drunk, turning and slowly lowering himself to his knees.

"Hands up," growled Rollie. "Higher, damn your useless hides!"

Both made it to their knees. Hands raised behind their heads, they wobbled and swayed.

Rollie kept the rifle trained on them but didn't want to risk a shot and bring folks running. He searched the ground for something stout. Although the yellow lantern light was dim, he saw what he wanted a few feet away and snatched it up. A length of kitchen stove wood as long as his forearm and thick as a wrist.

Without waiting, he gripped it by one end and swung

it hard, slamming it into the thin man's head, just behind the ear. That spot usually dropped a man quick, and it didn't fail.

The skinny fool gasped as the log smacked his bean, then slumped against his stout companion and flopped backward to the ground in a painful-looking pose, his legs tucked beneath him.

The big man looked over. "Skip? You okay?"

Giving him no time to wonder more, Rollie considered the brute's thick face and gave him the same treatment, but laced the swing with some added pepper.

The brute grunted, sighed, and flopped forward. His hands dropped to his side, his head smacked into the rails, and he sagged into them.

Already on the move, leaned over the rail. Beside him he heard a long, loud fart leak out of the big boy. He did his best to ignore it, but the foul cloud hung about him. He looked into the pen. "Pops?" Seeing the wide black-and white back end of a mammoth boar pig, Rollie gabbed the lantern's bail from the nail on which it hung, and leaned in farther. "Pops?"

"Yeah, shoot it. Shoot the pig. He's tearing at me with his teeth." Exhausted, Pops words were slurred and slow.

"Don't worry, Pops. I've got him." Rollie rehung the lantern and climbed the rail front of the sty. Between the stink of the place and the gassy mess the big boy was still releasing, he pinched his mouth tight and gagged a couple of times.

"Here, pig. Here. Come over here," he growled, then let himself down into the muck. It was drier than he expected, but in his experience with pigs, that didn't matter.

The stink would carry for a long ol' time. "Pops, hang on. I'm coming."

The pig finally turned to see what sort of creature dared to bother him. He swung his big, wide face around and Rollie saw the long, curving snout, the yellow tusks jutting upward, brown at the base. The tiny, deep-set eyes seemed to glow red in the lantern light.

Then the thing opened its mouth and lunged at him.

It wheeled on Rollie, toothy mouth wide and squealing. He backed up and clunked against the rails, his rifle jutting outward. The big pig advanced fast and Rollie shoved the rifle's barrel forward, straight into the boar's mouth as it nearly ran right onto it.

The hog squealed once again.

As much out of instinct as survival, Rollie shoved the gun barrel hard and deep into the pig. Nearly to his knuckles, he squeezed the trigger. The sound was barely a whisper of what it would have been had the gun not been lodged inside the maw of a killer boar.

The beast jerked to a stop, legs locked, and a high-pitched scream whistled out of its foaming, blood-flecked mouth. Soon its eyes quivered and danced in their tiny sockets and rolled backward in its thick skull, red-white and wet.

Rollie tugged hard as weight began to pull down on his gun-holding arm. His rifle slid out of the beast's mouth, slick with blood and phlegm and stink.

The boar wheezed and swayed, then flopped to the muck with a massive grunt. Almost as soon as it landed its feet quivered and its trotters trembled, sticking straight out in the air. It farted, a long, low, draining sound, and gurgled from its mouth at the same time.

Pops staggered forward from out of the darkness beyond the nearly dead pig. "My word. Glad you come along, Rollie, but I wish you'd aimed that thing some-wheres other than at me."

Rollie froze in place. "Pops, did I shoot you?"

"No, but the back end of that pig did. Oh . . . my." Pops walked with slow, gentle steps over to Rollie, lugging in one hand the chain tethering him.

Rollie saw it was fastened in a front corner by several bent nails. "Where's the key, Pops?"

"Huh?"

"The key . . . the key to your shackles," said Rollie, helping his friend over to the hog, where Pops sat down.

"About the only thing this vicious creature has been useful for." Pops shook his head and watched for the killer beast to roar back into life, but it didn't. "Oh, I think one of those animals"—he nodded to the unconscious men on the ground—"has it. You kill them?"

"I don't think we're that lucky. We'll find out." Rollie climbed out of the sty and began rummaging through the flopped men's pockets. "We have to hurry. That shot wasn't loud, but you never know."

"That's right, mister. But I know."

Rollie looked over his left shoulder at a dark shape about ten feet behind him. It was a short shape, and the voice sounded feminine, raspy. A woman. It also looked as if she held a weapon.

He paused and gritted his teeth. This is all he needed. He had to get Pops out of there. He looked like he'd been torn up by that huge pig. "Look," he said. "I need to get my friend out of that sty. I will kill you if I have to."

The woman snorted. "Mister, you don't look like much. I reckon I could lick you with both hands behind my back. As it happens, you don't need to strongarm me. I bet I know who you are, and if that's the case, I know why you're here."

"Oh, you do, do you?" Rollie began to straighten up. He was going to keep low, in a half crouch, swing the rifle and let her have it, but that would bring people running.

"You don't want to use that rifle on me, mister."

"I don't?"

"Nope. That'd just call attention to yourself. Besides, I know something that might help you. If you are who I think you are."

He stood straight. From the sty, Pops groaned. "You hurry it up? I don't like being chained, and I damn sure don't like being chained in a pig sty!"

Rollie smiled and shook his head. At least Pops wasn't too far gone to show his true self.

"Look, lady, I don't have time for riddles. If you're going to help me, then help me and explain yourself later. I need to find the keys to that man's shackles."

"What about Horace?"

"Who's Horace?" Rollie's eyes widened.

"The pig."

"Oh, I shot him. Somebody else can render him down."

"I wouldn't eat that pig if you paid me in gold."

"Why's that?" said Rollie as he kept rummaging in the skinny man's pockets. He couldn't be certain, but he thought maybe the man was dead. The other one, he wasn't so sure about.

"That pig feeds on people, mostly. Some table scraps."

"People?"

"Yeah, like your friend, yonder."

"I heard that!" shouted Pops.

His pard sounded more like himself with each passing minute . . . and that pleased Rollie.

"And," said the young woman, stepping closer. "You'll want to look in Moe's trouser pocket. Right front, I believe."

"For the key?"

"Yeah for the key. What else you hunting for down there, mister?"

Rollie grumbled and approached the big man. He shoved him backward and the burly brute flopped onto his back, arms spread as if he were trying to fly.

As he felt in the man's pocket, the fellow made a gurgling, groaning sound, faint but audible, from deep in his throat. Before Rollie could react to the sound, the woman stepped forward, bent low, snatched up his length of stove wood, and swung it hard. Rollie rolled out of the way and came up with his rifle leveled on her.

"Take 'er easy, mister," she said to Rollie, looking down at her handiwork. She'd slammed the wood hard into the side of the big man's head. "I wasn't aiming for you. If I was, you'd look like him by now."

The man's head spurted a thin stream of blood for a few moments, then it quickly fizzled to a seep. His head was bent at an odd angle and the eye nearest the fresh wound was open, half popping from its socket.

If the big man wasn't as dead as his companion, Rollie didn't know what else might do it. "Thanks," he said, still holding the key he'd found just before the man had groaned.

As he looked up at her, his breath hitched in his throat. "I—" He looked away and made for the sty once more.

Her dark, matted hair hung about her face in clumps. Her face was doughy, pudgy, as was her body. But it was the rest of her face that caught Rollie by surprise. A mass of criss-crossed pink, welted scars covered her entire face. Cuts that had gone right across from one side of her face on down through her lips and nose, even over her eyes. Her left eye had gone milky gray, likely from whatever devilish deal had caused the wound.

But her right eye, dark in color and clear and cold, stared at him hard. "Don't pretend you didn't see nothin', mister. I am downright cozy with reactions such as yours."

"I'm sorry, ma'am," he said over his shoulder. "It . . . must have been painful."

"You bet it was. Hurt like the hounds of hell themselves had slashed me." She shrugged as Rollie mounted the rails. "I guess in a way they did. One, anyway."

"Who did that to you?"

"The man you're here for, of course."

"Swearengen?"

"Who else? But I can't let you have him, you understand?"

"What?" said Rollie, fidgeting with the lock on the chain wrapped about Pops' left wrist.

"'Bout time you got here," said Pops. "Another minute, I'd have had to really lay into them."

"Well, I can always leave you here," said Rollie, turning away from his pard for a teasing moment.

Pops said, "What happened to you? Side of your head took a walloping."

"Yeah, long story."

"Tell me later, over a beer."

"Yep."

"Right now we need to get out of here," said Pops, wincing at pain from some wound Rollie could not yet see.

It was too dark in the back of the sty, but he knew Pops had been hurt by the pig, and likely by men before that. The story would come out in due course, but first Rollie had to get him out of there, then decide if Pops was going to be able to help him find Tish, and Pops' daughter.

From the sight of that young woman's scarred face, Swearengen was a sadist, so every minute was vital. For some reason, he also wanted Rollie dead. Judging from what he'd heard about the man, it was likely for little more than the money, but crooked as a dog's hind leg, Swearengen was probably familiar with any number of other criminals—some who would pay to have Rollie's head delivered to them.

"Come on, Pops," he said, helping his chum slog back through the filth of the sty.

Pops paused beside the big pig's head. "See you around, you surly old swine." He rubbed his own sore head and walked to the railing. Even that effort seemed to wind him.

Rollie helped him climb up and over the rails, noticing for the first time the damage dealt to his pard. The man's trousers and sleeves were shredded in places. His legs and arms were riddled with bleeding gashes and puncture wounds where the beast had savaged him with its fangs. He'd only been able to fend off the pig's attacks by wielding the slack in the chain in a determined, if feeble, defense.

The sight, coupled with the horribly scarred face of the once-pretty girl standing a few feet away, made Rollie Finnegan as angry as he'd ever been in many a long year. He had to get in the theater. No time to waste.

The young woman still stood by the head of the man she'd sent to howl at the gates of hell. "Good to see you're alive, mister."

"Okay, then," said Pops. "Who are you?"

She looked at Rollie. "Nice that somebody thinks to ask kindly questions." She looked back at Pops. "I'm Margaret, thank you. And you are?"

Rollie rolled his eyes. "He's Pops and I'm Rollie. Okay? Now, where's the water trough? He's a mess and I have work to do."

She nodded toward a dark shape a few yards to their left. Rollie had lifted down the lantern and they walked to the trough.

Standing on the other side of Pops, supporting him, Margaret nodded toward Rollie and asked, "He always like this?"

"Naw, mostly he's worse."

She snorted, making a slight piggy sound with her nose. "Sorry. Bet you had your fill of hogs for today."

Pops cleaned up as best he could. Discovering none of his wounds appeared to be a threat to his life, he limbered up and drank his fill. Water from the trough couldn't be any worse inside him than pig muck and blood could be on the outside.

"Why should we trust you, Margaret?" asked Rollie.

"Because I work here and because I know more than you do. And because I could scream right now and you'd be sunk. And because I have dedicated my life to killing Al Swearengen. That's why."

The two men looked at each other.

Pops shrugged. "Good enough for me. I just want to find Tish and my daughter, then get the hell out of here. This town has been hard on me." He rubbed his arms.

"All of that is reason enough," said Rollie. "But that last point, killing Swearengen, that breaks the deal right there."

"Nope," she said. "I have more reason than you to kill him."

"If you work here, why haven't you done it yet?" said Pops.

"Because I'm waiting for the right moment. I got to get him alone, make him suffer bad, bad." She seemed to drift from them a moment, gazing into the night. Then she looked at them and whipped open her skirt to reveal her upper right leg. "Look at that," she said, pride in her voice.

The men did their best to look away. "Ma'am," said Rollie. "We don't have time for games. Where can we find—"

"No, damn you. My knife." She slid a long butcher knife free of a homemade sheath strapped to her leg. Even in the low light from the lantern, they could see the blade was honed bright and keen. "Got it from the kitchen. They never knew. This here"—she held it up, turning it and marveling at it, a slight smile on her face—"this here is for Al."

She looked at Rollie, then Pops. "I'll help you get in

there, find whoever you need to, but I need a favor, too. One favor."

"If we can," said Rollie. "Sure."

"Don't give me away. Don't tell nobody what I'm aiming to do. And you got to let me have Al alive."

"That's two favors," said Rollie.

She shrugged. "So what. I ain't good with numbers."

Rollie was about to ask her to show them the best way inside, but she started talking again.

"Him and his men, they tried to kill me, but"—she touched her face—"this ain't nothing compared with what he did to Myrna. That's my sister. Was. She ended up in there." She nodded toward the sty. "Now I'm waiting for the right time. He thinks I forgive him, thinks I'm addled in the head and good for nothing but kitchen work and cleaning. But I put up with him. I'm just waiting for the right time. He's wily, but I'm patient. I'll get him. Sometimes you want to kill a snake, you got to crawl right down into the rocky ol' cave where it's sleeping all balled up. That's when you get 'em."

"Okay, then," said Pops. "Hand me that rifle, Rollie, and if Margaret would be so kind as to point the way, we'll get in there, do the job that needs doing." He described Tish and then, as best he could, his daughter.

"Yeah, they're both in there. That red-haired fool, she kicked up a fuss earlier today, then he shut her up somehow. Ain't seen her come out. I reckon it's 'cause she's pretty.

"The pretty ones always stay longer with Al. Same with the black girl. If it's the one I think it is, she's been here a while. He don't trot her out much. When I've seen her, she's been gone up here." She tapped her head. "He uses laudanum and whiskey, anything it takes to knock 'em cold, then he . . . Well, you're men. You know."

Neither Rollie nor Pops dared say what they were thinking, which was each hoped they weren't too late.

True to her word, the girl led them to a staircase along the left side of the building. "It's what the girls use. Al doesn't want them doin' much in sight during the daytime."

"Why don't they leave?" said Pops.

Margaret snorted. "And go where? Do what? He'd just hunt them down and throw them to the pig. Now, you take me. I am the worst thing ever gonna happen to him, because I don't care what happens to me. He already took it all from me, see?"

"Well, he's gonna have to get a new pig." Creeping toward the corner of the building, Rollie sounded grim and tight.

"Hell, that don't bother him none. Though I do believe he was fond of Horace. Kept him around a long ol' time. You go up those stairs, windows to the girls' rooms. Find an open one, then you're in."

"And then?" said Rollie.

"And then . . . I can't do much to help you. I'll see if I can't create a ruckus to keep him from noticing you up there. Some of the girls, though, they might get riled seeing you. He's got some of them thinking he's their god, you know? Like they can't do a thing without him. Mostly it's the drugs he gives them. They can't go half a day without what he gives them."

"This man is a sorry piece of work," said Pops.

They began their ascent up the narrow, moon-puckered stairwell. After a couple of steps, Pops looked behind, but Margaret wasn't there. He hoped she wouldn't do something foolish on their behalf. Something about her he liked. He felt almighty bad for her, but she had spine. More than most men he'd ever met.

In the lead, Rollie paused. "Before we get up there," he whispered. "We need a plan."

"I'm all ears, pard," said Pops. "My way of doing things only earns a man pig muck."

Rollie nodded in the dark. "Moon's not too bad. We'll flank the windows as we come to them, try to peek in. Maybe we'll see something. Should be one we can get in through, then do some real exploring. "

"But we best keep it down. Floors squeak."

"Yeah, but it's a working night for most of them, so they might be . . . between customers. Let's look for an empty room first."

Pops nodded and they proceeded upward.

Chapter 31

They came to the first window on their right, and flanked it. Rollie passed by and hugged the left side, Pops took the right. With a nod, they peeked in. A low-turned oil lamp lit enough of the room that they could see what sat inside.

They peered above the half-height curtains and dead ahead was a bed, and on the bed was a large shape. Or rather two large shapes, moving. Rollie's eyebrows rose high, as did Pops. No telling who was inside, but they had to move on. They weren't going to climb into that window any time soon. They low walked to the next window, taking each footfall with as much caution as possible.

They repeated their procedure, and saw an empty room. No lamp, but the curtains were parted and moonglow provided enough light they felt confident in their assessment. Pops nodded an indication Rollie should try his luck. He did, and was rewarded with the stubborn feel of a window locked from the inside.

He silently cursed cautious women and jerked his head along the narrow catwalk. He nearly tripped over a wobbly wooden chair and another farther on. His boot nudged a small empty food tin and he caught a whiff of spent tobacco stink. It must be where the women spent their off time, smoking and chewing tobacco and drinking and growing bitter and desperate and waiting for something, *anything,* in their paltry lives to change. He doubted anything ever did. Little for the good, anyway.

Rollie and Pops were about halfway along the building's side, creeping slowly toward the front, when Pops sensed the third window was the right one. He just knew it somehow. Raised a hand's width at the bottom, the window was about knee height, and a lamp, turned low, glowed inside. A bed stood in roughly the same spot as in the previous rooms. And there wasn't a soul inside.

Not certain how long the situation would be available, Rollie sensed what Pops did and gingerly raised the window. It stuck, then popped and rattled with the force of his hand pressing upward. They held their breath and pulled painful faces until the puckered, dried wood stopped stuttering in the wooden tracks.

Pops nodded to Rollie who bent and poked his head into the room and looked left, then right. He pulled it back out and nodded to Pops, then climbed inside. It took a few stifled grunts and groans from each of them, battered and abused as the day had made them, but they managed to get inside and stood still a moment before the window.

Then Rollie whispered, "Oh, Pops. Forgive me for saying so, but you smell godawful."

"Well pardon me for trying to stay alive in a pig sty!" His whisper was a pinch louder and more forceful.

Rollie said nothing, but was glad the room's low light

hid his smile. He didn't know if Pops could ever wash that stink off, but he certainly hoped so. Otherwise, business at The Last Drop was indeed going to drop. Like a stone.

Now that they'd made it into the snake's belly, the first order of business was to find the women. Specifically, the two they came for.

Rollie and Pops had already agreed not to split up, even though it would make finding the girls more difficult. Pity the strange creature outside, Margaret, didn't actually know where the women were held.

If they could get them out and safe without harm to them or anyone else, Rollie would consider going back inside to mop the floor with the Deadwood devil.

Pops walked up close beside him and whispered. "Too many rooms. We need to split up to see it all."

"I know, but how will we know what the other's found?"

In the moment of silence that followed, they heard a soft clinking sound. They looked at each other, sharing a thought. What if it were somebody chained up?

"We know he's not afraid to use chains on a body." Pops held up his chafed wrist.

Rollie nodded. "Up there, then."

They walked carefully along a dark hallway different from the one Pops had briefly seen earlier. Light seeped from under a closed door they'd just passed, then from another farther ahead on their left. They heard low voices, a man's and a woman's from one. Rollie flattened against the left wall, Pops across against the right, guns raised and eyes watching.

Moments passed, then they saw shadows cut across the sliver of light from beneath the door. The murmuring voices quieted a moment, then the door handle turned, the door swung inward with a low, quiet squeak, and a man stepped out, carrying what looked to be a gun belt in one hand and a hat in the other. Before the door closed behind him, they saw he was tall, broad of shoulder, and wore a full, dark beard.

Pops and Rollie exchanged looks, knowing each meant the same thing. Neither had any idea which direction the man would walk, but if he did turn toward them, he might see them in the shadows, and their foray would end with the thundering of gunfire in the tight hallway.

They waited and held their breaths.

The man dawdled, fiddling with his gun belt, strapping it on his trim waist, taking his time to adjust it. Arms half raised, he stood as if he were about to launch into a square dance, then readjusted how the holster rode on his left side.

Pops wanted to shout, "Get on with it!" but held his breath and waited. After all, the man wasn't but fifteen feet down the hallway from them.

Then the man half turned toward them, and set his tall hat on his head, going through the same ritual of adjusting the topper, seeing how it felt, then readjusting it. Finally satisfied, he looked their way a moment then looked back toward the direction from which they'd walked, and made his choice.

Rollie and Pops didn't breathe their sighs of relief at seeing his back disappear into the long, dark hall, for many more moments. Hearing his boots step firmly on the carpeted wood floor, they waited until the sounds diminished as he clunked down a staircase. At the bottom, he opened a door and for a brief moment they heard the faint din of far-off voices, a sound they had become aware of humming somewhere beneath them.

The bar room and gaming room, and whatever passed for a theater.

They didn't waste any more time, but moved once more down the hall, neither speaking, but each breathing easier. Another menace avoided.

They crept slower, listening at doors. From behind the next door with a sliver of light peeking beneath, they heard the unsteady drone of a man's snore. It wasn't what they'd heard earlier—the sound of chain clinking—but someone was napping. Doubtful it was Swearengen as he was known as an astute businessman and was likely downstairs, not far from the action of his business.

Rollie had guessed the man had an office somewhere downstairs. It was a room he intended to find before the night was out. But that was a long way off.

Pops moved ahead of him, creeping with a limp down the hall. Rollie felt bad for him. As awful as his head still felt, Pops looked a whole lot worse, yet he was soldiering on. The drive to find his daughter was so much more powerful than the aches of his own ailments.

Pops reached the end of the hall and paused. He motioned toward Rollie, beckoning him with a hurried hand, then pointed at a door nearly invisible in the dark.

As soon as Rollie joined him, Pops glanced down the hall behind them, set his hand on the doorknob and turned it, pushing inward. It was locked. He tried the other direction. Again it didn't budge.

They heard a sound inside the room, a grating, yet soft sliding, and both men knew what it was—heavy steel sliding on wood. Chain on wood. A soft, cough sounded, then more slow sliding.

Pops looked at Rollie, eyes wide as if to say, *My daughter's in there and I know it for a fact.*

Rollie nodded and gently pushed Pops' hand off the knob. Less fatigued, Rollie figured they'd be better off if they could force the lock with as little noise and fuss as possible. He nodded toward the hallway and then at Pops, indicating he should keep an eye out. Gripping the metal knob tight, Rollie turned it to the right hard, forcing the mechanism harder, harder. The sounds of metal pinging inside seemed to fill the dim hall, echoing up and down the long, narrow space. Rollie winced and squeezed tighter, turning harder.

Short of kicking in the door, a noisy prospect he hoped to avoid but wasn't opposed to doing, he wasn't certain what else to do. He didn't think he'd be able to pick the lock any better than what he was already doing.

About to let off the knob and try wedging his big knife blade in, he'd decided to pry the mechanism apart when something inside the knob pinged, clicked, and popped louder than any other noise they'd made since stepping through the open window. They both froze.

Feet sounded in the room the man had emerged from. They hugged the walls once more, just as that door opened and the occupant, a woman with frizzy, tousled hair, peered out, her robe hanging wide open, revealing her partially lit nude body. The light from her room cast her form in half shadow and she squinted down the hallway, but could see little save for darkness.

The men did not so much as flinch, though Rollie wanted

to sneeze to clear out the stink of pig sty from having Pops so near.

The woman angled her head left, then right, then muttered, turned and retreated back into her room.

Hoping that last bit of noise from within the lock had done the job, Rollie gripped it tight, his whitened knuckles nearly visible in the dark. As the woman's door clunked shut, he shoved the previously locked door hard.

It opened inward and he and Pops piled into one another to get in. Luckily, the room was not lit, for Rollie had not had time to close the door fully behind them when a door from up the hallway opened fast. They held still, assuming it was the same woman, again thinking she'd heard something.

Stomping footsteps approached, but she didn't walk more than ten feet, holding there a long moment. The men guessed she was looking for sign of something amiss. She didn't want to believe she'd heard nothing at all.

Again, the men held, not breathing. The woman gave up and stomped back to her room. As she closed the door once again, Rollie timed his closing of the door. Only then did he and Pops turn and look into the room.

It was a hot space, stifling, and unlit by a lamp. But it was lit enough by moonglow they could see a few dim shapes. A soft cough sounded across from the door, followed by that dragging sound once more.

Pops made for it, peered close, and then knelt. "Girl?" He reached out, touched the arm of whoever it was.

Rollie remained tense, eyeing the rest of the dark room. He didn't see much of anything, and the room was small enough it couldn't hold all that many surprises, anyway.

A ladderback chair sat in a far corner, angled toward the figure on the floor.

"Girl?" Pops moved closer, peering at the downcast face. He reached out gently once more and lifted the chin to look into the eyes of the chained woman. At the same time she looked up into his.

Chapter 32

She had heard a noise, metal, but not the chains she was shackled by. She heard the door, then other sounds. Boots. *Must be the demon who kept me here.* She'd fight him. Fight him like she always did. Well, like she always tried to.

A chance it wasn't him, though. Could be it was that foolish girl who sometimes came with the demon, sometimes alone. Maybe it was her, come to empty the slops bucket and set down the plate of food. Same thing she did every day.

But it was too late or maybe too early, wasn't it? Hard to tell—she had lost count of the hours a long time ago, wasn't even sure how long she'd been here. *Weeks? Months? Years? Two lifetimes?*

Something touched her arm, then her chin. She wasn't so pulled away with the drugs or whatever it was he forced into her that she couldn't see or feel or hear. Or smell. A foul smell that just came to her. *Foul.* Mostly, she was tired. Plumb tired. And she felt itchy all over.

The thing that touched her chin didn't let go, kept pushing upward, forcing her to raise her head. And when she did, she looked square into the face of a demon. No, no, a ghost, maybe.

"No," she shook her head and shoved backward with her feet, her chains dragging and clinking softly against the wood floor. "No, no way."

"Zadie?" said a voice, whispering to her. "Zadie? Is that you, girl?"

From somewhere in her mind, somewhere far back, far down, deep and buried, something told her to pay attention. To think of something more than the room with the high window and the itchy feeling.

"Zadie?" said the voice again, little more than a whisper. But it was not the demon's voice.

Might be it was a voice she knew somehow. *How is that possible?*

"Zadie?" said the voice again. "I'm here. I've come for you, girl. It's gonna be all right now, girl. Okay?"

Maybe none of this is real, she thought.

Another voice said, "Pops, that her? We have to go. Is that chain fastened?"

"Hang on, now. Hang on a minute."

The girl looked at the face, close enough in the moon-glow through the high window to see a man, but not any-body she knew. Or was it?

The man said, "Zadie, girl, we have to get out of here. You need to help us. We're here to take you out of here."

She looked at the face. It was someone she knew, some-how, but who? From where? And when? "This is not real," she whispered.

Pops shook his head and shuffled to her side on his knees. "It is real, honey, I tell you. It's as real as I am right now. I'm here, see? I tried and tried. I been looking for you all these years—" He reached again out for her.

She jerked away and kept shaking her head. "No! I've been telling myself . . . none of this is real. Now I know . . ."

"Pops!" Rollie leaned down close to his side. "We don't have time for this. We have to get out of here. He has a small army and they'll likely be coming soon."

Pops didn't look up. "Let them. I don't care any more. I got my baby, finally. I found my daughter."

Rollie growled in whispered rage. "I understand, but you have to snap out of this foolishness, Pops." He clamped a hand on his pard's shoulder and shook it hard.

Pops swung at him but Rollie, still standing, was more agile and jerked out of the way. "Knock it off, Pops! If you stay here you'll both be killed, but only after all manner of badness, man! Do you want that? For her? For your daughter? Do you want to be the cause of her death now that you've finally found her?"

That seemed to crack the odd shell the weary man had built up around himself. He shook his head, "No, no. Can't let that happen."

"Good," said Rollie nodding, too, in relief. "Now, Zadie, where is Tish? The red-haired woman? Where is she? Anything? Where does Swearengen keep the new girls?"

The girl kept shaking her head, her eyes were not focused on either of them. "Oh, oh no. Not the office," she said, wincing and backing up.

Rollie leaned closer. "Office? Al's office? Where is it, Zadie?"

Pops looked at Rollie, then nodded. "Honey, you have to tell us now."

She still didn't look up at them, but nodded. "Yes, it's a room. Downstairs somewhere. He sleeps there. Does things . . ."

Pops grabbed her wrist and pulled her close. "You're going to thank me for this later," he said, and even though she fought, he pulled her close and wrapped her in a big hug.

Rollie sighed. "Pops, we just talked about this. We have to get going. I have to find Tish."

With wide eyes, Pops looked up at Rollie over the struggling girl's shoulder. It took nearly a minute of the weak girl struggling, but her efforts became weaker and finally she seemed to collapse beneath his hugging arms and within seconds, Rollie heard deep, wracking sobs from her.

"The chains, Rollie. We've got to tug them free."

Rollie looked closer, grabbed the manacles close by her feet and wrenched them. It took two tries, but they came apart, away from her ankles. He nodded as if satisfied with the result, then did the same with the chains about her wrists, freeing her.

Rollie lowered them to the floor so they wouldn't clank, somewhat amazed he was able to deal with them so quickly. He walked softly to the door and peered out. So far there was no sound from nosey neighbors in other rooms. He slipped back in and closed the door once more.

"Pops, you'll have to take her back out the way we came in."

"What about you?"

"Never mind me. I'm going for Tish. You go back out. Cap and Tish's horse are tied out back behind the sty. I guess you know where that is."

"Yeah, I reckon I won't forget it any time soon. Where we gonna meet? I can get her situated out there and come back in and help you."

"No, too risky. She's in no fit state to make her own decisions."

"Hey," she said, in a slow, drawly voice. "I'm not a child."

"I know," said Rollie, suppressing an urge to shout. He looked back to his pard and shook his head. "Pops, we don't have time for this."

"Okay, okay. I'll meet you where?"

Rollie thought a moment. "Out front. In a half-hour."

"Not much time. You forget where you are and who owns this joint?"

"Nope. But I'm not going to pick a fight with him. Unless I have to. Tish is my first concern."

"Okay, then. You ready, girl?" Pops looked at his daughter. She was looking down at the floor, sort of swaying in place as if trying to keep her footing on a ship's deck. "Yeah, yeah. Tryin' . . ."

Rollie nodded. "Half an hour. Let's go." He went to the door first and peeked out once more, then leaned back in. "Clear. I'll go a few paces ahead. You follow. You manage with the rifle and the girl?"

"Hell, yes. Got my baby back. Nobody is going to take her from me again."

Rollie nodded and left the room, revolver poised. Pops and Zadie followed, though she was barely able to walk. Rollie sighed and waited for them. They were between doors in the hallway. He leaned close to Pops ear. "Take the pistol. Give me the rifle. You'll have to carry her. No other way."

"Yeah, looks so."

They swapped guns.

Pops stuffed the revolver into his deep left pocket, as good as it was going to get for grabbing easy, then scooped up the girl. She was awake enough that she didn't protest, but wrapped her arms around Pops' neck and laid her face against his shoulder. Before Rollie turned away, he saw tears sliding down Pops smiling face.

They nodded to each other, then Rollie walked ahead into the darkness, glancing back until Pops reached him in front of the room they'd entered through. Just their luck if the resident had returned while they were down the hall. Rollie risked it and turned the knob.

The first thing he saw was the bed to his left, still empty. The rest of the room, the same. And the window was raised high as they'd left it. He didn't suppose it would matter if Pops left it up behind him after he left.

He backed out and nodded to Pops, who entered. Rollie closed the door behind them, silently wishing them luck, and himself, too. Then he angled right, toward the staircase he'd heard the dithering man take some time before. He made it to a landing when he heard voices downstairs, along a passage he could not yet see.

The voices passed by the bottom of the stairs and kept going. Rollie didn't waste any more time. He was on a mission to find Swearengen's office, and some other room off of his office, if the girl was to be believed.

Something seemed familiar about the place. A sliver of a thought niggled at him as he walked with caution, but the simplicity of it came to him—the din of yammering, laughing voices from the barroom, the smell of tobacco smoke, the dull clink of poker chips, the piano. . . . Most of the sounds, save for the piano, brought The Last Drop to mind.

Rollie felt a quick tinge of homesickness for the place, and for Boar Gulch. An odd feeling, something he hadn't felt in, well, maybe forever. And suddenly he wanted to be back there, relatively safe and sound. With his friends in the same condition, all enjoying their days and nights, free of worry about who might be attacking them at any given minute.

The interesting and odd feeling served the immediate purpose of making him want to get Tish—and she'd better be okay or Swearengen would not only pay for it, he'd pay dearly, and slowly, hair by hair, fingernail by fingernail, tooth by tooth, one eyeball at a time, one razor cut at a time. Rollie was in no mood to tolerate cruelty to his friends, and he was in a hard mood enough to dole out cruelty to deserving recipients.

Judging from the distance of the sounds and smells of the place, clawing toward high pitch as the night wore on, Rollie figured he was a couple of doors with a hallway in between from the bar room, which suited him just fine. He had to find Swearengen's office. Three doors were coming up, one on his left, another a bit beyond, on his right, and the third faced him, forming the end of the hall.

The left side of the hallway was a little darker, in shadow, and he heard boots approaching from behind. He looked, saw nobody yet, but he'd be in sight any second now. He had nowhere to go. The end of the hallway was too far away to make a dash for it, and even then it was a closed door. He glanced behind once more and opted for the door on the left. It was unlocked and dim but not dark inside. Nobody shouted at him, so he closed it behind him, but not all the way.

He peered out through the crack and into the lamp-lit hallway. As the bootsteps approached, he had to be ready in case whoever it was intended to enter this room. He felt with his right hand and decided there was enough space between him and some sort of shelves for him to step to the side should the need arise.

In the next moment, he saw two things that heartened him. The man who'd walked down the hall was tugging out keys and unlocking the door across the hall and up a bit from him. And that man was Al Swearengen.

Rollie smiled.

Chapter 33

Swearengen unlocked the door, with a deftness that belied practice, and then closed it behind him. Rollie waited to hear the tell-tale clinks and clicks of the door being locked again, but apparently Swearengen wasn't paranoid enough to lock himself in. Or it might mean he was only going to be in there—whatever room that was, likely the man's office—for a short visit.

Rollie quickly glanced about the room he was in. It was lit only by the moonglow through the window. Opening the door to the hall, it squeaked a little. He held his breath, standing to the side, in shadow. The hall light, though paltry, was enough to give him more of a look inside the room. Nothing in it but stacks of crates of whiskey, food, and shelves with more goods stacked, none too neatly. He saw movement on the floor toward the back of the room and tightened, then spied a brown rat scuttling close by a torn and leaking sack of meal.

Good. Unless there was more to the room beyond what he could see, the odds of anyone in it were slim. He hoped the room across the way was Swearengen's office. If

Zadie's fuzzy memory could be trusted, a room off of that was likely where Tish was being held.

Time to barge in and see what would come of it.

Rollie crossed the hall and with barely a breath taken, snatched the knob and gave it a turn. Leading the way with his rifle gripped tight, he nosed into the bright room, trained the gun on Swearengen, and closed the door behind himself.

Behind a massive squat wooden desk stood Swearengen, a too-fat cigar pooching out of his lips. He looked at Rollie with raised eyebrows, and his cigar drooped a little. "Who the hell are you?"

"Don't recognize me, Al?"

Rollie waited for their previous—and only—face-to-face meeting to occur to the man. It had been a number of years before. He'd been passing through the region on his way back from east of there, having tracked a fugitive thief, a robber of banks by the name of Filson, who'd mistakenly believed crossing state lines would somehow exempt him from the grasp of the law.

Rollie had had to remind him that while the law might have been unable to drop its various and varied duties to chase after lowlife thieves, the Pinkerton Detective Agency was often hired by the law to deal with such annoying tasks.

He'd deposited the man to the law—after removing him from the embrace of a fat native woman with no teeth. The two had been holed up like badgers in a dugout shelter they'd shared with all manner of other vermin. The woman had tried to get the drop on him, so Rollie had been obliged to cold conk her and truss her up, naked, atop Filson's own pack horse.

As for Filson, Rollie had allowed the man to don his trousers, and then he, too, rode atop his own horse. The rest of their goods he left behind. Except, of course, the remainder of the stolen cash, which Filson had conveniently left in three withered bank bags.

On his way back westward, Rollie had decided to take a couple of days for himself and swung northward by a half-day's ride to take a peek at this bustling new burg called Deadwood he'd heard so much about, little of it favorable. But as it was anchored somewhat lawfully by his old friend, Seth Bullock, he thought he'd pass through, catch up with Bullock, and see what all the hubbub was about.

Bullock had taken him on a tour of the town, and though Bullock had seemed quite proud of it, Rollie had at the time not thought much of it. He realized his purview was tainted by forced visitations to many such crime-plagued mine camps. As he was currently a resident of a relatively crime-free mine camp known as Boar Gulch, his views on such places had softened a touch. And if he had to admit it, Deadwood had cleaned itself up in the years since he'd initially visited.

On that brief town tour with Bullock, they'd bumped into Al Swearengen haranguing a Chinese family about something they had or hadn't done for him. Either way, it had appeared as if he were about to strike one of their children and Rollie had snatched up his revolver and leveled it on the swarthy man before Bullock had even had a chance to intervene.

Rollie and Swearengen had exchanged cool, level gazes. Swearengen had lowered his hand from a striking position and had plucked the cigar from his mouth. "Good day, gentlemen," he'd said, and proceeded on down the dust-caked boardwalk.

"Who was that cretin?" said Rollie, watching the man disappear into some place with a sign above denoting it as The Gem Theater.

"That cretin you just braced is the infamous Al Swearengen."

"Huh." Rollie thought he might have heard of him, and he recalled it wasn't a comment of the flattering sort. All these years later, and many unsavory stories attributed to the man later, they were again face-to-face.

Swearengen shrugged. "Should I?"

Rollie waited, and then the eyebrows lowered and a slow smile crept onto the man's face. "The street out front, some years back. You accosted me with a firearm, as I recall."

"Not the way it happened, but believe what you need to."

Swearengen plunked down in the wooden chair behind his desk. It squeaked. "So you lived through it, eh?"

"By *it*, I guess you refer to that silly little gang of children you sent into the hills after me?"

"Me? Why, what on earth can you mean? I'm merely relaying gossip, sir. If there's one fault I have—just the one, mind you—it's that I do love a juicy shank of gossip to nibble on. Oh, I do, I do. Say, since you are here, why don't we have a drink together, hmm?"

"No, thanks," said Rollie, though he would sorely like a good slug of rye right about then. *Stay sharp,* he told himself. "Where's the girl?"

Swearengen poured a glass of amber-colored liquid. "From the looks of your bruised head seems those children who found you in the hills gave you a right smart beating."

"Answer my question, Swearengen."

"Oh, something about a girl?"

"Red hair, pretty. Came here this morning looking for work, I'd say."

"Hmm, no, no, that does not ring any bells with me. And I tell you, I have an eye for the pretty ones. And more often than you'd think, they seem to feel the same toward yours truly. Interesting, eh?"

"The girl upstairs. What about her."

"Girl upstairs? You'll have to be more specific. We have a number of women who live upstairs. Performers all. I run a theater here, in case you hadn't noticed. Maybe you were too busy slinking around here after dark."

Rollie stepped forward, the gun held steady, aimed at the seated man. "The girl upstairs, black girl, pretty. You had her chained, drugged."

That got him, thought Rollie as he watched a shadow pass before Swearengen's dark eyes. Rollie's smile drifted away.

"If your girls are performers, then why chain her? That's kidnapping, slavery, forcible restraint. None of those is lawful."

The bar owner looked around himself theatrically. "Law? What law?" He poured himself another short drink from the bottle on the desk, and leaned back in his chair. It squeaked again. "No, I understand your concern, really I do. You see, the truth is and you can ask the young lady this herself, I rescued that poor, abused thing from a certain den of depravity that shall, for the moment, remained unnamed. Rest assured, it is not anywhere near here. Something terrible must have happened to her there. Something I knew very little about when I rescued her.

"You see"—Swearengen leaned forward—"I suspect she had been drugged somehow. Oh, but she was in an appalling state. Yet at the time she was fairly docile. Enough so that I took her into my very own cabin on the journey."

"I bet you did."

'Now, now, Mr. Finnegan." He sipped. "Where are my manners? Are you certain you would not like a sip of this fine—indeed the finest—Kentucky mash I have had the pleasure of knowing for some years now?"

"No, the girl. Why chain her?"

"Ah, yes." The man behind the desk sighed. "Her actual condition became apparent to me shortly after my rescue of her. She became, well"—he shrugged—"she became violent. There's no other word for it. She became violent, lashing out, biting and cursing, kicking and punching. I had to chain her for her own good. Why, it was all we could do—"

"We?"

"Well, yes, me and a few of my . . . associates. I believe you've already met several of them."

"One man's vermin is another's associate."

"Oh, harsh words. You cut me to the core, sir."

"That's exactly what I intend to do!" Rollie launched himself over the desk, shoving upward with his legs, in time to avoid most, but not all, of the stray, biting stings of lead shot from the boom that sounded as he jumped.

The room filled with smoke and jagged chips of wood and the stink of gun powder. Sound was replaced with a whooshing pulse, like a smith hammering at his forge deep underwater.

Swearengen had triggered a shotgun blast from beneath his desk, aimed at whoever found him- or herself called before the self-important whoremonger.

"You—" That was all the bar owner was able to say before Rollie's left arm caught him about the throat and kept coming. The two men collapsed in a pile, the squeaking desk chair a splintered wreck beneath Swearengen.

Rollie thrashed like a tail-caught viper and struggled to gain a knee so he might land a blow. By the time he did, Swearengen had slid to the side enough he was able to swing an arching fist up at the unprotected left side of Rollie's face.

As Rollie spun, fighting an unexpected wave of sudden dizziness, he caught sight of the deadly below-desk contraption, a sawed-off single-barrel rigged on a leather sling hanging in the cavity below the desk top. Beyond it, the front of the desk was blown apart and he saw the spot where he'd been standing.

In that quick glimpse, several thoughts came to him. How many times in his life had he come that close to dying? How many more did he have left before he ran out of them? And had the pellets from the blast done much damage to his legs?

He knew he'd been hit, but he didn't dare look. He had to lay low the savage Swearengen and he didn't care what that half-demented girl, Margaret, wanted. She'd had her chance, plenty of them, and she'd not used them.

Swearengen was a devil of a man who was, even as Rollie threw himself once more at the bar owner, making a high-pitched, frenzied, whining sound, and clawing and crawling toward an escape. But it was an escape Rollie was about to cut off.

He drew his revolver and swung it around soundly, hoping to connect the butt of the handle with Swearengen's head, but instead it clunked part of the ragged jutting chairback first. The blow it delivered to the man's head would result in little more than a bruise.

That was all the reprieve Swearengen needed as he snatched up something off a bottom shelf of a feeble, leaning bookstand against the wall. It emerged out of the shadows and swung toward him fast. Swearengen jerked farther away from him and spun around so he faced upward, a teeth-gritting leer pulling his mouth wide in a rictus of rage. At the same time, he swung the long, thin thing held at one end in his clenched right fist. As it swung, Rollie saw part of it become disconnected and slide off from whatever Swearengen held in his hand. It whipped past Rollie's head and over the desk.

In Swearengen's hand was a long, gleaming steel blade, thin and as long as a man's forearm, not unlike a bayonet, but thinner.

The thing that had slid off and away had been its scabbard, but the blade was whipping toward Rollie fast. He had enough time to hold up his left arm and hope Swearengen hadn't gotten enough speed behind the blow to do much damage. But he didn't wait to find out.

With a shouted growl, Rollie drove the pistol downward once more. The blow connected with the left side of Swearengen's face as the thin knife's gleaming blade struck his arm. He felt it cut into him, but he moved his arm quickly, and regained a proper hold on his rifle.

He got the gun righted around with a flip of his hand,

and thumbed back the hammer. He was beyond caring. Swearengen had tried to kill him twice and he was about to get his.

Rollie gritted his teeth and jammed the snout end of the barrel into Swearengen's upward-facing left cheekbone. The man was trying to roll and buck out from beneath Rollie's partially pinning leg, but he stopped when he felt the gun barrel jammed hard into his face.

Rollie leaned close, his spittle flecking in the trembling face. The man's eyes were bulged, his nostrils quivered wide, and then . . . then Al Swearengen smiled. A wide smile that grew wider. Wide enough that his teeth showed, teeth that had a little scrim of blood over them.

"You might as well smile when you meet the devil. It won't last long."

Then Swearengen began giggling.

"What the hell's so funny?" Rollie all but growled the words. His finger tightened on the trigger as he asked,

Then he heard a throat clear behind him.

He froze.

Swearengen laughed louder, at first a chuckle, then it bubbled up out of him in a wheeze.

"You ought not to treat Al that-a-way."

Rollie heard a gun's hammer cocking back to the deadliest position of all. *Any second now,* he thought. A second thought crowded that one right out of the way. *Aw, to hell with this. I cheated death a couple of times already today. I bet I have one more lucky card in my hand.*

Without any further thought, without so much as a twitching muscle, Rollie Finnegan swung that rifle around to his left, hard and fast. At the same time, he dropped to his right, spinning to face his unseen attacker, Swearengen forgotten for the briefest moment.

He rolled onto his right shoulder blade and caught a glimpse of a wide, fleshy face sporting thick dark stubble and topped with a derby hat. It was the face of a hired moron and not one that looked overly intelligent. Rollie triggered the rifle and it barked flame and spat death.

What he caught was the man's leg, specifically the left knee. That close to the end of the gun, the meat and bone exploded in a burst of jellied pulp. Even before he spun and flopped to the floor the man was screaming. But Rollie didn't care. He knew such an agonizing wound would prevent the moron from trying to shoot him, at least for the next few moments.

And that's all the time Rollie needed.

He turned back to Swearengen, who was still laying on his back, half addled, and the shock of what he'd seen writ large upon his swarthy features. Rollie grabbed the edge of the desk and stood tall, the rifle aimed at the whore-monger's face.

"Now, where is the redheaded woman? Tish. Where is she, damn you? Tell me now and I won't kill you."

Swearengen shook his head as if to clear his thoughts. He wagged a hand behind him. That door! The door!"

"Good, get up. Hands where I can see them."

"But I'm wounded!"

"So is he." Rollie jerked his head to the side without taking his eyes off Swearengen. "And you don't see him complaining do you?"

The knee-shot man was curled up and mewling, writhing on the floor and gasping, trying to force out a scream but it kept ending in a squelching, bleating sound.

"Yes!" said Swearengen. "You shot him in the knee!"

"Yes, and I'll do the same to you in two second unless you get up. One."

"Okay!" Swearengen scrambled upright, more agile than expected.

Rollie shove him toward the closet door.

He fumbled in his pocket and tugged out a leather strap looping a half dozen skeleton keys. His hands shook as he tried several of them.

"Come on, fool. Open the door." Rollie glanced quickly at the doorway to the hall, surprised nobody was banging it down, what with all the gunfire.

"I'm trying," growled Swearengen, gaining some of his nerve back.

Rollie noticed and jammed the rifle barrel into the back of the disgusting man's head. "Unlock it, now." His voice was low, steady, and cold.

Swearengen dropped the keys and bent to retrieve them.

Rollie knew it was a ploy and he kicked hard, his right boot toe catching Swearengen under the jaw and nesting hard against his windpipe. He went down in a gagging, half-conscious mess. Rollie kicked again, this time at the doorknob. The solid door shuddered and burst apart under the hard boot of Stoneface Finnegan.

The room wasn't much more than a big closet, with a cot along the back wall and a slops bucket in the corner. Sitting on the floor with her back against the cot was Tish Gray. Her hands were chained on her lap and another chain led from them down to her booted ankles.

Even in the low light, Rollie saw she looked like hell. But she raised her head and, though her left eye was nearly puffed shut and her lip was split and the side of her face was swollen and bruising, she squinted up at him. "I knew it was you."

"Don't talk now." He snatched the keys off the floor, glanced at the office once again. "Can you unlock yourself?" He lightly tossed the keys to her. She caught them in one hand. "Watch me."

"Nope, got things to do. Hurry up now."

Rollie crossed the room to where the knee-shot brute was still writhing, making a low, mewling sound and holding his leg. The shot had made such a mess it wouldn't take much more for the thing to be severed.

He bent down and slammed the butt of the rifle against the man's temple. He didn't much care if it knocked the man out or killed him. Either way, he was shut up.

Grabbing the man's pistol, he returned to the closet. Tish was freed of the chains and was about to toss them on the floor.

"Nope," he said, and nodded toward Swearengen. Together, they manacled Swearengen and then Rollie looked at her. "You okay to walk out of here?"

She nodded. "Been better, but I'm good."

He handed her the knee-shot man's revolver. "We're leaving."

"Which way?" she said at the door to the hall.

"Right out the front."

She didn't slow, didn't hesitate, didn't question him.

Limping, Rollie snagged the chain in his right hand and dragged the weak, barely flailing Swearengen behind him.

Tish walked just ahead of him, a little unsteady but making it. The revolver gripped tight in her hand, she ignored her puffed face, her split lip, and her swollen left eye.

They shoved through a set of closed double doors and

the brightness, smoke, and din of the bar room washed over them. For a moment Tish hesitated, then she plowed ahead. She held her head up and with a defiant look defied anyone to approach her and her pistol.

Nobody did. They just parted like a drawn curtain and watched as the woman made for the front door. Following her, a bloodied and bruised man dragged another barely conscious and chained man behind.

"That Al?" somebody said.

Someone else replied. "Yeah."

"Should we help him?"

"Nah, Al always says to leave him be and mind our own business."

"Okay, then. He's the boss."

Out front, as they reached the top of the steps, Tish said, "What's the plan?"

About to reply he didn't know yet, Rollie suddenly knew what his plan was when he spied a dapper fellow in a striped suit and a tall, fawn hat standing at the bottom of the stairs.

"Rollie Finnegan," said the dapper man.

"Seth Bullock," acknowledged Rollie.

Chapter 34

On their way out, despite the appearance of his old friend, Rollie was tempted to toss a match into the now-wrecked guts of the Gem. He even said so, with as much of a dignified head nod as he could muster, before he descended the steps.

The infamous Deadwood lawman rocked back on his heels, hands in his trouser pockets, and hinted that torching the dive might be going a step too far. "Why, we could lose the entire downtown, and likely many lives with it. Then I'd have to hang you and your companions. And it looks to me as if you all have been through quite enough for one day. Besides that, I just got back to town and, boy, I'd rather not have to deal with a fire just now."

While Bullock spoke, Rollie and Tish descended the Gem's broad front steps, dragging the slowly reviving, chained Al Swearengen behind.

"Good to see you, Seth."

"Rollie, the same. What you got there?" He nodded toward Rollie's writhing, sputtering burden.

"Oh, this?" He lifted the chain and let it drop down again a couple of times. "Just doing a little vermin clean up."

"Justice . . ." said Swearengen.

"Hey." said Bullock, leaning down. "What's that?" He squinted. "Why, it's—" He squatted and, using a kerchief, raised the bar owner's head by the hair. "It is! Ol' Al. Say, looks to me you ought to be more careful walking down the stairs, Al. You've taken a nasty knock there."

"Ahh . . . Justice . . . where's the law? Unfair . . ." Swearengen squirmed and thrashed.

Bullock let the growling, groaning man's head smack down again, right into a heap of fresh horse apples. He considered stuffing the hanky into his pocket, but let it drop to drape on top of Swearengen's head, sneering at the filth of the man.

Rollie let go of the chains and he and Tish walked over by Bullock, who'd retreated a few paces.

"You know, Rollie, you've made yourself an enemy for life with that one," said Bullock, nodding toward the sputtering Swearengen.

Rollie shrugged. "What's one more?" He glanced about for Pops and his daughter, but failed to see them.

"I don't know," said the sheriff. "He's not like anything I've ever come across. He's relentless."

Rollie nodded. "And so am I."

Pops carried Zadie down the Gem's creaking side staircase. She seemed more boisterous and alert once they reached the night's fresh air. Halfway across the backyard, he set her down and kept an arm about her back, supporting her as they walked.

They made it to the sty without seeing anyone else— no sign of Margaret. The scene was still lit by the lantern's low, dull glow. The girl saw the two dead men and the bloodied mess that was the huge, dead boar inside the sty, but she said nothing.

Rollie's horse, Cap, was where he said it would be, along with Tish's mount. They were chomping and fidgety, but Pops was able to get Zadie up on Tish's horse, and he climbed aboard Cap, though it took him a couple of tries and a few more groans. Trying not to let his stiffening and wounds hamper him, he figured whatever he'd endured had been worth it.

Besides, they were likely nothing compared to what the girl had been through in her life. She'd tell him in time, he figured. And if she decided to never share that part of her life with him, that was fine, too. As far as Pops was concerned, their lives were beginning all over again, right now.

As they rounded the far side street to the west of the block, he heard the muffled blast and snap of gunfire from somewhere within the Gem.

He looked at Zadie, but she was still fighting the effects of whatever she'd been doped with. She looked to be winning, though staying in the saddle was a chore at the moment. He sorely wanted to go to Rollie's aid but wanted even more to not leave his daughter's side. Not now. Too soon. Far too soon for that. They were, after all, still in the damnable town.

And so they waited, sitting their horses in shadow just up the street from the Gem. His part of the rescue had been easy. He imagined all manner of foul situations in which his friend was now wedged, and hoped none were true.

After a good seven minutes or so, he slid out of the

saddle. Zadie seemed to sense his unrest and looked down at him, squinting in the dark. "I'll be okay here. I will."

Pops wanted to believe her and even took a few steps forward, though he still held Cap's reins. Then he heard the tell-tale sounds of a small group of people ahead. He stopped and listened and watched.

He saw a thin man with big moustaches in a dapper suit and hat approach the front of the Gem. Then he saw somebody, no, a couple of somebodies, make their way down the steps.

And one of them was dragging another person. The folks who'd walked down the steps turned in the light of a couple of lanterns hanging out front on hooked posts, and Pops saw Rollie's peppered hair and beard, and beside him a flash of red hair—Tish!

Pops let out a long-pent breath. Zadie appeared beside him, leaning against him a little. He held the reins of the other horse.

"That one on the ground," said Pops. "I think it's Swearengen."

Zadie leaned forward, looking. Then she nodded, looking revived, if but for a moment. "Let me kill him. Let me at him."

Pops' eyebrows rose. "What? No, no." He wrapped a big arm about her frail shoulders.

She offered a weak struggle. "Why won't you let me go?"

"No, no. Not now. We'll leave that pleasure for another person. It won't be long, I'd guess."

"Dammit! I want to kill him right now."

Pops looked at his daughter. "You ever killed another person? Hmm?"

She slowly shook her head. He saw the rage festering in her eyes.

"No, I didn't think so. Sure, I see pure hate in there, bright and sharp, like a freshly honed blade. But if you'd been used to killing, you'd be part dead inside yourself, nowhere near as shiny and bright. And while you have no doubt put up with a whole lot in your young life, you ain't dead inside. Not yet."

"I want to kill him."

Pops nodded. "You may want to and you may have good reason."

"I do!"

He nodded. "I ain't arguing that. But today is not the day for you to take that man down."

"Why?"

"Because first we need to get you away from here. You have to build yourself up. Get time and distance betwixt you and him." Pops looked deep into her eyes. "Trust me."

She finally relented, then said, "Your eyes . . . they aren't that clear and bright."

He looked away, back to the little crowd. "You're right. You don't want to go down the paths I been down. 'Cause part of me ain't never coming back. It's a devil's deal you make with yourself. But you"—he looked back to her—"you got the chance to change all that before it starts."

She stared back at Swearengen, then nodded.

"Good. Now let's go join our friends."

Chapter 35

Sheriff Seth Bullock tilted his hat back and surveyed the scene. He scratched his hair and rubbed his chin as if considering a weighty purchase. Finally, he said, "I'd be obliged, Rollie, if you and your companions would come to the house for a visit. My wife would sure enjoy the company of the ladies here and you and I can catch up on old times. If you don't mind me saying so, all of you look like you could use some rest and doctoring. And a square meal by my Martha wouldn't go amiss, I'll wager."

Rollie looked at Pops, who appeared to be about ready to drop in his tracks. Pops shrugged, a sure sign he was ready for a long bear of a nap. And the women looked equally as bereft of inclination.

Rollie nodded. "That would be fine, Seth. Just fine. But what about him?"

"Al?" he glanced over his shoulder as they walked toward the lawman's office. "Hell, he isn't going anywhere. He's too stupid and too greedy to skip town. I'll deal with him directly. The only thing he'll do is slink back inside his precious Gem and hole up and lick his wounds and curse at everyone."

After they retrieved all their gear and horses, true to his word, Seth and his wife, Martha, hosted them in high style. They were able to clean up, get doctored—Pops' boar punctures and slashes were nasty looking, but light enough he didn't require much stitching. Rollie's legs had taken a few rounds of shot, but he was able to pick them out without too much yowling and growling. Then they all enjoyed hot baths, in turn.

Later, as they sipped a first soothing whiskey, Rollie asked Seth about his lippy young deputy. Bullock nodded and scratched his head beneath his hat. "Yeah, the boy's an idiot, but he's got sand. It's hidden deep, but I think he has the makings of a decent deputy one day.

"The other one, though, the one you . . . disposed of up yonder in the hills, I had my doubts about him when I hired him on. Now that I know he was in the employ of Swearengen, or at least interested in dealing with him in a blackmail manner, well, it's a lesson I've learned the hard way. I'm shamed to say it affected you directly."

"It would have happened anyway, Seth. My life's been tall on fame and short on protection and truth for a while now. All the more reasons to make for home. No need to subject you to any more unwanted killings and treachery than necessary while we're here."

"Stay as long as you like," said Martha, setting down a nearly whole pie in the center of the table. "If Seth had given me more of a warning I might have been able to make something more elegant than that stew and dumplings and elk shank. And this pie, oh, it's not nearly enough for you all."

"It's just fine, ma'am," said Pops. "In fact, I've never

had the equal of such a meal. You truly are a life saver. I was about ready to expire."

The compliment reddened Mrs. Bullock's cheeks and she patted Pops on the shoulder as she whisked back toward the kitchen where she was holding court with the ladies. She'd been helping them doctor their wounds, plying them with food, and giving them what garments she thought they might require.

Pops kept an eye on the women through the propped-open door. Rollie understood without needing an expla-nation: His pard had lost his daughter for years, indeed had thought her dead. He sure wasn't going to lose sight of her now that she was in the other room.

She was still a little fuzzy and forlorn, likely due to malnutrition and neglect and whatever drug Swearengen doped his girls with. Rollie suspected, too, that she'd have a time in weaning off such vile things. Yes, the father-and-daughter reunion would be a long, slow one.

"High time I did something more about Swearengen than I've been able to do. I've been so short-handed and he's only grown more powerful. But no more." Bullock's color had risen in his cheeks, and Rollie didn't think it was just from the fine whiskey he'd poured each of them. "No more."

"Be glad to help, Seth." Rollie sipped.

"Thank you, Rollie, but no, you've done plenty. That's part of why I was out of town. I was recruiting new men—real, seasoned hands to help me quell the rising tide of filth in Deadwood. I'm representing the people here and the good ones have pledged funds for more lawmen.

"We're building a good community in Deadwood. A place with schools and churches, and most importantly, with families who want to sink roots and make a go of it. I won't have to put up with Swearengen's shenanigans much longer. Nor those of anyone like him."

Pops nodded. "And the new men? When are they due?"

"One rides in tomorrow, then the other two come in three, maybe four days. That's when the real fun begins."

"Well, if you don't need us, we'll leave you in peace tomorrow morning. We can camp in the barn, if that suits you."

"Better yet," said Seth. "I'll bed down here in the downstairs with you gents and the three ladies can have the upstairs to themselves."

"We heard that," said Tish.

"And?" said Rollie.

"And it's fine with us," said Martha.

Pops and Rollie knew this was largely because of Pops and his obvious need to not be separated from his newly found child.

"Good." Bullock smacked his hands together. "Then it's settled." He lowered his voice. "One more quick dram of the good stuff and then we'll wrap it up. You all look as tired as Methuselah's horse."

"Mr. Bullock," said his wife from the kitchen. "I believe you've had enough of the whiskey for tonight."

"No, no, my dove. I do not believe we have." He smiled at the fellows, though as Seth poured, Rollie saw that the lawman's ears had reddened.

All they heard from the kitchen was a quiet "Hmm."

The next morning, Martha fed them all a hearty breakfast of back bacon, biscuits, gravy, steaks, eggs, ham, fried thick-slice potatoes, and pots of hot, black coffee. They dawdled and chatted for a while longer, putting off the inevitable, then they made their way to the barn and saddled their mounts.

Bullock made a gift to Zadie of a fine merle mare he'd been boarding since the owner, a drunk gambler, had come to a bad end in a knife fight. The horse had been appropriated as payment for the town's funeral and burial services. He allowed as how he was a high-ranking town official, it was well within his capacity to make a gift of recompense to someone maligned within town limits. He drew up a transfer of ownership at the kitchen table and had each person present sign as a witness, then handed it to Zadie.

She teared up a bit and he apologized for the terrible time she'd had, saying the horse was far too little and far too late, but he hoped it would do her some good. He also promised he and his men would finally rein in Al Swearengen.

With many thanks all around, Rollie, Pops, Zadie, and Tish mounted up out front of the Bullock home. Martha left the house last, lugging two sizable canvas totes, and handed them to her husband. "Hand those up to the men."

"What's this?" said Rollie.

"Food. You men can stand to back away from the dinner table now and again, but these young women need good food if they're to put up with the likes of you two."

Another round of thanks volleyed about the group, then smoothing his reins, Rollie said, "Well, it was good to see you again, Seth." He nodded toward Seth's wife. "And you as well, ma'am."

"And you, Mr. Finnegan," she said, dabbing a hanky at her eyes.

Bullock patted Cap's neck and stepped backward. "Do me a favor, Finnegan."

"What's that?"

"Stay the hell out of Deadwood!"

Rollie grinned. "Ha! With pleasure."

Everyone offered the others easy waves, then rode out, westward toward the far mountains and home. Boar Gulch.

A few minutes later, Tish said, "I thought you said he was your friend."

"He is. Why?"

"The way you parted, him telling you to stay out of town."

"He's right. Doesn't need the likes of me there." Rollie hid a grin. "I'm a menace."

"Oh."

"Shoot," said Pops. "He ought to try being Rollie's business partner."

Up ahead, where he'd ridden to take up the scout position, Rollie smiled as he tugged out his briar pipe and packed the bowl. Pops would keep an eye on their backtrail for a while and Tish and Zadie were chatting.

He'd spell Pops in a bit. Just now he wanted to enjoy a few moments of quiet before the next batch of the world's ill-tempered and warp-minded fools got in his way.

Chapter 36

Hours later they nudged midday, but given their late start, at least by Rollic's standard's, they decided by unspoken mutual consent to ride on and not worry about stopping to eat. They'd fallen into an easy, slow rhythm, considering they had many days of riding ahead of them. The slow part came about because each was ailing from various afflictions, though physically, Pops seemed to be worse off than any of them.

He'd not told Rollie what he'd been through before the pig sty, but he reckoned it would come out eventually. Such things tended to.

Rollie and Pops had been trading off scout and drag positions. Drag was especially concerning since neither man was convinced Swearengen, having taken such a public beating, was inclined to let them go unmolested. The two women were more or less sandwiched between.

Rollie was pleased to see it riled Tish. He hoped that meant the young woman, who'd been unusually quiet since departing Deadwood, was regaining some of her former spunk. Finally she rode up beside him and cleared her throat.

"Tish," he said, glancing at her.

"I've been thinking I haven't properly thanked you. I owe you my life."

He shook his head. "Not hardly."

"No, it's true. You were right, I never should have gone against what you said. I almost ended up—" She glanced behind at Zadie, who was riding in emotionless silence beside her father. "I almost ended up like all the other women who get to know Swearengen." She shook her head at her own folly.

Rollie finally said, "There's nothing wrong with cutting across the grain sometimes. Makes life harder for you of course, and tougher to cut, but sometimes you get the best results."

"I'm not certain I understand you."

He smiled. "Let's say I can't fault you for your ambition."

"Just because I'm a woman doesn't mean I can't be a Pinkerton agent."

"Course not. But you can't ignore the value of experience. Sometimes you have to let life season you a bit."

"I don't have time to wait for that to happen."

"Who said anything about waiting? In my experience," said Rollie, packing his pipe bowl. He smiled. "There's that word again. In my experience, you have to keep doing what you think is the right thing to do at any given moment. Sometimes you'll make mistakes, hopefully not those that cost lives, but if you do, you do. Nothing can be done about it except to learn from it and don't do it again. Any of this make sense?"

She nodded. "I think so. What you're saying is to keep

moving forward, chase your dreams, but know that true experience comes with time."

"Sure, yeah. That'll do."

They rode in near-silence, side by side, Tish getting the sense that she'd ventured far enough down the Rollie apology hole.

Chapter 37

Riding westward late in the second day, they neared the foothills of the Big Horns. As if by mutual agreement, the quartet drifted to a slowdown, then to a full stop beside a pleasant green glade that sloped to a clear stream.

"Perfect," said Pops, walking his horse deeper in and finally sliding out of the saddle a dozen feet from the water.

The rest followed suit, relief softening their faces. Pleased they had ample food left in the stores Martha Bullock had sent with them, it was enough for several days yet.

With little talk, each fell to the tasks they'd tended the night before. But the mood was not grim. Horses were watered, fed, rubbed down, and picketed.

A bit later, Zadie said, "Anybody up for biscuits?"

Pops swiveled his head around. "You know how to make biscuits?"

"'Course I do. Not only that, it's Mama's recipe. Not sure if I have the ingredients, but I'll do what I can with what I have."

"Oh, girl, don't tease me now. Your mama was, hands-down, the best cook who ever drew a breath. If anybody could come close, I expect it'll be you."

"She was a good cook," said Zadie. "You remember her sweet potato pie?"

"Ohhh," Pops groaned. "Do I ever. He closed his eyes and shook his head slowly. "I could fall over in a heap a happy man right now if only I had a taste of that pie one more time."

"Well that decides it," said Zadie. "I'm never going to make it."

"What do you mean?" said Pops, eyeing his daughter hard.

"I just got you back. You think I'd dare risk killing you with a pie? I don't care how good it is, I won't make it."

"I take it back, then," said Pops, almost pleading. "Don't tell me you have that recipe in your head, too?"

Zadie nodded slowly. "I won't guarantee it, but I think I can come close. 'Course, it'll never be as good as hers."

"It'll be yours, though," said Tish. "Maybe you could show me some things about cooking. I'm hopeless in that area."

"What do you eat in Chicago?" said Zadie, eyes wide.

Tish shrugged. "I eat at restaurants, mostly."

"Oh, it's been ages since I've been taken out to dine."

"Then you should come to the city with me. We can dine on our own, any time we want!"

Rollie set his saddle down in a heap not far from a grown-in fire ring. He saw a look of slight alarm on his pard's face regarding that last comment but knew Pops was too polite to say what he was feeling. It would no doubt be something about how he just got his daughter back, and please don't run off just yet.

As Pops walked stiff-legged down to the water, rubbing the stiffness from his back, Rollie walked up beside him. "This riding takes a lot out of a man," he said, shucking his hat and bending low to scoop water to bathe his face.

In a few moments, Pops did the same.

Rollie glanced over at the young women. "They seem to have hit it off."

"Yeah," said Pops, uncertain how to feel about the development.

"How long you make it before we're home?" It was a question asked for the sake of changing the topic.

"Oh, some days yet."

Pops nodded, knowing the answer.

"Time to gather firewood. I bet it's going to be a nippy one tonight."

"How do you know?" said Pops.

"I can feel it inside. In my bones, I guess," said Rollie.

"Now you sound like Wolfbait."

Rollie recoiled in mock horror. "Oh, say it ain't so."

Pops laughed for the first time in a day. "Come to think of it, those eyebrows of yours have been looking a little bushy. And you could use a haircut. Unless of course you're going to compete with him for the crustiest, mangiest old long-hair devil this side of the Pacific." Barely nimble enough, he dodged Rollie's bear paw of a fist as it sailed in for a clout.

The moment of levity broke the spell of quiet lethargy that had draped over the little group of travelers. They all perked up and set to their tasks with renewed vigor.

"Where are those biscuits?" said Rollie, arranging everyone's bedrolls while Pops tended to the blaze. Then he whispered low, "Hey, Pops."

Pops looked over.

"I found a bottle of something fine Seth must have slipped into my saddlebags."

"Funny thing," said Pops. "I found one in mine, too. I like those friends of yours, Finnegan."

"Yep, true blue. What say we make sure that stuff hasn't gone off, riding in the hot sun and all?"

"I believe these bones and muscles and tusk marks of mine could use a dose of . . . what's Wolfbait call it?"

Rollie smiled. "*His medicinals*."

"Yep, that's the stuff."

They sampled the first bottle and agreed it was as fine as the stuff they'd shared with the Deadwood lawman two nights before.

"Why are you two giggling like little schoolgirls?" said Tish, helping Zadie with spooning out biscuit dough.

"Never you mind," said Pops, unaccustomed sternness weighing his voice.

"Now, now," said Zadie. "You all need to keep the mood happy or these biscuits are liable to turn out flat and hard."

"Are you serious?" said Tish.

"'Course she is," said Pops. "Learned that from her Mama. Never allowed a cross word spoken while food was being prepared. It tends to sour the taste." He smiled at the memory. "I'd all-but forgotten that."

"Not me," said Zadie. "I remember a whole lot about those times." She was silent a few moments, then said, "It's what kept me going."

"Me, too," said Pops.

The evening passed in amicable company, a small band of friends as close and closer in some ways than any friends or family could ever be, pulled together through the grimness of hardship. Chatter about the campfire rose and fell as the few drinks of whiskey smoothed away the lingering rough edges and evening slowly crept upon them.

"What we need to do now," said Pops, giving over to a full-on yawn, arms wide and head thrown back, "is get a good night's sleep." He rubbed his face. "I'll take the first watch." He set his hands on his knees and made to rise.

"No way is that going to happen while I'm drawing breath," said Tish.

"Now who sounds like Wolfbait?" said Rollie.

"Hey," said Tish. "Don't forget I know who he is. And that's not necessarily a flattering thing to say to a person, especially to a woman."

"Who's this Wolf-whoever you keep mentioning, anyway?"

"Oh, you'll like him," said Pops. "He grows on you."

"Yeah," said Rollie. "Like one of those odd things that grows on trees."

"A fungus?" said Zadie.

Rollie snapped his fingers. "That's it."

"I can't wait." She grimaced and cleared away the last of the bowls and spoons and cups.

Some minutes later, after each person had attended to their nightly washing and needs, they settled in. Rollie grumbled as he tucked himself into his blankets.

He had lost an argument with Tish and agreed to take second watch. Zadie was game, but had no idea how to go about keeping an eye on the camp. In the end, she sat up with Tish on a rock halfway between the campfire and the river. Hipshot, the horses were at rest some paces away.

Soon, the only things the two women heard were the

sounds of two old silvertip boar grizzlies sawing away at the mass of sleep stacked high before them.

"You think they'd just up and die, snoring so hard like that." Zadie shook her head. "Amazing."

They sat trading stories in a low whisper. Finally Zadie yawned, looking to Tish an awful lot like her father—same head thrown back and arms wide pose—but no accompanying big yawning sound came from her.

"Zadie, get some sleep. I'll wake Rollie in a while."

"I'm so tired, I won't argue with you."

Tish sat upright, sipping a tepid cup of coffee and paying careful attention to the sounds of the night—rustlings in the undergrowth and duff of some night rodent, maybe a snake hunting a mouse. Far off to the northeast, the plaintive, wavering cry of a pack of wolves echoed down to their foothills encampment.

An owl hooted now and again, not raising a response. Eventually, she heard it no longer and assumed it had moved on, looking for kinship elsewhere.

She wondered if she, too, might end up doing the same. She'd not had much in her life she could call friendships, even fewer close encounters with men of the sort she'd consider more than companionships. She'd long suspected she was not suited to such things, and events of late had not helped convince her otherwise.

A sound—a snort, perhaps, not unlike a horse's, reached her, cutting through her thoughts. It was not from their mounts, who still stood placidly not far away in the scant moonlight.

Her thoughts turned to the dangers Rollie had told her of on their journey to Deadwood—the Sioux were thick in these parts, angered, and she could not blame them a bit. Their homelands were forever being gnawed away by ever-increasing numbers of white settlers, vagabonds, and ne-er-do-wells looking for whatever it was people look for in life. Other threats, of course, were road agents, with whom she'd had plenty of experience since venturing West, then eastward trailing Rollie and Pops.

There—she heard it again. Slowly she unbent her legs stiff from the crossed position they'd been in the past hour. Wearing her camp moccasins, she soft-footed back to the barely glowing campfire.

Zadie was wrapped tight in blankets and mired in a deep sleep. Rollie was far into sleep. The same with Pops. The two men had risked all and then some to rescue Pops' daughter, and then her, too. Good men, together filling a place in her mind, much like the father she had forever wished she'd had.

She had to wake up Rollie. And with that, she suspected Pops and Zadie would awaken, too. She hated to do it. Maybe what she'd heard was nothing at all. If so, she'd feel like a fool. *Oh, what to do?*

"What's wrong?" came Rollie's low, straight whisper.

She felt relief as she bent low beside him. "I'm sorry . . . it's probably nothing."

He sat up in one move, silently, no groaning, as if he were a kid. "What did you hear?" he whispered.

"Sounded like a horse, I think. Far off, that way." She gestured toward the west.

"Good. Okay. I'll stay up. You can get rest if you want to. Thanks."

"I'll stay up, too."

Rollie nodded. That was fine with him. If it turned out to be something they needed to worry about, Tish would be useful in waking the others, getting everybody alert and ready. Well, Pops wouldn't take much prompting. He was an old war horse, about as ready at any given moment in life for a threat as anyone Rollie had ever met.

He'd nearly slept in his boots, in part because he'd been too sleepy to pull them off, but then had eased them off. He regretted the move, though his feet were thankful for the few hours of respite. He tugged them back on, seating his heels with the customary thunk.

Tish waited for him to carry his gun belt and rifle away from the fire and amble over to her, halfway to the horses. Then she pointed toward the west again. "I think it came from that way."

Rollie nodded, finished buckling his belt, and paused, checking his gun. He heard something, too. "Good ear," he said to her.

She did not even try to suppress a smile. In the short time she had known him, it had been a rare moment for Rollie to pay her a compliment. Indeed, she'd only caused him headache, so even a small amount of usefulness felt good to offer him.

"It's a horse," he said. "Some ways off, but the breeze is carrying this way, and the land slopes toward us. Nothing to interfere with sound."

They waited in silence.

In the moonlight, his profile looked just about what she had expected—hoped—he'd be all those years of hearing of his exploits. He was the very reason she had wanted to be a detective in the first place, and specifically a Pinkerton "man." And there she was, on a case, sort of, sitting in the dark, waiting for . . . something to happen. With the legend himself, Stoneface Finnegan.

"So," he said. "Is it what you imagined?"

"What?" she said, surprised he once again seemed to be thinking similar thoughts as she.

"Traveling out West, working undercover. All of it."

"Ah"—she shrugged—"I think I might feel differently if I hadn't made such a mess of things."

"Nonsense. Do you think anybody who's ever worked in this line hasn't made a hash of it now and again? Happens all the time," he said, waving her wincing look away with a dismissive hand. "The things I've done and not done that I should have done could fill a book. Maybe two."

"Now that I doubt." She smiled, appreciating his attempt to make her feel better. It didn't much work, but it was kind of him. "What do you think that sound was?"

"Well, as I said, I think it's a horse. Whether it's a lone warrior, a hunter, a trapper, a drummer with a wagon, or a whole group of such, I don't know. If it came from the road ahead, they might well be heading this way. Makes sense, as riding anywhere but a traveled lane in the dark is risky at night. And even then, it's not something I prefer to do. Nor would anyone with a brain."

The rest of that early morning passed in the same fashion—occasional discussions about his work, the trip, even Al Swearengen and why he didn't kill the man, even though he'd been given ample opportunity to do so.

"I wanted to. No, that's not quite true. I don't go around wanting to kill people. But as much as some folks deserve to be put down for their foul deeds, I was there for other reasons. And I made a promise to someone."

"A promise?"

"Yeah, seems silly now, but at the time I just wanted to

get in there and help Pops' daughter. And find you, of course."

Tish blushed in the dark. "I'm sorry about running off like that. I wanted to prove to you and to myself that I was able to do that sort of work. It was so foolish."

"Well, you're right on that score. It was foolish."

She'd admitted it, but it still stung to hear him say it.

"But it ended okay." They sat in silence for a moment more, then Rollie said, "So? Did you?"

"Did I what?"

"Prove to yourself whatever it was you needed to prove?"

"I don't know, to be honest. I had a better notion of it before Deadwood than I do now."

"Should be the opposite," said Rollie. "You've learned something, I think. That should help with whatever decision you need to make."

"You're right. Yeah." She chewed on that a while.

Nothing more was spoken for a long time, then finally dawn began to crack the skyline behind them. As it always did, the new day's light crept up in silence and gave itself away only by the faint purple glow of predawn.

Zadie rose first. Nearly as silent as a cat, only the slight rustling of her blankets as she folded them gave her away. As she walked into the nearby rabbit brush to relieve herself, Pops woke.

"Morning, all," he said. "Nobody woke me. That's not right. We all need to take our turn at watch."

"I know," said Rollie. "My fault. I'll fight you later."

"Okay," said Pops. "Keep your blows from the neck up. Rest of me is too tired to put up with much else."

"You got it," said Rollie.

"Do you two always talk to each other like that?" said

Zadie, returning to the campfire with a small armload of wood.

"Ha," said Tish. "Sometimes they fight."

"Just to make it clear—you two do like each other, right? I mean, you are friends and all, no?"

"I tolerate him," said Pops.

"Likewise," said Rollie, neither man smiling.

"Cold," said Tish, rubbing her arms and rummaging in her bag for another layer to pull on.

She ended up doing what Zadie had done—pulled a blanket about herself like a big shawl. Pops and Rollie had done the same. Not much was said while they all waited for the coffee to boil.

At long last, after they'd attended to everything they could think of—the horses, the bushes, packing gear, and unpacking breakfast food—the sharp, bitter smell of coffee on the boil filled the air of the little campsite.

They'd settled down to plates of hot food and the quiet that comes with a meal being enjoyed when the sound of thundering hooves closed in toward them from the west.

Rollie was up in a moment, with Pops close behind. Both men had weapons raised and ready.

It was a single horse, and riding at a pretty fair clip.

"Tish!" Rollie barked, nodding toward Zadie, who was beginning to walk toward where Rollie and Pops had taken up posts up the trail.

Pops glanced back. "Back, Zadie, like the man said. We can't risk you two being seen out here. I know how that sounds, but I'd as soon make you angry with me as have owlhoots getting the wrong idea."

From below and past the horses, a man's voice shouted, "Too late, friend!"

Rollie and Pops half turned, hesitant to give over fully to the fresh danger and turn their backs on the sound of a horse closing in fast.

The man behind the voice was walking toward them from out of the stream—from the west, just like the approaching rider. He held his right hand up in an open-handed wave as friendly as the grin on his face. His left hand, also raised, held the reins of a horse plotting out of the stream, water spraying off its hooves.

"Who are you?" snarled Rollie, raising the rifle to his shoulder and training it on the man.

The man held his grin and kept walking closer. Glancing at the women off to his left by the picketed horses, he touched his raised right fingertips to his hat brim. "Ladies." He nodded. "Allow me to introduce myself, folks. I am Mace. Mace Matson." He walked closer.

Pops glanced at him but kept his eyes on the road. In a moment, he said, loud enough for Rollie to hear him. "Here comes the rider."

"Okay." Rollie didn't look over from watching this newcomer who'd just introduced himself.

"Now, now, gentlemen. Oh, and ladies." Matson looked again at Tish and Zadie, and let his eyes linger a moment "Seems to me you all look as though you've come upon hard times. Unless you enjoy whomping on each other now and again. I mean no disrespect to you. Just an innocent observation. But you have to admit you all are mighty banged up."

"What do you want?" said Rollie, not lowering his gun a bit. He heard the approaching rider rein up and heard the horse stomping, breathing slightly hard. It told him the horse had run a short distance.

"What's the hurry, stranger?" said Pops, the words sounding even, but the edge to his voice was cold and direct.

The rider said nothing. Silent as he slid out of the saddle and stood twenty feet away from Pops. He stared at him, holding only his reins. He wore a single gun rig but made no motion to reach for it. The same with the man who called himself Mace, who continued to walk closer.

"That's far enough, mister," said Rollie.

"Okay then." The man halted and maintained his pose, hands up, and still he smiled. "I'll tell you what, though. I have a habit, some folks say it's annoying, of smiling too much. Taking life far less serious than most folks you are likely to meet. How's it look to you?"

"How's what look?" said Rollie, not moving the gun, confident Pops had the other one covered. He was trying to work out why this man came up on them from the river below them, and the other one along the road, both from the same direction. One riding to beat hell, the other relaxed as if he were dropping by camp for a cup of coffee.

He was starting to suspect the man on the road was a distraction so this joker named Mace could sneak up on them. But something was still off.

Then he saw what it was.

As he was partially facing their horses and Tish and Zadie, he saw slight movement behind them in the trees. He caught Tish's eye and nodded toward the movement. Armed and as ready as she could be, Tish turned with caution as if to check the nearest horse. She murmured something low to Zadie, who froze a little, then relaxed with more whispering from Tish.

That's when Pops said, "More from the east, and across the trail, too."

Rollie tamped down a groan and refocused his half glance back at the Mace character.

The man was chuckling and nodding, his eyebrows high. "See? Maybe it's just me, but I have a whole lot to be happy about, you know?" The man continued moving forward.

Rollie said, "I told you to stay put. Unless you want me to part your hair."

"Oh, Mr. Finnegan, why so surly?" Matson's mirth dissipated, replaced with a look of concern. "Yes, indeed. I know who you are. I know who your friend is, too. As a matter of fact, I know about all of you. How, you may wonder?" He nodded in four directions slowly, casually—once at the thundering rider from the west, past Pops toward the far side of the road, where two riders were spaced apart and guns bristling and aimed at Rollie, Pops, and the women, then another nod toward the east where a line of riders approached through the sparse trees, all with guns drawn, advancing at a walk.

One man looked away for a moment to whip a stream of chaw juice outward. It almost caught the fellow to his left.

"As I say, me and the boys here, we just paid a visit to a lovely little rat hole in the mountains by the name of Boar Gulch."

Rollie and Pops stiffened visibly at the mention of their town.

"Now, now, don't you worry none. Last time we looked on it, granted that was as we were riding on out of there, but most of the town was all still there. Most of the people, too. Some of them might not have fared so well in standing up to us, though. You see?"

The first and abiding thought, one Rollie had had for months and months, even a couple of years, came pounding back at him—by staying put and being selfish, he had once again brought vicious amounts of harm to innocent people. For it was obvious that this man was after him. Had to be.

Oddly, the stranger resumed walking toward Rollie.

"One more step," said Rollie, thumbing back the hammer, "and you'll be chewing gristle from the back of your head."

"Oh, I don't think so," said Mace, his smarmy smile spread wide. "Boys?"

A chorus of sharp steely clicks and snaps echoed through the otherwise silent camp. Rollie glanced about. They were surrounded by at least a half dozen hard-bitten, raw-nerved strangers. All with guns aimed at them, aimed at him.

Matson walked up and stood in front of him, forcing Rollie to raise his rifle barrel.

"You're crowding me, mister. That never ends well for folks who do that to me."

"And from the looks of that bruising on your face, and from the mess the rest of you are in, I'd say you've been crowded plenty lately." Matson shook his head, a knowing grin on his face. "So, you just come from Deadwood, did you?"

Rollie's eyes never so much as twitched.

Without waiting for an answer, the man continued. "Yeah, those fools in your little town blabbed and blubbered, they surely did. I do recall hearing them say you were headed toward Deadwood with a woman on some sort of rescue

mission. Huh. I'm seeing two men and two women,
Strikes me you two men either got yourself good taste in
woman flesh as well as horseflesh, or the women are
blind. Or beholden to you." Matson smiled as if he'd just
revealed the wonderful punch line of a joke and was waiting for his audience to catch on.

Through clenched teeth, Pops said, "You shut your
mouth right now."

"Oh," said Matson. "Sensitive soul, huh? Well"—his
smile turned into a sneer and he leveled a reptilian gaze
across the group—"I expect we can beat that out of you.
What little is left of you, anyway. And this one"—he nodded
toward Rollie—"I'll have your head, thank you kindly.
Attached to the rest of you, that's just too much bother
and, well, too much headache to deal with. Especially not
when I have to lug it all the way back to Denver City for
my reward."

The silent man grunted.

"Oh, my manners, Drake. Yes, I meant to say *our*
reward."

Quick as a snake strike, Rollie snugged the rifle to his
shoulder.

Mace Matson didn't move. But all about them, one by
one, in rapid succession, the metallic clicks and pops of
weapons being readied to shoot filled the otherwise silent,
still air of the otherwise-pleasant campsite.

"No, no, no. That's not the way this is going to play
out, pal. Not by a long shot. For a supposedly clever fellow,
you don't seem to understand we have you surrounded.
In a word, Mr. Finnegan, you're in trouble."

"Three," said Rollie.

"Huh?"

"You said 'in a word'. *You're in trouble* is three words."

The man smiled once more. "Why, so it is."

Rollie saw the man's ears redden as a little color bloomed up onto his face.

"Hand me that rifle."

Rollie held for a moment.

"You really want me to let them open up on you all? Happy to do it."

Something told Rollie this character might just follow through. He'd bide his time. He'd been in tighter scrapes, after all. He let go of the rifle as Matson's hand closed about the fore stock. Then Matson circled to Rollie's side and slid out his Schofield.

The silent man Matson had called Drake also relieved Pops of his weapons.

"Now," said Mace. "You two men will get back to your little fire and sit far enough apart I don't have to worry you'll play slap-and-tickle with each other, okay?"

A minute later found Pops and Rollie once more about their campfire. The near-silent man bound their hands behind them.

"But you women," said Matson. "Not yet. You just stay where you're at."

Rollie choked back his rage and tried a different approach. "How long did you grace our little town with your presence?"

"Ha!" Matson seemed genuinely amused. "What you really mean is, did we kill everybody in that dung heap. Am I right?"

Rollie said nothing, and continued to stare at him.

"Oh, we may have knocked a few heads. A little of that goes a long way. You'd be surprised at how quick your so–called friends gave you up. You know, I get the sense they are tired of you bringing down all manner of headache on them. What do you think of that?"

Rollie straightened as if stretching his back, but he kept his eyes on Matson. "I think you are a jackass. And these inbred messes you brought along are more of the same."

That got to him.

"You're in no position to lip off to me, man. I could kill you right now and be done with it. Save myself the headache later."

"Go ahead," said Rollie.

Tish spoke in a near-closed-mouth whisper. "Stop antagonizing him."

Rollie didn't look at her.

"Well now," said Matson. "It ain't only pretty, save for that bruised-up face, but it can speak, too." He guided his horse around Rollie and stood about five feet from Tish. "What say you and me take a walk."

"Not on your life."

"Oh, it ain't my life we'll be waging on. It's yours. And theirs." He nodded toward the rest of Tish's party. "You see, I just got an idea. They come to me like that. I'm what you call a thinker. Somebody others can't help but fall in line behind."

Tish stared. "He was right. You are a jackass."

Rollie smiled slightly at that.

Matson didn't. His face grew tight and grim once more. "Now, now, pretty lady—"

The gunshot was quick and sharp, a crack in the silent,

late-day sky. It carried past them and felled a branch, the only victim in its wake.

"What are you doing?" shouted Mace.

"That black girl run off!"

"Well, get her back! But not dead, you idiot. Well, what are you waiting for? Get on your horse and ride, dammit! Get her back before she's gone for good! I will not tolerate failure, you hear me?"

The two men making for their horses looked at each other but didn't respond. Mace sighed. "One more time, boys. You hear me?"

"Yes, sir," they said simultaneously.

"Good. Now go! And bring her back alive and unhurt."

As they scampered off, Mace walked over to Pops and kicked his boot sole. "What do you think of that? You didn't raise that girl to have respect, did you?"

Pops looked at the fire and said nothing.

Nobody said a thing, so Mace kept on. "Now don't any of the rest of you go getting ideas about running off. There ain't no way that's going to help any of you. Matter of fact, since she can't have gotten far, I think we ought to give her a little lesson, don't you think, Drake?"

The silent man shrugged as if nothing much mattered to him.

"Drake, bring that red-haired devil over here and tie her up now. Can't risk her trotting off, too. Not yet, anyway."

Drake stared at Matson for a long moment, then did his bidding. Tish complied, but stiffly. She was no match for the dour man, however, and he jerked her limbs as if he were roping a calf.

With no warning, Mace held his hands to his mouth and shouted, "Oh, girly! I know you can hear me! You don't come dragging yourself back to camp right now, I'm going to commence to laying down some serious pain on your friends!" He looked at Pops. "And I believe I'll begin with your pappy!"

Pops returned the stare, a hint of surprise on his face.

"Yeah," said Mace. "That's right. I knowed you was her pap. I mean, aside from the obvious, there's something about you two. A family thing. I had that with a sister of mine once, but she's dead. Long time now, gnawing dirt for nigh on twenty years. But you and her, why, I reckon she'd do just about anything for her pap, am I right?"

Pops looked away, then shouted, "Don't do it! Keep running! Go!" He had just enough time to get out that last word before Matson drove his boot into Pops' right leg. Right into a long, particularly nasty gash from the boar. Pops sucked in a hard breath and jerked his leg away. He reached to grab it but his bound hands threw him off balance and he flopped to the side.

"Knock it off!" shouted Tish. "You want a fight? Untie me, and I'll give you a fight."

"Now, now, little darlin', that's more like it. Been waiting for you to come around." Matson fetched a bottle from his open saddlebag and popped the cork, never taking his eyes from the redheaded woman. He approached her but stayed just out of range of her boots, even though her legs were bound at the ankle. "I expect we'll tangle, all right. Was waiting for a little later, but now'll do. Won't need to untie you, though."

"That's enough," said Rollie, who had been silent through the latest commotion. He sat stiff and upright and his gaze locked onto Mace's eyes.

The outlaw seemed held as if in a brief trance. Then he smiled. "I reckon I'll do what I need to, Stoneface."

"Come here," said Rollie, not even blinking. "Now."

"What? You ordering me about, mister? Why, you're not even a lawman. Come to think on it, you never really were. Being a Pink man don't count for much of anything, now does it, Drake?"

The silent man didn't respond, just gazed at the revived fire.

Rollie repeated his order. "I said come here. Now."

The brash, boldness intrigued Mace, and he smiled at his fellow skunks in turn, then offered a deferential side nod toward Rollie. "All right, then. I expect I have it in me to indulge a soon-to-be-dead man with a last, if annoying, wish."

He stepped over a couple of feet, then circled the fire, thinking better of coming up on Rollie from the front, where his legs were tied, stretched out before him.

Rollie didn't move, didn't flinch, didn't so much as shift his gaze from staring at his own boots.

An odd quiet settled over the cluster of people, none save for Mace looking as if they were enjoying themselves. Rollie's raw ordering of the boss of the situation had stilled the gathered like a hard, sharp slap across the face. Even the fire complied, hushing for a moment the crackle and snap of flames hungry to be fed.

Mace made his way around the outer edge of the ring of men and approached Rollie. Standing over his prime captive and behind his right shoulder Matson failed to notice the rawhide thongs he'd made certain had been so tightly wrapped about Rollie's wrists were severed and flopped.

The cause sat nested in Rollie's tight, right fist, his trusty old friend, the Barlow folding blade he'd carried with him for years. It had sliced ropes, feed sacks, fish bellies, deer paunch, steaks, apples, men, snakes, fingernails, and his own hair. Always honed and oiled, it nested in a trouser pocket, sometimes a vest pocket, sometimes a winter coat pocket, but *always* at hand.

"I said . . . come here."

Mace once more acted as predictably as Rollie knew he would. He'd seen hundreds of such preening jackasses over the years, dealt with his share and then some, and never did they deviate from how they wanted to, needed to, act. Always with the curiosity of a dog, led by their sniffer and lack of brain. Mace Matson was no exception.

After a few moments in which he smiled again at his few fellow fools, he bent low, confident all was as he expected, as he had ordered it to be. Confident Rollie "Stoneface" Finnegan was bound and rendered useless and near death by him and no one else. "Yeah, Pink Man? What have you got for me? Huh?"

"This." Rollie growled low and spun even lower. Rolling with it, he lashed out with his flexed right fist, the open, razor-keen Barlow seeking—and finding—soft flesh. The angle of his swing afforded enough power the blade slipped through Matson's boot leather, sagged gray wool sock, and severed, neat as you please, the man's hamstring before briefly embedding in a bone that should never have tasted the raw intrusion of steel.

But it did.

For a brief flash of time, nothing seemed to have been disturbed. Then a thin, high scream seeped from Mace's lips. His head whipped backward as he collapsed, nearly on top of Rollie, who had already rolled back to his left, slashing toward his own boots and at the ropes binding him at the ankle.

Still taking advantage of the attention Mace was drawing to himself by screaming and clawing at his injured leg and writhing in a squirm of agony, Rollie pulled off another jerking lunge.

Save for grunts and huffing, the dervishlike Finnegan worked in silence, burying his blade over and over again into the neck of the gagging, trembling Matson. Rollie delivered four clean, punching slices, each releasing a hot gout of blood, spraying from the shocked man's neck meat.

By then the entire camp was a-boil with commotion. Seeing what was about to happen Pops had tensed then pulled himself low like a log and rolled into the nearest captor, knocking the man backward. The man lost his grip on his cocked revolver and it hit a rock, snapping off a bullet that drilled like a sizzling lead bee up through another of the captor's knees. It exited through the top of the man's thigh before shoving once more into the same hunched man's body high in his bread basket, severing something vital deep inside the heart muscle. Then it whipped up and out through the man's shoulder and off into the air like a single-minded bee determined to keep traveling.

The second Rollie began his fateful knife-wielding lunge, Tish bent to the side and snatched up a double-fist-size river rock, still plenty warm from the fire. On her right side, the brooding, silent Drake had been bent on one knee, too close to her for too long. He'd had one hand on his left knee, the other alternated between resting on the handle of his gun and his fingertips brushing against her side, sometimes along her hair.

She felt it, flinched with each light touch, and gritted her teeth tighter and tighter until she was certain her teeth would turn to powder. She'd become increasingly certain he was showing the others he had spoken for her, would make some move on her soon.

Likely there would have been a squabble between him and Matson if Rollie hadn't spurred himself into action.

Finally she had her chance to do something about it. Holding the stone awkwardly but as tightly as she could in her two bound hands, she gripped it with her fingers, tucked low, and shoved off with her right knee. Wedged hard against the fire stones, the pain of the move jolted her into welcome, piercing alertness.

While the man was turning his gaze down at her, she was already on her way to delivering a dose of sudden hell to his exposed crotch.

The rock slammed him hard and he reacted better than she could have hoped. He gasped, his eyes rolled back in his head, and he curled into a human ball of gibbering, tearing, not-so-silent man. At that moment, even if he were somehow able to snatch free his gun and shoot her in the head, she would have died somewhat satisfied, knowing she'd at least rendered him nearly useless for the rest of his useless life.

But the sudden thought of his pistol snapped her from

that foolish thinking and she lunged for it, her hands still bound. One of her fingers felt hot, throbbing, broken from jamming the rock into him. And she didn't care.

Tish lurched forward on her knees. Her skirts bunched, fetching up on her boot heels. She shoved forward, tearing the skirt in her efforts, and as she slapped for the gun, his hand whacked at her with palsied, feeble efforts. He knew what she was after, but his pain—the pain she'd delivered unto him—was so intense it was barely an attempt.

It wasn't enough. She slid the gun free of its holster then felt a hand on her shoulder. She swung the gun around, intent on shooting whoever it was.

Pops. His hands were free, though his wrists were bleeding. She saw it all in a flash of a second as he was reaching, not for the gun, but for her hands. His big thick hands grabbed her wrists and held them in one hand. With the other, he reached past her, slid the groaning man's hip knife free of its sheath, and in the same sweeping movement slid the tip of the gleaming blade beneath the thongs binding her wrists.

Her hands were free and the gun she'd held onto rested in her right hand. She'd never shot a man but was certain she could do it. And more than one. In that instant, Pops bent low with the knife once more and opened the throat of Drake in a quick, slashing move.

Then Pops was gone. On to the next man, working in fast, silent fury alongside Rollie.

Tish looked down at the gagging, dying man, and felt nothing but grim satisfaction. She was one of them now, one with Pops and Rollie. She knew it.

As Pops and Rollie quickly, efficiently fought the

intruders, Tish backed away from the center of the odd, strangling melee of humans, turned and bolted, intent on tracking down Zadie, vowing to lay low as many of the killers and thieves and vicious men as she could.

By any means.

Chapter 38

It took Tish less than a minute to find the two men who had been sent after Zadie. She hadn't gotten far. They had her cornered against a massive rocky berm. Ignoring the screams and shouts from the camp, they flanked Zadie, pawing her, tearing at her dress.

Later, Tish Gray would not remember having raised the gun, cocking and raising it. None of it. Nonetheless, the gun burst out with two violent booms. Two men dropped to the earth. One of them twitched and screamed, then lay silent. The second didn't move.

Blue smoke drifted up and away and Tish saw Zadie, trembling, her hands covering her face. Her shoulders jerked in silent heaves.

Through the pulsing of hollow sounds in her ears, she heard Pops bellow his daughter's name, over and over, heard him drawing closer, his rasping breath hoarse and bull-like.

Behind him, she heard Rollie shout her name.

Tish lowered the gun and let it fall to the ground.

The fight was over.

Chapter 39

It was another fine, high-blue day in the Sawtooth Range of Idaho Territory. The weary foursome of Rollie, Pops, Zadie, and Tish arrived back in Boar Gulch to find Wolfbait and Nosey battered but alive, and The Last Drop, though a ransacked mess, had been tidied and was slowly on the mend. Bone and Bone Junior were there as well, lending a hand with repairs.

Pops assessed the group of their friends one at a time, taking in the limping Nosey, the bandage-armed Wolfbait, and the two men named Bone, father and son, each with opposite splinted, bandaged legs.

As if in response to a question Pops was about to ask, Wolfbait said, "You should see the other fellas!"

"We did," said Rollie.

"Oh."

Over the next few minutes, the new arrivals learned what Wolfbait and Nosey as presiding proprietors in the absence of the owners of The Last Drop Saloon—*that pit of vile iniquity* according to Mayor Chauncey Wheeler—had put up with a whole lot of headache.

They had borne the burdensome brunt of a righteous

onslaught of a town-wide morality clean-up launched by Chauncey and a couple of other self-proclaimed *respectable* Boar Gulch business owners.

"What brought that on?" said Rollie, pulling out a chair and settling into it with a sigh.

Wolfbait cackled and handed Nosey beers, who ferried them to everyone.

"You'll recall," said the journalist, "how a certain widow was on her way to the Gulch?"

"Yeah," said Rollie. "Sister of a preacher, right?"

"Yep," said Nosey. "Except the preacher never made it to town."

Half listening, Rollie nodded and sipped his beer. Not certain, even after so many weeks away, if he was in the mood for one of Nosey and Wolfbait's windies. Time a-plenty to catch each other up on all their various doings, the recriminations, the hardships, the fights, all of it. At the moment, he wanted a little quiet. A few minutes of quiet.

But Wolfbait was on a roll. "The widow arrived all right! Seems she was sniffin' as much as Chauncey was, but for different reasons." Wolfbait's bushy eyebrows rose in a conspiratorial way.

Before he could explain further, Boar Gulch Mayor Chauncey Wheeler stomped up the front steps. Hands on hips, he stood backlit in the sunny doorway, glaring at the six people quietly sipping glasses of beer. He licked his lips, then resumed his momentarily forgotten scowl.

"Chauncey." Rollie nodded. "Come on in, pull up a chair."

"I will not."

"Well, sir, if you want to talk with us, you'd best come closer," said Pops. "We are too tuckered to shout."

The surly mayor growled, but walked into the cooler, shaded interior of the bar. "I . . . find it difficult to set foot in such a place."

"Never used to," said Rollie.

"Never had a widder woman with four squallerin' brats a-hounding him, neither!" Wolfbait drowned his cackle with a deep swallow of beer, satisfied for the moment that he'd managed to get the meat of his slice of gossip out there.

"Do tell," said Rollie, nodding to Wolfbait, then turning once again to Chauncey. "With news like that, it seems to me you'd be happy to get a little break from what sounds like a busy home life you have inherited for yourself."

Even in the darkened interior of the bar, they saw Chauncey's face redden and his eyes narrow.

"I didn't come here to drink with you! And I certainly didn't come here to discuss my life with this . . . this riffraff!" He waved a pudgy hand at them all.

"Then why did you come, Chauncey?"

"I—"

"Let's cut to it," said Rollie. "You want me out of here, out of town, out of your life. You want to possess this real estate, isn't that it?" He stretched out farther and wagged his boots a little. Nobody else spoke.

"I never said that!"

"Oh, so it's not true?"

"Why? Are you . . . are you thinking of selling?" Chauncey's tone softened the barest bit.

Rollie shrugged and sipped his beer.

"What's that supposed to mean?"

Rollie sighed and looked about the room. It was a good place to be, and he was gently surprised by how much he'd missed it. It was . . . home. But he had some long, dark conversations to work through, to somehow make up for all the hardships and losses his presence in Boar Gulch had put the other residents through.

As Rollie looked around the room at his friends—Pops, Nosey, Wolfbait, Bone, Bone Junior, and Tish and Zadie—something deep inside, that little voice he'd relied on for his entire long career as a Pinkerton man—a *legendary* Pinkerton man, if Tish was to be believed—told him Boar Gulch was a place worth fighting for. It was worth it, even if he had to tangle with his own self to stay. Even if it meant going against that other little voice inside him that forever wanted to cut bait and run.

Rollie sensed someone had moved in close, too close, to his right side. Someone fat and sweaty and angry and . . . smelling a little of fear. Cutting his eyes to the side, he saw what he expected to see: Chauncey Wheeler's fat, fleshy red face shaking with rage.

"Don't ignore me, damn you!" shouted the mayor, spittle flecking his lips.

In one smooth, silent movement, Rollie stood as his revolver whipped into view and the end of the barrel disappeared into Wheeler's open mouth. He shoved the gun far back until the fat man gagged.

Not giving him the chance to pull away, Rollie walked Wheeler backward fast and hard right out the front door of the Last Drop Saloon to the edge of the porch, a good five feet up off the ground. "Don't you ever get tired of being so . . . tiresome, Chauncey?" Without waiting for an answer, he leaned closer, his face inches from Wheeler's, the gun barrel still jammed in the man's mouth.

In a quieter voice only the two of them could hear, Rollie said, "You ever threaten me again, it will be the last thing you ever do in this or any other life. You hear me, fat man?"

Wide-eyed, Wheeler nodded, grunting and snotting on himself and the gun barrel.

"Good." Rollie straightened and shoved Chauncey with the revolver.

The man fell through the slightly mended railing and tipped backward off the edge of the deck, his arms whipping as if he were having a hard time swimming. With a cry ending in a wheeze, he dropped backward and landed hard, raising a substantial cloud of dust.

Rollie turned away and said over his shoulder, "Mind that first step."

Walking back inside, Rollie "Stoneface" Finnegan looked at the odd assortment of friends. "Let's all try to remember to keep out the seedy ones. It's our civic responsibility, after all, to keep this place respectable."

Pops shook his head and chuckled. "It's good to be home."

"I'll drink to that," said Wolfbait, winking at them all.

Keep reading for a special excerpt!

WILLIAM W. JOHNSTONE
and J.A. Johnstone

BRANNIGAN'S LAND

First in a Brand-New Series!

**Ty Brannigan traded his tin star for a cattle ranch.
But the men he left to rot behind bars have their
own hash to settle with him . . .**

Once a respected lawman in Kansas and Oklahoma,
Ty Brannigan ended his career as town marshal of
Warknife while he was still young enough to marry,
start a family, and raise cattle. Now nearly sixty,
he's a proud husband, father of four, and proprietor
of the Powderhorn Ranch on the outskirts of his
old stomping grounds. Close to twenty years since he
hung up his six-guns, Brannigan's more content
wrangling cows than criminals.

But for every remorseless outlaw Brannigan put in jail,
noosed, or left to the vultures, he made even more
enemies. Thieves and killers looking to settle old scores
have tracked the ex-lawdog to his ranch. They've made
the mistake of targeting his wife and children—only to
discover that Ty Brannigan enforces his own law with
a lightning-fast draw and a dead shot aim . . .

Look for BRANNIGAN'S LAND, on sale now!

Chapter 1

"What do you think, honey?" Ty Brannigan asked his oldest daughter.

"Just incredible, Pa. I don't know that I've ever seen a finer horse anywhere."

"He is something to look at, isn't he?"

"He sure is." MacKenna Brannigan lay beside her father near the crest of a rocky-topped ridge in the foothills of Wyoming Territory's Bear Paw Mountains, a spur range of the Wind Rivers, near Baldy Butte. Ty and MacKenna were peering down into the valley on the other side of the ridge. "I could lie here all day, just staring at him and his beautiful harem not to mention those six colts of his."

Tynan Brannigan, "Ty" for short, adjusted the focus on the spy glass he held to his right eye, bringing the big, impressive black stallion into sharper focus. The horse milled on the side of the next ridge, a couple of hundred feet up from where his harem languidly cropped grass with their foals along Indian Lodge Creek.

The big horse was watching over his herd, keeping an eye out for predators or rival herds led by stallions that might very well prove to be the black's blood enemy. He was having a good time performing the otherwise onerous task. The stallion ran along the side of the ridge then stopped abruptly, swung to his right and dashed up the steep ridge to the very top. He ran along the crest of the ridge first one way before wheeling, mane and tail flying, the sunlight glistening beautifully in his sleek, blue-black hide, and running back the other way before swinging down off the crest and galloping full out down the side toward where his harem lifted their heads and turned to watch him, twitching their ears incredulously.

Ty and MacKenna were several hundred yards from the big black, but Ty could still hear the thunder of the horse's hooves and the deep, grating chuffs the horse made with his powerful lungs as he ran.

The black slowed at the bottom of the ridge, near the stream, then went over and nosed one of the mares—a beautiful cream with a blond mane and tail. He nosed her hard, brusquely but playfully, then nipped the rear of one of the younger horses, a half-grown gray. The gray bleated indignantly. The stallion lifted his fine head and ripped out a shrill whinny. He put his head down, reared high, pawed the ground, then lunged into another ground-chewing gallop, making a mad dash up the ridge again.

MacKenna, who at seventeen was in the full flower of young womanhood, lowered the field glasses she'd been peering through and turned to her father, smiling. Her long hair was nearly as black as the stallion's, and it shone in the high-country sunshine like the black's did, as well. Her lustrous hazel eyes—her hair had come from her Spanish mother, but her eyes were the same almost startlingly clear blue-green as her father's—flashed in delight. Her plump red lips stretched back from her even, white teeth. "He's showing off, isn't he? He's showing off for the mares!"

Ty chuckled and lifted the spy glass again to his eye, returning his gaze to the black as the stallion stopped suddenly halfway up the ridge then turned to stand parallel to the ridge and peer off into the distance, ears pricked, tail arched, again looking for danger. "He sure is, honey."

Ty was glad he and MacKenna were upwind of the beautiful stud and his harem. If they'd been downwind, the black likely would have detected him and the girl and hazed his brood out of the valley where Ty and MacKenna, having a rare father-and-daughter ride alone together, lay on the side of their own ridge, admiring the lovely, charismatic, bewitchingly wild black stallion.

"They're just like boys, aren't they—wild stallions?" MacKenna said, playfully nudging her father in the ribs with her elbow. "Showing off for their women."

"Just like boys and men, honey," Ty agreed, chuckling. He turned to look at MacKenna who was peering through the field glasses again. "Would you like to have a horse like that, baby girl?"

MacKenna, named after Ty's long-dead mother, lowered the field glasses and turned to her father. Her thin black brows furled with speculation. Finally, she shook her head. "No." She turned to gaze with her naked eyes into the next valley. "No, a horse like that needs to be wild. Breaking or even gentling a horse like that . . . civilizing him . . . would ruin him." She glanced at her father. "Don't you think, Pa?"

"I couldn't agree more, Mack."

"How did you find this herd, Pa? I've never seen wild horses out here."

"Matt and I were hunting yearling mavericks on open range a few weeks ago, and we stumbled on several stud piles." Matt was the oldest of Ty and his wife Beatriz's four children, all of whom had been raised—were *being* raised, with the youngest at age twelve—on their Powderhorn Ranch in the shadow of several tall bluffs and mesas that abutted the ermine-tipped, higher peaks of the Wind Rivers.

MacKenna furled her dark brows again, curiously this time. "Stud piles?"

"Big piles of horse apples the herd leaders leave to mark their territory. Apparently, that big fella moved his herd in here recently. I've never seen stud piles in these parts before. Down deeper in the breaks of the Snowy River and in the badland country north of town, but never here."

"So, they're new in these parts," MacKenna said, smiling in delight and gazing into the next valley through her field glasses again. "Welcome, Black . . . ladies and youngsters." She turned to her father. "Thanks for showing me, Pa. It leaves you with a nice feeling, seeing such beautiful, wild beasts, doesn't it?"

Ty smiled and placed a big, affectionate hand against the back of his daughter's neck. "Sure does, baby girl."

MacKenna shook her head again. "No, it wouldn't be right to try to tame a horse like that. Just like some men can't be tamed, some horses can't either."

Her eyes acquired a pensive cast, and she lowered her gaze.

Damn, Ty thought. He'd brought her out here—just him and her—to try to take her mind off her heartbreak, not to remind her of it.

"Oh, honey," he said, sympathetically. "He's not worth how bad you feel."

He meant the young, itinerant horse gentler, Brandon Waycross, who had once worked for Ty. MacKenna had tumbled for the rakishly handsome young man, five years her senior, one summer ago, and only a few months ago he'd broken her heart. Though they hadn't made any formal plans, and MacKenna had never confessed as much, Ty knew that MacKenna had tumbled for young Waycross and had set her hat toward marrying the young man.

"I hope he is, Pa. Or I'm a fool, because I sure do feel almighty bad."

"Even after what he did?"

MacKenna drew her mouth corners down and nodded, her now-sad gaze still averted. "'Fraid so." She raised her eyes to Ty's. "I don't think he meant to betray me with Ivy. Some boys just can't help themselves."

"Don't make excuses for him, MacKenna. He's not a boy anymore. Brandon Waycross doesn't deserve you. You hold tight, baby girl. You're gonna find the right man—a good, kind, loyal man. That's the only kind to share your life with."

"Sometimes I feel like Ma got the last one of those," MacKenna said, then leaned toward Ty and planted an affectionate kiss on his cheek.

Ty smiled, sighed. "Well, honey. It's getting late and we've got an hour's ride back to the Powderhorn. Don't want to be late for supper or your mother will send us each out to fetch our own willow switches."

"Ouch!" MacKenna said, grinning. "She doesn't hold back like you do, either, Pa!"

"Believe me—I know!" Ty grin-winced and rubbed his backside.

He crawled a few feet down from the lip of the ridge, so the stallion wouldn't see him, then donned his high-crowned brown Stetson and rose to his full six-feet-four. At fifty-seven, having married MacKenna's mother when she was twenty-one and he was thirty-six, Ty Brannigan still owned the body of a Western horseman—tall, lean, broad-shouldered, and narrow-waisted.

Just by looking at him—into those warm eyes, especially—most would never have guessed he'd once been a formidable, uncompromising lawman in several formerly wide-open towns in Kansas and Oklahoma—a town tamer of legend. Ty had been the town marshal of nearby Warknife for three years and had cleaned out most of the hardcases during his first two years on the job, before meeting Beatriz Salazar, a local banker's daughter, falling head over heels in love, and turning in his badge to devote the rest of his life to ranching and raising a family.

It had not been a mistake. Ty did not miss wearing the badge. In fact, he treasured every moment spent working with his wife and their four children, now between the ages of twelve and nineteen, on their eight-thousand-acre spread, even when the work was especially tough like in spring with calving or when Ty was forced to run rustlers to ground with his old Henry repeating rifle and his stag-gripped Colt .44, holdovers from his lawdogging days. That Colt was housed now in its ancient, fringed, soft leather holster and thonged on his right thigh. The Henry repeater was sheathed on the coyote dun standing ground-reined with MacKenna's fine Appaloosa that Brandon Waycross had helped her gentle.

Ty didn't like wearing the guns, but they were a practical matter. Wyoming was still rough country, and over Ty's years as a tough-nosed lawman who'd sent many men to the territorial pen near Laramie, he'd made enemies. Some of those enemies had come gunning for him in the past, to get even for time spent behind bars or for family members who'd fallen victim to Ty's once-fast gun hand. When more enemies came, and he had to assume they would, he owed it to his family to be ready for them.

So far, the Brannigan family plot on a knoll east of the big main house, was occupied by only one Brannigan— Ty's father, Killian Brannigan, an old hide-hunting and fur-trapping mountain man who'd lived out his last years on the Powderhorn before succumbing to a heart stroke at age ninety. Ty didn't want to join his father just yet. He had too many young'uns to raise and a good woman to love. At age forty, Beatriz was too young to lose her man and to have to finish raising their four children alone.

"Come on, baby girl," Ty said, extending his hand to MacKenna. "Let's fork leather and fog some sage!"

MacKenna accepted her father's hand; Ty pulled her to her feet. An eerie whining sound was followed closely by a resolute thud and a dust plume on the side of the ridge, ahead and to Ty's right. He'd felt the bullet curl the air just off his right ear before the crack of the rifle reached him.

"Down, honey!" Ty yelled, and threw MacKenna back onto the ground, throwing himself down on top of her, covering her with his own bulk, then rolling off of her, pulling her on top of him again and rolling first her and then himself over the top of the ridge to the other side.

As he did, another bullet plumed dust within feet of MacKenna's left shoulder, turning Ty's insides into one taut, cold knot, sending icicles of terror shooting down his legs and into his feet.

"My God, Pa!" MacKenna cried when Ty had her safely on the other side of the ridge from the shooter. "What was *that*?"

"Keep your head down, honey!" Ty said, placing his left hand on her shoulder, holding her down, while pulling his stag-gripped .44 from its holster with his right hand.

"Who's shooting at us, Pa?"

"Your guess is as good as mine!" Breathless, Ty edged a cautious glance over the lip of the ridge and down the other side.

His and MacKenna's horses had run off, the coyote dun taking Ty's rifle along with it. Fifty yards beyond where the horses had stood was a wide creek bed choked with willows, cedars, and wild shadbark and juneberry bramble. The shooter must have fired from the creek bed, hidden by the bramble. Ty saw no sign of him.

Turning to MacKenna, who now lay belly down beside her father, her face blanched with fear as she gazed at him, Ty said, "You stay here, Mack. And for God sakes, keep your head down!"

Ty started to crab down the side of the ridge. MacKenna grabbed his arm, clutched it with a desperate grip. "Pa, where you goin'?"

"I'm gonna try to work around the bushwhacking coward! You stay here." He set down his gun to pat her hand that was still clutching his left forearm, and his normally mild eyes sparked with the hard light of a Celtic war council fire. Messing with him was one thing. Messing with his family was another thing altogether. "Don't you worry. I'm gonna get him, Mack!"

He remembered the bullet that had plumed dirt just inches from her shoulder.

MacKenna, as tough as the toughest Brannigan, which would be old Killian, hardened her jaws as well as her eyes and said, "Okay, Pa. Go get him!"

Chapter 2

Ty picked up his old but trusty Colt, crabbed down the sage- and rock-stippled ridge, then rose, turned, and hurried down the side at an angle to his right. A quick glance into the valley's bottom told him the ambusher's shot had cleared out the stallion and his harem of mares and foals.

The black would take no chances with his family. Neither would Ty Brannigan.

His heart thudding with the heat of his anger, Ty bottomed out at the base of the ridge and headed west. Just beyond the ridge lay another, brush-choked creek bed that connected the stream where the mares and foals were milling to the creek bed from which Ty believed the shooter had fired on him and MacKenna.

The big rancher followed a game path through willows into the creek bed, which was about five feet deep and threaded down its center by a narrow, shallow stream that smelled a tad skunky here in the late summer. He walked quickly along the edge of the murky water, heading north now, toward the intersecting creek bed.

He walked at a crouch, trying to make himself as small as possible, not easy for a man his size, the Colt cocked

and aimed out from his right side. As he walked, prickly
shrub branches and brambles reached out from the bank
on his right to grab at his buckskin pants, blue wool tunic
with laces halfway down the front, leather suspenders, and
his neck-knotted red bandanna.

He kept a close eye on the intersecting ravine ahead of
him, wary of more lead being fired his way.

He was twenty feet from the intersecting ravine . . .
fifteen . . . ten. The brush-sheathed bank dropped away
on his right, and he stopped, bent forward, peered off
down the ravine through which the stream continued, the
water following the ravine's course as it angled off to Ty's
left, roughly fifty yards away.

This intersecting ravine was broader and deeper than
the one Ty had just left, its banks peppered with rocks,
Ponderosas, cedars, and junipers. As far as Ty could see,
there was no sign of the shooter.

Had he pulled out?

The rancher began following the ravine's course,
keeping the cocked Colt aimed out from his right side.
The dark water trickled along its stony bed, spotted with
dead leaves and cattail down. When the stream hugged up
tight against the base of the embankment on Ty's right, he
crossed it and walked along its left side, the bank on that
side roughly ten feet to his left.

He'd just started to follow the ravine's bend when he
stopped suddenly, sniffed the air. The tang of horse and
leather scented the nearly still, hot summer air.

He'd no sooner identified the aroma when a man
shouted, *"Hyahh!"* and Ty saw a horse and rider burst out
of a thicket dead ahead of him, not fifteen feet away. The
rider whipped his rein ends against his horse's left hip and

the horse reared slightly, whinnied shrilly, laid its ears back, and bounded toward Ty.

As it did, the black-hatted man in the saddle fired a revolver along the right side of the roan's neck. Ty felt the punch of the bullet in his left arm but still managed to snap off a shot just before the horse bulled into him and pitched him back into the shallow stream.

He landed on his back, splashing water and cursing then whipping up the Colt again, turning his body to follow the rider galloping off down the stream away from him. Ty cursed as he quickly lined up his sights on the man's back and squeezed the trigger.

The Colt bucked and roared.

The bullet puffed dust from the back of the rider's vest, between his shoulder blades. The man slumped forward in his saddle, rolled down the roan's right wither, struck the ground, and bounced several times before piling up against a rock. He rolled onto his back with a groan and a sharp curse, gave a spasmodic jerk, and lay still, his pale forehead where his hat shielded it from the sun glowing brightly in the late afternoon sunshine.

He'd rolled onto his hat. The dark green bowler peeked out from between him and the rock, its crown crushed.

"Pa, you all right!" MacKenna cried.

Ty glanced to his left to see his daughter scrambling down the bank through the thick brush, the branches grabbing at her black hair and pulling it back behind her. It ripped her black, flat-brimmed hat off her head, but she left it where it lay at the base of the bank and ran into the stream, splashing the water high around her long, slender, legs clad in blue denim and black chaps to squat beside her father.

"Dammit, you're hit!" intoned the hot-blooded girl of Irish-Spanish extraction, not minding her tongue.

Wincing against the pain, Ty inspected the bloody hole in his arm, up high near his shoulder. The hole was near the very outside of the muscular limb and a quick probe with his fingers, sucking air sharply between his gritted teeth, told him there was an exit wound.

"Not to worry, baby girl—it's just a flesh wound. Went clear through. Hurts like blazes, but I've cut myself worse shavin'!"

"I'll be the judge of that!" MacKenna lowered her head to closely inspect her father's arm, glancing at first the exit wound and then the entrance wound. She puffed out her cheeks and looked at Ty. "Hurt awful bad, eh?"

"Nothin' a few shots of Irish whiskey won't cure."

"Ma won't let you drink."

Ty smiled but it was mostly another wince. "I think she'll make an exception for this though she might accuse me of tryin' to get ambushed just for the whiskey. You'll have to testify on my behalf."

"Who's the bastard layin' over there?"

"Young lady, your tongue!"

"If Ma can make an exception for that arm wound, I think you can make an exception for my tongue . . . given the circumstances . . ."

Ty grunted his agreement with his passionate daughter. "Help me up, baby girl. Gonna go over an' have a look."

"Wait." MacKenna removed her bandanna from around

her neck, wrapped it around her father's arm, over both wounds, and knotted it tightly.

Again, Ty drew a sharp breath against the pain.

"Cut yourself worse shavin', huh?" MacKenna grunted at him reprovingly.

She draped her father's right arm around her neck and helped hoist his big body up out of the water and mud. Ty stooped to retrieve his hat, which lay at the edge of the stream, the caved-in crown taking the shape of a horse hoof. He reshaped the hat, set it on his head, glanced at the dead man, and turned to MacKenna. "You'd best wait here. You don't need to see him."

"I've already seen him."

Ty sighed and then he and MacKenna walked over to stare down at the bushwhacker.

He was obviously dead. Ty's bullet had plowed through his back and out through his breastbone, likely shredding his heart.

Ty crouched to closely study the man.

He was medium tall and slender, some would say skinny, and he had long, dark-red hair that hung to his shoulders. His face was round and pudgy, with a pencil-thin mustache that did not match the rawness of his features. He wore a small, silver ring through his right ear, and a cheap, spruce-green, three-piece suit with a wool, rose-colored vest. On his bare right hand, that lay beside him, finger curled over the palm, he wore a gold ring on his pinky.

A gold watch lay on the ground beside him, a gold-washed chain trailing from the near vest pocket. Ty picked up the watch, ran his gloved right thumb over the leaf-scrolling on the lid.

"Dandy," Ty said. "At least, he was trying hard to be."

The dead man, who appeared in his mid-twenties, looked like a farm or ranch hand who, having tired of all day forking a saddle for the usual thirty-a-month-and-found, had decided to try his hand at the pasteboard and poker way of life . . .

MacKenna frowned up at her father. "Do you recognize him, Pa?"

Ty shook his head. "I don't recollect ever seein' him before. I think I'd remember." He dropped to a knee and, mainly using his right hand because his left arm was throbbing miserably, he went through the man's pockets. He found only two combs, one larger than the other, a small, pasteboard-covered notebook with only blank pages remaining, a gray canvas tobacco pouch, a pencil stub, and a deck of cards residing with a few lucifer matches in his shirt pocket.

"Nothing with his name on it," Ty said, sitting back on his heels. "And I don't know him by lookin' at him."

MacKenna stepped forward, placed a hand on her father's right shoulder, very lightly. "Don't mean he doesn't know you, though."

Ty looked up at her and drew his mouth corners down. She was too wise for her years. But then, her wisdom had come from the regrettable experience of knowing that men had come for her father before. Ty had never talked to her about it, but he supposed she'd lived with the fear more would come again.

And now one had.

Ty just wished she hadn't had to witness such a thing. None of his other kids nor Beatriz had—he'd been alone when others had tried to trim his wick—but now MacKenna had been a witness to the violence. Ty wrapped his good arm around her and pulled her close against him. He didn't say anything, because there was nothing to say. Reassuring words would only sound hollow.

He rose and turned to her. "Why don't you see if you can run down our horses, Mack? I'm going to see if I can run down this fella's mount. I'll take him to town tomorrow, turn him over to Chris Southern." Southern was one of Ty's closest friends and the current town marshal of Warknife.

"You got it, Pa." MacKenna turned and started walking toward the embankment.

"You all right, Mack?" Ty called to her back.

She stopped, glanced over her shoulder at him, and gave him a crooked, reassuring smile, then turned her head forward and climbed the embankment.

Ty watched her with an expression of prideful admiration. She was tall for her age—tall like her father—and her figure was becoming more and more womanly every day. A tough lady was Mack. "That one's got the bark on. Always has, always will."

MacKenna might have witnessed what had happened here today, and even nearly took one of those bullets herself. But the one Ty worried about was his wife, Beatriz. The woman was strong, but she'd been born to worry. She'd worry about Ty now. He wished there was some way he could not tell her but with the bullet hole in his arm, that would be impossible. Besides, she hated when he kept secrets from her, and he didn't blame her.

Ty didn't have to look far for the dead man's horse. He merely stuck two fingers between his lips and whistled.

A couple of minutes later, the roan came walking around a bend in the ravine, reins trailing. Ty trained his own horses to come to a whistle, and he was glad the roan had been trained to do the same. He was doubly glad, in fact, because with the burning pain in his arm, he hadn't had the energy to run the mount down.

Not long after the roan had returned, MacKenna rode up to the lip of the ravine bank, sitting the saddle of her Appaloosa and holding the reins of Ty's coyote dun. Ty had just finished tightening the roan's saddle cinch. Now he crouched over the dead man's body, which he'd wrapped in the man's own blanket roll. He'd gone through the man's saddlebags and, as had been the case with the man's pockets, he'd found nothing that identified him.

Which likely meant he was just some nobody with a grudge—often the most dangerous kind of man. He'd likely tracked Ty and MacKenna after they'd left the Powderhorn headquarters earlier. He'd come packing iron and the determination to exact a reckoning for past injury.

What injury might that be?

Ty had no idea.

"Hold on, Pa," MacKenna said. "I'll help you with that."

"You stay there, Mack. This ain't a job for a seventeen-year-old girl."

MacKenna was already scrambling down the bank through the brush. "It ain't a job for a fifty-seven-year-old wounded man, neither."

"You're as stubborn as your mother!"

"Thank you. On the count of three . . ." MacKenna had already crouched to take the man's ankles in her hands.

"All right, all right," Ty said, resignedly. "One . . . two . . . *three!*"

They each grunted as they hauled the dead man up off the ground, carried him over to the horse, and then, readjusting their grips on the dead man's body, slung him belly down across his saddle.

Ty leaned forward to catch his breath and to wait for the pain the maneuver had aggravated in his arm to subside. He turned to MacKenna and said, "Now for the hard part."

She frowned curiously at her father.

"Tellin' your mother," Ty said.

Visit us online at
KensingtonBooks.com
to read more from your favorite authors,
see books by series, view reading group guides, and more.

Visit us online for sneak peeks, exclusive giveaways,
special discounts, author content, and engaging
discussions with your fellow readers.

Sign up for our newsletters and be the first to get exciting news
and announcements about your favorite authors!
Kensingtonbooks.com/newsletter